THE BEGINNING OF CIVILIZATION
Mythologies Told True

Book 6

THE PATRIARCH AND THE LORD

Beginning's End

Second Edition

Dennis Wammack

DCW PRESS

Birmingham, Alabama

~~~~~~~~~~~~

The Beginning of Civilization: Mythologies Told True Series
The Patriarch and the Lord: Beginning's End, Second Edition
v250331

© Dennis Wammack, 2025

Hardback: ISBN 978-1-965619-09-4
Paperback: ISBN 978-1-965619-10-0
eBook: ISBN 978-1-965619-11-7

The Patriarch and the Lord: Beginning's End, Second Edition is the sixth in the six-book series, *The Beginning of Civilization: Mythologies Told True.*

Disclaimer: Within the six-book series, historical names are drawn from Greek, Egyptian, and Biblical references to protohistoric figures. Other names are derived from Sanskrit and Proto-Indo-European languages. Many characters, places, and events are inspired by well-known mythologies, but the narrative is not necessarily consistent with the myth. No effort has been made to provide historical accuracy of time or place or a scholarly development of technologies and themes. Histories spanning thousands of years have been compressed into hundreds to provide a single narrative across the series. Connections are made between characters who would realistically have lived in different epochs.

For rights and permissions, contact Dennis Wammack, denniswammack@gmail.com. denniswammack.com

Cover design by the author using artificial intelligence resources.
Books are printed and distributed by IngramSpark, Nashville TN.
Digital format is available from most digital book resellers.
Published by DCW Press, Birmingham, Alabama, dcwpress.com.

Phoenicia, Jaffa, Rocky, Burlyman, Polydore | Astarte, T'jaru
Terah, Amathlai, Haran, Terahson, Nahor, Sarai, Isaac, Jacob
Kyrios-Olon, Teumessian, Nimrod, Nimbal, Nimlad, Nimisis, Asherah, Set.
~~~~~~~~~~~~

TABLE OF CONTENTS

The Appendix contains a Glossary of referenced names and places.
"Year" is referenced to the first Winter Solstice Festival.

Djoser, Hetephe, Incense/Hagar/Keterah
Horus, Serket, Azazil, Abram, Baalat
Ishmael, Maribah, Fatimah, Nebaioth, Basemath, Kedar | Anath, Astarte

Phoenicia, Jaffa, Rocky, Burlyman, Polydore | Astarte, T'jaru
Terah, Amathlai, Haran, Terahson, Nahor, Sarai, Isaac, Jacob
Kyrios-Olon, Teumessian, Nimrod, Nimbal, Nimlad, Nimisis, Asherah, Set.

~~~~~~~~~~~~

THE BEGINNING OF CIVILIZATION

Mythologies Told True

Book 6

THE PATRIARCH AND THE LORD

Beginning's End

Second Edition

Djoser, Hetephe, Incense/Hagar/Keterah
Horus, Serket, Azazil, Abram, Baalat
Ishmael, Maribah, Fatimah, Nebaioth, Basemath, Kedar | Anath, Astarte

5
~~~~~~~~~~~~

~~~~~~~~~~~~

1. Port Jaffa

Year 158, Season 9

Abram sat beside Baalat listening to their teacher discuss the nature of death. The fire cackled in the cool night sky as its flames reflected off Middlesea; a good time to discuss the unknowable.

But not for the thirteen and eighteen-year-old. Death was far away; an abstraction. For them, there were bigger, closer concerns. They preferred discussions on the Way of Horus which addressed real issues faced by real people, them especially.

Abram carried the weight of the world in his head. Horus had exposed him to too much, too soon. There was no easy reconciliation for all Abram believed to be true—knew to be true—even if these truths might be mutually exclusive.

These contradictions did not concern Baalat; she was too busy practicing her virginity. Baalat remained almost a virgin except for selected talkative Urfa Missionaries to whom she provided her spy reports and might prove useful to her in becoming a Living God. Oh, yes; and except for occasional liaisons with a priest of Horus who brought her warmth and affection and a temporary overwhelming feeling of belonging. Her time as a child church prostitute did not count—she was forced to do that. She knew that people made sex complicated and sexual exclusivity seemed to be sought after in many quarters and if she were going to become a Living God that followed the Path of Horus, she would need all of her resources.

That, plus a plan.

Abram's plan, as was commanded by Teacher Horus, was that Abram would someday return to his home and, with his acquired worldly sophistication, become an influential leading citizen of Urfa. He would take over his Father's idol-selling business and redirect the ultra-conservative thoughts and actions of Urfa's citizens toward a more liberal civilized worldview.

"Good luck with that," Baalat had told Horus. Her comment angered Horus, confused Abram, and brought a smile to Azazil.

Horus: "Baalat, I hope you will help Abram teach the people of Urfa."
Azazil: "Neither of you will be *commanded* to go to Urfa, of course."
Horus: "But you *will* go!"

<div align="center">Phoenicia, Jaffa, Rocky, Burlyman, Polydore | Astarte, T'jaru
Terah, Amathlai, Haran, Terahson, Nahor, Sarai, Isaac, Jacob
Kyrios-Olon, Teumessian, Nimrod, Nimbal, Nimlad, Nimisis, Asherah, Set.</div>
~~~~~~~~~~~~

Abram: "Yes! I will go back home and teach them!"
Baalat: *Save people that don't even want to be saved? Ha!*

Her silence did not go unnoticed.

THE NEXT DAY

The Port Jaffa women of power sat on the dock patio enjoying their highsun meal while being appreciatively observed by a Greek, a Crete, and a Canaan sailor enjoying their highsun beer.

The women bantered among themselves.

Serket: "Those sailors are staring at all my beautiful friends."
Polydore: "Staring at your friends and you in that little Oceanid outfit, Serket."
Astarte: "Don't be jealous, there are enough sailors to go around."
Anath: *Not one throat worth slitting in the bunch.*
Baalat: "Mother Serket, maybe you shouldn't wear an outfit that revealing. Some men might think you are inviting them."
Serket: "My appearance brings them peace. Plus, it's good for business and it does not displease my husband."
Phoenicia: "You couldn't displease Horus if you danced naked on the table for them."
Serket: "Perhaps, but my husband has changed since he anointed King Djoser as Pharaoh. He doesn't hold me as tightly or as long. He's more at peace but it's not a peace I bring him."
Baalat: "He lost his soul!"
All: "What!?"
Baalat: "He had to defeat God Set in that disgusting contest over Anath to gain the right to crown King Djoser as Pharaoh. My teacher won, but it cost him his soul. I thought everybody knew that."
Serket: "My husband?! No! What happened?!"
Anath: "Come on Serket. You know he plowed me in front of Set and everybody else. He plowed me real good!"
Serket: "He never told me! But it must have been the right thing for him to do."
Anath: "He *wanted* to plow me, Sweet Serket. He wanted to a lot."
Baalat, angrily: "Don't be a bitch, Anath! Horus told us what happened. Not in detail, but it was obvious what he did. He did it to preserve Ma'at. But it cost him his soul."
Anath: "You don't tell a god what to do, Baalat. I can have you killed!"
Baalat: "I, Baalat, student of Horus, the greatest of all Living Gods, *do*

tell God Anath what she won't do. Obey me, God Anath, or I will have my teacher spank your bottom."

Anath: "Promises, promises."

Astarte: "What's a 'soul?'"

Baalat: "Horus teaches us that it's what's left of you after you die. At least, that's what he says it is."

Serket: "My husband is very learned. That must be what one is."

All: Banter, banter, banter.

Canaan Sailor: "You think any of them women want to know what I got hard between my legs; ready to go?"

Greek Sailor: "Hey, friend. Don't let the older one hear you talking like that. She's an Oceanid. If you disrespect a woman around an Oceanid, then the only female you will ever have again will be four-legged."

Crete Sailor: "That's true. Be sure to respect women around here. At least talk nice to them. Don't call them names and you will do all right."

Canaan Sailor: "Talk nice to bitches? They need to know who's boss."

Greek Sailor: "Friend, where are you from? You won't make it working this job with that attitude toward women. The one in the little white outfit can tell a ship captain that if *you* are sailing on his ship, he can't port here."

Crete Sailor: "The mean-looking one will let you plow her on a table in front of a crowd just so she can cut your throat and watch you die while your blood drips on her face."

Greek Sailor: "The Oceanid? Don't even ask. There are a lot of good wine houses around here. Let's go. You can get all the plowing you want. Just show the women proper respect."

Canaan Sailor: "I'm new at this sailorin' and that idn't how we do it in Tophet, but I like the sound of the rest of it. You boys show me around and learn me. I'll buy the first round of beer."

The three men rose and walked past the table of powerful women. In passing, the Greek sailor nodded to Polydore, and said, "Good highsun, Oceanid Polydore. It's good to see you, again."

The Greek sailor was favored with an Oceanid nod and smile.

IN THE HOUSE OF SERKET

Serket's was the finest house in Jaffa. The sweet innocent child from Rusalem had blossomed into a worldly woman of sophistication and taste. She had walked westward along the beach until she found a small rise away from Jaffa activity. The powerful Portmaster of Jaffa had a large and inviting home built there befitting her rank. The house was large enough to have an interior courtyard with strategically placed doors and windows to ensure a constant breeze from the sea. The second floor contained six guest bedrooms plus a large one facing the sea for her and her sometimes-there husband, Horus. Her sister and sister's consort, Phoenicia and Rocky, were permanent guests. A bedroom was reserved for her mentor and friend, Assistant City Chief Oceanid Polydore. It was always available when Polydore reached her limits of consorting with Chief Jaffa and needed time alone with the sea. Two bedrooms were maintained for Horus's followers which always included Azazil, Abram, and Baalat.

Serket's bed was opulent; a large mattress made of fine Egyptian linen stuffed with reeds and palm leaves. Her two headrests were made of fine leather. She needed no headrest when Horus came to her; he was her headrest. When she undressed for his pleasure, she always put on the beautiful gold and turquoise necklace Horus had given her when they were in Memphis. He had ceremoniously removed it from the neck of High-Priestess Hathor and presented it to Serket as a gift of marriage.

On this night, under a full moon, she lay contentedly in his arms. He held her close and tightly. Peace washed over her as the sea washes over an Oceanid. He was troubled but Horus was usually troubled.

She whispered, "Whatever it is, Husband, will pass. Do what you must do. Peace will come."

"Peace is but a moment, Wife. And only when you are in my arms. I will leave you and peace tomorrow. Abram's training must be completed, soon. It will be months before I return. Maybe many months. My love remains here with you. I will do what I must do because it is my duty to do it, but my love of doing it is gone. Hope is gone. Still, my words do some good in this world; still help a few who will listen. It is my disciples and priests who still believe. My words are for them."

His embrace suddenly became intense. He half-sobbed, "I am broken, Serket! Broken!"

She half-laughed, "You are whole, my husband. It is the world that is broken!" Serket mounted Horus.

SUNRISE ON THE BEACH

The next morning before sunrise, Serket and Horus walked to his traditional gathering place on the beach. They were followed by Azazil, Abram, Baalat, and three local docent-priests. Townspeople and followers were already gathering when they arrived. The Jaffa Way-of-Horus senior priest stood beside a welcoming morning fire.

He and Horus chatted until the broaching of the sun was imminent. Horus then extended his arms toward the appearing sun and began, "Welcome, Osiris, bringer of life; bringer of love; bringer of all good things. We, your people, love you as you love us. Travel fast and safely to your High-Priestess waiting at the Great River to call forth life into you so that you will become Ra, the Living Sun. We are your disciples. We travel the path you have set us upon. We love everyone, even those who despise us. We rejoice!"

The crowd responded, "We rejoice!"

Having completed his welcome, Horus asked, "And now, knowing that life is sometimes difficult, what problems shall we solve?"

The problems of his people rained down upon him.

HIGHSUN GOODBYE

After his morning service was complete, Baalat walked with Horus and Serket to a secluded part of the public gardens.

Baalat said, "Here, I brought some fruit and nuts and a little wine. I and Azazil have everything packed and ready to go. I will bring them here after our highsun meal. Is there any more you need of me?"

Serket touched Baalat's cheek. "No. You have prepared everything, Baalat. My husband and I must pack many months of visiting between now and when he returns. Take care of my husband, Baalat. If his time of abstinence grows too long for him to bear, I ask that you relieve him of his burden. It is my wish."

Baalat laughed. "He spurns my lasciviousness, Serket Your husband will be my greatest conquest if I can ever seduce him. But for now, take this time to wear your man out. I will be slow to return."

Serket giggled, "He is already well-worn, Daughter. But still, be slow."

Baalat left them.

They found a large tree and sat leaning against it; she nestled in his arms.

He said, "My Father asked me to free the people of Urfa from the abomination of the teachings of Teumessian. My quest is simple. All that remains is how do I do it."

"Abram is so innocent. Making him an instrument of love will not be difficult. Use him as a sword to cut off the false teachings."

"He remains a sheep. An intelligent, dedicated sheep, but a sheep still. He follows me and learns my words but once cut free; I fear who will become his next shepherd."

"Then use Baalat as your sword. She will never have a master; not even you."

"I trust Baalat without question up to her next bed. She is a spy for Kyrios-Olon, you know. It was the condition of her release. She tells everything she knows to the Urfa Missionaries about what I am doing. They will know that I was well-worn when I left you. She beds the important ones along with my most influential priests in each city. No one knows this, not even me. It's her secret because she is 'saving her virginity.'"

"Well, my broken husband, use the sharp edges of your soul to lovingly cut their throats."

"I could use my once-lover Anath for that. Everyone wins."

"Anath is mean-spirited. Don't give her the satisfaction."

"Anath wronged me. That she lay with other men was not a concern. That she gleefully went to Set as I watched was of no concern. But it affected me badly that they rejoiced in constantly describing the intimate details. If I am away too long, Serket, lay with whomever might bring you peace. But, please, not to hurt me, but because you wish it for yourself. I won't be angry."

"I don't wish to lay with any man but you, Husband. You are my peace."

"Woman, you bring me peace in a world without peace."

She snuggled closer.

Horus became lost in thought. *It seems easy enough with Serket in my arms. My weapons of war are a faithful, intelligent, dedicated sheep and an innocent, opportunistic, ambitious collector of debts. How hard can it be?*

After highsun, Azazil and the students found Horus and Serket. After stoic goodbyes, Horus and his group departed Port Jaffa to travel into the rough-hewn lands of Canaan.

There to spread the teachings of Horus to the oblivious, turbulent children of Ra.

Djoser, Hetephe, Incense/Hagar/Keterah
Horus, Serket, Azazil, Abram, Baalat
Ishmael, Maribah, Fatimah, Nebaioth, Basemath, Kedar | Anath, Astarte

~~~~~~~~~~~~~

2. Baalat and Abram

Year 158, Season 10

Abram and Baalat walked behind Horus and Azazil along the road to Sur.

Horus suddenly stopped, turned to his two students, and asked, "Student Abram, what will you do when we arrive at Sur?"

Abram, taken aback but knowing not to appear unsure, answered, "I will do as you command, Teacher."

"Neither Azazil nor I will be with you. Only Baalat. And Baalat, I command your subservience to Abram while you are in Sur. Do as he commands. Don't offer suggestions. I again ask, Student Abram, what will you do?"

Abram, stalling for time, answered, "I shall teach those that I meet 'The Way of Horus,' Master."

"Very good, Abram. Do that—but before you do, find four hungry people and feed them. Once fed, if they wish to hear your words, then speak to them. I will find you tomorrow in Sur and you will tell me what you accomplished. We will then go and stay for a while in Byblos. When I leave Byblos, you and Baalat will no longer be my students. You both will have graduated and will be free to go your own way or follow me as a disciple. This will be your decision. But Abram, until then, I advise you to turn your thoughts away from what Horus desires to what Abram desires. Go. I will find you tomorrow."

Horus turned and walked away, signaling Azazil to come with him.

Azazil looked at Abram and shrugged, then at Baalat and rolled his eyes.

Abram was panic-stricken.

Baalat feverishly worked through what had just happened and why. Understanding, she said to Azazil, "Don't worry, Azazil. We will do just fine." And to Abram, "Don't just stand there, Abram. Command me to do something."

Abram readjusted his thinking and his role. and commanded, "Let's go to Sur!" With newfound authority, he bravely turned and began walking toward Sur. Baalat obediently followed.

They walked.

<div align="center">Phoenicia, Jaffa, Rocky, Burlyman, Polydore | Astarte, T'jaru
Terah, Amathlai, Haran, Terahson, Nahor, Sarai, Isaac, Jacob
Kyrios-Olon, Teumessian, Nimrod, Nimbal, Nimlad, Nimisis, Asherah, Set.</div>
~~~~~~~~~~~~~

Finally, Abram said, "I was to remain his student until I became a man."

"Well, you are a man."

"I'm still a child. I have no idea how to conduct myself as a man.

She walked on in silence.

"I mean, not *really* a man."

She made no suggestions. She walked on in silence.

"I mean, I know the words. I know 'The Way of Horus' and he has shown me the world and all the hopeless people in it. I know what should be done when something needs doing. But either Teacher or Azazil—or you —have always been around to command the doing. I didn't have to be the one to command it."

Silence.

"I mean …"

Abram went through many "means."

Finally, Abram said, "He is throwing me into the deep, isn't he? Teaching me how to become a man. No, not teaching me—forcing me to become one when I'm not. I don't like it. I like being a follower. I don't want to be a man. It will be too hard. You were a whore, weren't you?—when Teacher asked you to follow him. A whore to Teumessian and the others. Teacher saved you when they were going to throw you away. But you were already a woman even before you became one. You began as a woman, and I have not even become a real man. You didn't want to become a woman, did you? You were a child when they took you to make you into a whore. I will never know what to do. I will never be a man—a leader." Tears came into his eyes.

Baalat did not speak nor take his hand. There was a grove of trees in the distance. They walked on.

"They called you a whore to belittle you, but it wasn't you they belittled. It was themselves. No matter what word they said you were—you remained Baalat. Doing what Baalat had to do. My home, my city, my people, everyone in Urfa call the other half whores. It's not right! Teacher taught me these things without once saying it! That's why he will return me to Urfa when I am a man! To teach them! To change them! But they will kill anyone who does not believe like they believe or say words differently than how they say the words. Teacher knows these things, but he will send me back anyway! I should run away! Run away while I can! They will not learn. I cannot change them. They will kill me!"

He was quiet for a while.

"I know what to do, of course. I was well taught. I will do what's right."

They walked on.

They came to the trees. She took his hand and led him into the grove. She stood facing him—staring at him, as she let her tunic fall to the ground. He stared wide-eyed at her naked body. She did not speak.

"You were my sister, but now you are just a whore!"

He turned and ran from the grove back to the path that led to Sur.

Her eyes followed him as he ran away.

SUR

Abram came to the village of Sur. Baalat followed far behind.

Abram waited at the outskirts for Baalat to catch up. Upon arriving, he quietly said, "We must find the local temple."

The temple was one of the few buildings in the village and not hard to find.

Abram approached the priest. "Greetings, Great Chief. I am Abram of Port Jaffa, and this is my sister, Baalat. We travel to Byblos but wish to visit the great village of Sur. Are we welcome here?"

As he eyed Baalat, he replied, "My name is Marqat and we worship Heracles in this village. Your sister is a comely wench."

"Yes, she is. I have already castrated three men who tried to take advantage of my sister's innocence. She keeps their testicles somewhere. Are there poor nearby where we might find lodgings in exchange for food?"

Marqat snapped out of his fantasy and officially replied. "Yes, we have an abundance of poor people in Sur. Walk the trail toward the east. You will find your choice of lodgings."

They bantered on, admiring the temple and the carved idol of Heracles in its center.

Leaving, Abram asked, "Will my sister be safe, or shall I keep my hand near my dagger?"

"Our village is poor. A blade nearby is always advised, Lord."

Lord! He called me Lord!

Abram and Baalat took the trail toward the East.

Abram asked, "Did I sound all right back there? I was afraid my voice would crack."

"You were fine, Abram."

The huts appeared, as did the people. Abram commanded Baalat to cook a stew with their remaining food rations; it would go farther. As the villagers ate, Baalat told the women how to retrieve more edibles from the surrounding land and Abram told the men how they could build simple rafts and catch fish from Middlesea. Around the dying fire, after the food was eaten and the telling told, Abram taught them the gospel of Horus. The appreciative poor then showed them to an abandoned hut where Abram and Baalat could safely sleep.

They entered the hut and began preparing for bed. He said, "I'm sorry about what happened back there, Baalat. I guess I'm just not ready."

"I see your shadows in the night, Abram. I hear your sounds. You are ready!" With that, she bedded down and turned her back to him. "I will be asleep soon enough. You can do it then!"

SUNRISE

Abram and Baalat built a small fire on the beach at Sur. They issued no invitations, but the fire and their activities attracted the attention of nearby early risers. Abram's greeting of the sun interested the watchers; the braver of which inquired into which god Abram was worshiping. Discussion ensued. Baalat passed out the little bread she had remaining. The Way of Horus was mentioned. Three people were interested enough to stay and talk.

HIGHSUN

The two found a small trading market where they traded coins for food. They retired to the village park to eat bread.

"Teacher did not tell us what we will do after we leave Byblos. What do you think we will do?"

"I am under your command until Teacher arrives. I was told not to make suggestions."

Her coolness toward him since the grove was suddenly colder still. He tried again. "I'm sorry, Sister. Too much is happening. I'm too confused. I don't know what I'm supposed to do."

"I am not your sister."

"Are you still my friend?"

"We are both students of the great Teacher Horus and will remain so until we leave Byblos. After that, you are on your own!"

"I don't want to be on my own. I want to be with you and Teacher."

"Poor little boy."

"When we leave Byblos, he is going to Urfa, isn't he? We will no longer be his students. We can go with him or not."

"Yes. 'Or not' sounds good!"

Abram's world was crumbling around him. He stood. "I will go find some poor people and give them some bread."

"Good boy. Command me to stay here and wait for my teacher."

Soon after highsun, Horus and Azazil entered Sur and, soon enough, found Abram talking with several people. The gathering excitedly made way for Horus and Azazil to join them. Abram had just been telling them the gospel of Horus and here he was. "This is so exciting, Master!"

Horus visited with them, adding gravitas to Abram's previous words. Abram puffed with pride.

As Horus and Abram talked, Azazil looked around for Baalat, and, not seeing her, wandered off into the village. He bypassed the temple and went straight to where he knew a city park would be. She was there, sitting under a large tree, fondling a leaf from a nearby plant.

Azazil sat down beside her without speaking.

Finally, he said, "Are you concerned about what to do after Byblos? You know that Horus fully expects you both to continue to follow him."

"Where is he going after Byblos?"

"You know where. To Urfa."

"Yes. I figured it out as he was saying it. And everything is perfectly clear, now. Sitting here. Under a nice tree. Touching a nice plant. Feeling it. told me about weapons of war. He forged me and Abram, too. He is a sweet boy, isn't he? Not so much a weapon of war, but, still, a sweet boy."

"If you want to talk about what happened, I am here."

"I don't, but thank you. I will go with him to Byblos, but I will not follow him to Urfa. His quest is not my quest; his war, not mine. I am well taught, well trained, and a student of the strongest women in Canaan and Egypt. I paid attention. I am prepared. I will miss you, Azazil. You are a good man."

He reached to touch her but decided not to. "Whatever it is, will pass away, Baalat."

She laughed a gentle laugh. "Do you not listen to Teacher? What he leaves unsaid between his words? Nothing passes away. Everything is forever."

Azazil stood. "We will pick you up on our way out."

"I'll see you then."

~~~

Azazil returned to find Horus and Abram in the temple talking to the priest.

Abram was exuberant. His teacher had praised him for his actions last night and this morning. He was talking to a village priest as an equal and as a valued asset that had helped alleviate the suffering in Sur. Abram felt as if he were becoming a real man in good standing among men. He was beginning to feel like he was ready to return to his home city—with or without the support of his best friend, Baalat. Seeing Azazil arrive, Abram greeted him as an equal.

Azazil responded, "Well everyone, let's be on our way to the big city."

As the men passed through the village, Baalat quietly joined them.

Djoser, Hetephe, Incense/Hagar/Keterah
Horus, Serket, Azazil, Abram, Baalat
Ishmael, Maribah, Fatimah, Nebaioth, Basemath, Kedar | Anath, Astarte
~~~

~~~~~~~~~~~~

3. Byblos

They arrived at Byblos early after highsun several days later.

Horus did not have many followers this far north, but the Byblos priest remembered Horus from his previous visit years before.

The priest hosted the group as they talked of gods and Urfa missionaries and such.

Horus inquired about the road to Alashiya. "I may wish to travel there next to hear of their memories of Tartarus."

"That road is not well traveled. The better roads veer eastward into the old lands; to the old city of Urfa." The priest talked on and eventually said that he wished to send invitations to the local powerful citizens to join him and his distinguished guests for the next-day evening meal. "Would this be acceptable to my distinguished guests?"

"That would be delightful."

Banter. Banter. Banter.

All rose when Horus rose. He said, "Until tomorrow's Sundown meal."

They left the temple together. Horus said, "Azazil, have Abraham find us a night's lodging. If it's unacceptable, it shall be Abram's fault. Go!"

The two hurried off leaving Horus and Baalat standing awkwardly together.

Horus said, "Let's walk through the city and talk, Student Baalat."

"Let's. The three lounging on the temple fountain are the ones who will follow us."

She turned to walk toward the port area. "The taller one will come to me after sundown for my report. You wish me to tell him that you are traveling to Alashiya, and that Abram and I are no longer your students; that Abram will follow you, but I will not; that there will be a sundown meal for all holy men tomorrow in the temple where these things will come to pass. Are there any other secrets you wish me to tell him?"

"Will you not go with us to Urfa? Abram needs you. You two are always together; you are his support. Things will go badly for him without you."
~~~~~~~~~~~~

"I intend to become a Living God that follows the Path of Queen Kiya—or the 'Path of Horus' as you fondly call it. When I was a child, you asked me what I wanted. This is what I want."

"You were never a child, Baalat. Your childhood was taken from you by Teumessian and his Church. You, of all women, should want this abomination destroyed!"

"You teach the gospel to those who will listen. Let them believe or not as is their nature."

As Horus became more agitated, Baalat became calmer.

He said, "They send out more and more missionaries, Baalat Their words become harsher, meaner, more demanding. They teach that El created Pumi and then created Valki to serve Pumi and do his bidding and stay quiet. They teach that Valki sinned a great sin and should therefore be subservient to Pumi. The people listen to these missionaries and become confused. You see the nature of the people of Canaan. That is the result of the incessant teachings of the Urfa missionaries. They must be stopped, Baalat. They must!"

She slowed to look at what called itself a dock. "That is a horrible excuse for a dock. Look at it!" Her imagination began replacing the decrepit dock into a substantial one; complete with an office for the dockmaster and a dining patio. *This could even be a port. A city this size should have a port. Port Jaffa sent at least one ship here, I remember it. What do they have to trade around here?*

Horus scanned the dock area. "Yes. It's horrible. But not as horrible as the world will be if the Church of Urfa fulfills its dream of controlling the minds of all people!"

"Then you must stop them, Shaman Horus. You and your sweet little friend, Abram. Azazil can help. But I cannot. I intend to stay in Byblos. It's a big city with a lot of potential. I may not have many shekels now, but I am smart and trained and can earn shekels without going to my back. Shall I tell Nimrod's spies that you drove me away or that I walked away? I can tell it either way. Whichever best serves your purposes."

"Tell him I drove you away. Perhaps the Kyrios-Olon will forget you exist."

THE SUNDOWN MEAL

The priests, shamans, and other righteous men gathered at the temple for the sundown meal honoring the Living God and premier Shaman—Lord

Djoser, Hetephe, Incense/Hagar/Keterah
Horus, Serket, Azazil, Abram, Baalat
Ishmael, Maribah, Fatimah, Nebaioth, Basemath, Kedar | Anath, Astarte

Horus, son of Osiris, the supreme God of Egypt. Shaman Horus's following ranged from the great halls of Memphis, along the Road of Horus, and even into Canaan and beyond. Several local young men had expressed an interest in the Gospel of Horus and might like to study further and maybe create a small temple in Byblos for him.

Nimrod among them.

Everyone talked of righteous things.

Horus took the opportunity to introduce his students of many years; Abram and Baalat. "They know the way people should live; they know the ways and language of many countries; there is no more that I can teach either of them. From this moment forth, they are set free into the world to accomplish many good and wonderful things; teaching and showing people how to live with righteousness and honor. I, their teacher, Horus, hereby proclaim the woman Baalat and the man Abram to be educated, honorable people. May Osiris favor them all the days of their lives."

Nimrod led the applause. He ingratiated himself with Abram while ignoring Baalat. "I'm originally from Urfa. Maybe we could travel together for a while."

Horus listened without comment.

Toward the end of the evening, Azazil came to Baalat and whispered, "Meet me at the fountain."

They both discreetly disappeared from the temple and into the night.

Arriving at the fountain, Azazil asked, "May we talk in confidence? Neither sharing the words of the other with anyone."

She answered, "Yes."

"You are superior to Abram. You are more mature with more understanding and capabilities."

"Thank you."

"Abram will mature more—we hope. But you were the key to Horus's plan to rid the world of Urfa missionaries. Horus is too upset to come to you, but he understands your position, and, too, your reasons."

"I don't understand my reasons. I do what I must do. I owe Teacher Horus my life; my everything. If he commands me, I will follow him and do as he wishes until I die."

Phoenicia, Jaffa, Rocky, Burlyman, Polydore | Astarte, T'jaru
Terah, Amathlai, Haran, Terahson, Nahor, Sarai, Isaac, Jacob
Kyrios-Olon, Teumessian, Nimrod, Nimbal, Nimlad, Nimisis, Asherah, Set.

Azazil laughed. "Ahh, that is the pathway to ruin, isn't it? You know it, I know it, Horus knows it. No. Do what you must do. You plan on becoming a Living God that follows the Path of Queen Kiya. What could be finer than that? The higher one rises, the harder to remain on the path of righteousness. If you rise that high and remain true to your path, Horus will be vindicated in his choice of you. Do you have funds to live on until you begin your rise?"

"Yes. I have saved almost 16 shekels. That will last me a long time!"

"Excellent. Here is a pouch. Horus put away a half-denarii a day for each day you followed him. That comes to over 700 denarius with which to begin your new life."

Baalat was incredulous. "That's more than 200 shekels! Teacher is too generous. He saved my life. He taught me everything. That is more than enough. I need no shekels."

"Then be generous with those you meet along the way, Baalat. Whatever —whenever—you need, I will be there as will be Lord Horus. Be careful, my child! Be great."

Uncharacteristically, Azazil leaned in and embraced her.

She embraced him back and half-sobbed, "I just couldn't go with Abram. I just couldn't."

~~~

Inside, Nimrod and Abram laughed a laugh of Urfa brotherhood.

The next day, before the sun rose, Horus found Azazil and said, "It is best that you don't come with Abram and me to Urfa. Abram's new friend wants to join us and that is one too many. Baalat needs someone with her, but she is too independent to show it. Help her get started. I will help Abram. May Osiris be with us all."

The sun neared the horizon. Horus faced the east and greeted his father— Osiris. Abram and Nimrod stood on either side; Azazil and Baalat behind him. Several dozen people stood observing the ceremony. After the ceremony was finished, the visiting done, and the inspiring complete, Horus bid farewell to the local dignitaries and others gathered there.

He then turned to look into the eyes of Baalat and said "Soon, Daughter. I will see you soon."

With that, Horus, Abram, and Nimrod sat off to Urfa.

Djoser, Hetephe, Incense/Hagar/Keterah
Horus, Serket, Azazil, Abram, Baalat
Ishmael, Maribah, Fatimah, Nebaioth, Basemath, Kedar | Anath, Astarte
~~~

~~~~~~~~~~~~

4. The Story of Young Abram

Year 158, Season 11

Out of the city, Horus said, "You left Urfa a boy, Master Abram. You return a man—with the shadow of a beard. Are you nervous?"

"No, Teach … I mean Lord Horus. I am educated and eager to begin my new life and excited I will soon see my mother, brothers, and sister. I hope they are all well."

"Will you miss Baalat?"

"She is a whore. It's good we are parted."

Horus replied, "I found Baalat to be an intelligent, righteous, and loving woman. You judged her differently?"

"Yes. She was a whore."

"And what of Astarte and Anath, and even Polydore and Phoenicia?"

"It doesn't matter who they lay with. They did not pretend to be righteous women who would not betray me by laying with other men."

Nimrod said, "Well stated, Friend Abram. Well stated!"

Horus said, "I see." *I don't see at all, Abram. She betrayed YOU? Since when was she yours to betray? This does not bode well, my once-student Abram. Not well, at all. And your new friend is NOT your friend.*

They walked on. Nimrod mindlessly talked away.

Abram eventually interrupted Nimrod's soliloquy with, "But if Urfa is your home, why did you leave?"

"Well, I was not taken as a student by a great teacher like you were. My mother was stoned to death for being a harlot and my father was sent to the pastures because he was the husband of a harlot. The Church of Urfa took me in as an orphan alter-boy and trained me in the way of the righteous gods. When I became a man, they wanted me to become a missionary, but I was more ambitious. They kindly released me from my obligations. I go back to Urfa every year or so to rest in a land of righteous people and away from all the temptations and evil in the rest of the world. What about you? I know why you left, but why are you returning?"
~~~~~~~~~~~~

"Teacher Horus has taught me everything he knows, and I am growing a man's beard. It's time I return to my family to begin a new life."

"A righteous life, I'm sure. That may be difficult after being exposed to all the evil in the world."

"Teacher Horus taught me the Path of Horus and he is very righteous."

"Does your teacher lay with all manner of women?"

"Oh, no. He is married and he does not lay with any woman but his wife."

Their banter continued along those lines.

Horus, walking far behind, liked nothing of the words he could hear and repented of his decision to ask Azazil to remain with Baalat. Horus needed Azazil's thoughts on Abram's attitude toward sexual liaisons. *Sexual exclusivity is fine, as is sexual promiscuity and everything in between. It depends on the person, the circumstances, and the needs but it is not given to a person to judge another person in this matter, especially when the person has no vested interest in any of the parties involved. I assumed that this attitude would become ingrained into Abram during his exposure to the greater world. Obviously not.*

It was late in the day when the travelers arrived at the gates to Urfa.

Nimrod said, "Rest here, Lord Abram. I will scavenge a banner to carry before you into the village as I proclaim your grand return."

"Yes, Friend Nimrod. That is an excellent suggestion. I will ask Shaman Horus to build us a campfire. We can enter the village after sunrise tomorrow."

Horus smirked. *I, your beloved teacher, am now the builder of campfires? You grow in self-confidence, if nothing else, Abram. Arrogance, perhaps? Whatever shall I do with you? Love you, I suppose. No matter what road you take.*

Horus did not wait to be commanded by the boy-man. He began gathering wood with which to build a fire.

Abram patiently waited.

Soon enough, Nimrod returned carrying a tattered flag. He said, "This worn-out flag is the only thing I could find Lord Abram. I hope you will find it satisfactory."

Abram sniffed, "Yes, that will be adequate. Thank you, Friend Nimrod."

They ate the evening meal Horus had prepared and discussed the coming days' activities.

Djoser, Hetephe, Incense/Hagar/Keterah
Horus, Serket, Azazil, Abram, Baalat
Ishmael, Maribah, Fatimah, Nebaioth, Basemath, Kedar | Anath, Astarte

SUNRISE

Horus made no motion to rise from his blanket and perform his ritual sunrise ceremony. He would rely on Abram to honor the coming of the sun.

The sun broached the horizon. Neither Abram nor Nimrod made a motion to stir.

Horus stared at the emerging sun. *Ahh, Father. You rise even though I am not standing to greet you. So be it. I tried to create two weapons of war against the Kyrios-Olon and their missionaries, but my scheme is not going well. I planned the best I could. Dyohestia and the others are quite clever. Their little missionary spy Nimrod ingratiates himself with Abram. Abram accepts people as they present themselves. He remains innocent. Father Osiris, help me. Help us all.*

Nimrod rose and saw Abram still sleeping. Shaman Horus, too, lay motionless. He thought, *Interesting. The Shaman foregoes his daily ritual. Do you play a game? Have you yet abandoned hope? We shall see.*

Nimrod noisily prepared for the day.

The noise woke Abram. He saw the sun already rising in the sky. In a panic, he jumped up and ran to Horus, still lying on his blanket. "Teacher, Teacher. We have missed the rising of the sun. Wake up. Wake up!"

Horus sat up and sleepily said, "Lord Abram, is the coming of Osiris no longer of importance to you? I thought you would be first up and ready to welcome him to your homeland."

Nimrod walked up and said, "It's not Abram's duty to greet the sun. This is his day of triumph. He returns to his people, a man full-grown. I shall carry this flag before us, telling all we meet that Abram has returned."

Horus countered, "Yes. He left a boy but has now been exposed to great civilizations and a multitude of different cultures and beliefs. It will be difficult for him to face the narrow-minded attitudes of the people in his small, closed village of Urfa. He will have to slowly teach his people how to be tolerant and welcoming."

Nimrod replied, "Yes. Abram will be welcomed, and you will be tolerated. Perhaps Abram will now more fully appreciate the magnificent culture of Urfa; the mother of cities; the home of the Church of Urfa—the living voice of the gods. What do you think Abram? Do you have words to describe the wantonness of the women in the 'multitude of cultures you have been exposed to?' I have heard they will fornicate with any man and that they try to seduce boys before their time. Can this possibly be true?"

Abram, somewhat confused, said, "Most women are very respectful and nice and don't go out searching for men to lay with." He had never considered, more or less reconciled, the stark difference in local and worldly attitudes and expectations for women. Nor did he notice that Horus and Nimrod had locked stares.

Horus ventured a little smile. *Lord Abram, do I detect the beginning of knowledge? Perhaps all is not lost, after all.*

Nimrod coldly smiled back. *Soon enough you must leave, you son of a bastard god —And sweet, pliable Abram will remain.*

Abram snapped back into the present. "I am ready, Friend Nimrod. Raise my flag high and lead me back to my people."

So, it began.

As the three passed "The Pastures" in single file. Nimrod hailed five boys leaning against the fence enclosing the Pastures—peering in to hopefully catch a glimpse of naked women chasing men—always mindful of not getting captured by one of the insatiable whores.

Nimrod called out, "Young men, Lord Abram returns to his city ready to lead his people. Go before us and call out to all that can hear, 'Abram returns to us!' Go and loudly proclaim his coming!"

The boys were not sure who Abram was, but they were always ready for running and screaming. They enthusiastically began to do so. More children saw and joined in as they neared the village.

By the time they arrived at the village, people were leaving their homes to stand outside to greet the commotion. Terah and his two older sons stood on the road to greet the returning Abram. His mother and young sister, Amathlai and Sarai, stood ramrod straight, near their house, hands clasped in front of them. The Urfa perfect family waited for the return of their world-traveling child now become a man.

Abram saw his family and almost lost his new-found manliness by running to them, but sophisticated decorum held. He marched to his father, pounded his chest with his fist; and then repeated the gesture to his two older brothers. He did not dare acknowledge his beloved mother and sister who watched in proud admiration. He knew they could visit after the men had said all the things men should say.

Djoser, Hetephe, Incense/Hagar/Keterah
Horus, Serket, Azazil, Abram, Baalat
Ishmael, Maribah, Fatimah, Nebaioth, Basemath, Kedar | Anath, Astarte

With arm motions, Nimrod stirred up the gathering crowd.

Horus stood in the background observing. *Welcome home, Abram. I hope I taught you well.*

In the far, far distance, the drumming of the drums began. The crowd gasped with anticipation. *So much excitement all at one time. All hail Abram!, the returning son!*

The men standing in the road moved to the shoulder and sat down to make themselves comfortable. The women retreated farther into the surrounding yards. Several men signaled their wives to bring them a beer, which the women hurried off to do.

Horus thought *Drummers? They know what's coming. Sounds like a church thing. They are well prepared. Their spies are competent.*

The drums grew closer. Anticipation mounted. Finally, two columns of boys dressed in red uniforms holding church flags marched toward Abram and those gathered around him. The crowd became silent. Behind the two columns, came the drummers. Behind the drummers, came twelve attractive women dressed in finery giving little hand waves to the men. Behind the twelve attractive women came …

Horus searched for an apt description of the woman. *High-Priestess? Chief Courtesan? Holy Mother of the church parading lasciviously in front of the men? We have some contradictions in the land of Urfa.*

The twelve women parted so that their leader could stand in front of her parade. She nodded graciously to Abram and his entourage and then spoke to one of her attendants. The attendant went to Abram, spoke a few words, took Abram's hand, and led Abram to face the commanding woman. She placed Abram's hand into the hands of her leader.

Abram was not at all sure of what was happening, but he remembered his training. *"Never appear unsure."*

The leader said, "Abram, my name is Asherah. I am High-Horpriestess for the Church of Urfa. Welcome home." She placed her hand lightly on his shoulder.

Horus listened to the conversation with interest.

He watched as Asherah slid her hand higher up Abram's shoulder until it rested on the nape of his neck.

Abram spoke the appropriate words. *I feel strange. What's happening?*

Phoenicia, Jaffa, Rocky, Burlyman, Polydore | Astarte, T'jaru
Terah, Amathlai, Haran, Terahson, Nahor, Sarai, Isaac, Jacob
Kyrios-Olon, Teumessian, Nimrod, Nimbal, Nimlad, Nimisis, Asherah, Set.

Finally, with her fingers still resting on Abram's neck, Asherah turned to one of her Horpriestesses and said, "Bring Horus to me."

The Horpriestess walked to Horus and requested that he meet the High-Horpriestess.

He arrived.

They exchanged pleasantries then she strongly suggested, "I believe that your presence may be upsetting our precious guest. My Horpriestess will escort you to the Temple where you will be entertained."

He replied, "Thank you for your gracious request but I prefer to remain here."

She stared at him. "It is not a request."

"Oh, then I accept." He held out his elbow to the priestess.

She did not take it but instead said, "Follow me," and unceremoniously led Horus back down the path toward the temple. The beer-drinking men took note as they passed by.

Asherah returned to her delightful chat with Abram. Her fingers on his neck wriggled a little.

The priestess escorted Horus to the Temple entrance. Arriving, she said, "You may not pollute my temple with your presence. I will take you to the gardens in the back. You will find it pleasant enough."

She took him around behind the gigantic building to a landscaped area and said, "I have been commanded to offer you wine. Will you take it?"

"No."

"Very well. Wait here." She left and entered the temple.

He sat down on a bench on the walkway circling a large fountain containing two swans. Other exotic birds roamed the garden. He waited.

And waited.

Dyoares exited the temple with great enthusiasm. He rushed to Horus with arms outstretched. Dyohestia followed behind with two attendants.

"Horus! Our great nemesis. I'm so glad to see you again." Uninvited, Dyoares embraced Horus with a bear hug.

Horus pulled back. "Greetings, Dyoares. Your network of spies and agents is impressive. It is a pity that you and your kind are evil."

"You pay us great honor, God Horus. But I must correct you. *You* are evil. *We* are good. And evidently more impressive than you. If Nimrods' reports are accurate, you have failed miserably in creating these—what do you call them?—'weapons of war?' The girl you left on the docks of Byblos was last seen wandering the markets of Byblos wasting her money on trinkets, and the boy returns to us well-prepared to enter into *our* ministry. Your beloved father was a far more competent adversary, but no matter—you are here."

Dyohestia arrived with her hand extended.

Horus took her hand, and asked, "Am I to kiss it or spit on it? Which would excite you more, woman?"

"I'm too tired to play silly word games, Horus. Join me for a cup of morning wine—please." She turned to an attendant and said, "Three glasses of wine from the same bottle. Let our guest select his glass first."

Horus inspected the three glasses and made his selection. "There does not appear to be a skull engraved on any of them."

She did not offer a retort. "I am in the midst of serious planning, but I wanted to see for myself how far you have progressed toward becoming one of us. Nimrod reported that you appeared to have been broken the night before the coronation of Egypt's Pharaoh. A few judicious inquiries from the sheep and goats give us a fairly accurate picture of what happened. You tasted the glory of power and tried to spit it out. But the taste will linger, I have found the key to your conversion, and we are patient. Ambrosia gives us all the time we will ever need."

"The key?"

"The key to opening the door for you to pass through—from care taking the oblivious, turbulent sheep into the bright sunshine of the Kyrios-Olon. You will like it here."

"And what is this key?"

She laughed. "I don't want to make it too easy for you, Horus. It will take away our edge. Thank you for visiting. I will leave you to spar with my brother. Is there anything I can give you before you leave?"

"I am already in your debt for eliminating the Winter Solstice sacrifices."

"Oh, I had forgotten about that. But yes, send us a High-Priest for the Church of Urfa. Replacing Teumessian is impossible and using a priestess as a temporizing move is counterproductive. He must desire to obey us and never mention our existence to the sheep. Otherwise, send us a candidate and there will be no debt for either side. Just mention a name to any of our missionaries or tell Dyoares on your way out. Sadly, I have decided to wait until you are one of us before you may have me. Thank you, Horus. You make my life more interesting."

She took his hand, brought it to her lips, and licked his fingers. Lowering it, she smiled and said, "See, that wasn't hard? Are you?" She commanded the two servants to stay with the men and then she returned to the temple.

Dyoares commanded, "More wine. No poison."

Horus selected his glass, "Do you want a young man for the High-Priest?"

"No, no, no. The more like Teumessian the better. An old man will be more pliable. Between ambrosia, young handmaidens, and constant healing herbs, we can keep him alive for a long time. But a commanding, intimidating, arrogant voice and control over the sheep is a must."

"A barter. I tell you the name. You tell me the key."

Dyoares was momentarily at a loss for words. "No! Surprise and uncertainty are part of the key. I cannot possibly tell you of it."

"Very well."

"I mean, it would spoil the surprise,"

"I understand."

"Is it a good candidate?"

"A most excellent candidate."

Dyoares was agitated.

He commanded a servant, "Go consult with my brethren. Tell them that Horus will exchange the name of our next High-Priest for the key to his enlightenment." Then he leaned back, sipped his wine, motioned toward the swans, and said to Horus, "Beautiful, graceful creatures, aren't they? They mate for life! I much prefer the ancient belief that we are transformed into one when we die and can fly past the clouds to become a light in the night sky. Your Egyptian practice of preserving dead flesh isn't all that appealing, do you think?"

Horus found Dyoares to be far more knowledgeable in the teachings of shamanism than he would have thought. They had a nice conversation.

Dyoares asked, "Do you think we are some kind of monsters, Lord Horus? Taking delight in the suffering of the sheep? Quite the contrary. We want them to be happy, just not if it costs us anything. You understand, I'm sure."

Eventually, the servant returned, accompanied by Dyoathena.

Dyoathena spoke to Dyoares. "Accept his offer. We gain much and lose only a little. But give me the name first, God Horus. In case it is not to our liking. Is this acceptable?"

Horus said, "Set."

The two Dyos looked at one another in silence; considering.

Dyoares said, "A most excellent suggestion. I approve. And you, Dyoathena?"

"I agree, as will our brethren. I will tell them of our choice. Ask our guest if he will bring God Set to us or shall we send a Nim to bring him to us? Thank you, God Horus. Your debt to Dyohestia is paid in full."

She left the two men.

Dyoares said, "The key to destroying your sanctimonious self-righteousness is simple. We have another extraordinary candidate wishing to join the Kyrios-Olon other than Nimrod. His name is Nimbal. After we learned of your plans to bring Abram back to Urfa to disrupt our smooth-running organization, we sent Nimbal to Port Jaffa. He will travel fast and is already a day ahead of you. Nimbal was assigned an important task: seduce your wife. He will be armed with charm, wit, news of your travels, and bottles of Aphrodite-wine, but other than that, it shall be her own conscious decision and by her own eager free will that she decides she wants Nimbal to plow her. More wine?"

Horus contemplated the swans; swimming peacefully together; held out his glass, and said, "Please."

Nimrod smiled. *Well, my friend, you appear anxious to get back to check on your wife. You should have bought her a goat.*

<div align="center">~~~</div>

Meanwhile, Asherah continued to mesmerize Abram.

His mother Amathlai and sister Sarai watched in wide-eyed admiration as their youngest male captivated the heart of the great High-Horpriestess Asherah. Abram was most certainly now a man of consequence.

Phoenicia, Jaffa, Rocky, Burlyman, Polydore | Astarte, T'jaru
Terah, Amathlai, Haran, Terahson, Nahor, Sarai, Isaac, Jacob
Kyrios-Olon, Teumessian, Nimrod, Nimbal, Nimlad, Nimisis, Asherah, Set.

His father and two brothers were envious that the Horpriestess was slobbering over Abram, the youngest and most docile male in their family.

Asherah told Abram, "I am told that you are not yet married, that you have not found a pure and loving woman that you will honor and care for. A man such as yourself needs a loving woman to obey your commands. Surely you have considered taking such a wife."

Abram blushed. "I have been traveling in foreign lands. Most of the women there are whores and not pure at all."

"How horrible. How you must have suffered surrounded by such women as these. Perhaps you might take me as your temporary wife."

"T-take you? As my wife? But you are a Church of Urfa Priestess!"

"Yes. I am. I am a Horpriestess—sister-wife to all the good, faithful women married in the True Church. He who marries a pure woman in the name of the Church also marries me. The good and faithful husband may visit me when his wife is sick or unavailable. In this way, the man is always fulfilled and will care for his wife even more. I imagine you could take me as a bride even though you have not yet taken your first wife."

Abram panicked. *Never let them see you unsure!*

He said, "I will discuss this with my father. Marriage is a serious decision because it must last a lifetime. Father will help me decide."

"A very manly decision. I so hope that your father will look with favor on our spiritual and physical union." She smiled as she squeezed the back of his neck. "I must leave you now. Discuss with your father if you should take me as your willing, eager wife." She stepped back and motioned her attendants to escort her back to the Temple.

Abram was left staring at the departing woman in confusion.

Terah walked to his son, slapped him on the shoulder, and loudly said, "What about that boy? The Horpriestess will marry you and she didn't even mention a love offering. Most unmarried men have got to give a large love offering to marry her. Married men just have to make sure they keep up their tithing. This is wonderful. You bring a lot of pride to our family; more than those two worthless brothers of yours. Come on inside and let's talk about everything."

As they passed Amathlai standing there at attention, Terah commanded, "Hey, woman – bring me and my big-world son a beer."

Djoser, Hetephe, Incense/Hagar/Keterah
Horus, Serket, Azazil, Abram, Baalat
Ishmael, Maribah, Fatimah, Nebaioth, Basemath, Kedar | Anath, Astarte

~~~~~~~~~~~~~

5. The Story of Young Baalat

Year 158, Season 11

As the story of young Abram had begun, so began the story of young Baalat: Horus had stared into the eyes of Baalat and said "Soon, my daughter. I will see you soon." With that, he, Abram, and Nimrod had set off to Urfa.

So then, Azazil stood beside Baalat in silence.

She said, "Well, that's that. Will you walk with me, Azazil? At least until I learn about the city and its dangers. I will buy you highsun meal with my newfound wealth."

"I will walk with you until you cast me off, Baalat. You must acquire a title and choose your manner of dress. When you cast me off, you must have a self-protection plan. You carry too much wealth not to be noticed. Either take on a disguise or attract a strong consort. Hetephe once did quite well dressed as a man."

"Hmm. Then while I have you, let's walk to what they call a dock. It is a wretched thing. I can't believe Portmaster Serket once sent a Jaffa trading vessel to this place. I want to know who controls it and why."

They found the dock. It was lined with a few small fishing vessels. They walked to the shack at its north end.

She asked, "Will you talk with them Teacher Azazil? I wish to appear stupid and untrained."

Azazil nodded, "Yes," as they entered the shack. "Greetings Dockmaster. Are you the chief of this excellent dock?"

"Yea, Stranger. If you wanna use one of my fine fishin' boats, it'll cost you a denarii a day. Most of'em are seaworthy enough. If it sinks, then you gotta pay another two denarii for not returnin' it. Do you accept my fair offer?"

"Fair enough, dockmaster. I and my daughter have just arrived in your city, and I must catch food within the quartermoon. Will you have a vessel available when I return?"

"I don't promise, but there be few 'nough fishermen these days. I 'spect you'll have some boats to choose from."
~~~~~~~~~~~~~

Baalat asked, "Why are there no fishermen?"

The dockmaster laughed. "Probably 'cause there ain't no fish no more, at least not close in. City dumpin's drove'em most away."

Baalat unintentionally took over the conversation and gleaned all the information he knew about the water's approach to Byblos. He was a lonely man, happy to have someone that would talk with him. Baalat gathered all the information she could think of and signaled Azazil that they could now leave. Azazil bid farewell and as they turned to leave, Baalat suddenly asked the man, "Where is a good place for Father to obtain a good highsun meal for both of us?"

A new subject of conversation opened. The dockmaster took advantage of Baalat's offer of a free meal.

EXIT FROM BYBLOS

Baalat spent the next quartermoon walking the city, absorbing it. The city markets had stalls of carved ivory, olive oil, Myrrh, gold, cedar, carved ebony, and fashioned malachite. She had shekels. How could she use her wealth to her advantage? These things were affordable in Byblos. Too bad she did not have them in Port Jaffa. They would be worth a lot more.

In the meantime, she had to find a way to support and protect herself. She talked to people and made friends. She needed a brilliant plan if she was going to become a Living God. That failing, she would still need some kind of plan to stay alive.

She made several friends as she walked. Baalat told them of the glories of the great trading city of Port Jaffa. One of the women suggested Baalat buy some cheap malachite, take it back to Port Jaffa, and sell it for a big profit. Baalat gasped as she instantaneously visualized, in her mind, a brilliant plan.

<div style="text-align: center;">~~~</div>

Azazil stood on the dock with Baalat, Dockman, and Baalat's four new-found women friends. He was aghast. He said, "This is ill-conceived, Baalat. I should forbid you to even consider it. When Horus hears this, he will have me thrown into the sea, bound and gagged. You should not attempt it!"

"Not only will I attempt it, but with the help of Osiris and my four strong women helpers, I shall do it! Dockman will have riches beyond his dreams. My helpers will become women of great worth."

Djoser, Hetephe, Incense/Hagar/Keterah
Horus, Serket, Azazil, Abram, Baalat
Ishmael, Maribah, Fatimah, Nebaioth, Basemath, Kedar | Anath, Astarte

"And you, my daughter?"

She laughed. "One does not become a Living God without accomplishing great deeds. This will be my first great deed. All that, plus I may make some shekels and get to keep on living."

Dockman said, "Let her go, Great Shaman Azazil. If she dies, she has already paid for the loss of my boats. If she returns, I get a handsome reward and she will own the finest dock in Byblos. What could be finer?!"

Azazil said to Baalat, "Neither you nor any of your crew has ever been to sea before!"

"Dockman is a good teacher and the lives of we five depend on our learning. We are smart and motivated. Besides, we are not going to sea. We will hug the coast until we get to Port Jaffa. Middlesea is calm enough this time of year. We have five tethered vessels and I plan on losing at least two of them. Even if I lose three, there is still profit in it. I am excited, Teacher Azazil. Please be excited for us! Give us your blessing."

"Tomorrow at sunrise, Daughter. I will give you my blessing plus implore Osiris to guide and protect you. I will mention his son, Horus, which will hopefully attract his attention."

They laughed in the camaraderie of those about to do a great deed.

Or die.

PORT JAFFA

After a quartermoon of difficult boating, Baalat stood in the lead fishing boat looking at the skyline of Jaffa in the far distance. She fell to her knees and gave thanks for their safe travels to every god that might exist. The women in the trailing tethered boats saw Baalat prostrate herself and, not exactly sure why, also fell to their knees and bowed their heads.

Baalat stood, raised her arms to the heavens, and screamed, "Thank you Osiris—giver of all things—for your protection. You are great and great is your love."

Each of her sailors joined in, "Great is your love!"

Baalat moved to the back of her boat and faced the women in the trailing boats. She said, "We must avoid the trading vessels and all costs. The wake from their bow would be enough to wash us under. Let's rest until the moon is high. The sea will be calm, and the big ships will all be docked. We can find a nice stretch of beach and land and avoid the port altogether. At sunrise, I will find Chief Phoenicia at her warehouse. She will help us unload our wares to a place where we can trade. We are almost there, Sailors! By sundown tomorrow we will be on our way to riches!"

The five women excitedly chattered among themselves.

Darkness came soon enough. The women negotiated their way past the well-lit, boisterous port and found a long stretch of secluded beach. They safed their vessels long before the moon was at its highest.

Baalat instructed her crew, "I will find someone to assist us. If sailors come this way, they will be drunk. Don't let them see inside our boats. Entertain them, seduce them, or tell them you're diseased, just keep them distracted from our cargo. I will return with help as soon as I can."

Baalat departed toward the direction of the trade warehouse. *I'm so tired. Let someone nice be there. Please.*

She came to the darkened warehouse and climbed the steps to the front porch. Unseen, in the dark, Phoenicia sat in Rocky's lap as they drank wine looking out over Middlesea.

Baalat was startled by Phoenicia's voice. "Good evening, Student Baalat. Has Horus returned home?"

"Trader Phoenicia! I didn't see you there in the dark. Is this an inappropriate time to call on you?"

"Yes. Very inappropriate. It's late, but we are here. Sit down. Join us. Have a glass of wine. Tell us of your travels."

She did, but left out the, "I and my friends returned by fishing boats."

Rocky said, "That's quite a story. You are no longer Horus's student. You left him in Byblos, and you have returned with trade. Quite a story indeed. Where did you leave this trade of yours? You have a wagon someplace?"

"Not exactly, Master Rocky. What we did is …"

Both Rocky and Phoenicia were aghast upon hearing the story. After all the how's, couldn't have's, impossible's, and you can't be serious's, Phoenicia said to Rocky, "Let's go see this conglomeration before the sea reclaims it. Did you obtain port clearance to dock, Captain Baalat?"

"Well, no. Was I supposed to?"

Phoenicia glanced at Rocky and said, "May Poseidon help us all! Let's go to the port. Maybe someone's still there. Let's straighten out this mess."

They arrived at the dock. The patio was alive with drunken sailors. An assistant Portmaster was still on duty. Baalat had to spend two of her precious shekels but before high-moon, Baalat had paid her port fees, received permission to unload, had secured a trading space at the Port Jaffa warehouse, and had purchased enough beer that semi-sober sailors had lifted her five fishing vessels loaded with trade out of the water and deposited them, still dripping, in their stall at the warehouse.

In the warehouse, Phoenicia stared wide-eyed at the collection of finely carved pieces of ebony, ivory, and onyx; at the beautiful necklaces and bracelets of lapis lazuli and malachite; at the flasks of olive oil and myrrh. All from five rickety rowboats that had sailed the coastline of Middlesea.

The ranking sailor inspected the rowboats stacked against the wall. "Hey, come look at this. This is cedar. That's a real good wood. Hard to find."

Baalat walked to the ranking sailor and asked, "I have a shekel left. Is that enough to buy another round of beer for my new friends?"

The sailor looked at the shekel and announced, "Sailors! Trader Baalat is buying all the beer we can drink tonight. Let's keep the dock open as long as one of us is still standing!"

A roar of approval went up. The sailors loudly headed to the dock patio.

Captain Trader Baalat was off to a good start.

Phoenicia and Rocky were left staring at the wonders that lay before her.

Baalat asked, "Master Phoenicia, may I leave two of my sailors to be your servants and learn the ways of a great trading house?"

Phoenicia absentmindedly replied, "'Assistants.' We shall make them our assistants. Come Assistant-trademasters, we have much work to do before we open for trade tomorrow." She walked to the first table; her new assistants eagerly followed.

As they walked to the tables, Rocky said, "Let's discuss where to maximize our profits. I will tell you the things to look for."

With satisfaction, Baalat watched them walk away. She said to her remaining two women. "Well, *my* Assistants One and Two, let's go to the dock and learn what we may learn."

SUNRISE WITH MADDOG

Baalat was near exhaustion from a quartermoon without proper sleep, but it would be unforgivable not to greet Osiris as he breached the horizon.

She stood in front of the dock building facing the east, waiting. Osiris came. She bowed her head and closed her eyes. *Great Osiris, you protected my sailors from harm. For this I give thanks. You smiled with favor on my quest. For this I give thank. You inspired the strength for me to do a great thing, for this I give thanks. Protect and guide Abram. He needs your strength and wisdom so desperately. Grant him strength and wisdom. And, let Teacher Horus find the way to become whole again. Thank you for all that you provide your children.*

Aloud she said, "Let it be!"

From behind her, she heard several people respond with, "Let it be!"

She looked over and saw Maddog Burlyman, the patio manager, and several women standing reverently. The women hurried away to prepare the dock patio for the coming day.

Maddog walked to her and asked, "You're that woman that brought five fishin' boats full of expensive-lookin' trade from Byblos, aren't you?"

"Yes. We did well, didn't we? We are all first-time sailors."

Maddog snorted, "Unbelievable! God Poseidon looks upon you with great favor. You and your crew will join me for morning meal."

"I would be delighted, Lord…. 'Maddog' is it?"

"Yea. Maddog Burlyman. I'm Protector for Portmaster Serket and Lord Polydore before her. I wanna hear about how you and Poseidon did this."

They walked to Maddog's table and sat down. Hot meals appeared on the table. The server asked Baalat, "Beer? Wine? Water? Blackwater?"

Maddog snarled, "Bring her blackwater. Strong blackwater. She looks like she can use it!"

Baalat said, "Yes. Blackwater, please."

"All right. Now, tell me how—and maybe why —you did this thing!"

Baalat, tired as she was, began her dissertation. The blackwater renewed her strength.

The long story told; Baalat leaned back and sipped her blackwater.

Customers began arriving for their morning meal.

To Baalat, Maddog said, "You and your sailors can go curl up in the storage room. Come find me if you ever wake up." He commanded the server, "Bring me a beer!"

SUNRISE

Baalat woke in a panic. *The sun is rising! I must greet Osiris! Where am I? How long have I been here?*

She jumped up, roused her still-sleeping sailors, oriented herself, and quickly made her way to the beach. The sun was almost clear of the horizon as she bowed her head and reverently greeted Osiris.

Her bones ached, her hair was dirty, she had not cleaned her teeth, her clothes were filthy, and she was still groggy. She had not thought past yesterday, didn't know what to do next, and needed a plan.

But she *did* have a full night's sleep.

Her assistants stood behind her. One asked, "What now, Lady Baalat?"

Baalat turned, stared at them for a moment, and said, "Let's go get a beer."

Entry into the Dock facilities, even into the patio, led past Maddog Burlyman's desk. As Baalat and her crew entered, he said, "Send your crewmen to the patio eating area. Postmaster Serket wishes to see you in her in her office, immediately!"

"Thank you, Captain Maddog. Now we have a plan."

She separated from her two crewmen at the patio entrance, turned right, walked to the end of the hallway, and knocked on the door.

A sweet voice said, "Come in."

Baalat entered and was hand-motioned to sit at the chair in front of Portmaster Serket's large desk. A not-so-sweet voice said, "I assume you are rested enough that we can come to the understanding that you will *not* sail into my port unannounced, without signal of porting, without registration, without a proper manifest, without invitation, without permission, and without proper authorization of using my staff to unload your trade directly at the Port Jaffa Trade Building. You are attempting to bypass port taxes, port infrastructure, and port logistics. I will not allow this! Is there any part of this you do *not* understand?"

Baalat was blindsided. She had expected warm words of welcome and congratulations plus she did not understand one word Serket was saying— except "taxes." *My teacher's wife is furious with me. She does not even acknowledge me as a friend. She expects me to follow rules when I don't even know what they are. How could I? What can I do? I don't know what I'm doing. I thought we were doing good! I thought she would be pleased! I thought she would welcome me. Teacher, what am I to say?*

"Never let them see you unsure."

Baalat leaned back in her chair and calmly said, "I have not had my morning meal. Could I at least have a cup of blackwater while I clear up all misunderstandings to your satisfaction?"

Serket was irritated and taken aback but commanded her assistant to bring cups of blackwater.

Baalat said, "You are correct to reprimand me. I have not followed standard protocols and I had wrongly assumed that I could provide all necessary information after we docked. A list of merchandise we carry is at the Trade Center. If you think it appropriate, send one of your administrators with me now to the Trade Center so that we can provide a list of what we carry and pay appropriate taxes and port fees plus whatever penalties and fines you require. I will then consult with your staff on your docking requirements and never violate them again. Is this satisfactory?"

"Master Burlyman will be your liaison. Take your morning meal, then find Burlyman. Spend your day straightening out this mess you have created."

"Most certainly, Portmaster. This will not happen again!" *Bitch!*

"Very well. Clear this up by the end of the day. You may go."

Baalat rose, said, "Thank you, and by the way, your husband is on his way to Urfa. He is doing well," and walked to find Burlyman.

The voice behind her said, "Thank you for that information, Captain."

Baalat found Burlyman sitting at his desk and asked, "I did bad, didn't I?"

"Yea. It's hard managin' a big dock like this. They can't allow for mistakes or exceptions. I heard you were gettin' the big talkin' to. You'll be all right. We got all day to straighten it out. But we need to talk 'bout your sailin' vessels. You won't be able to pull this off again. They won't let you sail out of here in those things. Go get somethin' to eat. Send your two women to me. I'll start 'em on the way things gotta be to have a sea tradin' company."

"Thank you, Captain Maddog. You are a good man." She turned to, at last, start her day.

Maddog Burlyman almost injured his face.

He smiled.

Djoser, Hetephe, Incense/Hagar/Keterah
Horus, Serket, Azazil, Abram, Baalat
Ishmael, Maribah, Fatimah, Nebaioth, Basemath, Kedar | Anath, Astarte

~~~

Baalat, Maddog, and the two women port assistants, now named Paone and Patwo, walked into the frenetic Trade Center. The newly named trade assistant, Tatwo, saw them enter and scurried over to escort them to the designated Byblos trading tables. The other trade assistant, Taone, was negotiating the sale of finely detailed onyx pieces to a trader from Crete.

Tatwo told Baalat that they had done real good in bringing in small highly finished products rather than heavy, unfinished raw materials. "It will take a lot longer to trade everything but what we brought gets a lot more in trade. It might take a full season to trade everything but you're going to be wealthy when this is over." That, plus, "Phoenicia is going to help us through the record-keeping the Trade Center needs, and she said that knowing Serket, she will want some port taxes even if we didn't exactly come through the port. We did come over her water, after all."

Tatwo then scurried away to present some exquisite lapis lazuli necklaces to a waiting Egyptian trader.

Burlyman wanted to see the ship's manifest. He waited until Taone finished her transaction then walked over to talk to her and was given some parchments.

He returned to Baalat with the parchment filled with unrecognizable scribbles. "What *is* this? Does it say anything? Where are your tablets?"

"This is a detailed list of everything we brought with us to trade. It records everything about what we have."

"It looks like the scratching of a chicken."

"It is written in standard Old Language. The symbols were developed by Titanide Mnemosyne. Teacher Horus had an Oceanid teach me to read and write this when we were in Memphis."

"It needs to be recorded on clay tablets in Common Trade Language. Have someone translate this scratching before the day is out or Portmaster Serket will be furious."

"I need a scribe."

"Go get a Chief Mate off the dock before he has too many beers. Most of them can record trade transactions. Read this stuff to them. They can make it presentable."
~~~

"Yes, Captain Burlyman. Right away, Captain Burlyman." She hurried off to the dock carrying her precious parchment.

Had there been sarcasm in her voice, Burlyman would have detected it. He did not. It made him feel … useful?

Patwo waited until Baalat had left and walked over to talk with Burlyman. "Trader Baalat said that we will not be allowed to leave in our fishing boats. We have already decided that papyrus and gold would command high prices in Byblos but are inexpensive in Jaffa. We know that we couldn't carry much because it is so bulky and heavy. But even a little would be profitable. What can we do to be allowed to leave with our trade, Captain Burlyman?"

"I will think about your problem, Sailor. You say papyrus is valuable in Byblos?"

"Yes, it is much preferred over clay tablets, but it is so expensive, it isn't used very much."

"How much papyrus would you carry?"

"Well, certainly five full fishing boats. If we had a hundred fishing boats, then those, too."

Burlyman hesitated. "I will think about your problem, Sailor. You and your captain find me after your captain makes peace with Portmaster Serket."

He turned and returned to his desk at the port.

THE PLAN

Before sundown, Baalat had coins, clay manifest tablets, and the new-found knowledge that only a qualified boat captain is granted permission to dock at Port Jaffa.

Serket found Baalat's documents and payment to be in order. "Very well, Trader Baalat. Your indiscretion is recognized and corrected, and you realize you may not use your fishing boats in port waters. That being said, welcome to Port Jaffa. Your feat is impressive. Guard Burlyman asked my permission to counsel with you if I found your corrective actions to be satisfactory. You may tell him that I am pleased with your professional response. Perhaps we can meet socially after your affairs are in order."

"Thank you, Portmaster. I always endeavor to do that which is the right thing to do, and I would be delighted to join you for pleasantries at your convenience."

"Excellent. Guard Burlyman is waiting on you."

Baalat left Serket's office and released a great sigh of relief. It had been a long day, but she was thrilled with her newfound knowledge. Who knew that port operations could be so complex and intricate? And now she felt like an accomplished ... what? Not a captain, not a portmaster, not a trader, not a sailor. She now knew a little about all those things but was a master of none of them. *Dung. I'm a complete failure. Life is hard!*

She found Burlyman. He said, "Come on. Let's talk. I'll buy you a beer."

They found an out-of-the-way table on the patio and sat. A server rushed two beers and a bowl of nuts to their table.

He said, "The way I see it is that you have a lot of money, but you and your crew are either gonna stay here or else walk back to Byblos. Seein' you and four other women sail in on rickety rafts has me wantin' to set to sea again. I been here long enough —too long. You provide the money, I'll provide the know-how. There's some ships scheduled to dock soon. I gotta good reputation. I should be able to engage one of 'em for a season. You fill it with as much trade as you want. Nobody trades on that coast 'cause there aren't any proper ports. No trader is gonna buy cargo space with us, so it'll be just your goods. I might be able to find a couple of payin' passengers that had rather sail than walk up that way. I'll get us a smaller ship and if you fill half of it with trade, you should do all right. Gettin' your trade off the ship and onto land is gonna be a problem cause we will have to anchor out at sea. I thought about fillin' those rowboats of yours with trade. Maybe you can use'm to ferry your cargo since Byblos don't have a portmaster 'cause they don't have a port."

Her eyes stared into his over the mug of beer she held near her face. *The sea! How you love the sea. The fury of it. The calmness of it. Poseidon is your god. The ports. The docks. Horus took me to the port in Egypt. It is five, no, ten times the size of Port Jaffa. The Egyptians think big. Build things bigger. Better. For eternity!*

Burlyman was almost fidgeting under her gaze. He did not know why, but he wanted to please her. To impress her.

She stared deeper. She could see the dilapidated dock at Byblos. She superimposed an image of the Egyptian port. *Byblos! Gateway from the east to the lands of Egypt Greece! Crete! Lands of which I do not know!*

She held out her beer to salute him, saying, "Captain Burlyman, we are going to do well together. God Poseidon rejoices you again sail his seas!"

Burlyman nodded in recognition.

He was almost trembling.

~~~

They worked, the six of them, feverishly for a full half moon. Their ship was neither the smallest nor the largest in port. Baalat had almost no money remaining. She had invested her newly acquired fortune into this venture; the massive overhead of acquiring the ship for a full season, taxes, guarantees, insurance, and on and on. But she now commanded a trading ship filled with papyrus, gold, and turquoise. She owned a great deal of the trade outright plus she had leveraged the local oversupply of papyrus into profit-sharing consignments upon her ship's return. If the venture was successful, Baalat and her two trader-women had already decided that the return voyage would bring back raw materials of cedar, ebony, and uncut lapis lazuli. Baalat would reap great returns; assuming the ship didn't sink, the gods were kind, and they gained all permissions.

As an added profit, four people had booked passage to Byblos. All of this from the secondary port of Jaffa to sail to a non-existent port in Byblos—Gateway to the East.

The ship set sail. All thought, *Osiris be with us ... and Poseidon!*

BAALAT AT SEA

The ship would soon arrive in Byblos.

Baalat had taken papyrus from their cargo and had meticulously transcribed their manifest onto it. *Tablet markings are so basic. They contain so little information. Mnesomyne's characters are easily written onto papyrus. I can fashion her symbols into whatever words I wish and describe so much more. I must keep all of my transactions on papyrus and teach some local people how to read and write these symbols.*

She admired her work, rose, and set off to find Captain Burlyman.

Burlyman was on deck studying the night sky for signs of a storm. As she approached, he said, "God Poseidon carries us in his palm, Tradesman. He looks upon you with favor."

"I need all the help we can get. If you look toward God Poseidon for favor, I shall fall on my knees and beg for it."
~~~

"That would not be wise. The gods favor the courageous."

"Then courageous we shall be! I have a plan for Byblos. I remember abandoned buildings near the dock. I don't know who they belong to, but I will send my two assistants to the city to find out. We will unload our cargo into these buildings when we arrive and hope to find owners who will look upon us with favor. How many trips will it take to unload? Do we unload as fast as we can or as slowly as we dare?"

"If the sea remains calm, take whatever time you need. We will know more about the weather when we arrive."

They stood side by side on the deck looking over the calm sea toward a full moon.

He said, "The moon will be full tonight, a rare occurrence. In all my years, I have seen only one other full moon on Winter's Solstice."

"Then let all gods take note that this was the night courageous Captain Burlyman sailed into Byblos. May they bless Byblos and its people."

"The gods watch for signs that portend great fortune."

They sailed on in silence watching the moon rise toward its glory—hopefully portending great fortune.

~~~~~~~~~~~~~

6. Vignettes

SERKET AND NIMBAL

Year 158, Season 11

The day before the beginning of the Winter Solstice Season, Nimbal stood considering the city he was about to enter. *If I can do this, they will make me a Dyo. She is a woman. I cannot fail. I will take the name Dyoapollo. God of everything!*

He walked the city once more, re-familiarizing himself with its sights and sounds. He passed the home of Jaffa the some-teenth and his two powerful female keepers—Polydore and Astarte. Although, missionary reports suggested Astarte had left to be God Set's concubine; replacing the Dispatcher Anath woman who, according to reports, had humiliated him by eagerly fornicating with Horus while Set and the powers-that-be watched Horus do it. *Ah, yes. That will be useful information in Serket's upcoming seduction.*

He walked to stare at the impressive Trading House managed by the sister, Phoenicia. *Phoenicia was more or less a prostitute until she was saved from a life of debauchery by Serket. Another useful fact.*

Finally, the port office itself. *You are an accomplished woman. A confident woman. A woman quietly filled with the passion of life. I can not fail!*

He chuckled out loud. *I doubt that the cabbage thing is true but the mere fact that your name is associated with such a story is enough to make my mission easy.*

He stood looking at the port, reviewing to make sure he had all the tools he might need. *You will be closing soon, my soon-to-be lover. It is time to begin.*

He confidently strode toward the Port office and entered. A woman sat at the front desk. He looked around with a bit of confusion, and said, "I was told that a man named Maddog Burlyman would be here to greet me. Am I in the wrong building?"

"Oh, no. I am a temporary replacement for Captain Burlyman. He accepted an offer to set to sea as a Ship's Captain. How can I help you?"

"I met an interesting Shaman in Byblos. His name is Horus, and he is a man of many stories He was on his way to Urfa and asked me to stop by the port and deliver some messages to a woman named Serket. Do you know of her?"

<div align="center">

Djoser, Hetephe, Incense/Hagar/Keterah
Horus, Serket, Azazil, Abram, Baalat
Ishmael, Maribah, Fatimah, Nebaioth, Basemath, Kedar | Anath, Astarte

</div>
~~~~~~~~~~~~~

"Portmaster Serket!? Of course! She will be thrilled. Come with me!"

Nimbal followed the woman to an office door. She knocked, stuck her head in the door, and said, "Portmaster there is a man from Byblos bringing you messages from Lord Horus!"

The sound of a woman's squeal of delight, a chair moving, and footsteps were heard.

The bright face of Serket appeared. "I am Portmaster Serket! You bring words from my husband?"

He engaged.

~~~

They bantered back and forth.

Eventually, she accepted a second glass of his Aphrodite wine. He had told of Horus and seamlessly mixed in some Greek poetry and several risque anecdotes, each more risque than the previous. He made her laugh six times. He brushed his leg against hers, apologized profusely, and said, "But I *did* enjoy it. I hope you don't mind. I could talk with you all night and into the morning. I love hearing what you have to say."

He stood and walked over to admire the colored painting hanging on the wall behind the desk. He stood a little closer to her than one might expect. "This is gorgeous. Is there a story here? "

She rose to stand beside him. "Yes. This is a gift from my husband. It is a drawing of Isis blowing life into Osiris."

Suddenly, he grabbed her, embraced, and forcefully kissed her. He rejected her expected pushing away and at the exact moment she would submit, he pushed *her* away. With an agonized voice, he exclaimed, "I'm sorry Portmaster Serket! That was unforgivable! I was overcome by desire. Forgive me, if you can."

He backed away and quietly said, "Tell me to leave, and I will."

He gave her a look of sincere atonement.

She stared at him without speaking.

He said, "Command me to leave or else share another glass of my wine with me. I beseech Aphrodite to convince you to accept the wine."

"Perhaps one more wine but you will honor my refusal of any inappropriate suggestions you might make."
~~~

"I so swear but you must swear that if you *do* accept me then you will never speak of it to anyone. It must remain a precious memory only in our own minds. Do you swear?"

"Pour your wine, Nimbal."

As they drank their third glass, Nimbal, as he recited erotic Greek Poetry, pulled a small lyre from his traveling bag, and said, "Sit on your sofa so that I may sit in your chair and play my love song."

She did not notice nor care that he was now *telling* her what to do. Horus had initiated her into the physical pleasure and the emotional reward of sexual activity. She liked it—all of it. *I have not lain with Horus in a long time! Nimbal said Horus would not return for at least another six seasons! I wish Horus were here, but he's not. Sex—I mean SIX—more seasons!*

She obediently moved to her sofa and sat. The Aphrodite-wine coursed through her veins, he played the lyre beautifully, his voice full of passion. *Horus DID tell me that he wouldn't mind. That I could—if I really wanted to.*

Nimbal finished his song, laid down his lyre, walked to stand before her, fell to his knees, and gently pushed hers apart.

She stared into his eyes the entire time. *I really want to.*

HORUS

Horus and Azazil arrived in Port Jaffa two days after the quarter moon marking the beginning of the Winter Solstice Season. Decorations were appearing throughout the city.

Horus did not go immediately to the docks. Instead, he sat under the tree that he and Serket had sat under when he had left a lifetime ago. "Azazil, ask Serket to join me."

Nimbal watched from his secluded observation bench as Azazil entered the Port Building and watched as, soon enough, Serket left carrying a blanket and a basket. Nimbal discreetly followed her.

Serket walked past Horus sitting under his tree but said nothing. She kept walking to an out-of-the-way secluded area and spread the blanket on the ground. She placed sweetbread and wine on it, sat down, smiled at Horus, patted the blanket, and said, "Sweetbread and wine for my sweet. Come to me. We can do things."

He shook his head, "No," and motioned for her to come to sit beside him.

She did, and said, "You return, but did not come to my bed. I bring us a blanket, and still you will not come to me. Am I a scorned woman?"

He took her under his arm. She snuggled close.

"I worried about you, Serket. I lost Baalat to them. Now I am losing Abram to them, and they said they were coming to seduce you. I worried they would succeed. I worried they would fail. Are you all right?"

She sat frantically thinking. *I was right to go to Polydore. Oceanids are wise in these matters. Nimbal WAS an agent of Urfa. They want to destroy my husband through me. Be with my words, Oceanid Polydore. Make my words right.*

He said, "You are quiet, my wife."

She said, "Succeed? Fail? How will you measure those things, Husband? I lay with a man while you were away. His name was Nimbal. He wanted me to swear that I would not tell you. I did not swear. How can a woman keep this a secret from the man she loves? A man who is her life, her every breath. Nimbal told me you would not return for at least another six months. He was very accomplished; both in my seduction and my enjoyment. But he left me with nothing. You always leave me with peace and joy. So ... what is your judgment, Husband? Did they succeed or fail?"

He embraced her and cried for a while, then said, "Lead me to your blanket; but I need no sweetbread, nor wine; only you."

After they were sated, peace came to Serket.

An uneasy peace.

CELEBRATIONS

In Port Jaffa, Horus greeted the rising sun after the Winter Solstice and encouraged it to proceed to Memphis where High-Priestess Hathor would be waiting to call forth Osiris to become Ra. Horus had planned on performing this ceremony at Fort Rafah, the entrance into Egypt, but his local priests told him that the Living God Anath was scheduled to perform the ceremony. So Horus remained in Port Jaffa teaching of the path where each person respected their neighbors, where every person helped every other person. Several men blushed when he told of a man who loved his camel instead of a woman. "If neither man nor camel is hurt by this act, then what right do we have to condemn them? Every woman, child, animal, and man has the basic right not to be condemned unless harm is inflicted. Do no harm. Love one another. Be worthy."

Azazil and his priests mingled with the crowd passing out bread and offering kind words. The world was filled with hope and goodwill.

At the edge of the crowd, Nimbal stood listening.

When Serket finally glanced at him, he was grinning.

~~~

In Fort Rafah, Anath performed an impressive ceremony, supported by her sister, Astarte, who had traveled from Memphis to help her—and be observed by important people as she associated herself with Sister Anath, the Living God of Canaan. Set had been furious that Astarte was leaving him in Memphis to go help her bitch sister in the cursed places where Horus was held in such high esteem. But Astarte was not without her own ambition and, although she would not dare mention it, Sister Anath was held in much higher regard than Set everywhere east of Memphis.

And in Memphis, the sun finally breached the horizon and was greeted with the pomp and splendor of the world's greatest civilization.

Another year began.
~~~

~~~~~~~~~~~~~~

7A. Serket

Year 159, Season 1

SERKET'S SEASON ONE

Horus and Azazil had departed Jaffa to travel the Egyptian Trade Route.

After her husband had departed, Serket invited her friends to join her on the dock patio for highsun meal and gossip.

The women sat hunched over in deep conversation around a remote table on the dock patio. No sailor dared approach them.

Serket: "Horus cried when I told him that I had lain with Nimbal. Why did he cry? He had told me that he would be gone for a long time, and I had his permission to lie with someone if I wanted to! He wasn't mad or anything, but he still cried."

Polydore: "Sweet! Men are fragile creatures. It is not you. You have no blame. Horus understands."

Dispatcher Anath: "Horus cries over everything. He'll get over it."

Serket: "Horus performed a beautiful sunrise ceremony the next day. I stood listening knowing Nimbal was there. I did not glance his way until the ceremony was over. I caught him leering at me!"

Polydore: "Nimbal is some kind of Urfa missionary sent to create mischief. You told Horus what you did. Forget about it."

Phoenicia: "I have satisfied hundreds of men. Rocky neither knows nor cares how many or who they were."

Serket: "How many have you lain with after you lay with Rocky?"

Phoenicia: "Well, none, really. But still, I have lain with hundreds. You have lain with two!"

Polydore: "Oceanids do not form life-long attachments to a single male, but I understand. You did not sneak behind his back, you did not lie to him, he gave you leave, and you believed he meant it, you did not betray him, and you have done no wrong. Yet it causes you anguish. Did he ask you not to do it again? Forbid it?"

Serket: "He takes his pilgrimage, and he did not tell me what he wished me to do or not do. And I'm afraid Nimbal is going to come again."

Dispatcher Anath, excitedly: "Are you going to let him do it?!"

Phoenicia: "Are you?!"

Serket, hesitantly: "I don't know."

Polydore: "Therein lay the mischief."

<div align="center">Phoenicia, Jaffa, Rocky, Burlyman, Polydore | Astarte, T'jaru
Terah, Amathlai, Haran, Terahson, Nahor, Sarai, Isaac, Jacob
Kyrios-Olon, Teumessian, Nimrod, Nimbal, Nimlad, Nimisis, Asherah, Set.</div>
~~~~~~~~~~~~~~

~~~~~~~~~~~~~~

7B. Baalat

Year 159, Seasons 1, 2, 3

BAALAT'S SEASON ONE

Burlyman dropped anchor as close as he dared to Byblos. He lowered Baalat's five fishing boats into the water. All filled with as much cargo as he dared. Baalat reviewed her plans with her Trader and Port Assistants. "We are as prepared as we can be, People. Let's do it!"

Each lowered themselves into a different fishing boat and began rowing to the Byblos dock, such as it was. They arrived and began unloading their wares on the dock. Patwo rowed back to the ship to pick up Burlyman and two sailors. Trade Assistants Taone and Tatwo headed into town to survey what markets remained open during this raucous period of the Winter Solstice season and develop a plan for the best cargo to invest in for the ship's return trip to Port Jaffa. Baalat and Paone walked to the abandoned buildings near the end of the docks. Burlyman and the two sailors joined them and all wandered through the abandoned buildings.

Paone and Burlyman discussed which one would be best for storing and trading their wares. They took their decision to Baalat who said, "We will use the one closest to the docks."

She looked at Paone and said, "Stay here and start laying out what the greatest port in the world would be like if it were built here."

She looked at Patwo and said, "Get the rowboats and all our goods into the first warehouse."

To Burlyman, she said, "Come with me, Captain Burlyman. Let's go find our probably drunk dockmaster. He will live somewhere nearby."

They walked the alleyways where he probably lived. Baalat loudly repeated, "Lord Dockman. I have your investment ready to disperse."

Soon enough, a figure emerged from a doorway behind them, and shouted, "Woman Baalat, you are alive! Did you do what you set out to do? Have you made me rich!"

Baalat, somewhat repulsed, embraced Dockman. *For business purposes only because you are exceedingly valuable to me.*
~~~~~~~~~~~~~~

She said, "Lord Dockman. We will discuss business after you sober up. In the meantime, yes, I think you will be pleased, but now I have other needs you can probably assist with me."

"I will not begin another transaction before I complete the first one. How well did you do?"

"I remember that you said I could buy your dock and fishing boats for twenty shekels. As soon as you are sober, I am prepared to complete the transaction."

"TWENTY SHEKELS? I MUST HAVE AT LEAST FORTY SHEKELS FOR MY EXTREMELY VALUABLE DOCK!"

Baalat stared at him. *You are a foolish man Lord Dockman ... or drunk ... or both. You would have fared much better with Twenty.*

She said, "Oh, my goodness, Lord Dockman. As it turns out, the dock is useless to me without those nearby abandoned buildings. Without those buildings, I could not afford your dock for even ten shekels. My trade was successful, but unfortunately, your docks are not useful without some buildings to go with them. Whatever shall I do?"

Dockman began his inebriated calculations. "Fifty shekels and you may have the docks and the first building!"

Baalat pondered. "That's a lot of shekels, Lord Dockman."

After the back and forth, pondering, demands, hesitations, and negotiations, Baalat said, "You drive a hard bargain, Lord Dockman, but we will meet at the Chief of Byblos House tomorrow at begin of business. He will witness the sale of your docks and the adjacent six abandoned buildings for the high price of sixty shekels. I will have the tablets prepared and ready to be signed plus your five shekels return on investing in my first venture. Get a good night's sleep and appear there completely sober. Are we in agreement?"

"Yes. That will be satisfactory."

They saw him back into his room and bid him farewell until the next morning. Baalat left a shekel on his table to remind him of their talk.

The four walked back to the dock. Baalat said to Paone, "You heard the agreement. Find a scribe and document it but change the sixty shekels to eighty shekels."

Burlyman asked, "Can you afford that?"

"No, but I would have paid one hundred and twenty for all that we are getting. By the time I buy trade for your return to Port Jaffa, I shall have no wealth except what my Traders can negotiate for that which you carry to Port Jaffa. If you sink during the voyage, then I will have nothing but a slum in which to live. Worse yet, Captain Maddog Burlyman will never own his own ship. That would make God Poseidon so very sad!"

They returned to the dock. The two Traders had scavenged food for everyone plus a lot of beer. They had a little party on the dock for themselves and the worn-out ship's sailors.

The Traders were beside themselves with information. "There is always a shortage of papyrus in Byblos. I believe we should be able to trade all that we have quickly and with significant profit. Plus there is an overabundance of cedar here. We can get it for the taking. Land trade caravans are slow adjusting to supplies and demands!"

Burlyman wanted to be supportive of "his" women. He said, "You will have a quartermoon to fill our ship's cargo bays then we must set sail. My agreement is that the ship will be back in Jaffa by the next new moon, and you will need time to unload. I will begin finding another ship to charter as soon as we dock."

Baalat said, "After our return trade is secure, take whatever profit remains and attempt to buy a ship worthy of Captain Burlyman. If trading is good, you will have enough to at least offer a first payment. Purchase a good one. One that will not sink and take our fortune with it."

"Lord Baalat, to put all your wealth into one enterprise is not wise. One stroke of misfortune and you are ruined!"

"*We* are ruined, Captain Burlyman. Do your best. I will keep God Poseidon entertained and away from the mischief he can cause. Do well with the purchase and bring us back another shipment of papyrus and whatever else our Trader Women can steal. If the gods are on our side, invite Oceanid Polydore to return with you. I will ask her to build you a port such as you have never seen. When shall I expect your next return?"

Burlyman considered the question. "To find and negotiate purchase of a ship will take at least a season; probably two. To load it with trade and return, another season. By the fourth Full Moon of the year, I believe."

"Then I shall start looking for you by the fourth Full Moon with your ship and our wealth."

Djoser, Hetephe, Incense/Hagar/Keterah
Horus, Serket, Azazil, Abram, Baalat
Ishmael, Maribah, Fatimah, Nebaioth, Basemath, Kedar | Anath, Astarte

The women were giddy with excitement, the sailors exuberant with potential good fortune, Burlyman solemn with the responsibility laid upon him. Baalat considered her people. *What is the worst that can happen to us? No matter what, it will be glorious!*

After a beer and a while, Baalat slipped away and stood at the end of the dock looking at the peaceful three-quarter moon. *Great God Osiris—Thank you for my incredibly good fortune. And you, Great God Poseidon—Bless this city and all its people.*

She appreciatively sipped her beer.

THE PURCHASE

She and Dockman met the next morning at the Chief of Byblos's house. The Chief was more interested in celebrating the closing days of the Winter Solstice season, but he always took time to properly oversee the smooth operation of his city. The chief was impressed with Dockman's negotiating ability in getting such a high price for such worthless land, but if the woman had the money, then someone would probably help her depart with it sooner or later.

Dockman well remembered the negotiated price was sixty shekels. He was pleased that Baalat was evidently confused.

After the exchange was concluded, Baalat complained to the chief that so much waste was dumped into her waters and that the smell would be unbearable during the hotter months. The chief explained that he paid up to two shekels a day to keep city waste and filth and garbage picked up. Throwing it into the sea was the most expedient thing to do with it. If she had a better or cheaper solution, he would give her an audience.

Baalat and Lord Dockman, as he would now refer to himself, walked toward the docks together. He agreed, "Yes, the smell will be horrible when the heat comes. I'm so happy I no longer own this property."

"Well," she asked, "can you at least help me figure out a way to have the waste taken somewhere else?"

He would think about it.

Meanwhile, a line of papyrus merchants was already forming at Warehouse Number One with money in both hands.

Her two Trader women had secured massive amounts of cedar to export back to Port Jaffa and were now scouring Byblos for other profitable export goods. Especially for wheat and grain products which could be resold to Egypt now that their stores were being depleted after two years of drought.

BAALAT'S SEASON TWO

Burlyman with his crew and two trader women set sail from Byblos to Port Jaffa on the morning after the falling quarter moon. His ship was filled with cedar, grain, and colored metal mined in large quantities in Alashiya. They also carried intricately worked metal bowls, jewelry, and carved ivory; expensive items requiring only a little cargo space.

Baalat, Paone, and Patwo busied themselves with finding potential dock builders and warehouse workmen. As the three women walked the city, they observed the trash on the streets and how random workers would appear, place it in their sacks, and carry it to throw it into the sea. Patwo observed, "They are not very efficient or timely with their gathering. A port would fall into the sea if it were managed this poorly."

Baalat asked her, "And where would you place the litter they gather?"

Patwo answered, "Well, a farm would benefit from the excrement, some of the trash is only damaged and could be repaired and resold, the remainder could be thrown into a low area that needed building up."

Paone said, "Let's go find such a place."

They walked due east to the outskirts of the city. Nothing attracted their attention until the elevation began rising.

Patwo decided. "This is as good a place as any to build ourselves a little hut. Dig some trenches to throw the unusable things into. Use the dirt to build a little artificial water pond. We can throw the excrement onto a field downwind from our huts. Use dirt from the trenches to cover it. Make fields to grow whatever they grow around here or even make a vineyard. Nothing impressive; just make everything useful. We need a wagon and someday some kind of beast to pull it."

Paone said, "First we need a wagon, someone to pull it, and two people to pick up trash. Oh, and something to pay them with. Then Lord Baalat can get a contract to pick up trash from the chief."

Baalat said, "We have one shekel and some coins to live on for at least three seasons. We must live wisely."

They returned to the city market area. Patwo asked a lentil merchant, "Where do the poor people of Byblos live?"

The woman laughed. "We are all poor, my lady. The wretched live outside the city to the southeast."

The three women thanked the merchant and turned toward the southeast. Soon enough, the city ended, and the huts appeared. Old people, mostly crippled, stared at them as they walked the littered path. They came upon a shack with a broken-down wagon in the front yard. Baalat turned, marched to the doorless front entrance, and exclaimed, "Hello! Is anyone home?" She heard shuffling feet. An old, stooped, toothless woman appeared. The woman saw that Baalat was a person of rank and deferentially bowed. She said, "My lady, I have no taxes to give you or anything of value. Please do not beat me!"

"Do you own the wagon in the front yard?"

"That worthless thing belonged to my husband but then the cow that pulled it died and then my husband died. I have nothing but scraps of food that I find. Please do not beat me."

"I wish to inspect your wagon. May I?"

"Take the wagon, my lady. It is useless to me. Just leave me in peace."

"Very well. We will leave you for now."

The three women left to inspect the wagon.

They observed, "We need oil for the wheels, nails and pieces of lumber for the frame, a harness for whatever pulls it, three replacement spokes, and some binding rope. The bottom is in poor shape but usable."

The women completed their inspection and hurried back to the market to use some precious coins for repair parts.

As darkness came, they returned to their cramped hut on the dock and made their plans for the next day.

A BUSINESS

Sunrise came.

Baalat paused for a few moments and said a silent greeting to Isis and Osiris as he broached the horizon. *One cannot have too many friends. Remembering Isis will please Osiris.*

They made their way back to the wagon with their supplies and spent much of the morning repairing the wagon. The two Port women slipped into their harnesses and gave a pull. The wagon jerked into motion ready for a day's work.

Baalat put on a bright yellow vest and marched to the old woman's shack. Baalat said, "I accept your offer of the wagon. Here is your morning's meal. Eat it and when you are finished, put this on and report for work at the wagon. You will be fed all you can eat as long as you work for me. Your name is now Bybone. Are we in agreement?"

The astonished woman could only mutter, "Y-yes, my lady."

After more coaching, the woman took the food and yellow vest and disappeared into her house. Soon enough, she cautiously reappeared wearing the bright yellow vest matching the ones worn by Baalat, Paone, and Patwo.

Baalat said, "We have a new business, ladies. Collect what you can. Bring it to the Chief's House before sundown. I'm off to negotiate with the chief. Do well."

The women had partitioned the wagon bed into three sections.

Baalat left and her two assistants began picking up litter within a twelve-pace distance from the wagon. After a short time, Paone looked at the old woman and said, "You may be old and crippled, but you are not useless. Do your share!"

The woman stared in disbelief and then with slow understanding began to place litter in the wagon. Patwo had the shovel, so she was in charge of excrement. The first area cleared of litter, the two women pulled the wagon twenty-four paces toward town and began again. Soon, the rhythm of teamwork kicked in and their effort became effortless. They stopped for highsun meal. The old woman was ecstatic to be fed a second time in one day. After eating and resting, they began again.

Baalat was sitting on the front porch of the Chief's house when she saw the wagon appear in the distance. She called for the chief to join her and the two walked to greet the approaching wagon. Arriving, she said, "Well, Great Chief Maku. Does this quantity meet with your approval? We will bring you no less than this amount each day before sundown. You will give us a quarter of a shekel for each load. I will be responsible for disposing of this away from the city. You will offer the protection of Byblos to those workers wearing a yellow vest. Are we in agreement?"

Chief Maku stared at the wagon doing quick calculations. "Yes, we are in agreement. Take the wagon to the back. I will introduce you to the bookkeeper. He will give you payment. After the inspections and payment were made, Baalat said, "Excellent, Chief Maku. I and my people are honored to be in your employment. I will be allowed to add additional wagons in the future, will I not?"

"Yes, Lord Baalat. Our city has a lot of refuse."

"This is a challenge I will accept and don't you dare forget how nice the waterfront will smell this summer without all the trash being dumped into it. A party honoring the city leadership will be in order. By the way, this is Paone, Patwo, and Bybone. They will work very hard under your leadership."

The chief nodded toward the women in recognition.

Bybone almost fainted. *My husband! We are somebody!*

Baalat helped pull the wagon back toward the poor section. "Dung! We have to find a place to dump our trash before we can pick up another load and we have a new moon tonight. We will miss a day tomorrow until we can get settled."

Patwo said, "The woman was quite talkative once she warmed up to us. She told me how the land lays, who grows what, and where they grow it. We can trade excrement for a share of their harvest. Leave the wagon in front of the woman's house tonight. Have her tell her neighbors to take what they want. Whatever remains after sunrise, there is a washed-out gully not too far away that needs to be reclaimed and it's downwind. We will be back in business by mid-morning. I think we can get two strong-backed men to pull the wagon for food and beer. A quarter of a shekel will go a long way for food and beer."

Baalat walked on in silence. They would spend the night under the wagon awaiting the sunrise. *Anything is riches when you have nothing.*

RECRUITS

Sunrise.

Baalat greeted Isis and Osiris. Nothing remained in the wagon but excrement. A dozen men stood milling around hoping to be recognized. Baalat walked to the men and said, "I need two worthy men to pull the wagon while the women gather trash. I do not know you, but you know yourselves. Select two men you most respect and send them to me. They will have food this morning and beer this evening. Tomorrow they will have yellow vests. I hope this is the beginning of work for those who wish to work. If not here, then elsewhere. Good morning, men."

She turned and returned to the wagon. *This is going to work out well.*

ANOTHER BUSINESS

Days passed.

Baalat was pleased with herself as she greeted a rising sun. *Greetings Great Gods Isis and Osiris. I give thanks to you and to God Poseidon. You are kind to be merciful to one such as I. A woman with nothing. I rejoice in your blessings. Peace be with you. Always.*

She opened her eyes to face the coming day. *Patwo has two wagons, now. Four men pulling. Eight women gathering. The men don't even stop anymore; they adjust their speed to the speed of the women. Extremely efficient. A half-shekel a day. More than enough to feed them and buy them vests. They would work without food simply to receive a vest. It's a sign of rank to them.* "Anything is riches when you have nothing."

Baalat broke from her reverie when Paone arrived.

Baalat said, "We are out of shekels, Paone. Stop restoration of the warehouse. We have no money to pay wages. What we have accomplished must suffice until our ship returns."

"The men will work for food, beer, and their blue vest, Lord Baalat. I can go to my back to earn enough coins for that."

"No, Paone. Leave that to the young women with no other hope. Here are a few coins. Go into the markets and see if you can buy enough to feed your men for a day or two more. Patwo's project is bringing in money but it's best if she can keep it all and re-invest it. It's too bad we don't have a way for reclaiming the dock to bring in revenue."

Paone took the coins, stared at them for a moment, and vowed to do the best she could.

Baalat inspected her six warehouses—praising the workers. "If your gods are kind, you shall create a workplace of great value and pride."

At highsun, she stood at the end of the dilapidated docks and stared out into a vision of greatness.

The end of the day approached. Paone returned and threw down a blanket upon which she set out bread, beer, and dried fish. "This will get them fed nicely, I think. You can promise them more of the same tomorrow if you like. I did well in the market."

Baalat called the men to their "feast." They sat cross-legged on the dock happily devouring their bounty.

Two random men walked up. "Hey, whose beer? Can I have one?"

Paone quickly responded, "Food and beer are free to our workmen; for a small coin you may join them."

The two men looked at the food, then at each other. "It looks good. Let's do it." They offered two small coins and sat down to join the meal.

Baalat and Paone looked at one another with mutual revelation.

They would sleep well that night.

SUNRISE

Soon after Baalat's sunrise ritual, Patwo showed up at the dock carrying a sack. "Don't worry, your two cleanup teams are performing their day's work. I will meet them before sundown, have their wagons inspected, and collect our wages. We need more dung. The farmers are elated to receive it and happily promise us a share of their crops. The local people want to inspect the remainder of our daily collection. Affluent people discard the best things. I pulled out a lot of material I thought might be useful to you. A hammer and some nails and nice-looking ceramic tiles; that sort of thing. We don't have that much going into our landfill. One of the merchants gives me special prices on the fruits and vegetables because I buy so much, and I accept whatever goods he has too much of including the older things. Do you need food here? I have a lot left over."

Baalat said, "I was thinking about offering food and drink for sale on the dock. That would help us."

"The other people collecting trash are still throwing it in the ocean, aren't they? The docks will smell bad until you stop that."

"Ask them how much they get for each bag. Buy it from them for that price and throw it in the wagon. Pay double for pure excrement. Also, I need some tables and chairs to make a patio restaurant."

"If I see some worn out ones, I will offer to haul it away without charge. Or maybe just a small charge. I will let the teams know and pay a bonus to the wagon that brings some in. Anything else?"

"I will take all the food you can spare and here, take these coins and get whatever beer you can with it. We open 'The Port Byblos Outdoor Restaurant' tomorrow night at Sunset! I need some torches, too."

The next day, Patwo scavenged three almost perfectly good tables and a dozen almost perfectly serviceable chairs. Even with the bonuses, the day's work broke even. They were maintaining their resources and the grand opening of the PBOR would have actual tables and chairs and torches. That, plus additional scavenged items made perfectly good decorations for the restaurant. Patwo offered three city scavengers coins for their accumulated trash.

Paone incorporated the salvaged items into warehouse repairs. It was enough to keep her workmen busy and make small advances.

The tables, chairs, improvised benches, two torches, workman eating and drinking for free, and the dozen paying customers were enough to make the grand opening of the PBOR a rousing success.

By the end of the season, Baalat had added a third litter wagon, negotiated a city contract to maintain Byblos free of litter, was the provider of fertilizer to six farms, was developing a used goods market stall with goods recycled from the litter wagons, was well on her way to purifying the water around her docks, owned the almost finest restaurant in Byblos, one fully serviceable warehouse, two on their way, and three more being repaired.

And, oh yes, somewhere, Poseidon willing, she had a ship full of trade merchandise.

<p style="text-align:center">~~~</p>

Baalat's projects continued to make incremental progress. She had several which generated small amounts of revenue with enough she could reinvest creating even more revenue.

She had no resources to advance her goal of building a great port even though the surrounding port infrastructure slowly progressed.

She had no one who knew what the port specifications should be; nor the design, nor the where, nor the how, nor the materials, nor the thousand little capabilities that a smooth-running port should have. And, oh yes, she had no shekels to make any of it happen, anyway. She had to content herself with working on what she had and developing Byblos contacts from the poorest to the most powerful. The PBOR continued to grow and improve in quality.

Otherwise, she must wait for Captain Burlyman to come sailing in ... or walking in ... or swimming in ... with news of their trading expedition.

And each sunrise, she greeted the rising sun with encouragement for his daily travel across the sky and to give thanks to him and all the other gods —which Horus taught her did not exist—but which a clever, ambitious woman had to always take into consideration.

The third season approached.

They waited.

Phoenicia, Jaffa, Rocky, Burlyman, Polydore | Astarte, T'jaru
Terah, Amathlai, Haran, Terahson, Nahor, Sarai, Isaac, Jacob
Kyrios-Olon, Teumessian, Nimrod, Nimbal, Nimlad, Nimisis, Asherah, Set.

~~~~~~~~~~~~

7C. Baalat's Traders

Year 159, Seasons 1, 2, 3

BAALAT'S TRADERS SEASON ONE

Burlyman with his crew and two trader women set sail from Byblos to Port Jaffa on the morning after the falling quarter moon. His ship was filled with cedar and a colored metal mined in large quantities in Alashiya. They also carried intricately worked metal bowls, jewelry, and carved ivory; expensive items requiring only a little cargo space.

PORT JAFFA

A quartermoon later, Captain Burlyman received permission to dock at Port Jaffa. He had taken his time and hugged the coastline. *No need to taunt Poseidon.*

He docked.

The two Trader women scurried to the Warehouse to secure a trading space and find out what was trading well. Taone overheard two grizzled Damascus Caravan traders discussing the cedar from Byblos that had just docked and how in Egypt they could ten times what it would trade for in Jaffa. Taone scurried back to find Captain Burlyman. She found him on the dock engaging laborers to unload his cargo. She said, "Captain Burlyman, I have a problem. Can you advise me?"

Burlyman found time to sit with the women to discuss their problem.

He said, "We can't do it. I must have the ship unloaded and delivered back to its owner here in Port Jaffa by the New Moon. I don't have time to sail to Newport, unload, and get back in time. You will have to unload everything by tomorrow."

Taone asked, "How much to buy the boat outright?"

"With what Baalat gave me, all the trade from all of our cargo might do it, but maybe not."

"Dung! We would have a ship, but nothing left to buy trade. Very well, we will unload tomorrow, and you can return your ship to its owner. Let's make whatever profits we can. You wanted a bigger ship, anyway."

Tomorrow came.

Djoser, Hetephe, Incense/Hagar/Keterah
Horus, Serket, Azazil, Abram, Baalat
Ishmael, Maribah, Fatimah, Nebaioth, Basemath, Kedar | Anath, Astarte
~~~~~~~~~~~~

LADY OF BYBLOS ONE

Taone and Tatwo were finishing their morning meal discussing the busy day they were about to have. They had to oversee the placement of all their trade in the Warehouse and engage buyers. They both saw Captain Burlyman pass them on his way to Portmaster Serket's office and decided they would tarry a while longer.

Eventually, Burlyman came out, saw them, and walked over to join them. He looked like dung.

Simultaneously, the women brightly said, "Good morning, Captain Burlyman!"

"Yes. Yes, it is, my ladies. Lord Baalat now owns a trading vessel. We can sail to wherever we wish, whenever we wish."

The women listened with wide-eyed excitement as Burlyman recounted how he had found the ship's owner at a wine house after he had left them last night; of how he and the owner had drank and discussed the joy of a retired sea captain living in Port Jaffa, if only he had enough shekels; of how Burlyman made an offer which the captain rejected but countered with something do-able; of how Oceanid Polydore had found and joined them after hearing Captain Burlyman was in port; of how Burlyman's offer plus ten percent of their profit from the cedar sales at Newport might be sufficient to buy the ship; of how Oceanid Polydore would do anything to help her old protector Maddog Burlyman get his own ship; of how delighted she was that Burlyman and that Baalat woman were going to try to build a port at Byblos from nothing. "How brave and exciting," she had said. Of how, if this were satisfactory to the two trader women, they would all meet at the House of Chief Jaffa at highsun to complete the transaction; of how, if this came to pass, Captain Burlyman would dedicate himself to be the best captain, ever. *God Poseidon, let them choose to do it. I have missed the sea. The smell. The wind. Being a man of consequence. I have missed the sea. So much.*

Poseidon listened to the pleas of his faithful servant, Maddog Burlyman.

Everything came to pass.

NEWPORT

"Lady of Byblos One," captained by Captain Maddog Burlyman, sailed into the Egyptian port of Newport the evening of the rising quarter moon with a cargo of treasures including a massive amount of cedar.

Captain Burlyman negotiated a slot at the port and docked his ship.

The two confident traders hurried into the warehouse area to secure a trading space and observe what was happening. Unfortunately, they were overwhelmed by … everything. They were two young unsophisticated women from the hinterlands come to work in the big city. Every culture and every language in the known world were whirling around them. Suddenly they were frightened. They didn't know where to begin.

Tatwo said, "Let's go find a corner and cry!"

"You cry. I'll vomit."

They looked at one another, took deep breaths, and disappeared into the chaos of bartering, yelling, threatening, obnoxious, slimy-talking world-class traders from every nation known to man.

They returned to their ship at sundown and met Captain Burlyman.

Taone said, "We secured the smallest trading stall they had. It costs a fortune, but we can experiment with selling the small items before we try to trade the cedar and metals. How long before we have to unload."

Burlyman answered, "The docking fee is a half-shekel a day. Count your shekels."

"Unload the small items at this location," she said as she handed him a tablet, "Every trader in there is meaner than the last one."

Burlyman laughed. "Don't tell me that a sweet little trader woman is frightened of some big mean-looking man!"

"How do I deal with them? What is their weakness?"

"When it comes to shekels and trade, they have no weakness."

Tatwo snorted, "They are men! They will have a weakness. Come, Sister. Let's get back in there and watch them."

The two women went in together, and watched heated trades. After the trade was done and the traders were separating, each woman went to one of the traders and swooned, "You took such an advantage in that trade! How did you do it?"

They were met with varying degrees of "Get lost" to "He was not a good trader, was he?" But with each episode, they walked away with an insight.

Late that night, aboard ship, they decided. "They are not trading. They are doing battle with each other. We know what we paid for our trade. Let's set our price at a hundred times the buying price and refuse each offer with a 'thank you, but no' until someone will pay our price."

They slept well.

SUNRISE IN NEWPORT

The two women met Burlyman at sunrise. "We want samples of the cedar and the metal; not much. Just enough to show what it is. How long before you can have it there?"

"If I were doing it, before you finished your morning meal. Using their people with their rules, hopefully by highsun."

Taone said to Tatwo, let's get some parchment and make signs. No one there has a sign. They will look at our wares just for the novelty of seeing our signs."

"Put more liner on your eyes. We might as well look like women. We can at least distract them a little. And let's put all of our honey-bread nuggets into little bowls. If they talk nice to us they can have a piece."

"And beer, if they buy anything from us."

"All right, Trader-Sister. Let us do battle with men the way women have always done battle with men."

"We cannot lose!"

They happily gathered their papyrus, inks, candy nuggets, and some beer and headed off to prepare their trading stall for world-class battle.

THANK YOU, BUT NO

Their merchandise was delivered ahead of time thanks to Burlyman's constant attention. He knew not to speak or direct because the workmen would complain to their leaders. But hovering and watching intently was its own form of motivation. Besides, Newport was the most well-run port there was, as well as one of the largest.

A ship's captain did not engage in trading activities, but he removed his hat and drifted, inconspicuously, to the Byblos trading stall. The stall was surrounded by traders even though many were angrily storming away to the sound of pealing laughter. He thought, *They don't know what in the depths of Tartarus they are doing but they are having a glorious time doing it.*

He eased his way into the crowd. Taone was happily telling an Egyptian Trader, "Surely you jest, Sir. I don't have time for such nonsense. Now, excuse yourself, so that someone with adequate funds may make an offer on my cedar. Whoever buys the lot will make a handsome profit and I do not wish to waste either of our time talking of smaller lots."

The trader was incensed. "I represent the Pharaoh of Egypt. You should be honored to GIVE me the cedar. I DEMAND that you accept my offer!!!"

"Oh, Sweet. I'm so sorry. I hope you don't get into any trouble by failing to secure the cedar for our beloved Pharaoh. Here, have a honey-sweet to make your day more pleasant. NEXT!"

The Trader stormed off.

Burlyman followed him to the largest trading stall in the port. He took a deep breath, composed himself, walked to a trader, and announced, "I am Captain Burlyman of Byblos. I am in need of the largest trading vessel which might be for sale. Are you aware of any such vessel?"

The man eyed Burlyman. "Byblos doesn't have a port. How can you possibly need even a small vessel?"

"I am not here to answer questions. I am here to trade the finest cedar in the world for a sailing vessel of quality. Obviously, you are not the person to deal with." Burlyman abruptly turned and strode back toward the Byblos stall; not giving the tradesman time to respond. *That'll stir things up.*

The Pharaoh's traders made increasingly large offers on the cedar, *all* of the cedar. Each offer was graciously refused. "I'm so sorry, but my fine cedar is worth more to me than it is to you."

"Your cedar is worth nothing if no one buys it!"

"Oh, sir, you are so very wrong. My cedar is worth exactly what I say it is!"

"You will never trade it!"

"Byblos intends to rent a stall from this time unto forever. My cedar will be waiting until then or until it's sold. Of course, when I sell this consignment, I will return with even more. Here, have a honey-sweet. NEXT!"

Tatwo was doing a brisk business selling expensive, carved merchandise. The pieces seemed to be under-priced at a hundred times their original cost. Tatwo scaled up her asking prices.

They both handled inquiries into the raw copper ore setting off to the side. Some serious traders kept returning to inspect it. Eventually, a trader returned accompanied by a slight, intense man. The intense man inspected the ore and asked, "You can deliver this in quantity?"

"Yes sir, all which you might want."

The man said, "I will take all that you have but will require a much lower price if I agree to buy your next shipment. I will send a wagon to receive the ore from your ship." The man turned and left his trader standing there at the mercy of sweetly smiling Tatwo.

Burlyman finally had a chance to tell Taone of the inquiry he had made at the Pharaoh's tent.

During the remaining days of Season One of the new year, the trader women had a glorious time.

They had found their purpose in life.

BAALAT'S TRADERS SEASON TWO

The royal escort arrived to announce to the Chief of the Newport Trade Center that immediately after sunrise tomorrow, the chief would deliver to the captain of the escort the following: One: The captain of the sailing vessel "Lady of Byblos One." Two: A minimum of one trader from the Byblos trading delegation. Three: Samples of the different qualities of cedar available from the traders. Four: Samples of other goods Byblos had for trade. "We will return to this location at sunrise."

They turned and retired to their camp.

The Trade Center Chief sighed. *Bookkeeping. Traders with monstrous egos. Royal demands. There is always a problem!*

He sat off to the Byblos trading stall.

Arriving, he watched the two trader women laughing off insufficient offers with, "Thank you, but no. NEXT!" and occasionally accepting an offer for an exquisite work of art. The Chief thought, *Don't be dung-heads. Obey the Pharaoh's command without argument. Make your captain obey.*

He glanced at their contract, then approached the one he assumed would be named Taone. He brushed aside several traders waiting to speak to her and said, "I am the Newport Chief of Trade. Greetings Trader Taone. Today is a joyous day for you! Not only does your trading go well but the Royal Court itself wishes to meet with you. You and your ship's captain have been commanded to meet here immediately after sunrise to be escorted by the Pharaoh's honor guard to the Pharaoh's Palace in

Phoenicia, Jaffa, Rocky, Burlyman, Polydore | Astarte, T'jaru
Terah, Amathlai, Haran, Terahson, Nahor, Sarai, Isaac, Jacob
Kyrios-Olon, Teumessian, Nimrod, Nimbal, Nimlad, Nimisis, Asherah, Set.

Memphis bringing samples of your goods. This is all I was told. I trust this command meets with your joyful approval."

Taone blankly stared at him. *Commanded? Pulled away from my trade for Zeus only knows how long? Am I being arrested for refusing the Pharaoh's trader's offers? Who is this man to order me around? Is it to my advantage to create a scene? Other traders disappear after you tell them to go away. Is it to my advantage to go with "The Chief of Trade?" This man is only doing his job, I suppose. How should I respond? Portmaster Serket is to be feared and this is a much larger port than hers.*

She answered, "I am at your disposal, Lord. I will do whatever you advise me in the manner you advise me to do it. Perhaps you can counsel me in this matter so that I will not appear foolish and ignorant to these people. I wish only to uphold the honor and dignity of your great trading center."

He responded, "Very good. Bring your captain to my office and I will advise you as best I can." *Wonderful! She is as wise as she is vicious.*

He turned away to go and address his next problem.

Taone thought, *Lord Baalat, I wish you were here. I am a poor uneducated, unsophisticated woman from the poor side of Byblos unskilled in any way. But Captain Burlyman is a man of the world. I will place my faith in him. Great gods be with me!*

She found Burlyman on the dock drinking beer with other captains. She said to him, "Captain Burlyman, we are commanded to be escorted to Memphis tomorrow morning to meet the Pharaoh."

A hush of respect and disbelief settled over the usually raucous, domineering Sea Captains.

Burlyman played his part well, "Excellent. It will be good to see the Pharaoh, again. Be sure to bring your honey-candy."

GOING TO SEE THE PHARAOH

Morning came. The Pharaoh's guard came. Taone was prepared.

General Khaba, a high-level royal advisor, introduced himself. All the correct words were exchanged. The pomp of a royal carriage protected by a Pharaoh's guard always attracted attention. Taone and Burlyman were assisted into the drawn carriage by Khaba who took a seat in front. The carriers began the long pull from the Port back to Memphis.

Khaba told them:
"You will never refuse a request of the Pharaoh. Not that he would have you killed, but then again, I don't know what he would do because no

one has ever refused the Pharaoh. Certainly, don't attempt to negotiate."
"I understand he is interested in your cedar and was disappointed that his tradesman was not able to acquire it. The Tradesmen were not killed for their failure. At least, I don't think they were."
"The raw ore we purchased appears to be a rare and useful thing. The Pharaoh will want to know the source, how much you have available, and the asking price."
"The Pharaoh considers your asking price to be your final, non-negotiable price which he will either accept or refuse. You would not want a Pharaoh reduced to negotiating."
"The Pharaoh was surprised to hear that Byblos is now a trading port. Someone may be killed for that. That information is a matter of national security. Failure to be aware of this fact will be treated as a serious breach of military responsibility."
"I am to inquire into your favorite food, drink, entertainment, and preferences in the traits of the personal escort to be assigned to you."
"I am now prepared to answer questions you might have."

They talked on until Taone saw the skyline of the City of Memphis in the distance. Her eyes widened, her jaw dropped, and she could no longer talk; no longer hear; only watch the majesty of a great city draw ever closer.

~~~

They arrived at the palace and were shown through a back door into a receiving room where a dozen men and women stood waiting to be inspected. Captain Burlyman was immediately brought a beer and Taone a fruit-wine. Khaba said, "Whoever you select will escort you to the baths, scrub you, message you, and help you select dress suitable for this evening's meeting with the Pharaoh. It will be a public spectacle, I fear. Your escort will brief you on protocol and be with you every step of the way. Now sit, enjoy your drink, and select your escort."

Lord Baalat would be proud of how quickly her little country girl from outside Byblos adjusted to such an exotic situation. She chose the large, muscular Nubian male because he had such a nice smile.

SUNDOWN

Torches and lamps were lit illuminating the great pavilion to the Mastaba's of past kings. The people gathered to witness the event. The event was small; only the two guests with their escorts. The Pharaoh and Queen stood waiting beside the marble statues of Metis and Crius as the drums were heard from the Mastaba of chief Kemet. The procession of guests

Phoenicia, Jaffa, Rocky, Burlyman, Polydore | Astarte, T'jaru
Terah, Amathlai, Haran, Terahson, Nahor, Sarai, Isaac, Jacob
Kyrios-Olon, Teumessian, Nimrod, Nimbal, Nimlad, Nimisis, Asherah, Set.
~~~

was led by Priest Hotep. Upon their arrival, the guests bowed to the Pharaoh and followed him and the Queen into the palace. Inside, away from the crowd, Djoser and Hetephe held their arms out to their sides and attendants rushed to disrobe them down to their white tunics with purple trim. A beer was brought to Burlyman, a fruit-wine to Taone, a red wine to Djoser, and a brown-wine to Hetephe. Hetephe looked at the escorts and said, "Help yourself to whatever food and drink you wish." Djoser sat in an over sized chair; Hetephe stood behind him, her arm on his high-backed chair.

Djoser looked at his two guests and said, "Sit or stand as it pleases you. Now tell me of this port that does not exist."

Both Djoser and Hetephe courteously listened to the words, watched the body language, facial expressions, inferred from what wasn't being said, noted who said what, and who didn't say what. Their silence prompted more and more words from both Taone and Burlyman.

Hetephe finally said, "I see, Trader Taone. This great port exists only in the mind of your Lady. But perhaps it will someday be built. In the meantime, Sea Captain Burlyman docks at sea and transports goods to land by using five fishing boats your lady purchased with nothing. And from your lady's few shekels, you bring a sailing vessel into Egypt which Captain Burlyman says he purchased out of the profits from your fishing boats. And a vessel filled with enough cedar to bankrupt the treasury of Egypt. What an interesting tale you tell."

Taone straightened her back. She did not like the tone of the Queen. She snapped, "And which part of this *tale* does the Great Queen *not* believe?"

The Queen straightened *her* back. *This woman is challenging me.*

Hetephe snapped, "The starting with nothing part. What fortune is backing you?"

Djoser smoothly interrupted, "I have yet to hear the name of your 'Great Lady.' Perhaps that would shed light on your ... *tale.*"

Taone haughtily replied, "The name of my Lady is Baalat of Byblos, once of Urfa, student of Horus, the great teacher, daughter of no one knows who, builder of a great port, and backed by Poseidon, Isis, and Osiris!"

Djoser glanced at Hetephe and held out his hand for silence. He said to Taone, "Baalat is the name of a child priestess Horus took as a follower along with Abram when he was in Urfa. Is this the same Baalat?"

"It is, my Lord!"

Djoser looked at Hetephe and requested, "Bring Hathor to me! Tell her our guest's tale!"

She said, "Yes, Husband," and left to take the hidden passage to the Pyramid Mastabas and summon Hathor.

Djoser looked at Burlyman and said, "High-Priestess Hathor will be joining us in a few minutes. While we wait, talk about the ships you envision operating out of this nonexistent port."

He signaled to an attendant to "keep our guest's glasses full."

After more talking and another glass of fruit-wine, stronger this time, Taone saw a chamber door open and two priestesses wearing unimaginable finery enter the room. With anxious fear, she wondered, *Which one of these women is the High-Priestess?*

The thought was immediately answered as the unsmiling High-Priestess Hathor entered the room, stood between her priestesses, looked at Djoser, and nodded to him in recognition. Her dress overpowered the simple finery of her two priestesses; her presence diminished the presence of the Pharaoh into that of a common man.

Hathor then looked at Taone and said, "I have been told that you appear to be a low-born woman with a common accent and little education. Is this true?"

Taone was stunned to be talked to like this. Yet ... "This is true, my Lady."

"A low-born woman without credentials who commands the Pharaoh's finest traders and now talks with the Pharaoh of Egypt concerning matters of great wealth. A common woman who brooks no insolence from the Queen of Egypt who could have her put to death with the snap of her fingers. And this low-born woman looks in respect and admiration to her Lord and Master who was once a girl-prostitute ravished by whatever man might want her. A gutter girl who now commands sea captains and will build the largest seaport in the world. Are these things true?"

"Y-yes. These things are true, my Lady."

"I was told that Lord Baalat greets Isis, Osiris, and Poseidon each morning and gives them thanks for the bounty they give her. Is this true?"

"Y-yes, my lady."

Hathor said to Djoser, "Bring her to the Mastaba of Osiris. Isis demands it." She and her two priestesses turned and left the room.

Djoser said to himself, "I'm the Pharaoh! I'll finish my wine first."

To Trader Taone, he said, "Trader Taone, my traders tell me they must double their money with each transaction. Sometimes, if conditions are good, they can get five times return. And if they ever get a ten-fold return, they are ecstatic. Are these numbers consistent with your thoughts?"

"I am not trained in the art, Great Pharaoh. I make up my own numbers."

"I see. The amount my traders offered for your cedar was a large sum of money. I suspect it was more than ten times your investment."

"Yes, my Pharaoh. I refused thirty times my investment.:'

"I see. Then your asking price was, let me see, about one hundred times your cost."

"Yes, my Lord."

'I see. It is your cedar, and you must do what you must do. But I will point out that even if you get a hundred-fold profit, your sales will be few. At a ten times profit, your sales would be large, consistent, and ongoing. Did I mention that terms are very important in trading? Side benefits often are more valuable than the money received."

Burlyman thought, *So the Pharaoh does not negotiate!*

Djoser signaled to an advisor standing in the back. "Admiral, come and meet Captain Burlyman. He might be interested in purchasing one or more of the ships you are trying to retire from the Kingdom's fleet. Take him to Hostess House. Get to know one another. And, Trader Taone, you appear to have attracted the interest of High-Priestess Hathor. Come with me and let's go visit the gods. Bring your Nubian friend with you."

After spending an evening with the powers of the world, of visiting the actual body of Osiris, of talking of heritage and hopes, of being overwhelmed but not backing off, of acquiring immediate sophistication, Taone was finally led to a guest room. The Nubian stayed by her side offering periodic support as she suffered through the evening, but she graciously declined his offer to retire for the night with her.

Meanwhile, Captain Burlyman discussed the sea and ships with the admiral of the thirty vessels of the Egyptian trading fleet, most of which would be replaced with even larger ships if only the Pharaoh had cedar with which to build them. The admiral lovingly described each of his most worthy ships and hoped that they could retire to a worthy destiny.

Late in the night, Burlyman was shown to his quarters. He graciously, for Captain Burlyman, declined continued assistance by his lovely escort.

TOURISTS

Trader Taone and Captain Burlyman spent the next three days being shown the wonders of Memphis, including tours of places not usually shown to visitors. Taone remained wide-eyed throughout. Burlyman wondered what discussions were being held in the palace and why. On the first day, Taone had casually mentioned to her Nubian escort how she wished Tatwo could be here to see these wonders.

By nightfall, Tatwo showed up in Memphis with her own escort, a woman trained in the art of diction.

Tatwo said, "Th' Chief o' Trade assigned summun to watch our stall 'til we get back. He'll record names o' inter'sted traders."

Tatwo's escort suggested a more neutral pronunciation. Tatwo took note.

On the fourth day, the Pharaoh's Messenger was waiting when the three Byblosians emerged from their guest rooms. He said to each, "You are invited by the Pharaoh to attend a highsun meeting with his Chief Trader to discuss trading opportunities. The Pharaoh expects that you will be able to attend this meeting. The Pharaoh expects it to be mutually beneficial."

Trader Taone replied, "We will be delighted to attend this important meeting and hear your Chief Trader's generous proposal." The reply was with an almost neutral dialect.

They attended the negotiations. The once furious, obnoxious Chief Trader was now a well-oiled talking machine who presented the Pharaoh's proposal. The Chief Trader stated that a sailing date on the first day of the Fourth Season would benefit the kingdom. Captain Burly man quietly said, "I swore to my Lord Baalat that we would port in Byblos by the fourth Full Moon. No further comments on that subject were made.

The meeting adjourned for highsun meal so that the guests could discuss the Kingdom's proposal.

They were served a meal fit for masters of the sea while they discussed the proposal they were given. Burlyman warned them to show no emotions because they were surely being watched. They showed no emotion.

Upon returning to the meeting, the Chief Trader opened with, "A sailing date on the quarter moon before the fourth season is acceptable if it better fits your plan to arrive by the fourth New Moon." The two traders agreed, to Burlyman's unexpressed delight, to accept the Chief Traders "generous" offer even though it was far less than the original asking price and the delayed sailing date confused them, but they were happy enough.

They returned to Newport a quartermoon after they had left; richer, wiser, and still somewhat unsure of the required sailing date.

Upon return to their stall, the traders were presented with detailed entries of inquiries made, contact information, and receipts for the sale of twenty-eight high-priced objects at the marked price, which happened to be one-hundred-fifty times the original purchase price. Their agreement with the Pharaoh fixed prices at twenty times the cost of cedar and copper ore, to be reduced to fifteen times the actual cost on the second shipment; and ten times the cost on the third shipment. Negotiations would be re-entered for the fourth shipment including possible purchase of the Egyptian Trading vessel, "Ra-Four."

Taone and Tatwo were uneasy that they had been taken advantage of by wily Egyptian traders. Upon hearing this, the Nubian escort laughed and said, "Friend Taone, the Pharaoh's traders pray to Hades that he condemns you both to the pits of Tartarus forever."

Tatwo said, in a neutral accent, "Well, no matter. It is done. We did the best that little country women could do."

Their cargo of cedar and ore sold and delivered, the Byblosians spent their days making obscene profits from their luxury items and filling their ship with cheap merchandise such as papyrus. Tatwo observed to Taone, "We made a lot of profit, didn't we?"

Captain Maddog Burlyman toured the Egyptian Trading vessels that were in port and talked about what made for a nicely designed port.

BAALAT'S TRADERS SEASON THREE

At the beginning of the Third Month, they had done all they could do and were ready to cast off. But their agreement called for a two quartermoon delay; with Egypt paying the additional dockage costs.

A few days before departure, an agent of the Pharaoh called upon Captain Burlyman and said, "I wish to book passage for seven people to Byblos."

Understanding slid silently into the captain's mind.

~~~~~~~~~~~

7D. Set

Year 159, Seasons 1, 2, 3

SET'S SEASON ONE

Early in the first season, Nimlad entered Memphis, a far distance from his base in Urfa. He quickly determined that his assignment would be found in South Memphis. Quicker still that in South Memphis, Living God Set would usually be found at Hostess House or the House of Ishtar.

Nimlad entered the Hostess House and ordered a beer. He engaged his server in conversation.

Throughout the evening, she answered all his questions:
"Sure. Everybody knows God Set. We love him so much."
"Oh, he loves garnished lettuce and beer."
"Every morning meal. That's his table, over there."
"His wife is our beloved Nephthys, but Astarte is usually with him."
"He spends most nights with Astarte at the House of Ishtar."
"Yes, he is still in South Memphis. Sometimes he visits the High-Priestess or even the Pharaoh. He can go anyplace he wants."
"He is a person of the highest rank. Almost as high as the Pharaoh."

Nimlad contentedly sipped his beer. *This may work.*

He finished his beer, rose, and ventured into the city to explore.

SUNRISE

Nimlad entered Hostess House and requested a table next to the one his server had pointed to the day before. He ordered the Garnished Lettuce, bread, and fruit-wine. Soon, three people entered Hostess House and were shown to Set's table. Nimlad noticed that no one ordered but they were soon served what appeared to be their standard morning meal. Nimlad eavesdropped. The woman was "Astarte," and the younger man was "Anubis."

Nimlad finished his meal but sipped his fruit-wine until Set finished *his* meal. Nimlad then rose, walked to face Set, said, "Great Living God Set," and bowed deeply from the waist.

Set, pleased, said, "Yes. I am God Set. Rise and tell me your name."
~~~~~~~~~~~

Nimlad stood straight, looked Set directly in the eyes, and introduced himself using flattering words and hints of possible wealth and additional status that might be found in the ancient city of Urfa if only God Set would listen to a proposal.

The proposal contained the carefully chosen words of "building the greatest religion the world has ever known" plus "the greatest temple in the world" plus "a guaranteed longer and continued active life."

These words captured Set's attention. Astarte's, too. She assumed that wherever Set went, she would go.

Set said "Yes, yes, young man. Sit down. He motioned for wine to be served to his guest and for Astarte to accidentally brush her leg against Nimlad's. Set was a master of using others to increase his own self-worth and Astarte was his eager consort—concubine—whatever.

Set leaned back to reflect on what he had heard so far. He said, "I passed through Urfa long ago. It's at the edge of nowhere. I led many people from Urfa to build a magnificent city in Egypt which everyone wished to be named 'Charon City.' The name has since changed for some reason. No, Lord ... Nimlad ... is it? No matter what the glory, I could not possibly leave the luxuries of Memphis where I am held in such high regard and so well loved. I am sure you will find someone nice to be your High-Priest. Talk to my nephew Horus. He might be interested." Set chuckled. "Plus going from a Living God to only a High-Priest is not acceptable." He sipped his beer.

Nimlad engaged:
"The name Horus was discussed but he would not be man enough for the job."
"I fear you are incorrect. Memphis is now at the edge of nowhere."
"The lands near Urfa will produce mighty empires. This is where civilization now bursts forth."
"The Church of Urfa must teach people proper respect for the gods."
"The Church must not allow false thinking."
"The High-Priest must teach all men the nature of the gods."
"All men shall look to the High-Priest for wisdom and guidance. He will be adored by all men."
"His name will be exalted for all time."

By now, Set was leaning forward in his chair, elbows on the table, listening intently to Nimlad.

Nimlad continued:

"It's true. You would have to leave Memphis. But the luxury of your new temple would surpass anything I have seen so far in Memphis."

"You may not be interested in women, but if you were, know that the temple priestesses are selected for their beauty, poise, and adoration of the male body. They would, of course, fight among themselves as to who could best please you."

"You would be responsible for increasing the size of the temple into the greatest structure in the world."

"But your greatest responsibility would be expanding and growing the power of the True Church."

"If you feel that you are the man to make these things happen, then whatever you ask shall be given."

Nimlad leaned back and waited for Set to respond. It took all his willpower, training, and ambition to ignore Astarte's leg continuously accidentally brushing against his. She was, after all, well on her way to becoming a Canaanite god of sexual pleasure.

Set's only question was, "Building the greatest structure in the world, you said?"

Nimrod and Set talked until Set agreed to at least consider the proposal. Nimrod rose, looked at Astarte, and said, "If you can get us access to the top of that pyramid thing I saw as I entered your fair city, I will bring the Aphrodite wine."

Astarte beamed, "I *am* the High-Priestess's sister, you know."

DECISIONS

At their morning meal, Astarte said to Set, "I think you should accept Lord Nimlad's offer. Being the High-Priest of the Church of Urfa would be quite prestigious. They have missionaries all over Canaan and they bother Horus so much it *must* be a powerful church. It would pay back Sister Anath for that horrible thing she and Horus did to you and it's a way to show Horus that you are better than he is."

"No, Sweet Astarte. There is no way to Urfa except the high road through those dreadful Horus followers or else the low road through Canaan where Anath's dreadful followers are. Plus, I was in Urfa in my youth. It was a dreadful little place. Everything about this is so simply dreadful. We will remain here where we are rightfully adored as gods, me more so."

Both Astarte and Anubis agreed that was too bad because they would love to take an adventure to the land of Urfa.

Astarte glanced across the room to Nimlad who was sitting in a far corner eating his morning Garnished Lettuce. Nimlad was there every morning eating his breakfast lettuce.

He was leering at her.

SET'S SEASON TWO

Set had instilled into Astarte that the two of them should visit her sister Hathor the evening of each full moon. Set knew that this would be the period of maximum activity at the Mastaba, which was always good to be around. So it was that they sat at Osiris's old table drinking fine wine waiting for Hathor to find time to visit.

Festive fences had been erected across the front of the patio to provide privacy as the priestesses and priests performed their tasks. Hathor took advantage of the privacy and joined her sister and Set to sip a glass of wine and hear of Astarte's visit to Fort Rajah. The sisters gossiped. Set halfheartedly listened. The fact that Anath's Winter Solstice Celebration in Fort Rajah was a wonderful success was annoying. The fact that Horus was coming to Memphis was annoying. The fact that ... *wait .... what? ...*

Astarte giggled as she whispered secret gossip she had innocently overheard as she accidentally eavesdropped on a private conversation between Polydore and Phoenicia, "Serket had herself a little tryst with a certain Nimbal from Urfa while Horus was away. Horus is said to have cried. Can you believe it?"

Set sat back in quiet joy. *Nimbal? ... Nimlad? ... Brothers, perhaps? ... How interesting.*

~~~

After sunrise a few days later, Set returned to his usual table at Hostess House for his sunrise meal. Nimlad sat in the far corner. Set saw him and motioned him to come over.

As Nimlad sat down, Set said, "I am told there is a Nimbal visiting Port Jaffa getting into all kinds of mischief. Are you related by chance?"

"We are both high-ranking priests in the church of Urfa. Nimbal was sent to Port Jaffa to humiliate Horus by making his wife beg for Nimbal to
~~~

plow her—many times. Do you know if he was successful?" *Welcome to the Church of Urfa, Great Living God Set.*

Astarte could not wait to tell Sister Hathor that Astarte might be moving to Urfa with God Set.

If only Set didn't have to go through Canaan or travel the Way of Horus.

Phoenicia, Jaffa, Rocky, Burlyman, Polydore | Astarte, T'jaru
Terah, Amathlai, Haran, Terahson, Nahor, Sarai, Isaac, Jacob
Kyrios-Olon, Teumessian, Nimrod, Nimbal, Nimlad, Nimisis, Asherah, Set.

~~~~~~~~~~~~

7E. Horus

Year 159, Seasons 1, 2, 3

HORUS'S SEASON ONE

Horus spent his remaining time in Port Jaffa with Serket and his friends and followers.

Among his friends was Astarte, who had journeyed to Port Jaffa to visit her once sister-consort, Polydore. Astarte was delighted to find that her old, dear, influential friend Horus was also in Port Jaffa. A girl should always visit with a dear, influential friend whenever the opportunity arose.

Astarte visited all her old, influential Port Jaffa friends, especially Horus and Serket. Astarte had a delightful conversation; finding out that Horus would soon travel through Canaan teaching and would arrive in Memphis as the fourth season of the new year approached, and how Serket would, conditions permitting, meet him at the beginning of the Fourth month.

She was having such a delightful conversation; she did not even notice Serket wince when Astarte recounted the time that Horus ravished Sister Anath in front of everyone and humiliated Set beyond bearing and things of that nature. "Well, I have had a delightful time, but I simply must get back to Memphis and God Set. I hope I'm still his consort. He was so angry with me when I left for Fort Rajah. If not, Anubis may be ready for a faithful consort—or concubine—or whatever. He's not Living God material unless someone of consequence pushes him into it. Horus, do find me when you get to Memphis. Maybe we could relive the old days when we were both so young and we would, well, you know ... Well, I will see you in Memphis."

With that, she was off to Memphis.

~~~

After sunrise service and a poignant farewell to Serket, Horus set off to Memphis with Azazil. Scheduled stops were at Fort Rafah and then at each fort along the Trade Route.

Word that Horus was approaching Fort Rafah preceded his coming. His followers met him on his way in. Horus felt warm and at home with his people. He had been away too long from his devout followers. It had been many seasons since he could relax in the company of his own kind.

Nothing had gone well in a long time. First Baalat, then Abram, then Serket. He needed to rethink his two life goals—how to counteract the teachings of the Urfa missionaries plus how to find the land of the dead. And here were students with whom he could discuss such things.

Azazil was beginning to teach that they were the church of Horus. That Horus would someday die but his teachings would live on through them, his congregation—his Church. There was copious learned discussion. Horus's thoughts turned more and more to what might be happening in Memphis and less and less to what might be happening in Jaffa.

They met, they talked, they counseled, they ate, they taught, they drank, they rejoiced, and life was good once more.

That night, Horus lay down to hopefully sleep in peace.

He awoke to a rising wind. He lay awake, listening and thinking. *Losing Baalat was unfortunate. She understands the falseness of gods better than Azazil and Rocky. She should have been my heir instead of Abram. Once-student Abram doesn't have much of a chance to save his people. The Kyrios-Olon targeted him from the beginning. Nimrod will twist his beliefs to his will. Asherah will be able to make him belief whatever she wishes him to believe. My great plan is undone.*

From the sea came the rising wind and the sound of distant thunder.

He was answered by either Isis, Osiris, Djoser, or the wind. *You shall do that which is right!*

He thought, *What shall I do about the Urfa missionaries? They eliminated their human sacrifice teachings at my request. Teaching the lies of multiple gods mislead the people but otherwise does no harm. It is their teaching that the gods require women to be submissive and obedient to men that is the problem. Dyoares is clear that this is a powerful tool for keeping women in line and not competing with males. Males are easily controlled by the Kyrios-Olon; females, not so much. I need a new plan. Djoser and Hetephe can advise me. I will talk to them when I get to Memphis!*

He tried to keep it from his mind, but against his will, the thoughts came: Serket lying in the arms of another man. *I know I told her she could do it. But I didn't expect her to. She brought up the possibility of having children, again. What is it with women wanting children? I don't. I know she wanted to talk more about her Nimbal escapade, but I don't. It's over as far as I'm concerned. I didn't let her talk about it, and she will feel too much guilt to do it again. Maybe I should have told her not to do it again. Just to make sure she understands!*

Lightning split the night.

Phoenicia, Jaffa, Rocky, Burlyman, Polydore | Astarte, T'jaru
Terah, Amathlai, Haran, Terahson, Nahor, Sarai, Isaac, Jacob
Kyrios-Olon, Teumessian, Nimrod, Nimbal, Nimlad, Nimisis, Asherah, Set.

~~~

Morning came.

Horus and Azazil spent several days in Fort Rajah. It was the most important Fort along the route and the largest. Horus had the thought—actually, it was a pillow talk suggestion from Serket, but nonetheless—Horus had the thought that he could counteract the influence of the Urfa Missionaries by sending out missionaries of his own. If he could devise a way to successfully do this, then Fort Rajah, as the official entry point into Egypt, would be the center of his operations. In the meantime, he would visit two forts every quartermoon and be in Memphis within six more quartermoons.

MEMPHIS

Six quartermoons passed.

After arriving in Memphis, Horus went first to the House of Nephthys. There were women there tending the gardens, caring for the premises. One escorted Horus inside to his mother. He approached the old woman sitting on her chair. Another woman helped Nephthys rise to embrace her son. Tears of joy flowed down her cheeks. "My son. My son. You complete my life. Now I can join Isis."

He laughed. "You are much too young to think such things, Mother."

She laughed. "I choose not to believe the sweet lies of men anymore, Son. I have heard too many to care. I have not drunk the Ambrosia of the gods nor the Red Nectar of the Titans in a long time. Let time have its way with me. I am old. Set will not look upon me anymore. My sight is too painful for him to behold. I no longer know or care who he lies with. The local women treat me like I am some kind of god, yet I long for the embraces of Isis and of Osiris. But what about you? How is Serket? Is she with you?"

He laughed. "You ask me of Serket? What about my work? All my followers? My students? The evils of the world I teach against?"

Nephthys tensed. "Is she no longer your wife? She brought you love and peace, Son! What happened?"

Horus laughed and smoothed over his mother's concerns. They had a lovely chat; Nephthys was thrilled with all the wonderful words of her wonderful son.
~~~

"And what of Uncle Set, Mother? How is it he will not come to the most beautiful and worthy woman in Egypt?"

"Your Uncle still seeks that which he cannot find. He doesn't know its nature; only that he doesn't have it. I believe he and Astarte are in the western red lands with a new friend of theirs. Set is showing off how the nomads consider he and Astarte to be Living Gods. Set likes that sort of thing ... being a living god ... adulation. But you know that better than I."

"New friend?"

"Yes. A man from the east ... Urfa, I think. His name is Nimbob or something like that. He wants Set to migrate to Urfa to become some kind of important person there. Set is intrigued but as I understand it, there are two insurmountable obstacles."

She laughed, "You and Anath! He will either have to travel the path of Horus and constantly hear how wonderful you are, or he will have to travel through the Sinai where Anath is held to be the highest Living God —even higher than most of the dead ones. Both options are unbearable to him. So he roams the Western Red lands where he has no competition for adulation. I love him, still."

"You loved Charon, Mother. Charon went quite insane a long time ago."

"The mind and body of the Great Lord Charon remain in my husband. It is well hidden, but I still remember."

They talked on.

<div align="center">~~~</div>

Elsewhere, Azazil sought an audience with the supreme priestess in the world—Hathor. Stepmother of Horus, revered and feared by all people— even Pharaohs.

She granted the audience.

Azazil arrived, paid a proper greeting, and said, "My teacher longs to see his illustrious mother. He sends you his greetings, my lady."

Hathor said, "My son is too long from his people. He tries to save a world that does not wish saving. Come, sit here with me and tell me, does his wife and disciples comfort him adequately while he is away? Has he provided me a grandchild?"

Azazil sat and presented the short version of recent developments. He did not mention Serket.

Hathor said, "Horus will adjust to that which is. You did not mention Serket or grandchildren. There is a story there. Tell me."

Azazil said, "When Horus returns from his travels, he and Serket will meet with joy. There is no talk of children. Horus is visiting Nephthys now. He hopes you will see him after highsun."

"Tell him he is commanded to come to me at sundown tomorrow. He will stay with me until it is time for me to call forth his father. He may visit the Pharaoh and the others afterward."

"Yes, my lady."

He bid her proper goodbye, found Horus at the House of Nephthys, and told him that he would go to Hathor at sundown the next day. The three then went to Hostess House; there to hopefully find old friends and acquaintances. An entourage of women followed Nephthys; in case she might desire something done.

Anubis was there holding court. Hostess House Manager, Ba't, hearing of the gathering, tore herself away from managing the House of Ishtar's many businesses, and joined them. Ba't, in the ways of a modest woman, inferred that she would be available to Horus, if he so desired; all the while graciously refusing the continuous inquiries of Anubis. Horus mentioned several times, to several women, that he had a faithful wife to whom he was faithful.

Wine, beer, and good times flowed. Reluctant God Nephthys almost felt like the old days when she was Telchine Dexithea. *Philyra, Ariadne, Isis, Charon. I long for your touch.*

After a night of reunion and good times, Horus and Nephthys returned to the House of Nephthys, there to continue the lamentations of Horus.

The next morning, they groggily rose and went to the river to watch the sunrise ceremony. Nephthys was followed by her self-appointed attendants. Horus picked up an entourage along the way. They all came to Horus's favorite spot under the tree by the river. The multitude was gathering for the daily ceremony. All people of Egypt were expected to journey at least once to witness High-Priestess Hathor call forth Osiris to become Ra – the Living Sun. The spectacle was unimaginable.

Hathor and her people stood on the highest level of the Mastaba. Before the sun breached the horizon, sunlight would reflect off the top of the great obelisk jutting from the pyramid Mastabas. As soon as it struck the obelisk, hopeful women in the multitude would grasp their husband's crotch seeking the blessing of Isis—and in some cases, Nephthys. Then the Pharaoh and Queen would step from the Mastaba of Osiris to walk and salute the people and then turn to prostrate themselves toward the High-Priestess standing high above. The sunlight would slide down the obelisk until the sun finally breached the horizon. Dressed in the unimaginable grandeur of the High-Priestess, Hathor would then step forward and, with upraised arms, call forth Osiris.

As jaundiced as he was, the ceremony still moved Horus deeply. He wished that Serket was standing beside him; bringing with her the peace he so desperately wanted. *What is she doing right now, as I watch my father being called back from the Land of the Dead? Who is she with? What are they doing?*

Horus spent much of the day visiting his many disciples. Toward sundown, he said the proper things to his stepmother and disciples and set off to present himself to his second stepmother, Hathor, the unapproachable High-Priestess of Osiris.

~~~

Horus arrived at the Mastaba of Osiris. Hathor, dressed in the full regalia of her office, greeted him. The greeting was seen by the multitudes in the avenue far below. The multitudes, as were expected, were overwhelmed with the majesty of Horus—son of Isis and Osiris and who some already called a Living God—being greeted by Hathor, keeper of the gateway to powers beyond the imagination of mortals. Horus was well-versed in protocols of State. He performed the greetings with impeccable form. After the formal greeting was complete, Hathor turned and strode to the interior of the Mastaba.

Horus held back a few moments to acknowledge the crowd below. The crowd erupted with appreciative recognition. He waved good night, turned, and followed High-Priestess Hathor into the Mastaba. She stood waiting for him with outstretched arms wearing a simple gold-trimmed, white tunic.

Hathor said, "My son, you have finally returned to acknowledge the existence of the mother you have cast away."

"Cast away, Mother? You are the sunlight of my existence. I see you in every sunrise throughout every day until you leave me to my darkness. But you always come to me again with the light."
~~~

"My son has grown clever with words. So, cleverly tell me this ... where is my son's wife? Where is my grandchild?"

"My wife is well and in the land of Canaan performing important work. She can no more betray her duty as can you. Such is the curse of the powerful and needed. Your grandchildren remain hidden somewhere inside her. Neither of us has the time to properly raise a child."

"Cleverly said, yet you speak of everything but your wife. When you are ready to tell me, I will be ready to listen. So, tell me of the things you wish me to hear. Come with me to your father's table. I will have the flames extinguished so we cannot be seen, and we can drink wine. I will send word to Djoser that you are here, but of course, he will already know this and will come if he can, but I suspect not. Being Pharaoh severely limits his movements. You may lie with me tonight. Serket will approve because she knows the great peace I bring you. But, then again, perhaps you are not at ease with peace."

The patio flames were extinguished, and they went and sat at Osiris's old table. It was the night of a full moon and beautiful. The wine was exquisite. He talked of Baalat and of Abram; of Urfa and of Kyrios-Olon; of the failure of his grand scheme to eliminate the negative effects of the teachings of the Urfa missionaries; of Nimbal and Serket.

Even after two seasons away from his wife, he did not lie with Hathor.

He did not know why, but in the lonely night, he cried.

SET'S SEASON 3

Horus stood where he usually stood to watch the sunrise ceremony. He was disguised enough to prevent most people from recognizing him.

Djoser would know of Horus's arrival in Memphis and that Horus would be standing here where he always stood. But Horus recognized that Djoser could no longer move freely among his people as he undoubtedly wished to do. Djoser was Pharaoh—the God-King of Egypt. There were protocols to be observed. Where the Pharaoh appeared there must be planned pomp and pageantry; a spectacle to accompany him. For the glory of Egypt. For the unity of Egypt. For the people of Egypt.

The ceremony finished, and the crowd began to disperse. Horus enjoyed standing and experiencing everyday life. He was caught by surprise when a murmur ran through the crowd. He looked in the direction of the murmur and saw the crowd parting but not dispersing. They began falling on their knees with heads bowed.

Guards appeared with seven women in imperial dress walking toward him. Arriving, they stopped and stepped back. From the center stepped the Queen. She extended her hand for him to kiss and bow.

Horus bowed and kissed the ring of Queen Hetephe, wife of the Pharaoh.

The seven women began humming a soft gentle, but discordant, song sung so that those standing nearby could not understand the words spoken by the queen to her loyal subject.

She said, "My husband sends greetings to Horus, Son of Isis and Osiris, keeper of the sacred words, seeker of the understanding of the nature of death. You will share highsun meal with the Pharaoh in his palace. At sundown, you will share Sundown meal with him in front of the Mastaba of your father. The viziers are now planning this spectacle for the people of Egypt. It is a pleasure for my eyes to gaze upon you, Horus. Peace be with you."

She turned without waiting for a response. Her court surrounded her, and the troupe marched back to the palace.

The people looked at Horus with overwhelming respect and admiration; his thinly disguised appearance was no longer effective.

At this point, in this place, Horus usually cried.

On this day, he laughed.

HIGHSUN

The King's house had been enlarged many times and was now referred to as the Palace. Attendants in white tunics lined both sides of all the corridors. An official, dressed in white trimmed in red, escorted Horus from the entrance, through the halls, to the Pharaoh's private chamber. Hetephe sat beside Djoser. Djoser rose and strode toward Horus with extended arms. "My son, welcome home. You have been away far too long. I have need of your wise counsel for my many problems."

They both said all the proper words of greeting and reunion. All the proper words said, Djoser and Horus could finally talk together as father and godson. Hetephe offered to excuse herself so that "the men can talk."

It was Horus who said, "Stay, if you will." She leaned back in her chair in silence.

Djoser said, "Hete is wise counsel, Son. She once told me, 'Djoser lives a lie so the Pharaoh can live the truth.' Strange words, I think. Yet, I think of the life of Horus. A life more complicated than the Pharaoh's, perhaps."

Horus replied, "You suggest that Horus lives the lie so that Horus can live the truth. Yes, very strange words, Father."

"We have not talked since your contesting with Set over Anath. I have kept up with your adventures as best I can but, still, I have wanted to talk with you every day since then. Yet not even Pharaoh can command the impossible. It was not Horus that took Anath that night. It was someone else. Which Horus do I now talk with?"

"Neither. The first descended into the depths of the weakness of men and drowned there. The other rotted in the bright sunlight of day. I am now a shell without substance."

Djoser was somber. "A high price to pay for my glory. Your Mother and Father paid a high price, too. It appears my glory came with a high price ... a lot of suffering ... a little blood ... sacrifice of the innocent. I can roll in guilt, but then I would not be worthy of the unbearable cost of it."

Hetephe laughed. "Nephthys offered to teach me the fine art of sexual domination and humiliation in case my little immature prince needed it one day as he destroyed lives to rule the world."

Horus laughed. "And did Mother teach you?"

"Yes. But it is not my husband who craves this thing. It is his son." The room grew still. She rose, and said, "I will leave the men to talk."

As she left, Djoser said, "Before me stands a wonderful opportunity. The empty shell of a great man. With what shall I fill it?"

They talked about the problems and opportunities that lay before Horus. The empty shell gathered possibilities.

Eventually, Djoser asked no questions but took note of everything Horus told him—and didn't tell him.

Finally, satisfied that he understood Horus's view on all his issues, Djoser mentioned that they would attend an affair of state at sundown and this meeting was ended.

SUNDOWN

The word had spread throughout the city ... tonight the Pharaoh and high-born would be entertaining the great Living God Horus at the Mastaba of

Osiris. People packed meals and claimed a spot in the great viewing area on the avenue below to witness and join this spectacle.

It began.

The torches at the top level of the eight-story Mastaba suddenly flamed brightly. A sign that the High-Priestess, herself, would appear.

In her dress of office, she appeared.

Hearts on the avenue quickened.

She stretched out her arms to recognize the dinner of State below. To recognize the people that Osiris and Isis so loved on the avenue below. To Egypt.

She reached into the altar in front of her and withdrew fistfuls of silver confetti. This she threw this into the wind to slowly flutter to the landscape below. Each piece reflected the torchlight that fell upon it. Reflecting, glittering like lights in the heavens. She stood with outstretched arms until the last of the confetti reached the third level. One heartbeat after the sound of a drum, all torches above the third level were simultaneously extinguished; leaving the state dinner on the third level bathed in light; everything above it, bathed only in the light of the moon. Hathor had disappeared.

The formalities finished, music began on the third level and the guests retired to their tables for an evening of feasting and joviality. The people on the broad avenue below, with their picnic baskets, joined in as one, united Egypt.

After the meal, the guests stood and formed into small groups for individual discussions. This was a signal for the people on the avenue to disperse, which, of course, they didn't. As a matter of fact, many opened their own flasks of wine, and a few husbands danced with their wives to the sound of the music from on high. Few noticed the simply dressed woman who slipped into the company of the Pharaoh and Horus.

~~~

Djoser said, "Trader Hathor, you join us at last. Ready to yield to my imperial demands, I'm sure!"

Hathor replied, "Ready to hear my son's wise counsel on the matter."

Hetephe broke in, "Once more my husband and the High-Priestess are at each other's throats over a trivial issue!"
~~~

Both Djoser and Hathor repeated, in unison, "Trivial?!"

Advisor Khaba said to Horus, "The Pharaoh has decreed that Egypt shall create an official Calendar to be used by everyone in the world. One where a specific day, season, and year can be referenced with exact precision anywhere in the world. It is necessary because the world is growing ever smaller, and more events are happening between more and more countries. Timekeeping must be formalized and made common everywhere. A few problems exist. Astronomers measure time by the position of the lights in the heavens. Farmers measure time by the flooding of the Great River. Merchants measure time by the stages of the moon. Priests measure time by the location of the sun. So, what shall we base our new calendar on? The sun or the moon or the location of heaven's lights? And specifically, exactly when does our New Year begin? And what shall we call the units of measurement? And in what year are we living? Those sorts of things. So, Lord Horus, give us our answer. What does our new calendar look like?"

Horus was not impressed. *The world is drowning in problems and Djoser seeks to solve a problem that does not even exist.*

He said, "Call it the 'Political Calendar.' This is year Two of the Pharaoh. It began at the Winter Solstice. Divide it into twelve months. Each month begins at the new moon. Don't force it on anyone other than for affairs of state and trade. Now, that that's settled, I will have another wine."

Djoser looked at Hathor and said, "He tries hard, doesn't he?"

Hetephe said, "Saying Year Two of the Pharaoh may work well in Egypt but certainly not outside Egypt, and starting over for each Pharaoh would create many problems. Starting at Winter's Solstice completely disregards the fact that the position of the moon and the Solstice are not related. Quarter-moon to quarter-moon is the most used reference for the passage of time which your suggestion completely ignores. Some cultures say that this is the 159th Winter Solstice Season. Other cultures measure it from their estimated time since the founding of Tallstone, others from the Great Flood. There is no consensus, and even if there were, the numbers are estimates at best and ridiculous at worst. Plus, you have many days unaccounted for after the twelfth season is completed and before the new year begins."

Hathor said, "Calling it a 'Political Calendar' to be used by the States and for trade purposes is an excellent idea. We need not change anything. People can use whatever timekeeping method they have always used, so they won't be upset by being told to add another way to track time. Now, let's all agree that the New Year begins at Winter Solstice. That is a constant observable by all lands."

Horus replied, "Let the New Year begin at the Solstice and call this Year 159. Designate twelve 'months' in each year. Each month will contain thirty days. Give each month a name and on the five days left over at the end of the year, celebrate a different occupation—like farmers and laborers or even mothers. No labor will be performed on those days. The people will love that. Let New Moons remain the start of a season. A Month and a Season are two different things. There will be twelve months in a year and twelve seasons in a year. They will simply begin on different dates. I will have my wine now."

Djoser said, "You are having too much fun with my problem, Son."

Horus replied, "And my father is making a serious problem out of a bookkeeping exercise. Ask the portmasters what they suggest."

"My 'Political Calendar' is a worthwhile project regardless of what you think, but admittedly it's not like the challenges I had in my younger days. I am sentenced to remain in the background and do whatever I can do."

"You are too great a man for settling to be some kind of God-King of a remote kingdom. Come with me. Let's go save all the world's peoples."

"If the world is to be saved, then it is you who must save it. By the way, from whom do the people need saving?"

Horus answered, "From themselves, Father. From those who use the gods to control the people. Do you not remember the people of Urfa and their treatment of women? Father told me you were there. That you were all repulsed by their attitudes. Attitudes based on what the powerful told them the gods wanted of them. Nonexistent gods! Is this what you want for people? Or do you want people to understand the truth? How can you let these ideas continue to spread? Truth must be taught so that all may flourish. Help me, Father. I no longer know what to do."

Djoser sighed. "You will do all that you can do, Horus. Perhaps it is not our nature to want the truth, only to be told what to do. You teach them how to live good, meaningful lives. Keep doing that. Expand your teachings to cover the world. Let the people choose which truth suits them. Keep seeking the nature of death. If you ever find it, perhaps the truth of it will overpower lies disguised as truth. This is why your father gave us wine. So we can enjoy life while we seek the unknowable, teach the

Phoenicia, Jaffa, Rocky, Burlyman, Polydore | Astarte, T'jaru
Terah, Amathlai, Haran, Terahson, Nahor, Sarai, Isaac, Jacob
Kyrios-Olon, Teumessian, Nimrod, Nimbal, Nimlad, Nimisis, Asherah, Set.

unteachable, and reach for golden apples outside our reach. But I owe you a great debt. Now that I know your mind, I can suggest a plan. In seven days, I'll tell you what to do. Now, practice enjoying life, for a change."

~~~

A quartermoon later, Khaba found Horus and said, "By command of the Pharaoh, come with me."

Horus followed him through the back passageway to Osiris's Mastaba patio. Djoser, Hetephe, Hathor, and Nephthys sat at their table.

Hetephe said, "Sit."

He sat.

Hetephe: "Your life's successes, failures, desires, and conditions have been discussed. This is what you shall do."
Djoser: "The Political Calendar is of greater importance than you see."
Hetephe: "The Pharaoh can command it to be adopted for all business and political transactions involving Egypt. The portmasters and state tradesmen agree that it will significantly improve efficiencies and reduce misunderstandings if implementation is achieved."
Hathor: "But the common people will not adopt it by command, only if they can be tricked into it."
Nephthys: "My son, I'm sorry but Egypt needs you to do the tricking."
Hathor: "Horus shall teach the people that there is a new way to pay respect to the gods."
Nephthys: "Oh, Son. I'm sorry. I'm so sorry."
Djoser: "It is necessary to unite the people of the world but more importantly to you, it will be a great weapon with which you can crush the Church of Urfa."
Hathor: "Horus shall teach the people that the first thirty days of a new year is a 'month' named 'Osirismonth,' and that each morning they will pay homage to God Osiris and if they do so each day of his thirty days that the blessings of Osiris will shine down upon them. You shall teach them that the next thirty days will be a 'month' named 'Set' and if they pay homage to God Set every morning during Setmonth, his blessings will flow down to them."

Horus sat in cold fury listening to what he was being commanded to do.

Hathor continued: "The twelve months will be named Osiris, Set, Tehuti, Zeus, Poseidon, Ares, Ishtar, Astarte, Anath, Aphrodite, Dionysus, and Isis. The union of Isis and Osiris will be celebrated in

<div align="center">Djoser, Hetephe, Incense/Hagar/Keterah
Horus, Serket, Azazil, Abram, Baalat
Ishmael, Maribah, Fatimah, Nebaioth, Basemath, Kedar | Anath, Astarte</div>
~~~

Egypt during the five remaining days the year and whatever gods the locals want to celebrate everywhere else."

Horus: "You will have me teach the thing I have set out to destroy!"

Djoser: "By controlling what the gods say, you control what the gods wish. You can destroy the teachings of your enemies."

Hetephe: "You will tell the lesser lie to tell the greater truth."

Nephthys: "Love is hard."

Djoser: "A ship sails for Byblos at the next Quarter Moon, or as we now say, Hour 800, Day 25, Setmonth, Year 159. I have booked a passage for Set and his followers. Once Set hears there is a way to Urfa by sea, he will accept Nimlad's offer to become High-Priest of the Church of Urfa. The Kyrios-Olon seriously overestimate their control over Set. They have none. Set will destroy their church from the inside."

Hetephe: "I have requested General T'jaru retire from the Army and journey to Urfa with Set. A commanding man with his color will disturb the citizens. He will continually search for ways to increase the influence of Egypt and the Teachings of Horus."

Djoser: "In the self-interests of Egypt, I will support Lord Baalat in her goal of creating a major seaport in Byblos. If she is capable of doing it, trade in that part of the Middlesea will explode in Egypt's favor—and in Byblos's—and Baalat's. She will become a powerful woman who was once a dedicated disciple of Horus and from her reported words and deeds remains a disciple of his words. It can only help you to have a strong ally due west of Urfa."

Hetephe: "Do not dismiss Abram as a weapon of war. Allow Nimrod to use Abram in any way he wishes until the time of Abram's decision comes. Then, perhaps your teachings will prevail."

Djoser: "The ship sails on the 25th of the month. Your wife is scheduled to arrive in Memphis on the 28th. You could advance your goals if you sail on the ship. The name of the ship is 'Lady of Byblos One.' Book passage as you will."

Horus sat dumbly listening as his coming life was laid out before him.

An empty shell being filled with the detritus of life.

SET

HOUR 700, DAY 16, SETMONTH, YEAR 159

The Pharaoh's messenger arrived at Hostess House with a Message for God Set. Set was ecstatic to receive such recognition from the Pharaoh, himself. "Well, let's hear it, Messenger."

The Messenger recited, "Great Pharaoh Djoser of Egypt commands these words be delivered to Living God Set of South Memphis: Greetings, God Set. I invite you and any who might wish to accompany you, to enjoy the inaugural cruise of the good ship 'Lady of Byblos One' departing Newport Hour 700, Day 25, Setmonth, Year 159. The Lady of Byblos will arrive in Byblos by Hour 700, Day 30, Setmonth. I am pleased to offer you and your party free passage in recognition of your invaluable contributions to the kingdom. Your party may return to Newport at any future time of their choosing. My Messenger will return to Hostess House at 1800 this day to retrieve your decision and a list of the members of your party."

Set was stunned. He said, "How delightful. I and my friends can travel to Byblos by sea. The time sounds like some type of seafaring language. An interpretation in the common language will be expected but otherwise, how delightful! How many people may I take with me? Setmonth? What is that? Does that mean it's *my* month? How delightful! You want to go, don't you, Anubis? Should you go, Astarte? Or stay here? And what of my new friend Nimlad? Can I invite him? This is all so delightful!"

HORUS

HOUR 545, DAY 17, SETMONTH YEAR 159

The sun rose.

Horus stood under the great Sycamore Fig tree from where he always watched Hathor call forth his father. Nephthys beside him.

Nephthys said, "You can stay in Memphis and meet her. Azazil knows your mind and will act in your best interests on the voyage. Azazil can travel to Urfa with Set and the others. It's best for you not to return to Urfa, anyway. It will be good for you to stay here with your wife. She will renew your spirit; make you whole, again. You will both have a wonderful time in Memphis; side by side."

"You are right, Mother. It is difficult for her to travel here simply to see me. It is a sacrifice on her part. I owe it to her to be here."

Sadness clung to Nephthys. She did not know why.

DEPARTURE MORNING

HOUR 600, DAY 25, SETMONTH, YEAR 159

Set, Anubis, and Nimlad, with all their luggage, sat in the docking lounge a full hour before departure time. "We are going to have such a delightful time. Especially with my tour of the Church of Urfa. I am undecided as to whether to take the position or not, but this tour will make up my mind."

Set was somewhat disappointed to find that Astarte was also on the voyage as the guest of General T'jaru who was to visit Byblos on a fact-finding mission.

Also on the voyage were Azazil and the now ex-Portmaster of Newport, Ahumm; a man who knew everything there was to know about efficient port design and operations.

Horus and Nephthys stood watching the port activities; waiting to bid good voyage to the ship and its people.

Nephthys said to Horus, "You made the correct decision, waiting here for your wife. There would be little for you to do sailing with them, a word in Set's ear, perhaps. A few words to confuse Lord Nimlad. A suggestion to Astarte that might advance your purposes. A conspiracy with Anubis. To wait here for your wife will be better for her and for you."

A whistle blew indicating 300 heartbeats until a ship would depart; in this case "Lady of Byblos One."

Horus stared blankly at the ship. "Tell Serket I love her. She is my peace!"

He broke into a run and boarded "The Lady of Byblos" as it cast off.

SERKET

HOUR 1700, DAY 27, SETMONTH, YEAR 159

Serket sat upon Arrow staring at the majestic skyline of Memphis. *He has missed me so. I know it! The love and the peace that I bring him is not matched by any other woman or any other thing. He desires me over all other things. Our reunion will be glorious. We will drink wine under the tree by the river that he loves so. I may be brave and let him express his love for me under the tree. Or in it! Oh, Horus, I love you so!*

PORT JAFFA

HOUR 1900, DAY 28, SETMONTH, YEAR 159

By request of Trader Taone, "Lady of Byblos One" detoured and stood offshore at Port Jaffa. Ahumm and Taone were delivered to shore by rowboat. The two set off to find Oceanid Polydore and inform her of Egypt's plans for the remote outpost of Byblos and to inquire if she might be interested in journeying with them to Byblos.

And glory.

Phoenicia, Jaffa, Rocky, Burlyman, Polydore | Astarte, T'jaru
Terah, Amathlai, Haran, Terahson, Nahor, Sarai, Isaac, Jacob
Kyrios-Olon, Teumessian, Nimrod, Nimbal, Nimlad, Nimisis, Asherah, Set.

NEPHTHYS

HOUR 630, DAY 29, SETMONTH, YEAR 159

Serket accompanied Nephthys to witness the sunrise ceremony. They were surrounded by South Memphis women who revered Nephthys as their savior and probably a god. The two witnessed the calling forth of Ra-Osiris-Dionysus under the spreading Sycamore Fig Tree so favored by her stepson Horus. The ceremony was especially beautiful that morning. She asked her son's wife, Serket, to sit under the tree with her for a while. She grew tired and laid her head in Serket's lap. There Telchine Dexithea rested until a beautiful white light filled her mind. She gasped with surprise. *Philyra! Is that you?*

A priestess was sent for. As they waited, the women mourned. Serket sat still, cradling her. *I'm so happy that I did not tell you about Horus leaving me. You looked so old. So tired. I did not want to burden you with my sadness. You look so happy, now. So at peace.*

A priestess and four priests came. There would be a State funeral. She would be placed in front of Osiris's Mastaba and many comforting words would be said. All of South Memphis would attend. She would most likely be granted her own Mastaba.

Serket watched the body of Nephthys taken away. *Mother Nephthys, I told him that I would be his wife until he no longer returned to me. I suppose his leaving me here is the same thing. I will go to Hathor and declare myself divorced. He will be free of me and I of him. He brought me such peace. No woman could be more blessed than I. My assistant will make an excellent replacement Portmaster. I will be free to travel the deserts of Canaan and heal those stung by scorpions. I can heal many people. I can visit Rusalem and counsel my people. I can bring peace to many. Will you be proud of me, Horus? Will you remember my name?*

~~~~~~~~~~~~~

PART II. THE PATRIARCH

7F. Abram

Year 159, Seasons 1,2,3

ABRAM'S SEASON ONE

Abram sat at evening meal with his father and his older brother.

Mother Amathlai, younger Sister Sarai, and Sister-in-law Milkah stood in the cooking area talking and making sure the men were properly cared for.

Terah was agitated, "I don't understand, Abram! This Horus fellow took you away for more than five years to teach you and returned you not knowing anything. What in Hades' name were you doing all that time?!"

Abram tried, once again, to explain the teachings of Horus and how Abram had seen the world during this time.

Terah interrupted, "Yeah, yeah. I understand, but you don't know how to hunt, skin, farm, build, sculpt, or make anything. How do you intend to make a living? I'm already taking care of Haran and Terahson down at Haran's camp. I don't sell enough idols to keep three of you busy. So, what are you gonna do?"

"I will ask Lord Nimrod if he can get me a job working at the temple. A groundskeeper or housekeeping, maybe. Me working in the temple might be good for your business."

Placated for now and finished with his meal, Terah stood up and said, "Yeah, maybe so. Come on boys, let's wander down to the square. Somebody will give us a beer.

PROBLEMS SOLVED

Nimrod had been told that there was to be a massive buildup in control of the southern lands of Mesopotamia and that an unending source of idols was needed to support this project. Nimrod and Asherah held many meetings discussing how to best use Abram.

Terah controlled all idol trade. He had a trading depot a day's journey south of Urfa manned by his sons, Haran and Terahson.

If Nimrod could control the thoughts and actions of Abram, Abram would be a perfect addition at Haran's Outpost. Abram was, by Urfa
~~~~~~~~~~~~~

standards, worldly, well-spoken, well-connected, reasonably well-known through his connection with Living-God Horus, and well-versed in the nature of gods. But could he be controlled?

The sole purpose of Asherah's first meeting with Abram was to size up Abram. Her conclusion was, "He is afraid of women. It will be easy to convince him that all women are whores and I believe Lord Nimrod can mold his thoughts to whatever he wishes them to be."

Nimrod said, "I agree. He has strong opinions until I present a contradictory opinion and then he becomes confused. Horus controlled his mind for more than five years. I can undo all of Horus's teachings before the next Winter Solstice."

The Dyos always sat in darkness whenever they met with Nims and Hors. The less they were seen, the better. Nimrod presented his report on Abram.

A man's maniacal laugh came from the darkness. "How delicious. The great Shaman Horus is undone. We may have to reconsider the possibility of issuing him an invitation to join us. He is no match for our missionaries, more or less our Nims. We will use Abram against Horus. We will turn Terah's little trading camp into a major city and significantly expand our influence in the south by massively expanding Terah's idol sales and flooding the south with more missionaries far away from Horus's little 'Way of Horus' trade route. I *love* being a Kyrios-Olon!"

A female voice from the darkness commanded Nimrod. "Orchestrate a wedding of Lord Abram to High-Horpriestess Asherah. She will indoctrinate him with the usual woman-is-man's-submissive-helpmate. The church's wedding gift will be the lucrative trade assignment to the Harran outpost to provide all idols and trade in the south. We expect Abram to become a great lord there."

<center>~~~</center>

The pious women of Urfa met in the annex of the great church building at sunrise the day after each quarter moon. They had their separate but equal meeting room away from the men. No woman wanted to tempt a male to think impure thoughts by her presence. The meeting was usually led by one of the priestesses, but this morning was a special treat; Horpriestess Asherah herself would lead the discussions. "Have any of our sisters dressed provocatively this last quartermoon? Have any of your friends caused a male to look upon her with impure thoughts? Come, sisters. We are among friends. Tell us. Who has acted impurely?"

Discussion was always lively and contentious, but borderline activity was usually identified, and the woman was guided back to the road of purity.

As the teachings ended, Asherah asked Amathlai to remain for a private conversation. Amathlai was unsure whether to be pleased or frightened.

Alone together, Asherah suggested things such as:
"Abram is such a good man."
"But he is young and I can see in his eyes that manhood wages a great war inside him."
"He wishes to remain pure until he is married, but his manhood urges him to impure thoughts."
"If he has no immediate plans for marriage, I'm so afraid a whore will tempt him into lewd actions."
"Whores from the pastures sometimes slip into town to try to find a man to ravish."
"Consider convincing your husband that Abram should take me as his horwife. He must of course eventually marry a pure woman from within the church or I would become an adulteress and stoned to death."
"I imagine employment in the church would know no limit if I were Abram's horwife."
"Abram comes from such a righteous family, I'm certain he will do what's expected of him."
"Do make sure it's all right with your husband for Abram to marry me."

Amathlai left deciding that she should be exceedingly pleased.

THE WEDDING

Pillow talk between Terah and Amathlai was non-existent, Terah always fell asleep immediately after consummation. The best time to negotiate her desires was after serving a large portion of his favorite meal and offering an additional beer and sending away her children. A promise of honey bread after talking was also helpful. The possibility of Abram marrying Asherah did not require a great deal of convincing; especially after potential work for the church was mentioned and the traditional gigantic contribution to the church did not appear to be required.

All that remained was for the reluctant, unsure Abram to issue a formal proposal to the virtuous horpriestess Asherah.

~~~

Phoenicia, Jaffa, Rocky, Burlyman, Polydore | Astarte, T'jaru
Terah, Amathlai, Haran, Terahson, Nahor, Sarai, Isaac, Jacob
Kyrios-Olon, Teumessian, Nimrod, Nimbal, Nimlad, Nimisis, Asherah, Set.
~~~

Abram marched to the gates of the church square. He was escorted to Nimrod who greeted him graciously. Abram requested an audience with Horpriestess Asherah. He was shown to a nice place to wait while Asherah finished up some pressing work with whom she was currently involved.

Soon, Abram, with a written request in hand, was escorted into Asherah's immaculate quarters. He said, in a well-rehearsed way, "Pure and lovely Asherah, it would pay me great honor if you would accept my proposal of marriage and become my loving, adoring wife for now and all of eternity as blessed by the Church of Urfa, which teaches the righteous, loving words of the gods."

Asherah had already decided upon her best response to his proposal. She lowered her eyes and demurely answered, "It would be my great honor to become your wife, Lord Abram. Neither of us would ever cause the other to be unsure of what to do. Yes. I accept your gracious and manly proposal of marriage."

Abram returned home. He suspected, from the teachings of Horus, that he was being played.

~~~

So it was that within a quartermoon, the invitations were sent. The first, to the House of Terah. Three Church Attendants dressed in their finery, marched to the House of Terah and knocked. Amathlai answered. She called to her husband, "Husband Terah, there are three Boys of the Church here to see you."

Terah walked to greet them.

An Attendant said, "May we extend invitations to the women in your household to attend the wedding of Abram of Urfa to the pure woman named Asherah?"

"Why, yeah, sure."

The Attendant turned to Amathlai and handed her an ornate box. He said, "Inside are two garlands signifying the loving purity of the wearer. One for you and one for your daughter, Sarai. Those wearing a garland and modest white tunics bringing a dish of food prepared by their own hand may enter the Temple at highsun three days hence to witness this holy marriage blessed by the gods."

He turned and all the boys marched away.

<div align="center">
Djoser, Hetephe, Incense/Hagar/Keterah
Horus, Serket, Azazil, Abram, Baalat
Ishmael, Maribah, Fatimah, Nebaioth, Basemath, Kedar | Anath, Astarte
</div>
~~~

Terah grunted, "Well, what about that!"

Amathlai turned and stared at Sarai. Both had stars in their eyes.

THE WEDDING

The day of the wedding was magical.

All girls and unmarried women were there as were their mothers plus reluctant boys and men. The large grounds in front of the temple were covered with tents under which the women placed their food offerings. The grounds were an ocean of white. Presumed virgins of marriageable age had forced their favorite male to accompany them. Young boys had come for the sweetbreads and other delicious food. Mothers flitted around exchanging recipes serendipitously inspecting the unmarried young people for signs of suitable mates for their unmarried children.

Abram, with his father, spoke to all the husbands. Lewd comments were made. The citizens of Urfa, bound by this glorious common experience and shared values, bonded more closely.

Unseen, high in a temple tower, without emotion, the Kyrios-Olon observed the festivities unfolding below them.

At highsun, a temple bell pealed.

Alter boys marched double-file out the temple door and stopped. One continued on to escort Amathlai, followed by Sarai, into the temple where they were each given a bouquet and were sat in the front, near the altar. They were beautiful in their white dresses; heads crowned with a garland of white flowers.

The married women were then allowed entrance and directed to sit on the sides of the auditorium. Next, all the girls in their white dresses and white garlands were allowed entry and directed to sit in the middle of the auditorium between the married women. They were each given a single white flower upon entering.

Anticipation grew.

Unmarried women, with their male escort, were marched down the long aisle and sat behind the altar facing the gathered congregation. Each woman was given a beautiful bouquet. The mothers and girls swooned with admiration as they watched the procession of eligible unmarried women march down the aisle escorted by an eligible man.

The only males allowed entry were the musicians, the escorts, the father and brothers of the groom, the presiding official, and Abram. The women were thrilled to be here since they were allowed entry only on special occasions such as this. And none had ever seen as fine a ceremony as this.

It was time. A church bell pealed. The musicians began playing a lyrical melody punctuated by marching drums.

The presiding official, Nimrod, strode to the front of the altar.

Terah marched beside Abram down the long aisle to stand before Nimrod. They turned to face the Temple entrance.

Cymbals clashed. The volume of the music doubled; the drums became louder and more demanding. Six beautifully gowned priestesses entered— tiaras of flowers on their heads. They solemnly marched to stand on either side of the altar and turned to face the Temple doors.

Complete silence.

The temple bell pealed. Cymbals clashed. Drums rolled.

Asherah appeared, framed by the gigantic Temple doors. White gown. White veil hiding her face. Long train. She stood motionless. The girls let out a collective sigh. The hearts of the unmarried women beat faster. Their escorts fidgeted.

Asherah began her slow march down the aisle. Every female reveled in the pride of being female. The promise. The hope. The dreams. The glory. Making babies. Having a house. Having a husband. What could be finer? It was glorious!

Asherah arrived at the altar. Nimrod signaled Abram to remove the veil from her face which he clumsily did.

If there is one thing any Horpriestess knows how to do, it is to make her face beautiful. Desirable. Inviting. Asherah was the High-Horpriestess— the most accomplished priestess in the church of Urfa.

Terah's eyes widened when he saw her unveiled face. Even Abram gasped a little gasp in appreciation of her beauty.

Nimrod began. He said the things one would expect him to say such as, "Asherah, do you vow before Zeus to lay with no man that is not married to a sister-wife?" Also, "Abram, do you vow before Aphrodite to lay with no other woman but your wife, and if you do, to come immediately to the temple, confess your sin, and pay the appropriate repentance offering?"

Djoser, Hetephe, Incense/Hagar/Keterah
Horus, Serket, Azazil, Abram, Baalat
Ishmael, Maribah, Fatimah, Nebaioth, Basemath, Kedar | Anath, Astarte

Nimrod instructed the groom to kiss the bride and knew immediately that he had made a mistake. He saw, as did Asherah, the panic in Abram's eyes. Asherah, being a horpriestess, expertly removed the problem by coyly looking away and shaking her head, "No."

Laughter filtered through the congregation.

Nimrod introduced the newly married—albeit temporarily—couple to the audience and instructed Abram to take his bride to the wedding chamber in the back of the Temple.

Asherah expertly let him take her hand and lead her away to their bed. She had already discreetly unclasped her massive dress so that the bottom of the dress remained in place as she stepped out of it clad only in a thin, short white skirt that barely covered anything. She looked at the congregation and coyly said, "I won't be needing that!" She guided the panicking Abram toward her bedroom and whispered calming words as they departed.

They entered her bedroom with hundreds of burning candles and the scent of fall.

Her instructions had been clear, "He *must* be the aggressor. He *must* take you of his own volition. It *must* be his desire to have you and you *must* submit only because he is your loving husband. IS THAT UNDERSTOOD?"

She understood.

Things she huskily murmured were:
"Oh, husband. I am so disturbed right now. Would you permit me to have a glass of wine to calm me down?"
"Would you care for a glass, too?"
"But it would make me feel protected if you had a glass with me."
"Yes, just a small one."
"Would you remove the top of my dress so I can feel more relaxed?"
"Wonderful. Would you rub my shoulders for me, too?"
"Ohh, that feels soo good."
"I think we would enjoy another wine."
"I hope this will be your first time. I'm not really that experienced. We could learn together."
"My heart is still beating so fast. Here, put your hand over my heart so you feel it."

She wasn't the Church of Urfa High-Horpriestess for nothing.

Nimrod had shepherded the congregation into tents filled with food. The band had moved outside and begun playing lively music. The men headed for the beer. The married women gathered around the unmarried women and their escorts extolling the glory of marriage. The boys stuffed their faces with sweetbreads. The girls discovered the enclosure containing ponies decorated with festive ribbons they were allowed to ride.

Everything under control, Nimrod discreetly entered the hidden balcony overlooking Asherah's bedroom. He was pleased with her progress. Abram had gained self-confidence and the illusion he was the master of the scene. His testosterone level was rising. After his second glass of wine, he reached over to boldly stroke Asherah's now bare breasts.

She giggled.

Nimrod smiled. *What do you call them, Horus? "Weapons of war?" Well, my friend, mine are better than yours. I wish you were here to watch them doing battle. We could have a deep philosophical discussion.*

AFTER THE WEDDING

Abram's wedding night lasted two days which included subliminal indoctrination to foster his growing self-confidence in how to please a faithful wife. After the two-day training period, Asherah informed Abram that she, unfortunately, had many upcoming appointments she simply could not reschedule. Abram understood, she was sure. "My beloved husband, it is time that you consider all the young maidens within the Church of Urfa and select one to be your loving, submissive wife. Soon!"

Abram retired to his father's home where a large celebratory evening meal was prepared.

By Abram's command, the appreciative women were allowed to prepare their plates and join the men at the table.

Milkah listened intently with feigned indifference as Sarai peppered her big brother with questions about his wedding night and being married to the Horpriestess and everything. Amathlai continuously interrupted with "Sarai! That is not a proper question! Sarai! You are too young to know about these things! Sarai! I don't want you to grow up to be an impure woman thinking impure thoughts!"

Sarai's only defense was, "Well, he's my brother and I don't want him to be hurt or anything."

Amathlai said, "No one wants Abram hurt."

Then Sarai stunned her mother with the question, "Mother, Horpriestess Asherah is your sister-wife. Does Father ever go to her?"

"SARAI! WE DO NOT DISCUSS SUCH THINGS!"

Abram was happy enough not to discuss his wedding night. He turned the conversation to Milkah and how happy he was that his oldest brother had married the daughter of his half-brother, Haran.

Milkah was thrilled to be part of the extremely high-class family of Terah. "Bein' a country girl gets lonely, sometimes. With all the milkin' and farmin' and cleanin.' Father was always on the road sellin' idols and stuff. It was real nice when Terahson got sent down to the camp and I got sent up to marry Nahor. I was real fortunate. Of course, Sister Iskah has gotta do all the work keepin' house now. An' now there's *two* men. I worry about her sometimes. Mama never complained but I always thought she jus' worked herself to death and that was jus' takin' care of one man. She was jus' always so grateful that Father agreed to marry her when she started showin' so she woodn't get stoned to death."

The conversation was now back in Amathlai's area of expertise. "The gods *are* merciful, aren't they?"

Abram listened politely but eventually excused himself to walk outside into the cool, crisp air.

He was followed closely by Sarai and Milkah.

EMPLOYMENT

The next morning after sunrise, the messenger came. "Terah and Abram, you are commanded to join Lord Nimrod for evening meal. Lord Terah will present Lord Nimrod with his plans to increase trade through Harran Outpost by a factor of ten. Good day."

The messenger turned and left, leaving Terah in wide-eyed terror. *A command from the church. I have never had a command from the church before, but I know what happens to those that get one and fail. Ten-fold? It's all I can do to create idols and trade them with only Terahson and Haran there. Tenfold? What in the name of Zeus am I going to do?*

Abram said, "That sounds like fun! How long does it take to sculpt a new idol and make casting molds? Is there a lot of material nearby? How many pieces are you trading now? Can you train more sculptors easily? How many shekels do you make? Do the people come to trade at Harran Outpost or do Terahson and Haran go out and sell among the people?"

Phoenicia, Jaffa, Rocky, Burlyman, Polydore | Astarte, T'jaru
Terah, Amathlai, Haran, Terahson, Nahor, Sarai, Isaac, Jacob
Kyrios-Olon, Teumessian, Nimrod, Nimbal, Nimlad, Nimisis, Asherah, Set.

Terah, still terrified, took some unknown comfort in the questions coming from his young son's mouth. *The boy sounds smart. Maybe this Horus fellow actually taught him something. Like how to get things done. I hope you can make some kind of plan, boy. Cause I can't.*

The man and his son returned to their home where they discussed things.

~~~

Nimrod joyously greeted Terah and Abram as they entered the guest dining hall of the church. A young church priestess, not worthy of being a Horpriestess, provided them with food and drink. Nimrod listened with rapt attention as Terah nervously explained how he, with the help of Abram, planned on increasing his idol trade tenfold within the year. *Not bad, Terah. The boy told you what to do, didn't he? Not bad plans at all. You might actually do it.*

Nimrod said, "Excellent, Lord Terah. The church will provide you with all the resources you need. More sculptors, you say! Of course, how obvious! And they can sculpt idols of the local gods rather than offering the same old idols of Zeus, Aphrodite, and their kin. That alone will triple sales and be a way to bring the local gods into the folds of the One True Church. And you also need a fleet of carriages to travel the land with the missionaries. This will open an entirely new avenue for the spread of the True Word. Excellent. I am excited. But you must make one small change. Abram can advise you, but he will be working full-time directly with me as my chief assistant. He applied for work for the church and has been accepted for one of the highest positions available. It is his if he marries a local woman before the next full moon. The position is highly visible to the people and must represent all the teachings of the church; especially when it comes to marriage. I will assign one of my best missionaries to you as your assistant since I will be taking Abram. What a glorious plan you have given me, Terah. The world awaits you!"

Ecstatic Terah and uneasy Abram were dismissed.

~~~

Late that evening, Amathlai and Sarai were thrilled to join the men for talk and visitation. Sarai stood behind Abram messaging his tense shoulders as Terah recounted their wonderful evening meal with Lord Nimrod.

Sarai felt Abram grow more tense when Terah recounted how Abram must take a wife before the full moon to receive the high position within the church. She messaged more aggressively.

Abram felt himself respond to her demanding fingers. He crossed his legs.

Sarai moved closer, her body lightly touching his. Her fingers became stronger.

Amathlai immediately took note of what was happening between her son and daughter. She was as ferociously ambitious for her children as she was protective. Staring coldly at Sarai, Amathlai made untold calculations of what was proper. What was practical. What was acceptable. What would best benefit the House of Terah. What would best benefit her son.

Sarai, with confusion, defiance, and fear returned her mother's cold stare.

Amathlai decided. She innocently interrupted her still-rambling husband with, "Husband, did you ever tell Sarai who her birth mother is?"

Stillness is not a thing that can be described. It must be experienced.

There was stillness.

Sarai asked, "M-my birth mother?"

Amathlai answered, "Yes. My good friend had no husband and one night she confessed to me that your father had accidentally impregnated her after they had drank too much wine. So many problems went away when I agreed to pretend to be your birth mother and not accost your father over this indiscretion. You are the most beautiful young woman in Urfa and must soon select the man who will ask you to marry him. I thought your father would have told you by now."

Terah frantically searched his memory. *Oh Zeus, help me out here. What am I supposed to say? It might be possible but Amathlai never mentioned it! I don't think!*

There was much discussion coming up with a story that would be acceptable to the pious. Terah kept mostly silent. They finally agreed that their story was that Amathlai had discovered a foundling by the side of the road near the Pastures and that her love for the baby and the teachings of the Church compelled her to take the child as her own.

This tale solved so many potential problems. Whether the tale was true or not was known by Amathlai and, possibly, her husband.

This was the chance of Sarai's lifetime. *Abram is comfortable around me. He feels safe. I know he has feelings for me. He always has. And now it's acceptable! He will be the most powerful man that Urfa has ever produced. He could give me babies that would create nations. I would be the mother of nations. All that is needed is for him to ask me to become his loving wife. Sarai! Mother of Nations!*

Her hormones went full speed ahead: *He IS my half-brother but half-brother isn't at all like a full brother. It's more like a cousin, really. Yes, it's not like a full brother, at all. I am a woman. He is a man. We can make babies!*

Abram tore away from the discussion to go outside and think in solitude.

Sarai followed him out, crept up behind him, and placed her strong fingers on his shoulders. "You are so tense, handsome stranger. Here let me relieve your stress." She pressed her body against his back as she messaged his shoulders. She had crushed fragrant flowers with her fingers. "I wanted to remind you that I am a foundling and that you and I are not really sister and brother. I am a pure woman suitable for marriage. Mother has instructed me about the nature of being a woman, how to please a man in his bed, and all of the secret knowledge of women. It would be impure to imagine myself lying naked on my back with a man on top of me, wouldn't it? But I do wonder if I will writhe in ecstasy at my husband's touch. What do you think, Abram? Will I? Well, I had better get to my own bed. I hope I don't have any impure thoughts. Good night, Abram."

She bumped her body firmly against his as she left.

Abram knew what Sarai was suggesting. She made his decision less difficult. He had always felt comfortable around Sarai. And now he finds out that she isn't his sister; at least not his full sister. The story to be told was that she was found as an abandoned baby, which meant she would not even be suspected of being his half-sister.

Nimrod had commanded him to take a wife before the full moon but none of the other women in Urfa interested him. He knew his father didn't care and that his mother seemed to secretly approve of Sarai. No. It would not be difficult at all for Abram to propose marriage to his one-time sister Sarai.

But his mind could not quite form the image of Sarai "writhing."

<center>~~~</center>

Theirs was a standard wedding and not near the opulence of Abram's first wedding to Asherah.

The two newlyweds moved into a nice apartment in the Church building, a symbol of the highest status. Sarai was beside herself with self-importance as she went about her stately wifely gathering duties in the villages of Urfa.

Now she needed to get on with the baby-making.

Djoser, Hetephe, Incense/Hagar/Keterah
Horus, Serket, Azazil, Abram, Baalat
Ishmael, Maribah, Fatimah, Nebaioth, Basemath, Kedar | Anath, Astarte

THE ORGANIZATION

Nimrod would become Chief of all Chiefs in the administration as soon as he could find a High-Priest to replace the long-dead Teumessian. High-Horpriestess Asherah did a fine job of temporarily presiding over the church, but she was a woman, and this was man's work. Finding a man with the necessary stature that could be controlled by the Kyrios-Olon was more difficult than one might think. The missionaries searched for such a man, but the patience of the Kyrios-Olon was running out.

Abram was in the newly created Ministry of Church Expansion. He was assigned to build a church every half day's journey into the south. He must convince the residents to finance such a building and to pay a monthly tithe to the priests necessary to operate the church. In return, they would receive the blessings of Zeus or whoever the local god was. Church members in good standing would be allowed to buy idols of their choice at a discounted price. The local priests would then go about the business of ministering to the residents, recruiting missionaries to spread the good news, and teaching the residents what to think.

Terah reported to the Minister of Missionaries. He would send traveling idol sales representatives behind the missionaries. The sales of his idols would reinforce the teachings of the missionaries and keep the Church of Urfa in the minds of the people. At Abram's suggestion, Terah added a line of Prayer Cloths that had been blessed by the Urfa priestesses. They were said to bring many blessings to whoever owned one. Also, they were available in a number of colors.

Nimrod had everything just as he wanted except for one thing—Nimlad had not delivered Set to Urfa.

In the meantime, Nimrod traveled with Abram to inspect the Harran Outpost and meet with Terahson and Nahor. The outpost was not much of an outpost and neither Terahson nor Nahor were thrilled with the new quotas that had been laid upon them. They were quite content to sit around drinking beer and sculpting idols and selling one occasionally to anyone who came in and asked to buy one.

Although not under Nimrod's control, the two men *were* familiar with the Fiery Furnaces of the Church and had attended the trial of three men accused of being "unworthy" by the church. The trial consisted of the men being found guilty and then being thrown into the furnace. If they walked out alive, they were judged to be forgiven by the gods. Nimrod suggested that Terahson and Nahor had all the appearances of being

Phoenicia, Jaffa, Rocky, Burlyman, Polydore | Astarte, T'jaru
Terah, Amathlai, Haran, Terahson, Nahor, Sarai, Isaac, Jacob
Kyrios-Olon, Teumessian, Nimrod, Nimbal, Nimlad, Nimisis, Asherah, Set.

"unworthy." A perception both men were eager to shed as soon as possible.

Abram and Nimrod continued south for a day's march but found no sign of human activity but the next day, they came upon a village of some size.

Abram waited until sunrise and then performed Horus's "Greeting to the Sun" ceremony. Six people noticed and wandered over to see "what was happening."

Nimrod did not at all approve of the words being said, but it *did* attract people's attention and they *did* stay to talk with Abram after he had finished and they did need some place to pay homage to Nisaba, the Goddess of Harvest, and yes, they might be interested in buying an idol of Goddess Nisaba. "Would this building with a priest ensure that Nisaba is always pleased with our village and continue to bless our harvests?"

Nimrod listened with approval. *Let the boy say whatever he wants. Once the church is established, the priest can teach them church-approved dogma.*

They got directions to the next closest town where the scene was repeated. Nimrod was elated. *Two for two! This will work!*

They returned to Urfa.

Nimrod was delighted to report Abram's success to his superiors, but he also had to report that Harran Outpost needed significant infrastructure expansion. Nimlad was elated to be informed that a ship named "Lady of Byblos One" had anchored off the town of Byblos and that it brought with it Nimlad and the Living God Set who was reportedly exhilarated to be traveling to the ancient city of Urfa with its magnificent church and amenities.

Everything was falling into place.

~~~~~~~~~~~~

8. Vignettes

Year 159, Season 4, Zeusmonth

BAALAT IN BYBLOS

In Byblos, Baalat enthusiastically showed one-time Portmaster Nahum and Polydore her vision and what she had accomplished so far. All three were wide-eyed with ideas and excitement.

Captain Burlyman directed the offloading of the cargo into Warehouse One while visions of a fleet sailed through his head.

Paone and Patwo told Taone and Tatwo what they had accomplished since they had been gone. Taone and Tatwo reciprocated.

Ex-general T'jaru and Azazil found the dock cafe and ordered beers to continue discussions on how to best approach their issues.

Set, Anubis, and Nimlad set off for Urfa.

Horus stood alone on the dock looking back toward Memphis. He had done all that he could do and sacrificed all he had to sacrifice.

SET AND ASHERAH IN URFA

Set was escorted into the Church of Urfa with all the pomp available.

Crowds of excited townspeople lined the streets and watched his every step thrilled with the knowledge that this was Teumessian, or maybe even Zeus, himself, reborn. Reborn to guide and minister to them, to share the glory of the words of the gods. To tell them how pious they were—how worthy. They had been too long without affirmation that they were worthy and everyone else unworthy.

Set walked toward the large church doors along the path lined with church staff standing at attention dressed in their finery. Inside the magnificent nave stood the priestesses, each one more beautiful than the last. He came to the nave. To the right, he saw magnificence, to the left he saw magnificence, straight ahead was the altar and, too, the pulpit of the Living Word of the Gods; a wonder of the world.

He was shown the living areas of the Living Word of the Gods and the young girls who would be assigned as his assistants if he were to accept this extremely important position.

Phoenicia, Jaffa, Rocky, Burlyman, Polydore | Astarte, T'jaru
Terah, Amathlai, Haran, Terahson, Nahor, Sarai, Isaac, Jacob
Kyrios-Olon, Teumessian, Nimrod, Nimbal, Nimlad, Nimisis, Asherah, Set.
~~~~~~~~~~~~

Nimlad said, "While you are inspecting your sleeping area El Set, let me introduce the Horpriestesses who will report directly to you."

The twelve were introduced, their beauty far surpassing that of the simple priestesses he had seen as he entered.

"Oh, yes, and here is High-Horpriestess Asherah who will explain their function and duties."

Asherah entered. Upon seeing her beauty, Set gasped.

Nimlad commanded a servant girl, "Bring Aphrodite-wine to the great El Set and High-Horpriestess Asherah. Everyone but the Horpriestesses leave them as their functions and duties are explained to El Set. I hope that El Set will accept our invitation to become the new Living Word of The Gods and join us in front of his altar after Asherah has fully explained her responsibilities to him."

The touring group left El Set under the tutelage of Asherah.

The Kyrios-Olon silently observed her excellent presentation from their darkness on high.

EL SET

The installation of El Set, "The Living Word of The Gods," was worthy of Set's high expectations. He was pulled through the villages of Urfa on a carriage of black ebony. The people were overwhelmed to see the actual Living Word in their midst. The Ambrosia was already at work and a far better recipe than the Olympians had developed. He felt years younger.

Anubis discovered the Pasture and its loose women. He was now trying to determine how to get into the good graces of the church priestesses.

El Set, or El, as he would come to be called, had achieved the pinnacle of his career. He wished only that Philyra, Dionysus, and Dexithea could see him. He had no idea that the self-appointed Kyrios-Olon gods observed everything from their darkness on high.

INITIATIONS

The opulence of the inner sanctums of the Kyrios-Olon was not shown to Lords, Kings, High-Priests, the wealthy, or the famous; only to the Kyrios-Olon.

Initiation into their ranks was a ceremony of significance. The anteroom into the Inner Sanctum was the room of initiation and seen only by their devout followers; mostly simple priestesses, Horpriestesses, and Nims.

Djoser, Hetephe, Incense/Hagar/Keterah
Horus, Serket, Azazil, Abram, Baalat
Ishmael, Maribah, Fatimah, Nebaioth, Basemath, Kedar | Anath, Astarte

Nimrod had performed his duties well. He had the attitude, intelligence, cleverness, and desire for raw power that permeated members of their secret society. Nimrod had been invited to become Kyrios-Olon.

Two nude priestesses led Nimrod into the cavernous room lit by a single candle burning on an altar in the center. They stopped in front of the candle. Three hooded figures stepped from the darkness to face them. A soft low chant came from the darkness; words were said and repeated; blood was drawn and smeared; ancient words were recited. The two nude priestesses removed the hooded cloak from Nimrod's body, leaving him, too, nude.

From the darkness came the chant, "You have become one of us. You have become a god. You have become Dyoapollo."

Light suddenly blazed from lamps spread throughout the room. The naked bodies of the Kyrios-Olon and the Horpriestesses and the priestesses were illuminated.

The Horpriestesses fell upon Dyoapollo.

DELIGHTED PEOPLE

Sarai quit attempting to find delight in servicing her husband; she, instead, took delight in the possibility that this time he might impregnate her. She did remember to writhe now and then to keep up appearances.

Milkah returned to Harran with four married couples to learn the art of idol-making and to support a busier and better outpost. A route of traveling sales wagons full of local idols was established between Harran and points south. A generic goddess of fertility and one for crops was created as was a generic god of war and one of storms. These four idols were suitable to represent most local gods.

Terahson and Haran were invited to see the Church's Fiery-Furnace-of-Judgment. Their productivity increased significantly after their visit.

El Set took delight in explaining the desires of the gods, as related to him by the ever-present Nimlad, to his faithful people. Set was delighted that Lord Nimrod accepted his suggestion that each new church should promote the worship of Set and Asherah as gods.

Asherah was delighted to become El's concubine.

Abram was delighted to continue establishing churches as he traveled evermore southward into the lands of Mesopotamia. Spreading the Word of Horus relieved his guilt of not feeling the closeness with his nagging wife he had once felt with Baalat.

Nimrod was delighted with his success in promoting Church-educated missionaries into local priests and assigning them to the churches Abram had founded.

Nimrod was NOT delighted to become chief of Church operations. Dyo's should not be expected to do actual work.

Terah was delighted that profits from idol sales were going up tenfold even though the new idols were not as finely crafted as the old idols. At Abram's suggestion, Terah increased the price of an old idol one hundredfold and dictated that all newer idols were to be made in the form of impressionistic "modern art." He was considering moving his home and family to Harran, which was rapidly becoming a small city fueled by Terah's idol industry.

In the land of Urfa, everyone was simply delighted.

Toward the south, T'jaru, Astarte, and Azazil explored the lands of Mesopotamia making friends and spreading the Word of Horus.

Toward the west, the harbor in Byblos had been dredged, ample docks of cedar built, and warehouses modernized. The docks smelled of fresh ocean spray, the finest cafe north of Damascus sat on the dock. The city of Byblos was immaculately clean; local harvests thrived.

The trading ships of Captain Burlyman plied the route between Byblos and Newport providing large supplies of cedar to Memphis and returning with large supplies of papyrus and other goods for Byblos.

A port at Alashiya had been built to accommodate the trade of the fine copper ore found there.

Horus returned to Port Jaffa in search of Serket. He was disappointed to be informed that Serket had never returned from a pilgrimage to meet her husband in Memphis. He searched for a while. He was told about the death of Nephthys in the arms of Serket and how Serket had announced her divorce from her husband; of how Serket returned to the land of Canaan, healing those stung by scorpions, bringing peace to the people, teaching the Way of Horus.

He sought her in Rusalem. She wasn't there. She had prayed at the grave of her grandfather and continued her travels. It was as if she did not want to be found.

Djoser, Hetephe, Incense/Hagar/Keterah
Horus, Serket, Azazil, Abram, Baalat
Ishmael, Maribah, Fatimah, Nebaioth, Basemath, Kedar | Anath, Astarte

As Horus searched for Serket, he also searched for the Land of the Dead; for anyone who had ever talked to the dead. It was as if he could not save the people from themselves, then he would find his once-wife.

Failing that, he would keep moving.

The stars remained in their courses.

Phoenicia, Jaffa, Rocky, Burlyman, Polydore | Astarte, T'jaru
Terah, Amathlai, Haran, Terahson, Nahor, Sarai, Isaac, Jacob
Kyrios-Olon, Teumessian, Nimrod, Nimbal, Nimlad, Nimisis, Asherah, Set.

~~~~~~~~~~~~

9. Abram and Byblos

Year 165, Season 5, Poseidonmonth

Abram shrugged and said, "Whatever will be, will be."

This was Abram's answer to his mother's constant inquiry, "When will you present me with a grandchild?"

The gods knew Abram tried hard enough. He inseminated Sarai at least once each quartermoon. What more could he do?

He and Sarai visited his parents every evening. She to seek commiseration from her Stepmother-In-Law Mother over Abram's inability to impregnate her. He, to counsel with his father on his father's growing idol trade.

They left Terah's house well after sunset and walked to their apartment on the church grounds. Sarai was the envy of her friends, married to a successful man high-up in the church. He was handsome and she was beautiful. What was there not to like about the life Sarai had?

Sarai fussed all the way back to their apartment. She fussed about many things, but especially about not being impregnated.

He said, "Whatever will be, will be."
She said, "I want you to bed me every day until I get pregnant!"
He said, "Every day?! Wife, that would wear out our private parts. I don't think even a priestess is bedded every day."
She said, "Every day, Abram! Until I get pregnant."
He said, "I will talk with Asherah. She is knowledgeable about a woman's body. She can advise me."
She said, "Don't you dare bed that woman, Abram! I won't have it! You may bed only me! You have to get me pregnant!"
He said, "Whatever will be, will be."

~~~

The next morning, Abram went to his office early. Problems were beginning to overwhelm him. He requested an audience with Asherah.

The obviously pregnant Asherah happily danced into his office with "How can I please you today, Lord Abram?"

Djoser, Hetephe, Incense/Hagar/Keterah
Horus, Serket, Azazil, Abram, Baalat
Ishmael, Maribah, Fatimah, Nebaioth, Basemath, Kedar | Anath, Astarte

They talked of Asherah's promotion to El's wive from that of his concubine. She was also promoted out of her priestess position. "Getting pregnant made it all happen. No one in the church wanted me pregnant but me. It's my way out of servitude to the church. I am too far up in their church to ever get away from Urfa but at least I can now just look pretty and not have to do anything. That's the best I can do. I'm El's wife and he is older than Zeus. He can't live much longer no matter how much of that potion they pour into him."

This led to his sharing his problem with Sarai.

She suggested that he bed several different priestesses. "If one becomes pregnant then we will know if the problem is with you or with Sarai."

He dismissed the suggestion but for the first time, wondered if the problem was Sarai."

"Have her come see our Healer. She has potions for everything including getting pregnant."

"She does?!" Abram grew excited.

"Oh, yes. I needed a potion for this ..." she said as she patted her abdomen, "... and El needed a potion to put it inside me, both the baby and himself. Potions are wonderful things."

"Can she make a potion for me?"

Asherah considered the problem, "You lay with her once a quartermoon? Yes, Lord Abram. I believe several different potions may be in order."

Abram felt much better after his conversation with Asherah. He had a sudden insight into how much Asherah was like Baalat; except Baalat was a whore and Asherah wasn't because Asherah did not lie with other men after she had become Set's concubine. Not that Set cared, but Asherah did. That, and she wanted to leave the church, but the church wouldn't let her leave for some reason.

Abram was called to Nimrod's office to discuss the resistance to the church being met in the Mesopotamian region. "The farther south you go, the poorer the results you are getting, Abram. Why is this?"

"The Way of Horus is already being taught in the Mesopotamian lands. Azazil and General T'jaru—they call him Ninurta, "Mighty Hunter" because of his size and presence—travel the land spreading the good news. I need not establish a church in those areas."

Nimrod almost exploded as he said, "Get out of here!".

Abram was at a loss. Nimrod had never spoken to him in that manner. He stood up, left, shrugged, and said to no one, "Whatever will be, will be."

~~~

On the morning after the Full Moon, Abram began his journey south to visit his new churches and establish new ones. He had his usual retinue of six missionaries, but this time he was accompanied by Chief Nimrod and his primary assistant, Zedek. They stopped at the Harran Outpost where Haran joined them with his wagon filled with idols. The new idols of Set and Asherah were growing more popular.

They set off. Haran was enthusiastic. Nimrod was sullen. Zedek more so. Abram offered a happy, "Let's find out what today will bring!"

Sixteen churches had been established. El Set and Asherah were honored in them all.

Abram noticed that his churches were teaching the subservience of the wife to the husband and the general attitude of male privilege. This was not at all in line with the teachings of Horus that Abram had assumed would be taught in the churches he had established. Feelings of unease and confusion planted themselves in the back of his mind.

Nimrod found less acceptance of church dogma the farther south he traveled. *Horus is still at work. Will you never give in, you son of a bastard?*

Haran remained enthusiastic. Idol sales were brisk at every stop.

~~~

Nimrod wasn't certain where Mesopotamia actually began, but the sixteenth church must certainly be in the collective of organized villages and settlements that the Kyrios-Olon referred to as Mesopotamia. Nimrod saw that women had power, rights, and were not at all subservient to men. But men tended to work outside the home and women tended to maintain the home; a perfect situation for the church to formalize its teaching of the patriarchal control of the man over women, children, property, and power.

Nimrod listened as Abram found the local religious leader and extolled the Way of Horus as the way of worthy people. He listened more intently as the leader replied that was what the teachers Azazil, Ninurta, and Astarte had taught, and that perhaps the Church of Urfa, who respected all the local gods, might find a welcoming home here. "Do you have idols of Zeus and Aphrodite? They have many followers here."

Sales were brisk.

The six missionaries went to work finding a suitable location for the soon-to-be-built Church of Urfa.

Nimrod inquired as to where Azazil might be found.

He was told, "Two villages to the southwest."

That is exactly where Nimrod, Zedek, Abram, and Haran found Azazil, T'jaru, and Astarte.

~~~

The reunion of Azazil and Abram was long and warm.

Astarte flirted with Nimrod, obviously a man of importance.

Nimrod interrupted by introducing himself to T'jaru. "Greetings, I am Nimrod of Urfa. You appear to be friends with one of my friendly competitors. What brings you so far from the lands of Canaan?"

T'jaru knew well who Nimrod was, even before Djoser enlisted him to explore countering the church's incursions into this area. "I am General T'jaru of the Egyptian army and friend of Horus. I return the question. What brings you so far from the land of Urfa?"

Nimrod laughed. "Ah, so our competition of who controls the world has begun. I tell you now, Mesopotamia will be under the influence of Urfa. Egypt is far away and can control many other lands. Leave this land to us —General!"

Azazil heard the exchange and interrupted. "Gentlemen! Delicate diplomatic posturing seems to be a talent neither of you has. The world is large. Both our nations wish to expose our systems of belief and way of life to all people. Let the people decide which approach best suits them."

Nimrod said, "The people are sheep and need shepherds to tell them what to think. The Church is righteous. The Church will be their shepherd. The Way of Horus does not separate the duties of the male and the female into their proper divisions of responsibilities. It is abhorrent to the gods."

T'jaru listened with disbelief and then laughed. "Lord Nimrod. You are a loyal lap dog to your masters. You believe none of the nonsense you so mechanically spout. Come over to our side. You will sleep better at night."
~~~

Abram listened to the two men without fully understanding.

Astarte decided maybe she should stop flirting with Lord Nimrod.

Nimrod grew more agitated. "Our churches, idols, and priests will remain long after your traveling preaching show has left. Better to be a god's lap dog than an itinerant madman from the desert teaching that women are as good as men to mindless creatures that cannot understand any of it!"

Azazil said, "Lord Nimrod, the Way of Horus teaches the people how to be worthy and righteous. The world is made a better place when people treat others with dignity and respect. Surely, we can agree on that."

Nimrod growled, "Kiya was an evil whore taking from the gods that which belonged to the gods. Her memory, her words, and her followers will be eliminated from the face of the earth and natural order restored."

An always suppressed thought flashed through Abram's mind. *I wish Baalat was here to explain what's going on.*

Astarte, wishing to calm the confrontation, said, "Lord Abram. You are looking wise. What are your thoughts on these things?"

Abram thought, *Never let them see you unsure.*

He said, "Whatever will be, will be."

Azazil said, "Lord Abram, we have not visited in a long time. Join me tonight at evening meal and we can talk."

Nimrod said, "Lord Abram cannot accept your invitation. We are here on church business and have many plans to discuss tonight. We will leave you three to your business, such as it may be."

With that, Nimrod turned to go and glared at Abram to follow him.

Abram looked at Azazil, shrugged, and said, "Perhaps another time."

Azazil watched the three depart and said, "That went well, I think."

T'jaru replied, "Yes. We know their strategy. They don't know ours."

Astarte watched Nimrod depart. *Perhaps next time.*

<div align="center">~~~</div>

Abram decided to ask no questions until he found someone he could confide in. Someone like—who? *Baalat is back there someplace. I don't know where Teacher Horus is. Nimrod keeps me from Azazil and is behaving strangely. I'm not sure I trust him anymore. I have no one to talk to!*

Djoser, Hetephe, Incense/Hagar/Keterah
Horus, Serket, Azazil, Abram, Baalat
Ishmael, Maribah, Fatimah, Nebaioth, Basemath, Kedar | Anath, Astarte

He followed Nimrod in silence. *Never let them see you unsure.*

Nimrod asked Abram, "So, what do you think, Abram?"

"I think you and General T'jaru don't like each other."

"Is that all you think?"

"Yes."

"Very good. You and Haran join the missionaries for evening meal. I will be in later tonight."

After Zedek and Nimrod had walked away, Zedek said, "Lord Nimrod, with your permission, I have a plan would like to try."

"Well, let's hear it!"

Zedek explained his plan to the great approval of Nimrod.

The two men found a busy beerhouse. They entered and walked to a table where loud words could easily be overheard. The server arrived and Zedek threw a shekel on the table and proclaimed, "I'm buying beer for everybody!"

Having attracted their attention, he began, "Did y'all see that big black man struttin' around town like he owned the place? Well, did you! He's gettin' all the white women wonderin' what he's got in those pants of his. They real curious what it would be like bein' plowed by a big black man like that. It excites them. Back where I come from, he wouldn't be struttin' around. He'd be hangin' from a tree someplace without anything to excite the women with. You know what I'm sayin'? Yes sir, where I come from, men's men and we protect our women folk."

"That man is buying the beer. We should listen to what he's got to say."

"Yes sir, those darkies are that color because they disrespected the old gods—the righteous gods. The old gods were the whitest white a man could be—the darker, the farther away from righteousness you are. The gods cursed his tribe makin' em all real dark skinned and I'm here to tell you, that darkie was pitch black—and big—and your wives and daughters are wonderin' what it would be like to be ... Well, never you mind. A darkie just better not be in *my* town after sundown. We got one of those new Churches from up north. They tell the god's truth about everything. Here's another shekel—another round for my friends, here."

A cheer went up. A man said, "I did see a big black man in town. What's he doing here, I wonder."

Zedek shut up and let the crowd talk among themselves. He was pleased with himself and his improvisation.

Nimrod said to Zedek, "That was glorious, Assistant Zedek. You are going to go far in our organization! *He needs to put this performance on in every village where we have a church. Every village, really. As long as we can keep people afraid of the "Others," they will never notice the Kyrios-Olon.*

~~~

Nimrod, Abram, and Haran returned to Urfa in relative silence.

Nimrod made his report directly to the Kyrios-Olon which included Zedek's newly conceived and sure-to-be-effective strategy of "Fear-your-neighbor." With only a few words and a few beers, Zedek had left the male population of a village in deep philosophical discussions of whether it was justifiable to kill a man because he was black. Any quantifiable difference between people was open for exploitation. The church was so focused on controlling women through male domination that they had never considered the power of pitting one group against the "Other." The "Other" being anyone not in a specific group. Nimrod had the audacity to suggest the Kyrios-Olon were short-sighted. They used the Church of Urfa as their institution of control. They should begin nurturing kings and merchants. Everyone with great power was now a candidate to receive the unconditional love and infinite support of Kyrios-Olon. All that was required was blind, unquestioning obedience.

The Kyrios-Olon were delighted with these new and powerful concepts. There was a special celebration honoring Nimrod that involved candles and Horpriestesses.

~~~

When Abram returned to his office, Asherah came to him unannounced and told him to prepare himself for an enraged wife when he got home. The healers had told Sarai it was her fault she was not pregnant. Her insides were faulty. Sarai had screamed that it *wasn't* her fault—that it was Abram's fault—that a more powerful man would get her pregnant—that she would never be the mother of a nation as long as she relied on Abram to impregnate her.

Abram resigned himself to a constantly fussing wife.

Along with a fussing wife, Abram began agonizing over the implications of what he had learned on his trip south. Not implications, really. It was obvious that he was on the wrong side. The churches he was establishing were plainly promoting the worship of gods but worse, the subjugation of women to the whims of men. These were things his beloved Horus was teaching against. Now Abram had become his Mentor's enemy. He looked around and could see only the teachings of the Church of Urfa at work—his father and mother—all the men and the subservient women—all the girls whose only goal in life was to catch a husband and get pregnant. But it felt so natural. The men were happy. The women were happy. Why was this wrong? Maybe the church was right. Maybe Horus was wrong. That could be. It had to be. Else Abram was living a lie.

Nimrod called Abram in for serious discussions. El Set was still vigorous in the delivery of his quarter moon teachings, but Abram could help by practice-teaching the women's group. When El Set retired, Abram might be considered for his prestigious position. Abram continued to be pulled into the church's inner circle teaching things that Abram did not want to think about.

And in a conspiring tone, Nimrod said, "Asherah refused to remove the child Set placed inside her and Set supported her decision. She is no longer of use to the church, but she is too powerful to be cast out. Having her stoned for adultery wouldn't work out well. We ... I mean, I'm not sure how to proceed with this delicate situation. Do you have a suggestion?"

A memory flashed through Abram's mind. What Asherah had once said. *"No one in the church wanted me pregnant but me. It's my way out of servitude to the church. I am too far up in their church to ever get away from Urfa but at least I can now just look pretty and not have to do anything. This is the best I can do."*

Abram answered, "Send her to travel to our churches in the south as a representative. Show them a happily married, loving mother. That's your message, isn't it? She can be the thread that unites the churches as a single vision." Abram wasn't sure why he wanted to help Asherah, but he did.

"Set won't like losing his wife."

"Send different priestesses to his bed. He won't notice the difference and if he does, he won't care."

"That's an interesting suggestion, Abram. I have been looking for new ways to influence the sheep. Your suggestion might just be a way."

"Happy to be of service." Neither man recognized any hint of sarcasm in Abram's voice.

~~~

Several days later, a priestess rushed into Abram's office and said, "Asherah calls for you, come quickly!"

Abram rushed to Asherah's room where she sat squatting, panting, and sweating. She was surrounded by midwives giving her words of encouragement. A midwife told him, "We have given her all our herbs and ointments and potions, still the babe will not come. She called for you."

He went and stood before Asherah. She glared at him and hissed, "Call upon your damnable Horus to bless me and deliver this child to me. DO IT!!!"

Abram's training came to him. *Never panic. Never look unsure. Do something even if you don't know what you are doing. Do the best you can.*

He went to her and took her hands in his hands. He pulled her to an almost upright standing position, her eyes wide. The midwives were panicking. "A man must not do the job of a midwife. They know nothing of these things."

Asherah duck-walked with him to the tall replica of the obelisk of Osiris which Set had insisted be installed in the center of their room. She wrapped both arms around it; half-standing, panting, pushing, and grunting. Abram had no idea what he was doing or why he was doing it, but he took her head in both his hands, forced her to look him in the face, and intoned, "Isis, hear me, hear my words. You delivered your son Horus to the world from the seed of a man once dead. Deliver, too, this babe from this worthy woman, Asherah, from the seed of the man who killed your husband so that your blessings of forgiveness shall flow over the land even as Osiris's blessings of love flow across the land from on high. In the name of the mighty Titans of old, I beseech your mercy. In the name of your son, Horus, I beseech you to allow your faithful servant Asherah to give new life to your loving people."

Asherah glared at him unblinking. The midwives rushed to catch the babe as it came forth.

Abram stared out over the room of midwives. He said, "Tell no one of me or my words. I command it." He turned and hurriedly left the room.

Abram did not go to his father's house that night. Or to his own apartment. He went instead to the altar in the church and leaned against it. *It was a long time coming—clarity. I was a child. I knew nothing. Now—clarity. I*
~~~

don't know what to do or what matter it will make. But I now see the things that I do with clarity. Whether right or wrong, I cannot tell. But I now see what I do clearly.

Exhausted, he lay down on the floor and slept.

The next morning the church began brimming with life. Cleaners stepped over and around him until someone woke him.

It was Asherah, holding a baby. "Shemesh wanted to see her Uncle Abram. She is excited to be here. Come to my suite as I nurse her. I want you to witness the mercy of Isis."

He went with her. She closed the door, lowered her blouse, and nursed her baby girl.

She said, "The midwives are beside themselves with excitement. They have discovered a new position from which to give birth—standing clutching a birthing pole. They believe the pull of the earth helps the woman. I told everyone to never mention that you were even there. Your words would not be pleasing to the church. It will be our secret."

"... and a dozen midwives, and what the walls heard, and what the ceiling saw."

"I don't think they will kill you for your words."

"Of course not. They know they teach dung. If I don't tell the sheep, they don't care what I do or say. Just don't tell the sheep."

"You have become cynical, Abram. I'm sorry that had to happen. No, you will not be killed. You are becoming one of us. But you were kind to me. Because of your suggestion, I have been ordered to travel to Mesopotamia and spread the gospel of our church and I will be able to share my experience of giving birth with the women. I am forever in your debt."

Abram laughed. "Then I shall tell my father to create a new line of idols. He should call them Asherah poles and make them large enough and sturdy enough for a woman to cling to when giving birth. He will make quite a profit."

She sighed. "You will be a good one of us, Abram. Welcome, I suppose."

"Perhaps they will allow me to go with you. Maybe I could help the sheep without angering my betters."

"Who are your betters?"

Phoenicia, Jaffa, Rocky, Burlyman, Polydore | Astarte, T'jaru
Terah, Amathlai, Haran, Terahson, Nahor, Sarai, Isaac, Jacob
Kyrios-Olon, Teumessian, Nimrod, Nimbal, Nimlad, Nimisis, Asherah, Set.

"Nimrod. You. Others of whom I do not know. Nimrod refers to consultations. With whom is he conferring? I have been cursed with the knowledge of how to think, Asherah."

"It's best not to think, Abram. Sheep are so much happier not thinking."

"I will ask Nimrod to assign me to your project."

~~~

Nimrod granted the meeting with Abram. Abram sat to face Nimrod in Nimrod's office.

Nimrod said, "I know what you're going to ask, Abram, and the answer is no. You have the church expansion project going very nicely which we can now grow without your help. We have a much larger project for you. We want you to establish our largest church in the biggest city we have ever attempted. Byblos is growing rapidly. It is establishing an international influence that the church wishes to cultivate. You will report to Nimbal in Byblos at the Baal Inn before highsun two days after the next quarter moon or '1000, Poseidonmonth, Day 30, Year 165' as they say in Byblos. If you can establish our church for us, your future with us is unlimited. What about it? Any questions?"

"We?"

"I'm sorry. What?"

"We. You said 'we.' Who is 'we?'"

Nimrod laughed. "Bring us Byblos and you will find out."

<div align="center">

ABRAM AND BAALAT

Year 165, Season 5, Poseidonmonth

</div>

Abram would have preferred traveling with Asherah into Mesopotamia, but that request had been refused and this assignment would get him away from his nagging wife. He accepted the assignment.

~~~

He arrived in Byblos a day early and familiarized himself with the Egyptian Calendar posted throughout the city, complete with sand clocks to indicate the time of day, a city bell to ring the hour, and a map of the city indicating major points of interest including the Baal Inn.

The friendly receptionist at the inn already had Abram's room prepared. She said, "It's one of our nicest rooms. It has a view of the sea you can

Djoser, Hetephe, Incense/Hagar/Keterah
Horus, Serket, Azazil, Abram, Baalat
Ishmael, Maribah, Fatimah, Nebaioth, Basemath, Kedar | Anath, Astarte

127

enjoy after your long journey. We have complimentary wine in the common area. Your friend, Lord Nimbal, is a frequent guest there. Enjoy your stay with us, Lord Abram."

Abram went to his room, cleaned himself, and changed into his fine clothes. He went to the common area hoping to find Nimbal.

He found, instead, Baalat.

She sat by a window looking out over the harbor. She wore a white tunic trimmed in red and held a glass of red wine close to her red lips.

Abram stared at her; flooded with memories. *And so ...*

He walked to her table and silently stood there.

She glanced up at him, signaled him to sit, and then signaled her server to bring her guest wine. "Hello, Abram. It's been a long time."

"Yes, Baalat. It's been a long time."

They chatted. He told of his marriage and work for the Church of Urfa. She told of her career as a Byblos businesswoman.

Eventually, she said, "Lord Nimbal tells me you are here to help him establish one of those churches of yours. He has been relentlessly trying to buy me off and obtain leverage over me. First by seduction, then by offers of unlimited power, then by outright bribery. The poor man is in over his head. I suppose he called you in to finish what he couldn't do."

"I know nothing of Lord Nimbal or his goals. My project is to establish a church like I have already done in the south of Urfa. Now we wish to expand to the west. I did not come to ask for your help. I didn't know you were here. But from the sounds of it, I best not make you my enemy because if Baalat does not want my church in Byblos, then I will not get my church in Byblos."

"I do not delve into the matters of gods. We have every god ever conceived in Byblos. Our teacher will never have his desire to rid people of their belief in gods. They need gods like they need food. If your church teaches only religion, then I do not care. If your church begins teaching how to run a government, then I will care. That, plus encouraging prejudices between the sexes would be a problem."

His laugh was bitter. "You were always so superior to me, you know. So mature, so wise."

Baalat said, "You were always so quick to understand things. Eager to help me understand. You were my protector. You let no man harm me. I felt safe with you. Loved."

"I was too young, Baalat. You know that."

"You were a man. You needed only a woman to complete you. I was that woman. I remember the feel of my tunic sliding down my body. The feel of the warm air surrounding me as I exposed myself to you; inviting you to share the love I felt for you; the only love I had ever felt for a man. I had been slave to a hundred men but I never felt bad about myself. I never felt dirty. Until you labeled me. Until you told me what I was. And by Abram telling me what I was, then so I was—forever. And at that moment, all love inside me died—rotted—fell forever to the earth. Poor Nimbal still doesn't understand that I will never desire a man to touch me. He thinks it is him and all the while it is Abram."

"I was too young, Baalat. Forgive me. I never wished you harm."

"It no longer matters, Abram. I am what I am. You are what you are. It simply makes no difference."

"And what am I, Baalat?"

She looked at him. "You are the same as I, Abram. A whore."

He sat in silence.

She finished her wine, rose, and said, "This was nice. Closure, after a fashion. Goodbye, Abram."

She left him there. Fingering a glass of her red wine. Looking out over her harbor.

THE CHURCH OF URFA

Hour 1000, Poseidonmonth, Day 30, Year 165

Nimbal entered the Baal Inn common room, saw Abram, walked over, and said, "You must be Abram-the-Wonderful. I'm Nimbal. Leadership told me that you are our best hope for taking over the local powers that be. Aphrodite knows that I tried and failed. My prospects with the church continue to fall. My best hope for a longer life is to help you succeed with your church strategy. Baalat has ears all over this inn. Let's go to the central park to talk."

They strolled to the city square. Nimbal pointed out places of interest as they walked. "Baalat owns most of the city. She lets the chief maintain control, but she says what will and won't be done; exactly the power the church wants but that Baalat has, and she is not about to share it. We thought our best strategy was seduction. That's where I came in. The priestesses trained me in the art, and I thought I was good at it. I plowed through Horus's wife like she was warm butter. When I followed her to Memphis, her husband had left her stranded there. I thought there was no way to fail with my follow-up seductions. Our plan was that she would fall in love with me, and I could publicly humiliate Horus so that he would lose whatever self-respect he had left. He would be eliminated as a threat to the church. I couldn't get her the second time, but I claimed partial success because I got her the first time. I was reassigned to seduce and take control of Baalat. The best I can tell, she isn't warm-blooded. She's focused on nothing but business. You and I must figure out how to either control her or get rid of her or neutralize her."

They arrived at the park and found a secluded area in which to plan. Neither man noticed the street sweeper sweeping closely behind them nor the groundsman picking up litter near the bench where they were discussing the various approaches to their problem.

Over the next quartermoon, the problem solved itself. Religious leaders approached Abram knowing that he was once a student of Horus's and now a leader in the church of Urfa. They offered, "We wish for Abram to establish a large and powerful church in Byblos. And how wonderful it would be if Lord Nimbal could lead the church after Abram returns to Urfa. Oh, joy. Everyone will be so happy."

These things being done, Abram victoriously returned to Urfa with his report of success.

In her office above the first floor of the squalor of Warehouse Six, Baalat, a priest, and several sanitation workers discussed Nimbal and his church.

She said, "That should keep them occupied for a while!" She thanked them for their service to Byblos and asked what type of duties they would like as a reward. She dismissed them and retired to her private quarters on the third floor. A room fit for a pharaoh with a panoramic view of the Harbor of the greatest port in the world—that Baalat had built.

BAALAT AND HORUS

The Byblos Church of Urfa began to take shape. The hierarchy for the church was made and recruitment for missionaries had begun.

Phoenicia, Jaffa, Rocky, Burlyman, Polydore | Astarte, T'jaru
Terah, Amathlai, Haran, Terahson, Nahor, Sarai, Isaac, Jacob
Kyrios-Olon, Teumessian, Nimrod, Nimbal, Nimlad, Nimisis, Asherah, Set.

It was then Living-God Priest-Shaman Horus arrived in Byblos seeking his once-wife. He went first to Baalat. Horus was one of the few people allowed access to the third floor of Warehouse Six. He found her there.

Baalat replied, "No, Serket never comes to Byblos." She gave him a detailed report on Urfa; the growth of Harran, the new Byblos Church of Urfa, and the work of Abram within the church. "Abram is ready, Teacher. He will either melt like wax or become strong like iron. You'll know when you throw him to the fire."

"You do more to hold strong the word of Queen Kiya than I."

"Teacher is simply a tired old man seeking compliments from a former student. Keep standing, teacher. You may be tired and worn out, but you must continue your fight and mustn't stop until you find someone to replace you. Abram may be the one, but he must be thrown into the fire. If he is forged into strong metal, then you can roll up in a corner and find the Land of the Dead first-hand."

"You have become the Lady of Byblos and hold true to the enlightened path, Baalat. You are the one thing I have done right in my life."

"Then it is time to do another. Go to Urfa. Throw him into the fire."

~~~

Horus remained in Byblos. He did not know how to throw Abram into a fire and was unsure where he should go or what he should do. The gods decided for him.

A missionary from Urfa brought an urgent private message to Nimbal. "He Whose Name May Not Be Spoken lies dying. You are to return to Urfa immediately!"

A cleaning woman overheard the private message.

Nimbal set off immediately for Urfa.

Horus, who knew where and why Nimbal was going, because a cleaning woman had told Baalat who then told Horus, followed closely behind.

Djoser, Hetephe, Incense/Hagar/Keterah
Horus, Serket, Azazil, Abram, Baalat
Ishmael, Maribah, Fatimah, Nebaioth, Basemath, Kedar | Anath, Astarte
~~~

~~~~~~~~~~~~~

10. Land of the Dead.

Year 165, Season 10, Aphroditemonth

Horus caught Nimbal on the road to Urfa. He asked, "May I join you, Nimbal? I wish to pay my respects to my uncle before he dies. Will you make this happen for me?"

"Yes. I won't promise that Nimrod or Dyoares won't have you killed afterward; but yes. I suppose I owe you that much."

"You owe me nothing."

Nimbal took the opportunity to attempt to inflict injury on Horus. *My assignment was to weaken Horus. I couldn't get to her a second time but maybe I can still get to him. That would help my prospects with the Church.*

"I disagree, Friend Horus. I had a delightful time plowing your wife. She really enjoyed it! Did she describe the perverted things she did for my enjoyment?" And on and on and on.

Horus listened in silence. *Serket, I left you alone so many times. It was I who betrayed YOU.*

They arrived in Urfa and were met at the Church entrance by Guards who escorted Nimbal into the church and Horus into the Visitors Center; a walled garden with entrance and exit through the same gate—protected by a guard.

Horus sat and waited.

Abram came to him. "I was with Nimrod when Nimlad reported in. Nimrod wasn't happy to hear that you were also here."

The two men talked on—about life and living—about death and dying—about gods.

~~~

In their sleeping room, Asherah held El Set's hand as she extolled the great life he had lived. Anubis stood behind her.

Set wheezed, "Yes. I have done many great things, but I never defeated my nephew in a contesting. That's so sad, don't you think?"

Abram entered the room.

Set said, "Ahh, there you are my boy."

He paused to catch his breath. "My beloved wife Asherah wishes for *you* to replace me as High-Priest. I'm sure you will accept this honor and responsibility."

Set paused, again. "Some tell me it is the most powerful position on earth." Pause. "Even greater than being Pharaoh." Pause "Perhaps, it is. I don't know." Pause. "You will accept it, won't you?"

Abram knelt beside the ancient man. "I will consider it Great El Set. But only because it would please you. For no other reason."

"Good boy. Good boy. Is Nephthys with you? She will want to know."

"I will tell her, but perhaps you can tell her yourself when you see her."

"Yes. That will be better. I will rest now."

Set closed his eyes and fell asleep as Abram whispered into his ear, "Horus is here. He will come if you call him."

Set tossed in his sleep. He may or may not have heard. He may or may not have understood. He may or may not have cared.

Horus was escorted to El Set's visiting room outside his sleeping quarters. He met a charming Dyoares and an angry Nimrod.

Horus said, "Set is my uncle. That is the only reason I am here. I have not come to challenge you or influence Abram. I come to see Uncle Set."

Nimrod hissed, "Abram does tremendous work for us. One word to him against us and a dozen arrows will pierce your body in the blink of an eye. Am I understood?"

"Yes."

"Abram came to you in the garden. What did you say to him?"

"That he was a disgrace to the Word of Kiya. That he had betrayed everything he had been taught. That you are evil, that the church must be destroyed, that kind of things."

"You are a brazen bastard."

"My father was the bastard. My mother was married to my father and, unlike yours, knew who impregnated her."

Dyoares laughed and said, "I like you, Horus. You may turn out to be one of us, after all."

Djoser, Hetephe, Incense/Hagar/Keterah
Horus, Serket, Azazil, Abram, Baalat
Ishmael, Maribah, Fatimah, Nebaioth, Basemath, Kedar | Anath, Astarte

"Then I may see my uncle?"

Dyoares said, "If he calls for you, I will allow it."

Nimrod was not pleased.

THE DEATH OF SET

Set had become incoherent. The room had been cleared of everyone except attending priests. The senior priest comforted Set as best he could.

Set's eyes suddenly opened. He stared at the ceiling and tried to raise himself. Only an incoherent gurgle escaped his throat. He fell back dead.

The Priest meticulously examined the body to make certain. But Set was most certainly dead. The priest called for the embalmers.

The embalmers soon came but then Set raised his hand and wheezed, "Bring Horus to me."

The excited confused Priest called for Horus and waited in the uncertainty of "what's happening?"

Soon enough, Horus came. He asked, "Are you sure he was dead?"

"Yes, Lord. El Set was undoubtedly dead. Then he returned to life and called for you."

Horus moved to look into the face of his once-powerful adversary. *So, Uncle Set. You have been there and returned. Have you talked with them? Why didn't you stay? It can't be easy to return. What drove you back to this place?*

Horus put his hand on Set's chest, knelt, and whispered, "I am here, Uncle. Did the light come to you?"

Soon, the body jerked a little jerk. The body murmured, "… yes … the light was glorious … it was Nephthys come to welcome me … but it wasn't Nephthys … it was Dexithea … or maybe a Telchine dancing naked … or maybe all of them … but it was *really* your father … I cut off his hands and feet you know … but Isis put him back together … the light was all of them … and Philyra … they were welcoming me … but then Osiris said, 'stay if you wish, Brother … but you are strong … if you choose, you can return to the land of the living and defeat Horus in a contesting … I will tell you how to defeat him …'"

What was meant to be a chuckle tried to escape from his throat but he choked on it, spasmed, and began coughing deep gasps. He tried to raise himself but did not have the strength. Two priests rushed to raise him to a reclining position. A third brought water to his lips.

Set eventually swallowed the water, leaned back, and said, "So, my little Nephew … I return to at last defeat you … All our other contests have been meaningless … even over the Whore of Canaan."

He paused to collect his strength. "You have spent your life seeking the nature of death and now I know it and you don't!" He rested. "Do you concede defeat?"

"If your words are true, Uncle, I shall concede defeat."

Set laughed a raspy laugh. "It is the words of The One, Horus. The One told me everything … EVERYTHING! I return to at last defeat you! I know the nature of death and you don't!"

"Is Father with Mother?"

"They are ALL there, you fool. EVERYONE!"

Excited, Set began breathing rapidly but then calmed himself. "My life has been wonderful, Horus. Even in my agony. I am rich with the experience The One craves. I have climbed to the greatest heights, fallen to the deepest depths, and risen again to become a god … Neither you nor your father can claim to have experienced all that I have experienced … They wait with excitement that I will soon join them. They wait for me to become them."

Set closed his eyes with exhaustion and gasped deep breaths until he lay in complete stillness.

Horus whispered into his ear, "Take your time, Uncle. You won't leave until you defeat me. When you are ready, I am here."

Set stirred and whispered, "I swear The One told me the nature of death. I return to tell you and at last defeat you."

Horus said, "Tell me true. I will tell the world that you have defeated me."

Set chuckled and then recited the words of The One:

"We are the Tree of Life. The One. The All. Experiencing all things.

"Once our bodies were constrained by the passage of time. We experienced the 'Now,' but neither 'Past' nor 'Future.'

"Death is the body being shed. After death, time no longer exists. You experience everything you have ever experienced and know everything you have ever known. Without beginning or end. You will simply 'Be.'

"And know this …

"You are connected to every person and everything you have ever known. The connections are gateways. You will pass through these gates and experience all to which you are connected …

"And all things are eventually connected to all other things. You will enter all gates. Experience all things. You will become The One. The All.

"The Tree of Life is everything that has ever existed—seen and unseen— seeable and unseeable—known and unknown. The sun and all within its reach are only one branch, people but leaves on a limb, all so closely connected as to be as one.

"What you do to another person, you also do to yourself. After you shed your body, everything you did to others, you too will experience as they experienced it. You will experience all these things and all other things …

"Without end.

"This is the nature of the Land of the Dead …

"We are life unending—The Tree of Life. The One. The All.

"Join us as you will."

Set closed his eyes and rested. Finally, he looked at Horus and said, "My words are true. Admit that I have defeated you!"

"You have discovered the nature of death, Uncle. You are the better man. You have defeated me."

"Yes, I have. Yes, I have!" With growing excitement, Set's gaze slowly shifted to a corner of the ceiling. His eyes grew wide as he tried to sit upright. "The light! It is beautiful beyond words!"

The light Set seemed to see, seemed to hold out its arms and say to him, *"You know who I am and why I have come."*

With wide eyes, Set jerked to an upright position, screamed, "Philyra!" and fell back dead.

Horus called for the priests and told them, "He was a good man. A better man than I. Treat him with the respect the greatest of our kind deserve."

Horus turned, walked to the door where Abram was standing, and said, "Set returned from the Land of the Dead. He finally defeated me by giving me the answers to what I have spent my life searching for—the nature of death—the meaning of life—why we are. At last, I am complete."

Abram said, "The people will be ecstatic as you teach them these things."

Horus considered the people. *Most believe the Land of the Dead to be where their enemies and those that have wronged them live in eternal anguish and torment. The more enlightened see it as a land of eternal bliss for themselves, their friends, and like-minded people. But it appears to be neither Hades' Hell nor Ra's Heaven; it is both at the same time. Will people be confused when they learn everyone experiences the same things there?*

He said, "Tell the people, Abram? Perhaps not. People have eaten from the Tree of Knowledge and shown little benefit for the doing. If people knew of The Tree of Life, they would know they will live forever. Then they would begin to think and act like gods. I shall teach people *how* they should live; to love one another, to treat everyone the way they would want to be treated, to help those less fortunate. I will teach them the 'how;' they need not know the 'why.'"

"You have the power to spread this knowledge throughout the world. There is only *one* God and God is us. All people will rejoice with the knowing! You *must* tell them!"

"Don't you understand? With the knowing, they would become like the Kyrios-Olon—gods! Monsters that think only of themselves and neither feel the pain of others nor care. What is theirs, is theirs; what is yours, is theirs; and you are expected to adore them as they abuse you. My father was the only person called a god who cared for humanity, and he rejected godhood with his every breath."

"So, Teacher, what will you do?"

Horus was lost in the indecision of infinite possibilities of right and wrong; of good and bad; of the wrongness of any decision. *The worthy heed my teachings without knowing of the Tree of Life. Let the unworthy live as is their nature. All will someday be joined as The One. They can learn the "why" of it then.*

Finally, Horus said, "I shall hide the Tree of Life from the people. I will not allow them to become gods."

"You think the sheep are not worthy to be their own masters."

"It is no longer what *I* think, Abram. It is what *you* think. I will not teach them. But if you decide to become a teacher to sheep, I shall give you land in Canaan—near Rusalem. Go. Take your family. Your people. Teach the sheep. But know this, it is far more difficult than you think. Decide! I will be at Tallstone."

They walked from the sleeping room into the anteroom and were met by Nimrod, Dyoares, and Anubis.

Nimrod asked, "Well, is he dead or not?

Horus said, "Dead to the still living."

Nimlad said, "Then it is time for you to leave us, Shaman Horus. Unless you are ready to pledge your allegiance to us!"

Tiredly, Horus answered, "I am not yet ready, Lord Nimrod. My allegiance remains at Tallstone."

Nimrod said, "Then I will have the guards escort you out of Urfa."

Dyoares thought, *"Lord" Nimrod? Did the death of El get to you, Horus? Are you ready to accept your final destiny and become one of us?*

Dyoares, Nimrod, Anubis, and Abram watched Horus escorted away.

Nimrod asked Abram, "What did he say to you?"

"That I am a disgrace to the Word of Kiya. That I have betrayed everything I have been taught. That you are evil. That our kind devours those we protect. Those kinds of things."

Hopefully, Nimrod asked, "You didn't believe him, of course."

"Not believe him. You amuse me, Nimrod. Every word is true. The question you should be asking is, what will I do about it."

"And?"

"I appear to be much like you, Nimrod. A devourer of sheep."

"Good boy, Lord Abram. Good boy!"

Anubis watched as the others walked away leaving him alone. *You accomplished all things, my father. Yet only I grieve for you. You called your nephew to be with you to die; not your son. Your son who has followed you through deserts— through life—asking nothing of you. But your love.*

He choked back a sob. *Well, the good son will escort you to complete your journey. I will take you across the waters to your home. To Tartarus.*

~~~~~~~~~~~~~

11. Birth of the Patriarch

Year 165, Season 12, Isismonth

Abram stood at the altar listening to a hidden voice extol his accolades.

The voice said, "Lord Abram established more than twenty churches in Mesopotamia. They all thrive. Our control spreads."

Abram thought, *My teacher told me your name. What you are.*

"Lord Abram has shown his father how to increase his trade in idols a hundred-fold!"

Baalat told me my name. What I am!

"Lord Abram has conceived of entirely new classes of idols!"

Whores.

"Because of Abram, Asherah travels the land of Mesopotamia, increasing our power.

Devourer of sheep. Enemy of humanity.

"Because of Lord Abram, the Harran Outpost has become a thriving city. Our entry into Mesopotamia!"

Whores!

"Lord Abram did what Nimbal could not do. We are on our way to establishing our power in Byblos!"

I am a Whore! A destroyer of humanity.

Lord Abram was chosen by El Set to become El Abram—Living God— High-Priest of the Church of Urfa.

A devourer of sheep.

"Abram, you have only to ask, and you will be shown the True Power of the church. Ask and it will be given!"

And become one of you!

"Do you wish our power in its fullest revealed?"

I have the ability to think. Wisdom. Clarity. A label for what I am. Do I really want anything more? What do I want?

Djoser, Hetephe, Incense/Hagar/Keterah
Horus, Serket, Azazil, Abram, Baalat
Ishmael, Maribah, Fatimah, Nebaioth, Basemath, Kedar | Anath, Astarte
~~~~~~~~~~~~~

Abram answered, "No. Before this knowledge is revealed, I must make peace with my family. With my wife. With my father. With my brothers. With myself. Having done these things, then I will be prepared to decide this thing."

"Then you are given a quartermoon away from all responsibility. Return then in full peace and stand again before us. Go in wisdom, Lord Abram. You stand upon the verge of greatness."

"Thank you. I shall do what shall be done."

He was dismissed to his family.

TALLSTONE

Abram set off well before sunrise, but he journeyed northward toward the abandoned entrance to the city rather than southward toward his father's house in Harran. He walked past the Pastures, on into the abandoned courtyard of the old city. He stood reminiscing of his adventures here; of the time he marched into the square and invited those strange exotic people to dine at his father's house; of the years in between; the infinite, infinite years.

He walked on. Toward Tallstone.

It was well after highsun when he entered the desolation and stood before the ruins surrounding the hill where the tall stone had once stood. Now it lay broken into rocks at the base of the hill. A fog covered this world; a mist obscuring the "now;" making the "what was" more visible.

Abram looked to his left. Horus sat where Abram knew he would be sitting; at a flat table of stone, silently looking out over the ruins of long ago. Horus did not acknowledge Abram as Abram walked to sit across from him.

Abram quietly said, "Tell me the stories, again."

Horus told the stories again:
"Here is where civilization began."
"Destroyed by the anger of the ancient gods. The ones to whose successors you now bow."
"The gods destroyed the Titans—bringers of hope and peace and goodwill to all people."
"The gods killed Kiya, but not her teachings. Her teachings lived on through my father. Through me. And here they may well die."

The fog thickened. The past came closer.

Horus said, "Behind you is the burned-out shell which held the original teachings of the righteous; the building from which my father dragged the chest containing the teachings; the golden chest which my father and Set and Djoser recovered and took to the land of Egypt where they built it a Mastaba upon which the Obelisk of Osiris sits. Djoser moved the chest from its Mastaba to rest beneath First Mother on the plateau near the sea. What the chest waits for, I do not know. But it is not for me."

Horus looked at Abram, and continued, "I have an empty land of beautiful rolling hills south of Rusalem in Canaan that I named Hebron. If the path you travel takes you there, I give this land to you and your children in the hope that you will stay true to the path of righteousness; that you will teach your children how to think and not be sheep to those who would control them with meaningless loud words; that your sons will respect your daughters and not subjugate them to their own needs and inadequacies; that your children will embrace and love all people no matter their tribe."

Horus rose, said, "You, like I, can only do what you can do," and walked into the mist.

Abram continued to sit there. It was too late in the day to set off for Harran. He spent the night at Tallstone, sometimes sleeping; sometimes listening to older voices; sometimes watching shifting fog and shadows as they, at times, appeared to become living people.

DESTROYER OF IDOLS

He rose at sunrise.

The mist and fog had already burned away. He journeyed rapidly throughout the day and arrived at his father's magnificent new home in Harran after the sun had set. His brothers and their wives came to visit.

Abram was greeted with enthusiasm. His mother gushing her love. His father giving infinite praise. His wife constantly fussing. Cloying patronage from his brothers.

He listened to them in silence without emotion.

Wisdom. Clarity. The ability to think. What more could I want?

Their voices were a deafening noise within his ears.

I'm going to live forever. With them. As them. What more do I want?

Djoser, Hetephe, Incense/Hagar/Keterah
Horus, Serket, Azazil, Abram, Baalat
Ishmael, Maribah, Fatimah, Nebaioth, Basemath, Kedar | Anath, Astarte

Haran began describing the new molds they had just finished specifically for God Sin. "We are going to make a fortune!"

It's simple enough. To do what's right. To love them. How hard is that?

Finally, Abram rose and said to Haran, "Show me your idols."

They walked to the warehouse; Terah followed. Haran showed Abram hundreds of idols. Thousands.

Abram thought, *Each one is a lie—for the sheep. So the sheep will not have to think for themselves. So that imaginary gods can tell the sheep what to do. So the sheep will be united with their flock. And when commanded by the just and merciful gods, to go forth and kill the flocks that are not like themselves. With pious self-righteousness. And if the gods so desire, to hate the other sheep. The white sheep hating the black sheep— hating the sheep that lies with the goat—the sheep that's different. All in the name of the gods. If this is to be, it will not be of my doing.*

Abram walked to the sculpted statue of God Sin; raised it above his head and threw it to the ground; then to the mold of God Sin, raised it and smashed it to the ground; then to the cast idols.

He became a force of nature. Smashing idols.

Terah and Haran looked on frozen in disbelief and fear.

Finished, Abram turned to his father and brother and whispered, "There is no god but God!"

Frantic observers were already on their way back to tell Nimrod to bring forth the fire of judgment.

Terah was wild-eyed with disbelief. He screamed, "What have you done? Why did you do this? Our family will be judged unworthy! Why?"

Haran asked, "Brother, you have destroyed our idols. The Church will be furious. Why did you do this?"

Abram let the scene play out. He then told his father and brother of the way of Horus, to place their trust in the One-True-God, and to fear nothing—for in Abram's God was life everlasting.

He led them back to Terah's house where Abram changed into heavy woolen garments and donned a heavy cape.

He told all gathered, "It is only me they will judge but the church is going to be extremely angry."

His father was in tears, wailing that his family would be judged, that he would lose everything he had ever worked for.

Abram told him, "It is me they will judge but the House of Terah will be looked down upon and the making and selling of idols given to someone else. My teacher said he would give us land south of Rusalem in Canaan. It will be best for you to take our family there. Don't look back. The sooner you can leave, the better."

Terah said, "I must face the judgment of the church. My son must face it. If the mercy of the gods burns my son, then I must witness it."

"There are no gods, Father; only the One True God. What shall come for me is the mercy of merciless tyrants. Rather than despair, let us rejoice that we have this time together."

THE FURNACE

Nimrod was being berated by Dyoares for his complete failure with the Abram project. "Failure cannot be tolerated. You should burn in the fire with Abram."

Nimrod responded, "When you are finished, I'll take care of this matter!"

Dyoares stormed from the room to discuss this with the other Dyos.

Nimrod told Zedek to call for the keeper of the furnace.

Zedek called for Eliezer and told him, "Prepare the Furnace of Judgment. Have the guards bring Abram in for judgment—and my trusted production chief, Haran, too. Gather those who will attest to the righteous judgment after they are both thrown into the furnace. Schedule judgment at the break of the sun tomorrow. Command the people of Urfa to witness the righteous wrath of the gods to those who betray them. Let's at least get a teaching moment out of this debacle."

~~~

They came in the night and found the family of Terah nervously laughing and telling stories. The guards took Abram. To Abram's horror, they took Haran, too. Terah followed them back to Urfa and the Furnace of Judgment.

Arriving, their wait would not be long. The sun's glow was lighting the horizon. The coals were burning. Citizens were gathering. Eliezer stood before the jurors—six priests of the church and six random generous donors to the church.
~~~

The sun breached the horizon. Eliezer stepped forth, held out an arm, and pointed toward Abram and Haran. These two men are accused of insulting the gods. Are they guilty?"

The twelve men responded in unison, "Yes. They are guilty!"

Eliezer intoned, "The children of the gods find them guilty. Let the gods execute their just and righteous punishment! Bring forth the unrighteous Haran to be punished!"

Abram glanced at Haran, trying to reinforce the instructions Abram had given him. "You can survive this, Brother. Don't panic. Stay calm. Focus on the exit. Once you start for it, don't slow down. Keep moving at all costs. And most of all, don't panic. You can survive this thing."

Abram called out to the jurors, "Haran is a pious, righteous, innocent man! He did not disobey the gods. You condemn yourselves when you send an innocent man to be punished. Release this innocent man. It is I who have cursed the gods. Let your gods judge me. Let my brother go!"

Eliezer commanded, "Silence! Bring forth Haran to receive his punishment!"

Abram glanced at his father who was trembling in fear of the wrath of non-existent gods.

Abram remained calm and composed even as Haran grew more agitated.

Guards dragged Haran to the entrance of the furnace. Eliezer instructed, "Walk through the fire. If the gods do not condemn you, then you will not be consumed by the fire. The wrath of the merciful gods is upon you!"

With that, Haran was shoved through the entrance gate into the burning coals. Haran panicked. Haran was consumed by the fire as his father and the righteous men of Urfa watched.

As the body was consumed, Abram was brought to the entrance. The words were repeated. On the words "upon you" Abram did not wait for the guards to shove him into the furnace. He fixed his sights on the exit, jumped full force into the flames, dropped, rolled, stood, tumbled, rolled again, stood, and with quickly moving feet, found the exit.

He ignored his burns as best he could, composed himself, strolled away from the furnace, stood to face the jurors, and said, "Your false gods have judged me. Now, beware else the One True God judge *you*!"

Phoenicia, Jaffa, Rocky, Burlyman, Polydore | Astarte, T'jaru
Terah, Amathlai, Haran, Terahson, Nahor, Sarai, Isaac, Jacob
Kyrios-Olon, Teumessian, Nimrod, Nimbal, Nimlad, Nimisis, Asherah, Set.

He walked to his father, took his hand, and said, "Haran died a righteous man and has found peace in ever-lasting life. Rejoice."

He walked to face Eliezer, and said, "The Church of Urfa has wrongly accused my Father's son of wrongdoing as judged by your test. He is due compensation, which begins with his release from this city and its church. My father is free to take all that he possesses to a new land. Acknowledge this now. Here! In front of the people."

Eliezer desperately tried to stall and wait further instructions. "T-the gods are not ..."

Abram thundered, "You have witnessed the judgment of your gods! Do not tempt me to show you the judgment of the One True God! Release my father or be judged by the One True God!"

Eliezer capitulated, "Yes. That is just compensation. It shall be. I so swear in front of your God and the people."

To the smell of his brother's burning flesh, Abram whispered, "Join us. Your masters are going to take out their anger wherever they can."

Abram returned to his father, and said, "Now, take us to the land we were promised."

<p style="text-align:center">~~~</p>

Terah left his heart in Urfa; where he had owned the greatest collection of idols the world had ever known, where he had married, where his children had been born, where he was a man of consequence, where his son had been burned alive.

But so it was that Terah must lead his family out of the land of Urfa and into the land of Canaan. Taking with him, everything he possessed, save his idols, which the gods kept.

Terah took refuge in the assurances of his youngest son, Abram, that the One True God would never abandon them, and that they would one day be joined in peace and harmony for all time.

But until that day, he must take his family into the land of Canaan. To the rolling hills of Hebron.

Djoser, Hetephe, Incense/Hagar/Keterah
Horus, Serket, Azazil, Abram, Baalat
Ishmael, Maribah, Fatimah, Nebaioth, Basemath, Kedar | Anath, Astarte

~~~~~~~~~~~~~

12. Famine

Year 166, Season 3, Setmonth

Her Grandfather was long dead and buried when Horus came to Rusalem in hopes that Serket might be there. She wasn't. She had vanished and never returned.

Horus also came to ensure his claim to the land of Hebron was in order. He told of Abram's possible future claim and right to it.

Not that the land was desirable these days. It no longer produced the lush crops it was capable of when there was rain. Canaan suffered the same endless drought as Egypt. There had been almost no rain in four years. Hunger ran through the land. The Egyptians themselves were running low on grain reserves and no longer exported grains to Canaan or any other country. Canaan was the hardest hit; human suffering was rampant.

The elders told Horus that the sounds of a woman screaming in agony were heard during the Winter's Solstice.

That night, he lay in the bed where he and Serket had once lain. He could not cry.

The next morning, he traveled to Hebron and the rolling hills that contained so much promise. There he stayed for a day, then returned to Port Jaffa to assist Phoenicia.

Phoenicia had become the de facto assistant to Chief Jaffa. Chief Jaffa had lost his consort Astarte years ago to Living God Set. His wife, Polydore, had divorced him and immigrated to Port Byblos to assist Lady Baalat.

Chief Jaffa had been left alone to govern and even at his most excellent, he was less than mediocre.

Phoenicia had grown into the city leadership that Port Jaffa was so badly in need of. The famine hit the port harder than most cities because it was the last Canaanite city before Egypt and the famine was beginning to impact Egypt. Pharaoh Djoser restricted the number of immigrants allowed into Egypt. They were stopped at the border. The closest city to the border was Port Jaffa. Port Jaffa was overrun with starving people trying to gain entry into Egypt where not *everyone* was starving to death.

Phoenicia fed as many as she could but had little food to work with. She asked traders and ship captains to contribute whatever excess food they
~~~~~~~~~~~~~

might have. She set up shelters and community kitchens. Those who had food were asked to share what little they had. Stews became soups became nourishing water. Those who would not live were given gentle words instead of food. Animals that could no longer work were no longer retired to a peaceful pasture; they had one more service to provide.

It was as if the gods had turned their backs upon the people.

The missionaries and priests of the Church of Urfa were quick to point out that the people had turned their backs on the righteous gods, and if only the people would pray to the right gods, buy the right idols, and tithe to the church, then the righteous gods would once more favor them.

Phoenicia worked all the harder.

JOURNIES

So it was that Terah and his family arrived in Port Jaffa and pitched their tents in what was once a lovely city park but was now a city of tents and lamentations. Terah sat morosely in his tent with his family.

So it was that Abram found Horus tending the dying.

Horus came to Terah and said all his comforting words. Terah stared at the ground with no strength left to speak.

Horus finally rose and left the tent; Abram followed.

Abram said, "When he still talked, he blamed you for corrupting me into destroying his idols. His life ended in Harran. He takes no comfort in the knowledge of everlasting life. He only remembers he was once a man of importance because the gods of old had favored him with maintaining their idols. I destroyed all of that and he and his family were banished from the lands of Urfa. He has a right to be bitter. That, plus he has not had food enough to sustain him. My wish is to get him to your promised land and let him die there. That will be his last comfort, I suppose."

Horus volunteered, "Your father would not be allowed entry into Egypt. I will take him to Hebron and help him die. There are caves. I will select a suitable one for him and mark it for you. It is not the time for you to continue to Hebron. The sooner you can get your family into Egypt the better. Your word alone would be enough to gain your entry into Fort Rafah. My priests will remember you and assist you. Once in, each fort will provide enough food for you to live on. Your name and contributions to Egypt are still remembered by the court. You and your family will fare better than most but even the Pharaoh is gaunt and will not eat a full portion as long as any of his people are hungry."

"My father was a good man but he was not born for times like these."

"That's why we have death. Most certainly, it's time for him to embrace his ancestors."

"Do you really believe the dying words of a madman, Teacher?"

"If Set's words were not true, there is no reason for life, Abram. I choose to believe that Set talked with the One. Now, go say farewell to your father and leave him with me. I'll take him to Hebron after we greet the morning's sun."

Abram returned to Terah and talked with him as Haran directed the breaking of their camp. There was still daylight left in the day. Abram commanded Amathlai to embrace her husband and bid him good day until he returned to her.

Amathlai did as her son said but could not hold back her tears.

Abram then led his family toward Fort Rajah leaving a confused Terah sitting on the ground with Horus.

As they watched Terah's family leave, Horus said to Terah, "At sunrise, we will greet the mighty god Osiris. Then we will journey to Hebron. There I shall give you the food of life."

~~~

Abram's entry into Fort Rajah was not without confrontation. The 'too many people' objection had to be overcome but the local priests remembered Abram and his devotion to the teachings of Horus. Abram's family, including Sarai, was impressed that Abram was well-known and important in such an exotic land as Egypt.

They were allowed entry. The meager rations of food they were given were more than they had eaten the last season. Their journey to Memphis was wonderful with an almost adequate meal every day.

Along the way, Abram explained to Sarai that, in Egypt, she was not bound by the customs of Urfa such as her vow 'to obey' her husband. She was her own person and should always do the right thing regardless of her husband's wishes.

Sarai, uncharacteristically, remained silent.

Phoenicia, Jaffa, Rocky, Burlyman, Polydore | Astarte, T'jaru
Terah, Amathlai, Haran, Terahson, Nahor, Sarai, Isaac, Jacob
Kyrios-Olon, Teumessian, Nimrod, Nimbal, Nimlad, Nimisis, Asherah, Set.
~~~

~~~

They were assigned to camp north of Memphis on the road to Newport.

Sarai was indignant that this was the best site her husband could obtain.

As it turned out, this was considered to be a prestigious address reserved for high-ranking immigrants.

Sarai was delighted her husband had obtained such a delightful location.

The day after each phase change of the moon, the Pharaoh was carried along the roads of Egypt; he, sitting stone-faced with crossed crook and flail; Queen Hetephe standing behind him graciously nodding to those gathered along the way. Two nursing handmaidens rode with the queen. Upon observing a baby, the queen would stop the procession, and a handmaiden would retrieve and nurse the baby as the Pharaoh stood and solemnly observed this miracle of life and its promise.

But on this day, General Sanakhte, heir apparent to Djoser, ceremonially walked the road toward the port with Princess Incense, daughter of Queen Hetephe and Pharaoh Djoser. The two stopped to talk with and encourage the inhabitants of the tent cities; people who, in better days, might be guests of the pharaoh in the palace and whose future good-will would contribute to the continued power of Egypt. Scribes followed, making records of who they talked with.

The men—Abram, Nahor, Haran's son Lot, and Abram's servant Eliezer —were at Newport assisting port operations any way they could.

The women—Sarai, Amathlai, Milkah, and the child Iskah—remained at their tent. The women stepped out as an approaching commotion attracted their attention but not before Sarai applied color to her face just in case she should be looking her prettiest. She heard her mother exclaim, "Oh my goodness, he must be someone *very* important!" She applied a little more color and stepped from their tent to stand beside her mother-in-law.

So it was Sarai met Sanakhte.

Sanakhte and Incense came strolling up to introduce themselves; he in full regalia; she in a simple unadorned white linen tunic.

Incense said, "Good day, Ladies. I am Princess Incense, and this is Lord Sanakhte, General of the Egyptian Armies. We welcome you to Egypt.
~~~

Sanakhte said, "Be patient, gentlewomen. This drought will end. The rains will come as will the bountiful harvests. We can then all return to the life we once knew."

Incense said, "My father has commanded we use this time of trouble to meet our neighbors from the east; to better understand your customs and problems and hopes. When the troubles pass, all people will be closer." She looked at Amathlai and asked, "Are you from the lands of Canaan?"

Sarai glanced toward General Sanakhte and went for it. She gushed, "I am Sarai, sister to Abram, loyal student of God Horus. This is Abram's mother, Amathlai. We are honored to be in the presence of a powerful and generous lord such as yourself."

Incense was being raised to be a Pharaoh. She might one day become Pharaoh or might not. Sanakhte might precede her or might not. Regardless, she did not need the skills of a Pharaoh-in-training to recognize what every female regardless of age instantly recognizes—competition. She was amused. She would marry Sanakhte if she were so commanded but that probably wasn't going to happen. This pretty young interloper was welcome to him.

Incense offered, "General Sanakhte is certainly powerful and, as I understand from his many concubines, quite generous. Where are you from, Lord Sarai?"

Sarai did not remove her gaze from Sanakhte.

Sarai replied, "My family is from Urfa where father was a powerful trader. Our beloved father did not survive the long journey. We miss the protecting arm of a strong man."

Sanakhte replied, "Surely, a woman as beautiful as you has a husband."

Sarai responded, "Oh, General, if I had a proper husband, I would have birthed many children by now. I hope to meet you again, General Sanakhte. Perhaps we can share stories of our beloved countries and strengthen our bonds."

Incense wanted to roll her eyes, but Pharaohs-in-training would never do that. Instead, she dryly replied, "Perhaps the general has need of another concubine." *Forward woman. The general always has need of another woman. Perhaps he will favor you.*

Sarai said nothing but continued to stare at the general.

General Sanakhte chuckled and said, "Perhaps ..."

Incense said the proper "nice-to-meet-you's" and she and the general left to continue their goodwill stroll.

Amathlai was almost speechless. "Sarai! You led the general to believe that you are not married!"

Sarai snapped at her, "*Am* I married, Mother?! Where are my children?! A husband would have given you grandchildren by now! If I am to ever have children, it will not be by my brother! Abram is not nearly as powerful as the general! You will support my innocent deception if you want grandchildren, Mother. Do you want Abram to have an heir? *Do* you?!"

Amathlai was conflicted but she *did* want Abram to have an heir.

Sarai smiled in excited hopeful anticipation.

THE GIFT

A quartermoon slowly passed. A messenger arrived at the tent of Abram in the early morning. He presented a gift and an invitation to the woman Sarai from General Sanakhte.

Sarai's breath quickened.

Amathlai's eyes grew wide.

Abram was puzzled. "A gift from a general? Is this the person who passed through the tent's last quartermoon? Why would he be sending gifts?"

Sarai snapped back into reality. A powerful potential mate had sent her a gift and her husband had witnessed its arrival. A thousand plans flashed through her mind. *I will have a baby! But Abram will not be the father!*

She stared coldly at Abram and said more coldly to everyone in the tent, "Leave us!"

Amathlai was close to fainting, but Amathlai wanted Abram to have an heir. Amathlai obediently led everyone from the tent "to let Sarai and Abram talk."

The tent emptied except for Sarai and Abram.

She stared at him defiantly.

He sat down, looked up at her, and said, "So the pious and righteous family of Terah is soon to have a cuckolded husband. How interesting."

"It's not like that! It's not like that at all. He will make me pregnant. It's the only way you can ever have an heir. It's my duty as your wife. I'm in Egypt. I'm allowed to do what's right."

He stared at her. Her constant complaining, fussing, whining, and fault-finding had taken its toll. He casually said, "It is *you*, my wife. Not me. I can sire a child with any woman but you. Is that what you want? Then go pick out the woman you want to bear my child. It's as simple as that. You cannot conceive and you know it! So, what is it you plan to do?"

"I CAN CONCEIVE A CHILD! I WILL! I WILL BE THE MOTHER OF A NATION. IF YOU CANNOT PLANT A CHILD IN ME, I WILL FIND A MAN THAT CAN! I HATE YOU! I HATE YOU!"

Abram looked at her with understanding tinged with pity. "I understand, Sarai. You must at least try. I truly hope he is the one. *No need to hurt you more than you are already hurting. I no longer care what you do.*

"Accept his gift. Take whatever potions might help you conceive. You have my blessing."

She ran to him, embraced him, and cried and cried and cried.

Sarai eventually emerged from the tent and said to the messenger. "Tell the General that the necklace and little sleeping gown he has given me are beautiful. I accept his invitation to dine this evening and talk about further co-operation. Tell him I hope the gown will please him."

The messenger left.

Sarai stood there. Empty, but for the thought, *I will mother a nation.*

<div align="center">~~~</div>

She returned to her tent before sunrise wearing a beautiful necklace and a hardly used sleeping gown. She crawled into bed beside her husband, pressed herself firmly against him, and cried.

Abram with eyes wide shut, did not stir.

<div align="center">~~~</div>

The seasons wore on. Sarai visited the General at least twice a quartermoon, sometimes more.

And then ...

Djoser was casually reading random scribe's reports of whom his staff and attendants had visited in the tent camps. He noticed the entry "Abram—

student of God Horus." He read the entire entry, paused, read it again, and thought, *Abram was Horus's student years ago. He married but there is no mention of his wife. Did she die? Did she not come with him? Is there a story here?*

He sent for his daughter who arrived immediately. He asked, "Incense, this report says that you and General Sanakhte visited the tent of Abram of Urfa. Do you remember this visit?"

She glanced at the report and said, "Yes, Father. His sister Sarai was as forward with the general as a Nubian maiden performing a fertility dance. And if my chamber spies are correct, the general is exhausted after her every visit. Is Abram of interest to us?"

"Yes. Yes, he is. I wish to know about Abram's wife. Why isn't she mentioned in this report? Does Abram wish his sister to become an official concubine to Sanakhte? Revisit this tent. Use discretion but bring me a more detailed report. Horus is a national treasure. His student Baalat is a national treasure. And Abram? What is his status? Yes, he is of interest to Egypt. Go and find these things."

"Oh, Father. What fun!"

A SIMPLE MISUNDERSTANDING

Incense donned the simple disguise she wore when she wished to mingle unnoticed among her people. She arrived at the tent of Abram and asked for permission to enter. Appearance can be altered but a command by a Pharaoh-in-training, not so easily. Amathlai most certainly granted this vaguely familiar person entry into Abram's tent.

Amathlai said, "I am Amathlai, Mother of Abram. Welcome to our tent, my Lord, but I fear that I have no nourishment to offer you."

"Nourish me with wisdom, Lord Amathlai. Tell me if your son is married."

"He is my Lord. His wife is Sarai."

Sarai stepped forward but then froze with horror.

Incense said, "But you are sister to Abram. Are you not?"

Words and worlds came tumbling down.

~~~

That evening, Incense made her report to her father.

He merely said, "Call your mother to me. Have her bring wine."

Djoser, Hetephe, Incense/Hagar/Keterah
Horus, Serket, Azazil, Abram, Baalat
Ishmael, Maribah, Fatimah, Nebaioth, Basemath, Kedar | Anath, Astarte
~~~

Djoser and Hetephe sat together in quiet joy, drinking wine, discussing things. Improbable, unusual things.

He asked, "Woman, why did you marry me?"

She answered, "I found you to be an immature, but extremely interesting, little boy who needed a woman to grow him."

~~~

Djoser called for General Sanakhte to join him for wine. They, too, discussed things. Improbable, unusual things.

The general offered his resignation.

The Pharaoh laughed.

~~~

A messenger arrived at the tent of Abram. The messenger told Abram, "By royal command, Lord Abram and his wife will present themselves for a State dinner at the palace tomorrow at sundown."

A STATE DINNER

The pageantry of the Pharaoh and Queen greeting representatives of State always gave hope to their people. The pageantry finished; all were seated for the state dinner. The Pharaoh sat at the head of the table, the queen at the foot. Abram and Sarai sat on the Pharaoh's right. Princess Incense, General Sanakhte, and the general's beautiful chief concubine on his left.

Sarai was so sick to her stomach that she wanted to vomit. Abram was steeled and prepared to explain the unexplainable.

Hetephe and Incense kept the conversation going. It did not take a Pharaoh-in-training to see that Sarai wanted to throw up and that Abram would jump from the top of Osiris's obelisk when commanded.

Eventually, General Sanakhte opened the door to the true subject when he said, "You can imagine my surprise when I found out that the beautiful and charming Lady Sarai is married to our illustrious guest in an admirable trusting and open marriage sophisticated even by Egyptian standards; two people dedicated and determined to do whatever necessary to produce Lord Abram of Hebron an heir."

Incense said, "They are among the most interesting people I have ever met!"

Djoser said, "So we are here tonight to learn what Egypt must do to rectify our general's inability to impregnate Lord Sarai. Tell me, Chief Abram, what are your thoughts on what we are dealing with here tonight."

Abram opened his mouth and began. *Never let them see you unsure.*

Djoser let him say the words he needed to say. Djoser then said, "This is what shall be done as compensation for Egypt's failure to help Chief Abram produce an heir. To Abram, I shall give food for his family to return to Hebron and live for a year. To Sarai, I shall give a handmaiden. If she someday wishes the handmaiden to produce Abram's heir, then she may give the handmaiden to Chief Abram as his concubine. Egypt, the general, Lord Sarai, and Chief Abram will emerge from this unusual situation all the stronger and the people of Egypt will rejoice rather than question and be weakened by rumors and gossip. Tomorrow, General Sanakhte and his lovely concubine will provide Chief Abram and Lord Sarai carriage tours of our city. An official proclamation introducing all parties to the citizens will be made at highsun. Princess Incense, meet with the vizier, finalize the itinerary, and prepare prettier words than I have presented. I and the queen will now retire to select an appropriate handmaiden. Take time and get to know one another better."

He rose along with the queen. "Goodnight, all. May Egypt and Hebron find everlasting friendship and peace." They retired to their quarters to do the hard part.

THE DECISION

In their chamber, attendants changed them into bed clothes. They sat by their open window looking out over the great river."

He: "The general's concubine ate enough to feed three people."
She: "Sarai ate nothing. Which is good. She would not have kept it down."
He: "I expected Abram to handle this well. He is a student of Horus."
She: "You put them under extreme pressure. Sarai pulled herself together after she realized she wasn't going to be stoned to death."
He: "So what is it I want and who shall I select to do it? Abram may never be of consequence to Egypt, especially in the southern lands below Port Jaffa. If he were in Mesopotamia or Phoenicia, he would have more potential. But Hebron? Maybe I should just select a pretty maiden for him and be done with it."
She: "As inconsequential as soon-to-be Living-God Baalat of Byblos?"
He: "Horus *did* select him as a student. I should not underestimate him.

Djoser, Hetephe, Incense/Hagar/Keterah
Horus, Serket, Azazil, Abram, Baalat
Ishmael, Maribah, Fatimah, Nebaioth, Basemath, Kedar | Anath, Astarte

Perhaps he can make Hebron the capital of the world."

She: "And let's not overlook his wife. She is determined to be the mother of nations and she has the will to make it happen."

He: "I love my daughter. I want the best for her. What will she say?"

She: "She will find Sarai arrogant and obnoxious and difficult. And then she will give birth to a nation bound by blood to Egypt."

That evening, Djoser wandered the labyrinth from the palace to Osiris's Mastaba. He talked to his dear, but long dead, friend.

They agreed. *Love is hard.*

HAGAR

At 1000 the day after his fun-filled day of carriage rides, waving, and esteem building, General Sanakhte stood on the concourse and addressed the people of Memphis. He introduced Chief Abram of Hebron and his lovely wife Sarai, whom the general had unfortunately been unable to impregnate as per Chief Abram's most fervent desire. The general made several self-deprecating remarks which drew laughter from the crowd, a smile from Abram, and blushes from Sarai.

Finally, he introduced Egypt's gift to Hebron, a handmaiden for Sarai now known by the Canaanite name of Hagar.

Once known as Incense, Princess of Egypt.

DUTY

What once-Incense thought was of little consequence. She was trained to be a Pharaoh. She would do what must be done without question or regret. She sat with her father for a long time, listening to his thoughts, to the possibilities, to what she was giving up, to destinies that might be or might never be. If she accomplished nothing more than living a good life, Ma'at would be served.

Once-Incense did what any once-in-training Pharaoh would do, began laying out long-term plans, possible plans, contingency plans, "What is it that I want and what shall I do to accomplish it?"

She asked for a full medical examination of Sarai, especially of her reproductive outlook. And of Abram, also.

Sarai and Abram spent a day giving blood samples, urine samples, stool samples, hair samples, and skin samples. Their heart rate, breathing rate, and skin color were measured throughout the day. Endurance on flat land, inclined land, and rugged land were observed. Every orifice was poked and probed. The preliminary results were given to each subject. "Everything looks good. You're in great shape for a person your age."

Final and more detailed results were placed in files and a copy was given to Hagar for future reference. Hagar understood the abnormalities and idiosyncrasies of Sarai's reproductive system in great detail. She wondered, if she ever chose to attempt to do so, if she could mix potions to overcome Sarai's problems.

It was, however, not in Egypt's best interests to attempt that at this time.

HANDMAIDEN HAGAR

Hagar spent days getting to know Sarai. "How can I best serve you? What do you like to do? My mother taught me archery. I can teach reading and writing in seven languages. She did well with, "We could discuss ways that Abram might give you a baby. I know many potions we could try."

Sarai grew comfortable confiding in Hagar

Hagar emphasized repeatedly that she would not allow Abram to touch her unless Sarai officially appointed her as Abram's concubine.

But more important than Sarai was Abram, whom she only visited in the company of Sarai or Amathlai.

Abram once remarked to Eliezer, "Hagar is a pleasure to be around. She reminds me of a girl I once knew."

The day soon came that their wagon was hitched to a bull and a cow. It was loaded with provisions including nesting hens. Their departure was orchestrated to obtain the maximum approval of the people of Egypt. It was a glorious departure scene.

High on an eight-level Mastaba, hidden from the people, two figures watched this glorious departure.

An unwanted tear slid down the female's cheek. The male watched the departure as he held the female closely.

They both knew, *Love is hard.*

~~~~~~~~~~~~~

13. Hebron

Year 166, Season 11, Dionysusmonth

Twelve Egyptian soldiers accompanied the wagon over the Way of Horus. A wagon that might contain food would certainly be attacked for the cattle if nothing else. Reaching Fort Rafah, the captain turned due south, in the middle of a moonless night, to bypass all civilization, and then east again to journey along a non-existent road into Hebron. The soldiers assisted Abram and the other men in building a large communal house in a location that could be defended against anyone not trained in warfare; especially when defended by a well-equipped accomplished archer.

A spring was found near the communal house. It was small but provided enough drinking water with some left over for watering a garden. The women planted a portion of the crop seed and cuttings in the hope that they could harvest enough to feed themselves by the time their wagon of provisions had been consumed.

The chickens were provided with a safe nesting place.

Abram went to the highest point in the area. There he found a map to a cave. There he found the remains of Terah—a trader in idols.

Throughout most of Canaan and Egypt, the famine raged on. Those living in Hebron subsisted well enough.

Such was the birth of Hebron which was the land promised to the breaker of idols—a student of Horus—follower of the Path of Kiya—believer in the One True God—to Abram.

~~~

Few people ventured through Hebron. A nomadic tribe came to the spring and demanded to know why the water no longer pooled so that they and their animals could drink from it.

Abram explained that most of the water returned to the land; that he had built cisterns and jars to harvest the water so that it would be conserved and support many people. He led their animals to the water troughs where they drank their fill. He let the women fill their pouches and jugs with all the water they needed. "This land will always provide water to those that thirst and food to those that hunger. Hebron is a land where all people are united as friends."

Phoenicia, Jaffa, Rocky, Burlyman, Polydore | Astarte, T'jaru
Terah, Amathlai, Haran, Terahson, Nahor, Sarai, Isaac, Jacob
Kyrios-Olon, Teumessian, Nimrod, Nimbal, Nimlad, Nimisis, Asherah, Set.

The tribe contributed nuts and dates from their meager food supply to add to the almost-stew that Amathlai had made. They sat on blankets under a peaceful night sky telling stories of better days past and better days to come.

~~~

A scout found the village of Hebron and inquired about its residents. The scout was excited to learn this was now the home of Abram, once of significance in the Church of Urfa. He said, "Priestess Asherah will be pleased when I tell her of your whereabouts."

Within three quartermoons of the scout leaving Hebron, Asherah and her companions arrived to joyously reunite with Abram. Among her companions were T'jaru, Astarte, Anubis, Zedek, and a handmaiden to help care for Asherah's child. Knowing that the famine reached far into Canaan, they brought wine and feasting food with them.

Upon meeting, Asherah embraced Abram, saying, "We have been parted far too long, my once-husband."

Abram: *I had forgotten, we were married. once.*
Sarai: "When Abram married me, you were no longer his wife, Priestess."
Hagar: *Wife? That's interesting.*
T'jaru: "Be careful what you say in front of our good friend, Zedek. His task is to report to Nimrod everything that's said."
Astarte: "Lord Anubis tells me I have said some naughty things that need to be reported."
Asherah: "You are correct, Sarai. The man I most loved is now married to you and not to me. I have brought you a gift to show that I forgive you for taking him from me."

She motioned to her handmaiden to present the gift. "It is called an Asherah Pole and it can help you when you give birth. The women in Mesopotamia and Canaan adore the poles. Some claim they can rub their parts against it and it inspires them to conceive; others that it helps them give birth. Whichever, it is a constant reminder of the love all the gods have for them—and you—and Abram."

Abram said, "I will have no idols in Hebron, Asherah. Take it away."

"It's nothing more than a birthing pole, Abram. Your wife will thank you for it when her time comes."
~~~

Anubis said, "Let your wife keep it, Lord Abram. It costs you nothing and the missionary gives credit to Asherah. Let it remind you of all the false gods you are fighting against."

Hagar approvingly observed the progress being made in Hebron.

All was going well except Sarai would not get pregnant, even though she had taken to rubbing parts of her body against the Asherah Pole.

Phoenicia, Jaffa, Rocky, Burlyman, Polydore | Astarte, T'jaru
Terah, Amathlai, Haran, Terahson, Nahor, Sarai, Isaac, Jacob
Kyrios-Olon, Teumessian, Nimrod, Nimbal, Nimlad, Nimisis, Asherah, Set.

~~~~~~~~~~~~~

14. Ishmael

Year 170-184

Hagar had grown into an extension of Sarai; always with her, counseling her, teaching her, and sympathizing with her inability to conceive.

Sarai drank various potions and tried different mating techniques at all times of day under every position of the moon to no avail. Sarai grew ever more impatient. Abram, ever more weary.

Sarai often whined at Hagar. "You said that you would show me how to get pregnant. You said that you would mix herbs to make me pregnant. Why can't you do what you said you were going to do?"

Hagar would act repentant. *She is a three-year-old not getting her way. Be patient with her. Be forgiving.*

Sarai stood with Hagar on a hill overlooking the countryside. "Will the gods ever send forth the rains again? Abram doesn't want us to pray to any of them, not even Persephone."

Hagar replied, "Abram teaches of the One True God but still you pray to Aphrodite every night and Zeus every morning. I believe that if a thing is to be done, it is best for us to do it and not rely on gods."

"I have tried so hard to give him a son. I have done all that I know how to do. He must have a son. He must. I have failed him."

Hagar was silent for a long time. "Abram can sire a son whenever you command it."

"I don't want him to have a concubine. That just isn't right. I am his wife."

"I need no title to do what needs doing. The New Moon is coming; that is my time. The potion I mix will be strong. The child will be a male. It will be a single act that is over quickly and never spoken of again. We will raise the boy together. He will be strong like you and wise like his father."

"You will do in a single act what I could not do in a thousand."

"You provide the love. I will provide the body."

"Will the rains come?"

Hagar laughed, "That, I suppose, depends on what is offered to which god and if it's what that god wants."

<div align="center">

Djoser, Hetephe, Incense/Hagar/Keterah
Horus, Serket, Azazil, Abram, Baalat
Ishmael, Maribah, Fatimah, Nebaioth, Basemath, Kedar | Anath, Astarte

</div>
~~~~~~~~~~~~~

AN ACT OF LOVE

As she mixed her potion, Hagar considered the best way to handle this somewhat awkward situation. *Should Sarai hold his hand or should she be somewhere else? Do I show pleasure or hide it? What about him? It would help with conception if we both took pleasure in it. They both do it because it is their duty, not out of any great lust —or small lust, for that matter. It's her pride I must preserve. How do you mate with a woman's husband so that she is proud?*

Hagar met with Sarai. They discussed things. "I am a virgin and unsure of what pleases a man. Here is an ointment to apply to his man-parts as we do it. It will stimulate him to his maximum performance and make up for my lack of experience. Do you have suggestions on how I can best please him? Will it hurt?"

Sarai failed to notice that Hagar had gone from an expert in mating to a virgin.

Hagar met with Eliezer. They discussed things. "He must not compliment me or be happy to see me. He would rather be out plowing a field instead of me. He should ask Sarai, 'Must I do this, Sarai? This is disgusting.' If he must shout out, he should say, 'I love you, Sarai.'"

The new moon came. Meals eaten. Words said. Retiring for the night could be put off no longer. Sarai wore a beautiful silk night dress Hagar had given her. She and Abram lay in their bed side by side, arms by their sides, rigid. Hagar entered the room carrying a lamp wearing a long woolen dress. She lay down beside Abram, pulled the gown to her waist, stared at the ceiling, and said, "Mistress Sarai, help me do this thing."

Sarai rose, retrieved the fragrant oil, pushed on Abram until he rolled on top of Hagar, and began applying oils on him as she coldly said, "Now, in the name of your god, create me a son."

Sarai did not want to notice that Abram's lovemaking became far more intense than normal.

Hagar was too focused on the performance of her life to notice Sarai's cold stares. Hagar used little tricks to prolong the act. *It helps with conception if we both take pleasure in it.*

At the end, he shouted, "I love you! I have always loved you!"

~~~

The rains came.

Phoenicia, Jaffa, Rocky, Burlyman, Polydore | Astarte, T'jaru
Terah, Amathlai, Haran, Terahson, Nahor, Sarai, Isaac, Jacob
Kyrios-Olon, Teumessian, Nimrod, Nimbal, Nimlad, Nimisis, Asherah, Set.
~~~

THE PREGNANCY

It began innocently; two women thrilled with Hagar's pregnancy.

She began to show in the third month. Sarai placed her hand on Hagar's abdomen and said, "My child begins to be seen."

After that, Sarai began saying things like:
"Don't do that, it will hurt my baby."
"Do this! It will help my baby."
"You should feel fortunate that I let you carry my baby."
"My baby can't wait to get outside of you!"
"You are not fit to be a mother!"
"You're nothing but a whore!"

It was constant. It was unending. Abram was helpless in controlling either woman. Pharaohs have no limits. Pharaohs-in-training do.

Hagar packed her things, walked into the morning meal, and announced, "I'm going to Memphis. Goodbye." With that, she stormed out the door and headed to Rusalem, and from there to the road to Memphis.

Sarai screamed after her, "You can't take my baby from me! I won't have it! Do something, Abram! Kill her! Cut the baby out of her! We can raise it together! Kill her, Abram! Kill her!"

Amathlai rushed to Sarai to console the inconsolable.

Eliezer counseled Abram, "My Lord. You must subjugate your wife."

Abram thundered, "Quiet, woman! You displease your husband! Eliezer, bring Hagar back to me. Tell her that Sarai will not be allowed in her presence until the baby is born. I will build Hagar her own house away from Sarai. She can bear her child in peace."

Sarai screamed, "It's not her child. It's mine! It's mine!"

"SILENCE, WOMAN! SILENCE! Go, Eliezer. Bring Hagar home!"

She was halfway to Rusalem when Eliezer caught up with her. She did not stop but listened as they walked. They both recognized the problems.

Eliezer believed that Abram would control Sarai now that he faced the certainty of losing Sarai and his son if he did not. "But you must accept that Sarai will take your child away as soon as it is born; that she will raise him as her own and will soon enough forget that it is you who bore him. Master Abram is fond of quoting Horus—'Love is hard.' Come back to Hebron, Lady Hagar. Else it will remain a dirt village."

They spent a peaceful night in Rusalem. The local women oohed and ahhed over her pregnancy. It was enough.

BIRTH

Hagar grasped the Asherah pole. Amathlai delivered the baby.

Eliezer mercifully kept Sarai from the birthing room and gave Hagar a little time to swaddle and hold her child. She cooed and smiled at the babe who was content at its mother's breast. Finally, she kissed her child, steeled herself, and tearfully handed her baby to Abram.

Abram touched Hagar's cheek, gave her a sad smile, said, "Whatever will be, will be," and took their son to the adjacent room.

There, Sarai shrieked with excitement, "MY BABY! MY BABY! IT'S BEAUTIFUL!"

In another room, Hagar took comfort in what she had accomplished and that another woman was overwhelmed with excitement to be a mother at long last. A mother that would move mountains to enable her son to build a great city. A great civilization.

A great friend of Egypt.

ISHMAEL'S CHILDHOOD

Sarai claimed the child, Ishmael, as her own. Amathlai and other family members knew that it wasn't, but a thing repeated often and loudly enough becomes truth. Especially if one is screamed at for daring to suggest otherwise.

The newcomers who located in Hebron—mostly from Rusalem, Tophet, and Port Jaffa—did not know the difference but all the women noted the contentious relation between Sarai and her son.

The child never bonded with Sarai. Sarai could not comfort him. Ishmael became more turbulent as he grew.

Abram could sometimes play with the boy. Talk to him. Teach him. And sometimes even laugh with him. Abram taught the boy the Way of Horus and of the One True God.

Ishmael would sometimes sneak to find the handmaiden Hagar. He would sit at her feet and listen to stories of great deeds and great people. The stories enthralled the boy. He did not suspect that this was the woman he had bonded with at birth; this was his birth mother.

THE VISITOR

When Ishmael was six, a man came to see Abram.

Ishmael was beginning to understand that his "stupid" father was an important man and he was becoming accustomed to people coming to consult with him. Most of these people were "stupid and mean."

This man, however, carried himself with the weight of the world upon his back. Upon his arrival, Sarai stormed from the house with, "How can you possibly allow him into my home?!"

Nevertheless, Abram received the man and asked Hagar to bring them bread and wine.

Ishmael took am interest in the visitor. *Mother doesn't like him. Why is that?*

Abram said, "Welcome, Lord Horus. Are you well?"

"Well enough, Abram. Hebron appears to be growing into a significant village. Your people seem to follow the path. Did everything work out to your liking?"

"The land you gave me is a place of greatness. The people come here because it is a righteous place without false gods. Many people from Tophet have moved here. We work and live in harmony. Is Serket well?"

"We have been separated for a long time. Divorced, I was told. I would have found her if she had wanted to be found. Azazil has assumed my role as Teacher. He continually travels the road between Memphis and Byblos. I wander. I teach. I search for meaning. I help those whom I can. It is enough, I suppose."

"Do you teach the people of their immortality—The Tree-of-Life. The One. The All?"

"No. It would do more harm than good. Is this your son? I thought your wife was barren."

"Yes. This is Ishmael." Abram nervously introduced Ishmael without mentioning who his mother was.

Ishmael conversed as a polite adult. *Barren? What does barren mean?*

Horus asked Ishmael his thoughts on gods and women.

Ishmael had never participated in such conversations. For the first time, Ishmael was intimidated by an elder. He answered as best he could but felt his knowledge lacking.

Horus completed his visit, bid goodbye to Abram, Ishmael, and Hagar, and then said, "Tell Sarai you did the right thing. That all will be well."

The three watched Horus as he began his journey back to Rusalem.

Abram said, "Horus is the greatest Shaman to ever live. He would be a living god if there were such a thing."

Ishmael watched Horus disappear in the distance. *Great Shaman? Living God? Barren? What is barren?*

EXPLORATION

As he grew older, Ishmael would descend from the hills and disappear into the sandy desert for days at a time. Abram was at first concerned over his disappearances.

The boy sullenly said, "The sand is endless and pure. There is peace in the desert. Here there is dirt and dung and filth and anger. Only in the desert is there peace and serenity."

By the time he was eleven, Ishmael had become an expert at finding water below the surface of the desolation by inserting his walking staff into the sand until he found signs of water seeping up. Once he discovered an oasis surrounded by trees and other greenery where a nomadic tribe was camped. The boy was fascinated with the stories these strange people told.

The wilderness landscape was varied and endless. The boy would sit and stare at a location; imagining his father's walled city being suddenly transported there. He wondered what would be necessary for the city to thrive. The answer was always the same. Water.

The more water, the more successful the city.

He dreamed of building cities in his beloved desert. *The desert is so big. So vast. So serene!*

Being still a boy and not well-traveled, Ishmael had no concept of the word "vast."

The seasons became the years.

Phoenicia, Jaffa, Rocky, Burlyman, Polydore | Astarte, T'jaru
Terah, Amathlai, Haran, Terahson, Nahor, Sarai, Isaac, Jacob
Kyrios-Olon, Teumessian, Nimrod, Nimbal, Nimlad, Nimisis, Asherah, Set.

~~~~~~~~~~~~

15. The Sundering of Ishmael

Year 184

In his thirteenth year, Ishmael came into manhood. His disposition worsened. He had no tolerance for fools or vapidity. He began calling Sarai a fool and an idiot. One night he screamed at her, "You are not my mother! My real mother cannot be a stupid fool like you!"

With that, he stormed from the room into the night.

Abram looked at Sarai and said, "I will go talk with him. He will settle down."

Sarai stared at him and said coldly, "Kill him! Take him to the hilltop and cut his throat. I demand it! That god of yours demands it! Do it!"

Abram said, "I'll go talk to him."

Sarai screamed, "DO IT!"

Abram followed his son outside.

Hagar had listened to the exchange from a corner of the room. She stood and walked into the cool night air. She heard the tumultuous argument between Father and Son in the distance. She walked toward it and, finding them, sat on the ground beneath a tree. She said nothing but soon enough the man and almost-man saw her quietly sitting there.

Ishmael thundered, "And what does Handmaiden Hagar have to say?!"

She quietly said, "That you two should come and sit beside me."

The two men stared at her and then went and sat beside her.

She said, "Once, long ago in the land of Egypt, there was a plan where Lord Abram and his wife would found a city and grow it into the most powerful city in Canaan. They would have a son who would be taught the Way of Horus. His son would eventually continue the noble work of his father. The world would become a better place. But the Pharaoh of Egypt knew that the wife, Sarai, could not conceive a child and could not bear Abram a son."

She continued, "The Pharaoh gave his only daughter to be Abram's concubine because the concubine could and did bear Abram a son. The plan was good. But it did not work out well. Nor will it ever work out well.

Djoser, Hetephe, Incense/Hagar/Keterah
Horus, Serket, Azazil, Abram, Baalat
Ishmael, Maribah, Fatimah, Nebaioth, Basemath, Kedar | Anath, Astarte
~~~~~~~~~~~~

She hesitated, then said, "Your mother and father will now leave you to resolve what you have been told. When you understand and have to come to terms with the truth, return to Sarai in peace."

Hagar led Abram back to his home. They found a still-furious Sarai fussing at Eliezer.

Sarai ignored Abram's commands to calm down.

Hagar walked to Sarai, and quietly said, "I told him."

"W-what?"

"I told Ishmael the truth."

"You told him?"

"He is outside coming to terms with the truth; that I am his birth mother; that you are barren. The truth, sweet Sarai. The truth."

Sarai collapsed. Amathlai ran to cradle her head in her lap.

Abram and Eliezer exchanged glances.

Abram said, "Whatever will be, will be."

Sarai's eyes fluttered open, and she stared at the ceiling muttering unintelligible words.

Soon, Ishmael entered the room, walked to Hagar, and said, "Mother."

Sarai stood up screaming, "She is not your mother! She is a whore! She did nothing but birth you! I AM YOUR MOTHER. DO YOU UNDERSTAND ME?!"

Ishmael quietly replied, "Now I know why I always hated you. You are a liar and a thief."

Sarai rushed Hagar with the intent to kill, screaming, "YOU KILLED MY SON YOU TOOK HIM FROM ME HE LOVED ME SO MUCH AND YOU KILLED HIM YOU WILL DIE FOR THIS YOU ARE EVIL I WILL KILL YOU."

Eliezer took her in a bear hug and lifted her off the floor.

Hagar walked to Sarai who was still screaming and spitting. Hagar quietly asked Sarai, "What do you wish me to do?"

Sarai jerked loose, and with crouched venom, answered, "Take your bastard son and leave this land. Both of you never existed. Before morning's light, you will be gone from Hebron. You and your bastard son will never speak of the House of Abram, again."

Sarai glared at Abram and hissed, "That is what shall be. MAKE IT SO!" and stormed off to her sleeping quarters.

Hagar walked to Ishmael, stroked his cheek, and said, "Come my child, we must pack our things for a long journey to meet your grandparents."

They packed and planned late into the night.

Hagar said, "We will travel across the Redlands directly to Fort Rafah. We can sleep during the heat of the day. Two flasks of water should be sufficient to see us across the desert."

The predawn light came. All was prepared. Abram, Eliezer, and Sarai came to watch the departure.

Hagar looked at Sarai, and said, "I have never been alone with the father of my child. We have never talked without you or Amathlai in our presence. Abram and I will now walk to the gardens so that I may bid him proper farewell. You approve, I'm sure."

Sarai replied, "Do it quickly and go!"

"Come, Abram, walk with me."

Abram glanced at Sarai, and said, "Very well."

They left the house to walk to the garden. Hagar said, "In my quarters are three potions. Tonight, give her the first potion, tomorrow night give her the second potion. The third night, lay with her and then give her the third potion. Pray to that god of yours and Isis and Asherah for a son. Perhaps it will come to pass. I care for you, Abram. You did well with a difficult marriage. I shall remember you with extreme fondness."

He was silent for a long time. "You were my strength. You remind me of a girl I once knew. In my way, I suppose I love you. Don't be angry with me. Be well, sweet Hagar. Take care of our son. May peace be with you."

With that, he strode back into his house where Sarai was standing with her hands on the water flasks. Abram motioned Ishmael to load up their travel packs. Then they walked to join Hagar in the garden.

Abram glanced at Hagar then turned and said goodbye to his son.

As they left, Abram called out after them, "Ishmael, her name is Incense. Your mother's name is Incense!"

Djoser, Hetephe, Incense/Hagar/Keterah
Horus, Serket, Azazil, Abram, Baalat
Ishmael, Maribah, Fatimah, Nebaioth, Basemath, Kedar | Anath, Astarte

~~~~~~~~~~~~

PART III. THE LORD

16. Return of the Princess

Year 184

MEMPHIS

They traveled the direct route to Fort Rajah through the desert because it would be quicker, and they would bypass the people in Rusalem and Port Jaffa. They traveled until the day became too hot; then they stopped and slept beneath a makeshift tent. As the day cooled, they began again and walked throughout the night until the morning sun heated up the day. Again they stopped, drank, rested, and slept. Before they began again, they drank the last of the first flask of water and continued on until the next morning. They pitched their makeshift tent between large dunes of sand and opened the second flask of water.

Incense drank and spit the water onto the ground. "It's salted!"

Ishmael tasted it and agreed. "Somehow salt was inadvertently poured into our water!"

They looked at one another and simultaneously said, "SARAI!"

Incense said, "How far are we? Is it quicker to go back or continue on? Either way, we are doomed without water. The sun will not forgive us for being foolish!"

"Don't you think a better plan is to find water, Mother? I have my walking rod. Let's go on. I'll find water soon enough."

The travel slowed to a crawl as Ishmael, with sharp, trained eyes, scanned the sand for any sign of moisture. Six times he made exploratory digs into the sand without finding water. The seventh time, water began pooling in the hole he had dug.

Incense shouted, "Fill! Fill! Give us water to live by, Osiris and Poseidon and Zeus and god of Abraham and whoever!" She looked upon her son with the sudden reverence of a mother suddenly seeing her son as a man. *He is worthy to be my father's grandson!*

Their two water pouches filled, they traveled on and came to the Way of Horus Road. They joined a caravan traveling to Memphis but left it outside the city gates.

<div align="center">

Phoenicia, Jaffa, Rocky, Burlyman, Polydore | Astarte, T'jaru
Terah, Amathlai, Haran, Terahson, Nahor, Sarai, Isaac, Jacob
Kyrios-Olon, Teumessian, Nimrod, Nimbal, Nimlad, Nimisis, Asherah, Set.

</div>
~~~~~~~~~~~~

She said, "We will camp here tonight and watch the Sunrise Ceremony in the morning. I will show you the glory of civilization and then we will enter the court of my parents."

The arrogant, wild, exuberant boy-man, first humbled seeing the skyline of Memphis, was then further humbled by the calling forth of Osiris by High-Priestess Hathor. As full of himself as he was, he was still a small village boy being exposed to the most sophisticated city in the world. He tried not to expose his awe, but this would be only his first encounter with a wonder in a city filled with wonders.

Incense looked at his wide eyes and said, "Don't be concerned, Son. By the time you are introduced to greatness, you will have seen it in many forms. We will walk the city. I will show you South Memphis. If you want revenge on Sarai, bring her to South Memphis and introduce her to Ishtar and the other upright honored women who live there."

Ishmael then realized that his mother was part of this—accustomed to this—and could have remained part of this. He asked, "Why did you leave, Mother?"

"Had I not, then you would not have been born. I had no choice."

They spent the day walking and looking; gawking less and less.

Incense said, "We will rest in our tent tonight. Tomorrow, we will dress in our finest, watch the Sunrise Ceremony, and you will enter the world of gods and Pharaohs. Prepare your will and your mind. You are the grandson of a Pharaoh, and you will act the part whether you are ready or not. Am I understood?"

"Yes, Mother." *You are commanding me. You have never commanded me before. I don't like people telling me what to do, but they were sheep and fools and stupid. Are you preparing me, Mother? For people who are none of these things?*

Ishmael slept fitfully that night; overwhelmed with new experiences; preparing his will and his mind.

ISHMAEL'S ENTRY INTO THE PALACE

They rose and dressed in the predawn light.

Things Incense said:
"Your clothes are fine. It is not what you wear but the confidence with which you wear them. Be confident no matter what finely dressed person is addressing you."

"Don't assume the person is a fool because they speak as a fool; nor that they are wise because they speak big words. Judge them by their deeds."
"Be confident."
"Understand what your father taught you. You thought him a fool. He was not a fool. His words are wise."

They watched the sunrise ceremony, then proceeded to the Concourse of Chief Kemet. Incense did not stop at the guarded entrance to the Chief's Mastaba where the public was directed to leave the concourse but instead marched to the entrance and announced, "I am Princess Incense bringing my son, Prince Ishmael, to meet the great Chief Kemet. Grant our entry and send a message to the queen that her daughter has returned with her son. You tarry, Go! Now!"

Ishmael had never heard his mother use such a tone of voice. *She could have destroyed Sarai any time she wished. She did not wish to. What game does she play?*

The guard was young but well-trained. "Wait while I ensure your entry will be satisfactory, my Princess." He quickly entered the Mastaba to consult with the ranking priest.

The priest hurriedly rushed out to inspect this person demanding entrance, recognized the princess, bowed in recognition, and said, "Princess Incense, Chief Kemet will be delighted to see you plus you bring another member of his family for him to meet. How wonderful. I will send a messenger to inform our queen of your arrival."

Ishmael observed the postures, voices, and relationships carefully. He subconsciously began mimicking his mother's carriage and voice all the while seeing, for the first time, the chamber of a man deified and being cared for in case he returned from the land of the dead. He was overwhelmed with new and shifting knowledge. *My mother commands high-ranking people as if they were slaves. These are strange people. I am far from Hebron. Am I worthy to even be standing here?*

In the back of his mind, he heard, *Confidence!*

In a while, a courier returned with the message, "You and your son are to be entertained in the Osiris Mastaba until sundown. Then you will walk the Great Concourse and be officially received by the Pharaoh and the queen in front of the citizens of Memphis. Your Mother rejoices with your return." He handed Incense and Ishmael royal cloaks to wear when they were greeted.

Ishmael inspected the cloak. *This is the finest thing that I have ever seen.*

He handed the cloak back to the courier with the words, "I am who I am. I need no cloak to disguise who I am." He paused for a moment, thought, and added, "You will thank Queen Hetephe for her generosity, but I wish her to see me plain."

The courier was frozen with indecision.

Incense asked, "Do you not understand the command, Courier?"

The courier replied, "Yes, Princess. Immediately Prince," and hurried off with the rejected robe.

Ishmael thought, *This place suits me!*

They were escorted through the back corridors to the second level of the eight-level Mastaba where they were met by two Mastaba priestesses.

The older priestess said to Incense, "Welcome home, Princess Incense. I will escort you to visit Osiris."

The younger priestess said to Ishmael, "I am Maribah, a priestess to Osiris. I will take you and introduce you to our beloved Osiris."

Three moved to continue on.

One stood frozen in place. He thought, *She is the most beautiful creature I have ever seen. More beautiful than the dunes under a full moon. Her skin is darker than the desert night, itself. She will bear my son!*

Ishmael said to the priestess, "You will bear me a son. He will found a great tribe in the vast wilderness desert. I will name him Nebaioth. When the time is right, I shall come for you. We will celebrate the fullness of life and you will conceive our child!"

The priestess was momentarily without words. *What manner of man is this? Dressed as a commoner and addressing a Priestess of Osiris in such a familiar— extremely familiar—manner. How shall I handle this gross impropriety!*

She coolly replied, "I shall consult with Lord Osiris. If this is his will, then it shall be done. If not, then no. Follow me. I will introduce you."

Both Incense and the older priestess silently approved of the exchange

Ishmael happily followed behind the three. *She did not hesitate. She was extremely confident. She is not like the sheep. She is a person of consequence. She is going to bear my son!*

The visitation went well. Osiris is said to have been pleased.

REUNION

The sun set.

The people gathered.

The ceremonial attendants came forth on the Great Concourse.

At the top of the well-lit concourse appeared Princess Incense, eighteen years gone from the kingdom. Beside her, her son—Ishmael, Prince of Egypt. Wearing a common man's clothes.

The drums began

The Princess and her son began their march to the entrance of the concourse.

The Pharaoh and the Queen appeared at the concourse entrance and the hundred-voice chorus began singing the love song of Isis and Osiris.

The crowd was breathless with the glory of it.

The two arrived to be introduced to the Pharaoh. All proper words, gestures, and protocols were perfectly performed. The Pharaoh turned without acknowledging anyone and began his journey back toward the palace. Queen Hetephe turned to the crowd and enthusiastically acknowledged them with waves and gestures. The people melted into love, cheers, and shouts.

Incense and Ishmael followed the queen into the palace.

Once inside, the Pharaoh and the queen faced each other and held out their arms. Attendants rushed to remove their royal clothing and dress them in simple, but fine, tunics. Once dressed, they turned to face their prodigal daughter and their grandson.

Hetephe threw out her arms and rushed, in tears, to embrace her daughter.

Djoser strolled over to Ishmael, staring at him the entire time. He held out his arms and said, "Welcome, Ishmael. I believe you will prosper here. Before we have even met, you attempted to seduce a priestess, and your choice of a common man's clothes to greet the Pharaoh thrills every Egyptian witnessing your arrival. Your attire brings me even closer to my people. I am well pleased."

The two women stood embracing, crying, both talking at the same time, catching up on many years apart.

Ishmael said to Djoser, "I am unlearned. I arrogantly thought I knew everything. Father Abram taught me all that he knew of God and gods and good and evil and Horus and the sheep and those who control them. I now see that I know nothing. I do not wish to bring shame to my mother. I will dedicate my life to becoming worthy of being her son."

"Do you drink wine?"

"No, Pharaoh Djoser. I have never tasted it."

Djoser laughed, "Well, follow me back to Osiris's. We will sit at his table, and I will introduce you to the gift that Osiris, once named Dionysus, gave the people of the world. It is either a blessing or a curse, you know. What is the name of the priestess you are going to seduce? Maribah? She is your grandmother's great-niece, I think. I will see that she is our attendant while we drink wine and tell each other of our great conquests. Call me Grandfather when I'm not dressed in power."

The two men left the two women.

Hetephe stared appreciatively after them. She then looked at Incense and said, "You did well, Daughter. If he is not Abram's heir, he will have an even greater destiny. Now tell me of it. His conception. His birth. His childhood. Why you come without his father. Every word."

The women spent the rest of the evening being women.

The men, men.

ISHMAEL'S EDUCATION

Ishmael began the rigid educational process of a child of the court: diction, speaking, reading and writing in five languages, healing potions and herbs, battlefield surgery, astronomy, mathematics, diplomacy, warfare strategies and tactics, agriculture, history, religious studies, and much more.

Maribah was high-born Nubian. Nubian's adored and excelled at archery. Ishmael took up archery. He excelled.

But at each full moon, Ishmael returned to the great desert to spend days under the open sky of his beautiful desert. He spent this time reviewing all that he had learned, how it related to him, and how he could apply the information. He searched for water and kept detailed notes on areas with the highest potential of supplying sufficient water for a possible city. Now, instead of imagining Hebron suddenly transported to the desert, he began imagining Memphis being transported there. *How many wells? How many cisterns? How much irrigation and where?*

Cities tended to form on the water's edge or high in mountains or on fertile plains or along rivers. Of the great civilizations, none prospered in the magnificent, endless sands of a desert.

How sad, thought Ishmael. *How can this be?*

Phoenicia, Jaffa, Rocky, Burlyman, Polydore | Astarte, T'jaru
Terah, Amathlai, Haran, Terahson, Nahor, Sarai, Isaac, Jacob
Kyrios-Olon, Teumessian, Nimrod, Nimbal, Nimlad, Nimisis, Asherah, Set.

~~~~~~~~~~~~~

17. Ishmael—Prince of Egypt

Year 185

A year passed.

He and his mother grew closer.

Ishmael was an eager, able student who soaked up all the knowledge to which he was exposed. He could assume the dialect of any of the noble countries. He could read and write the Byblos scripts fluently. He was an expert archer and was the country's leading authority on the nature of the Sinai Desert and how to prosper there.

He had been introduced to the House of Ishtar and had become the house favorite. The original courtesans had long since gone on to even greater careers, but the House continued to maintain the highest standards and most accomplished courtesans in Egypt—that is to say, the world. He had considered trying to become involved with Maribah, but Ishmael did not *try* things—he *did* things, and he wasn't at all sure that Maribah was doable at this time. He would wait until she could not refuse him. Patience was not his strong point, but success was.

He met God Set's son, Anubis, with whom he had a common interest in the House of Ishtar, and, as it turned out, the Redlands. Anubis had followed his father through all the deserts as Set had built his following so that Set would be considered a living god. Anubis had extensive knowledge and experience with deserts. Despite the age difference, they became good friends.

As a Prince of Egypt, Ishmael traveled the Nomes learning the people. He always inquired if anyone would be interested in living in a great walled garden city in the eastern desert. The response was mostly laughter, but he took note of those who did not laugh. He traveled to Ogdoad City where a dozen men expressed interest. As children, many had been nomadic people living in the great desert of the Sinai. Ogdoad City was a wonderful place but the desert still beckoned them. Ishmael recorded these things.

He and his grandfather held many discussions on the politics of nations and how to best utilize their resources. So it was that on the night of a full moon, the two slipped to the top level of the eight-level Mastaba and sat looking out over Egypt. The lights in the firmament excited Ishmael. The sky was not as impressive as in the desert, but it was impressive enough.

Djoser, Hetephe, Incense/Hagar/Keterah
Horus, Serket, Azazil, Abram, Baalat
Ishmael, Maribah, Fatimah, Nebaioth, Basemath, Kedar | Anath, Astarte
~~~~~~~~~~~~~

Ishmael said, "Father taught me that there is only one god but you are a god and some call Lord Horus a god and Mother said that she called on many gods when she gave me birth. What do you think about gods?"

"There are no gods, Ishmael. I assumed the title to give me power. Horus is not a god and would be upset if you called him one. My stepson has dedicated his life to understanding death, the dead, and the gods. He insists that consciousness continues after death and is caught up in some kind of group consciousness he refers to as 'The One.' I suppose you could call that God if you wanted to. Otherwise, the concept of gods is a device by which powerful men control less powerful men."

"Your stepson? Who is that?"

"Why, Horus."

"LIVING GOD HORUS IS YOUR STEP-SON?"

"Yes. You must meet him. He hasn't been to Memphis in many years—too many. I will send word to him that he must attend this year's Winter Solstice Festival. He has been remiss in not meeting the son of his student to check on how things are working out."

"But I *have* met Lord Horus—long ago when I was a child. I had better refresh myself with his teachings. I don't want to appear uneducated in front of your stepson." *There is so much to learn. It will take me a long time to know everything there is to know. Grandfather is commanding the greatest Shaman who has ever lived to come and talk to me. Life is good.*

A TIME OF REFLECTION

Year 185, Season 12, Isismonth

The palace, Mastabas, city, and villages were decorated with greenery and red berries. Families visited, rejoicing and reviewing their actions during the previous year, a time of quiet reflective togetherness.

Horus arrived in Memphis and stood under the Sycamore Fig tree staring at his father's Mastaba. *So many years ago, Father. So many years.*

He then went to the House of Nephthys. It was not a Mastaba, but it could well have been. The priests had prepared her for the afterlife. Self-appointed South Memphis women attended her every need—such as they were. The women were overjoyed with the appearance of Horus on the porch for they knew that Nephthys, herself, would be overjoyed to be visited by her son. He looked at her lifeless body. *I was not here when you died.*

I am told that Serket held your head. How many ways can a man fail so many people at one time? I am sorry, Mother. I am sorry, Serket. I am sorry, Father. I am sorry.

He went to the Mastaba of his father. He was escorted to Hathor—the High-Priestess. They stood staring at one another.

"Hello, Mother."

"My son will not embrace me?"

He ran to her and she took him into her arms.

He wept.

~~~

It was required—the welcoming ceremony—for the people of Egypt.

The people held Horus in only a little less regard than the Pharaoh himself. If the truth were known, perhaps more so. This was Horus, son of Isis and Osiris, teacher of the way of Horus—the way of Kiya, known and respected in every land with followers throughout the known world. Horus! Anointer of Pharaohs! The great Shaman Horus who some called a Living God.

The drums beat. The voices sang. Horus walked the Grand Concourse.

Ishmael was allowed to stand beside Princess Incense who stood behind her mother. He watched wide-eyed as Horus strode the concourse with supreme confidence to greet Pharaoh Djoser. Here strode a man who knew pomp and grandeur as well as Djoser. He was born of pomp and grandeur. Horus was thinking, *Forgive me, my fathers and mothers. I could not save the people. I could not teach them the way.*

The two men greeted one another and stood talking to allow the crowd to erupt with emotion. Spectacle was required for a well-run kingdom. This was Spectacle.

Then Djoser regally escorted Horus to the palace. The queen, princess, and prince followed. The women gaily waved to the masses.

~~~

Djoser and Hetephe were changed from their ceremonial robes into practical dress.

Djoser held out his arms to Horus who came and embraced him.

"You have been away too long, my son."

Djoser, Hetephe, Incense/Hagar/Keterah
Horus, Serket, Azazil, Abram, Baalat
Ishmael, Maribah, Fatimah, Nebaioth, Basemath, Kedar | Anath, Astarte

The family talked of family and worldly things well into the evening.

After dining, Djoser and Horus returned to the Osiris Mastaba to visit Osiris and then sit at his table and discuss deeper subjects. Ishmael was allowed to follow, but he knew his place in this trio.

Maribah was one of the several attendants. She held eye contact with Ishmael but did not engage him.

Djoser asked, "Where does your quest stand?"

"I was with Set when he died. Set's priest insists that Set died and returned to life just to speak to me. If this was a devious scheme on Set's part, then he took the concept Osiris insisted upon and spun it into a tale of immense proportions as only Set could do. He would do this in order to finally defeat me in a contesting. Such a thing would be a fitting end to Set's life. If, on the other hand, Set actually died and returned from the dead, then …"

"Then you have discovered the land of the dead."

"Yes. But the knowledge is strangely unfulfilling. It's as if we should be born knowing it; live knowing it; rejoice in knowing it. Every person would love every person. The strongest men would always reach down to pick up the weakest men. Every man would respect every woman. No one would inflict unnecessary pain on any living creature. There would only be hunger if there was no food left anywhere in the world. We would worship no gods because we are the very god we would worship. The most powerful would work to raise up the weakest. Whatever asked for would be given. We would treat everyone and everything the way we would want to be treated. Yet everywhere I look, I see so little of this. My followers believe these things and teach these things and live these things, and yet everywhere I look …" His voice trailed off.

The attendants stepped forward to refresh their wine.

"Did you record Set's words?"

"Yes. The parchment is in my quarters."

"I would like to read it. You plan on putting it in the Chest of Tallstone, I suppose."

"Yes. Father would want that."

"Yes, he would. Perhaps we could all take it there after the season ends. Have a little ceremony of some kind. I could have security arrange something. This is strong knowledge. When you teach these words to the people, how do they receive it?"

"I don't teach it. Only Abram knows of Set's words."

Ishmael gasped. *Abram! My father! Only my father knows the secrets of the dead that Horus knows! My father!!!*

Djoser frowned. "You don't teach it? Why is this? Surely the people deserve to know!"

Horus explained why he would not teach it.

Djoser asked, "And Ishmael, what do you think of these matters?"

Maribah glanced at Ishmael with sudden interest in her eyes.

Ishmael froze. *Father said to never let them see you unsure. Answer questions without wavering. What you say matters less than how you say it. Be confident.*

He began. "The people are sheep. They need shepherds to tell them what to think. No person appreciates the riches they have; they always want more. Such is their nature. Lord Horus wishes to change the nature of men, but he withholds the knowledge that might change it. I have always thought my father was a fool. Now I see he is only following the path Lord Horus taught him."

Maribah froze. *The prince just called Lord Horus a fool. He spoke to Horus in a disrespectful manner and my Pharaoh heard. Prince, if you are fortunate, they will damn you to the depths of Tartarus without torturing you too much!*

But Horus laughed and responded, "Well said, Prince Ishmael. Well thought out! You have identified my problem. You would make a fine addition to the Kyrios-Olon. I can give you a recommendation if you like." He held out his wine glass in salute to Ishmael.

Ishmael was close to soiling himself but kept his face stoic and merely nodded in recognition. *Kyrios-Olon?*

Maribah had just heard more information than an assistant priestess should hear. She scurried off to find her superiors. They would want to know. *Ishmael should be thrashed for his insolence! He certainly needs it! He is so arrogant! So self-assured!*

Djoser said, "I wish to read the words of Set. Deliver the parchment to me. I will be in the Land of the Dead soon enough. I should prepare."

He rose and left them.

Djoser, Hetephe, Incense/Hagar/Keterah

Horus, Serket, Azazil, Abram, Baalat

Ishmael, Maribah, Fatimah, Nebaioth, Basemath, Kedar | Anath, Astarte

~~~

The days of reflection brought forth the night of the Winter Solstice.

As always, Hathor felt the weight of the world upon her. If she did not perform her duties correctly, Osiris might not rise higher into the sky the next day and the world would plunge forever into darkness; a world without the love of Osiris shining down upon it. Once, in the privacy of her quarters, she vomited with fear of it.

This sunrise was no different but, as always, once the drum sounded and she stepped forward with arms extended, Hathor became what she was—the High-Priestess of Osiris—the most confident and powerful person in the world. Upon her command, he always rose higher.

Horus admired her performance from the Sycamore tree near the river behind the gathered crowd. *Are you worthy of all this spectacle, Father? Bastard son of a self-appointed god. Wasn't your only glory in life inventing wine? Did you ever do any more than that? But I haven't invented anything near the wonder of wine. If you placed the significance of your life into your only begotten son doing something significant, well, then … let there be wine!*

The ceremony ended. He no longer wept.

He had no tears left to cry.

Phoenicia, Jaffa, Rocky, Burlyman, Polydore | Astarte, T'jaru
Terah, Amathlai, Haran, Terahson, Nahor, Sarai, Isaac, Jacob
Kyrios-Olon, Teumessian, Nimrod, Nimbal, Nimlad, Nimisis, Asherah, Set.
~~~

~~~~~~~~~~~~

18. The Seduction of Maribah

Year 186, Season 1, Osirismonth

Osiris rose higher!

The week of celebration and abandonment began.

Ishmael was allowed to attend the yearly afternoon reception hosted by Hathor and the priestesses for the high-born of Egypt. This was the only time that the masses could witness the Pharaoh behaving as a normal king rather than a god. This was a calculated risk on Djoser's part, but the gathered masses seemed to revel in witnessing that he might indeed be "one of them."

And the masses were gathered to watch this spectacle. They had brought their own wine and food which everyone shared with everyone else. This was a time of camaraderie, brotherhood, and revelry.

Ishmael watched Maribah and positioned himself on the path she would take when she returned to refresh the platter of food she was serving. She stepped through the door; he grabbed her by her shoulders and butt, pulled her to him, and kissed her forcefully full on her lips. She was momentarily stunned but then pushed back and slapped him across the face as hard as she could.

With blood-red cheek, he stared at her, grinned, and said, "It was worth that and a thousand more! I will trade another kiss for another slap!"

She stormed off to refill her platter.

~~~

That night, Ishmael cuddled his favorite courtesan and said, "I understand what a man gets out of this. What does a woman get?

Through much giggling, protests, patronization, and lies, the courtesan was finally seduced into providing a man with a woman's secret knowledge. It began with, "There are parts of a woman's body men do not know about," and went on from there.

Ishmael tested this new information. At morning light, he stared with self-satisfaction, at his courtesan almost passed out from pleasure.

He lay back and held her in his arms. *Maribah! Soon I shall come for you!*

Djoser, Hetephe, Incense/Hagar/Keterah
Horus, Serket, Azazil, Abram, Baalat
Ishmael, Maribah, Fatimah, Nebaioth, Basemath, Kedar | Anath, Astarte

FIRST MOTHER

Hetephe, with her man-mustache and ill-fitting clothes, led the bedraggled pilgrims into the presence of First Mother.

They were met by the Chief of the Site who offered them refreshments. Although this was a working quarry, travelers, especially Nubians, especially Nubian Women, would often stop to visit and gaze in wonder at the carving of First Mother. The Site Chief was always gracious.

The pilgrims either admired or stood in awe of the carving for a long time. Finally, Hetephe said to the site chief, "Now we would like to enter the sanctuary and visit the Ark."

This, unfortunately, could not be allowed. "The Ark is off-limits to travelers by order of Osiris, himself."

Hetephe said, "I understand, but come, let me show you something."

She led the Site Chief into the darkness under the head, removed her mustache and ill-fitting clothes, and stood before him in an elegant, purple-trimmed tunic. She said, "I am Hetephe, Queen of Egypt. I bring Pharaoh Djoser and Horus, son of Isis and Osiris. I bring their friends. You will never speak of this to any man or woman. You will grant us entrance to the Chest of Tallstone. You tarry! Go. Take us to the Ark."

The man was site chief because he was smart. He did the smart thing.

They were led into the Chambers between First Mother's feet. Lamps were lit. The cavern filled with light. Djoser fell to his knees. There, he told the story, to himself as much as to those gathered, of transporting the ark from Tallstone to the Obelisk Mastaba and then to this resting place— First Mother. The reference and wonder in Djoser's voice permeated into those around him. The Site Chief nervously shifted his feet as if he were not supposed to be hearing such intimate stories of the gods. Ishmael listened with increasing respect to such men as these. Including, he supposed, his father Abram.

Djoser finished with, "We have come to add to the wisdom of our kind."

Horus stepped forward and, as commanded by Djoser, told First Mother —or Osiris—or Kiya—and whoever might happen to be listening—the story of the words of The Tree-of-Life, "The One, The All" as told to God Set who was once called Lord Charon. He ended with, "I place these words into the ancient Chest of Tallstone. May our ancestors be pleased. May our children prosper."

With that, he opened the chest and placed the Papyrus into it. He closed the chest. A murmur of contentment passed through the room.

The Site Chief excitedly said, "I wager that the Crocodile Clan Truth-teller would love to be here right now." He stopped himself, remembering that he was among the most elite Egypt had ever produced.

Hetephe was quick to ask, "Crocodile Tribe? Truth-teller? Who are they? Why are they interested?"

The Site Chief had stepped into it. He was now the center of attention of what may as well have been the gods themselves. He stammered, "Th-they are nomads from the western Redlands. Th-they camp nearby every Summer Solstice and always pay their respects to First Mother. I hear that their Truth-teller had heard that an artifact from Tallstone had been placed between her legs and that the Truth-teller was upset when she wasn't allowed to see it, but she never asked me, so I don't know if it's true or not. Just that they camp near here every year and some of the women come and sit and stare at first mother for days at a time and sometimes they chant things."

Hetephe was full-blooded Nubian as was, supposedly, First Mother. All Nubians held First Mother in high regard and there appeared to be new knowledge here. *Crocodile Clan? Truth-teller? Why would such people be so interested in First Mother?*

She said, "Husband, send emissaries to find this clan. Have them bring this Truth-teller person to you to tell of her interest in this matter."

Horus said, "I have a better suggestion. I and Prince Ishmael shall grant them entry into First Mother."

So it was arranged that in six months hence, at Summer Solstice, Horus and Ishmael would sit under the imposing head of First Mother at the gate to the Chest of Tallstone. There to wait for the Truth-teller. There to grant her entry into the chamber of the ark in exchange for Truth.

CITIES AND DESERTS

Year 186, Seasons 1-6

Ishmael had returned to Memphis with the excitement of having been given an important role in an important meeting. He sought Anubis to share his excitement and found him at Hostess House extolling the hardship of being responsible for the initiation of new courtesans into the House of Ishtar. "It was my father's duty back in his day, but the responsibility fell to me as his son. God Set has since journeyed to the Land of the Dead. I escorted him there."

Ishmael had joined the group, ordered a beer, and listened in.

Anubis accepted all of the "Ahh, that's too bad," and "Well, somebody has got to do it!" He then leaned back and welcomed Ishmael.

Ishmael inquired into the fact that Anubis was the son of Lord Set of Urfa. After much discussion and explanation, Ishmael asked, "But, why weren't you invited to take God Set's words to be added to the Ark of Tallstone?"

"I *was* invited. Horus was insistent that I go. But that would have displeased my father. My father was jealous of Horus beyond telling. He would not even travel the Way of Horus. If there had been a southern road across the Sinai, I would have returned my father's body first to South Memphis and then to Tartarus by escorting it through the great deserts where my father was so revered. But the only road was the Way of Horus, so I took his body by sea from Byblos. I found Oceanids willing to sail with me. We anchored over the remains of Tartarus and the Oceanids guided my Father's body to rest on the top floor of the House of Gods that Father had built. I think I did what he would have wanted."

Ishmael listened to every word, but he replied, "A southern road across the Sinai?!"

"Well, any road but the Way of Horace would have worked, I suppose. But we often complained to one another during our desert travels how much easier it would have been with a road of some kind. Faster, keeping our bearings, those sorts of things. You are a student of the Redlands, what do you think?"

Ishmael was transported to a new world. His world. A world of cities in the deserts. His cities.

Eventually, he asked, "Would the Pharaoh fund such a road?"

"Djoser became Pharaoh because he invested in Egypt's future. Convince him of the value of such a road and that you can build it. He will fund it."

"I will give Mother heirs beyond number. It shall be my revenge."

"What are you talking about?"

"Cities. Cities in the desert. Twelve cities. One for each of my sons. I must prepare for them"

"You've had too much beer, boy. You need to slow down."

Phoenicia, Jaffa, Rocky, Burlyman, Polydore | Astarte, T'jaru
Terah, Amathlai, Haran, Terahson, Nahor, Sarai, Isaac, Jacob
Kyrios-Olon, Teumessian, Nimrod, Nimbal, Nimlad, Nimisis, Asherah, Set.

Ishmael leaned back in his chair and signaled for another beer. *I will build a walled city. I shall name it Shur. It will be in the exact middle of the Sinai desert on a southern road. One gate will lead to Memphis, the other to Hebron. A third shall lead south into the heart of the desert. I will raise my children there. As each becomes a man, I will build him a city. Another glorious city in the deserts of The One God.*

Ishmael then guided Anubis into talking about the deserts. He listened with half his mind and planned with the other half.

After thanking Anubis for an informative afternoon, he went to the quarters of his mother. There he asked again of why she had been given as a handmaiden to Sarai, why she had lain with Abram, what had been expected of all of this. Incense answered with the plain and sometimes hard truth of the way of the powerful; good and not good.

Ishmael was pleased.

The next day he went to the City Builders and requested a meeting. Receiving it, he proposed a project requiring significant resources from the kingdom. The builders were always searching for projects requiring significant resources that the Pharaoh might approve. They were delighted to discuss his vision of a southern trade route through the Sinai with a major city in the center.

Ishmael was pleased.

The day after, he found and boarded a barge on its way up the great river which would dock at Ogdoad City. He recruited those who were willing to build a new paradise in the desert.

He led builders across the river into the Sinai desert where they traveled to a high plateau near the center of the great desert, near the foothills of mountains with a spectacular view. Water runoff was available from the mountains; the water table was accessible for wells and irrigation; it was cool, even cold, at night; there were many wild animals and birds both permanent and migrating. In his mind, Ishmael saw the fruit trees already growing—apples, pears, apricots, peaches, dates, grapes. Nut trees— almonds, mulberry. Crops of barley, wheat, and corn. Gardens built on the wadi floors surrounded by massive walls to retain the soil and protect against animals. The placement of the wells. Seeing all these things in his mind, he walked to where the location of his fortress would be, sat down, and looked out approvingly at the location. He said, "Very well, builders of great Egyptian structures, what must be done to build me a city here?"

They took their notes, they made their plans, they designed a permanent city in the middle of the great Sinai desert. Then they took their plans to the Pharaoh.

~~~

Djoser looked at their plans. He asked his chief builder, "So you think it's possible to build a permanent settlement in the middle of the desert?"

The builder replied, "It has never been done before, my Pharaoh. The desert supports the Bedouins well enough. Prince Ishmael has convinced us a permanent settlement would not only survive, but thrive. His plans are sound. He has the will to try. We can lay a basic road without a great deal of expense. If he prospers, we can invest in the upgrades and complete a road into the Rusalem area which would relieve a lot of pressure on the northern trade route. If he fails to build a viable city, you still get a working road to support your mining efforts in the area. At worst, he fails. At best he succeeds spectacularly."

Djoser looked at Ishmael, "This will require at least ten years of your life and probably your entire life. You aren't old enough to know what you want to be doing next quartermoon!"

Ishmael glared at Djoser, "I shall build a city in the desert for each of my twelve sons. Their wives will be women of the highest order. My children will be educated in all the arts. My mother will be the grandmother of nations. This shall be done!"

Djoser stared at Ishmael. "I see. Then bring me one of these sons of yours." He motioned that this meeting was concluded.

As Ishmael and the builders left, Ishmael told the chief builder, "Priestesses gather gossip like spiders gather flies around a lantern. Let slip the nature of this meeting. Let slip the name Maribah was mentioned as the mother of my first son. Let slip the Pharaoh waits to meet my first son before he decides on the fate of my cities!"

Ishmael waited a week before he found his way to the Mastaba of Osiris. His pretext was to sit at Osiris's table with Anubis, drink wine, and plan great deeds. Neither he nor Anubis had on-demand access to the Mastaba patio, but because they were both accomplished in appearing regal for the masses who would certainly be watching them and they were both Egyptian high-born, access was usually granted. So, they sat looking out over the expanse to the great river, seeing and being seen, and discussing great cities in the desert. And, at Ishmael's request, Anubis had requested
~~~

the service of the young priestess—Maribah—who was assigned to stand in the background and tend to the needs of those on the patio. Ishmael did not attempt to engage her in conversation but talked loudly enough about his vision that she could accidentally hear the conversation including the infinite prestige his first son would receive if only he could find a woman worthy of bearing his first son.

But finally, being two worldly men, the conversation turned to a more earthy subject. The joyful act of impregnating a woman.

Anubis loudly told of the time he and a modest high-born woman of the court sneaked to the top of the eight-level Mastaba with a flask. Well actually, two flasks, of wine. "The view was magnificent. We could see everything, but no one could see us or any of the things we did. The combination of wine and view intoxicated her. She abandoned all pretense of modesty. We had a magnificent frolic!"

Ishmael replied, "If I ever have such a frolic, I will leave the story untold. It is between the man and the woman. Thank you for meeting me here, Lord Anubis. I can see the future clearly, now."

"Best of fortune with your project, Prince Ishmael. It will be a great and lasting benefit to Egypt." Anubis rose, nodded toward Maribah with thanks, and left.

Ishmael rose with him, but walked to the patio ledge, looked out over the crowd, and raised both his arms toward them. The crowd was jubilant at the acknowledgment by a prince. All that saw, waved back and shouted joyful salutations.

Ishmael then turned and walked back to the wall of the Mastaba where Maribah stood. He said, "Gain access to the rooftop for us tomorrow night. I will bring the wine."

"Very well. But I will get the wine from High-Priestess Hathor. It will be much better. And we will not meet tomorrow night, we will meet under a full moon. I must drink the potion that ensures my baby is a male."

"As you command, Priestess Maribah. I will return under the full moon and when your evening duties are complete, we shall make a child. I rejoice in our union." He turned to go.

She added, "And thank *you*, Prince Ishmael, for not asking me to tell you how masterfully you seduced me. That would have been a sign of needy male ego."

He turned to look at her. "You and I have no need for the admiration of others. We will rejoice with the company of one another under the fullness of the moon, Priestess Maribah." He turned again and left her.

She watched him depart. *Will our son be mighty? Will I abandon all modesty?*

~~~

The next night, the view was wonderful. The wine, excellent. Modesty, abandoned.

~~~

Summer solstice approached.

The excitement of traveling with Horus at Summer Solstice had worn away and was replaced with excitement of Maribah's pregnancy. The concept was overpowering in his mind. *I placed my seed into Mari! She is growing our son inside her body. She is providing the nourishment for my seed to become a human being! The seed of a man delivered into the wonder of a woman's body. Great Osiris, or One God, or whatever you are, bless the woman for, through her body, she brings forth life! Let her do well!*

Horus was adamant, however, that Ishmael travel with him to First Mother. "You are a scribe accomplished in writing the old words. You are the first son of my student, Abram. The words we hear may be of importance to our history. You *are* going with me as my scribe. You did your part! Maribah will continue to grow your son in your absence."

But until he must leave with Horus, Ishmael went every day to visit Maribah. She grew tired of his incessant touching of her abdomen. She refused all offers of becoming his official concubine, even discussions of becoming his wife. "I will give you a son to build your cities. You will give me a daughter to become a High-Priestess. I don't want some title interfering with my life!"

Also, every day, Ishmael worked on the design of the city of Shur and planned for the resources he would need. The Pharaoh had neither approved nor indicated that he would financially support this endeavor, but Ishmael fully intended to present his son to Djoser and if approval was not granted, Ishmael would rain fire from the sky until approval was given.

And, as he felt Maribah's body grow, he also discussed what resources she would need to raise their son into a feared and respected chief of a great desert city. "What kind of quarters will we need? What teachers and trainers will we need?"

She tolerated his "too-much" attention because she had been impregnated by every woman's dream, and she was not about to compromise his devotion to her and their child. *He is determined to raise a son of great power and worth. What more could a woman want from a man?*

However, when Ishmael inquired if they should lie together for the pleasure of it, he was informed that she could not become more pregnant than she already was but to ask her again after she had delivered their child to him. "I will present you with a son, then you will impregnate me with a daughter. This is equitable. We will take pleasure in it then."

~~~

Horus, in the meantime, sought all knowledge concerning First Mother, but there was simply nothing more to know than the legends from antiquity.

As the day of departure approached, Queen Hetephe told Horus that she would travel with them. She would not interfere, but if there was something to be learned about First Mother, the queen certainly should know of it; she was a Nubian Princess, after all.

Horus, Ishmael, Hetephe—with her mustache and loose garments, and a small support staff—set off for First Mother the day before Summer Solstice. They made camp away from the monument but with a view of who came and went. Soon, the Site Chief alerted them that the Clan of the Crocodile had set up camp over the horizon.

The next morning, well before sunrise, Horus and Ishmael took their position in front of the door into the chamber containing the Ark of Tallstone. At sunrise, the chief of the Clan of the Crocodile led his tribe in single file around the First Mother site three times and then marched back to their campsite. But three older women left the procession and marched down the ramp to stand in front of the monolith. They saw Horus and Ishmael and then sat on the ground to consider them.

Finally, one woman stood and approached the two men. "Are you the guardian of the Ark?"

"I am."

"We wish to enter First Mother and see that which she protects and nurtures."

"I wish to know who created First Mother and why!"
~~~

The woman turned, walked back to her tribeswomen, and sat. They discussed the exchange for a long time. Then, the three rose and walked to Horus and Ishmael. A woman asked, "Who are you to wish to know the creation of First Mother?"

"I am Horus, Son of Dionysus, who brought the Ark from Tallstone to Memphis. This is Ishmael, grandson of Djoser, who moved the Ark from Memphis to the protection of First Mother."

"You must never speak aloud the words of a Truth-teller. Your telling would change a word. Each retelling would change more words until no truth remained."

"Ishmael will record the words exactly as spoken. These words will be left in the Ark. The words will be only read and never spoken aloud."

The oldest woman considered, nodded, and said, "That is satisfactory."

The women were shown inside. There was much discussion, explanation, and questions but after all was said and settled, Ishmael recorded the words of the Truth Teller.

She recited, "The tribe of our great Chief Eazim-Rayiys encountered a tribe in the far south. They called themselves the 'People of Nubia.' Goods and women were traded, and stories were told. Chief Eazim-Rayiys told the story of his great Scout Mustakshaf who had traveled all lands and seen all things. In the far northeast, Mustakshaf found the strangest tribe he had ever encountered. The tribe did not move but stayed in the same camp. Their tents were permanent and did not move. Stranger still, their chief was a woman who did not command. The woman had learned to make plants grow wherever she wished them to grow. Her people were castaways from other tribes. The men no longer hunted but built things of wood and mud."

She continued her story at length and finished with, "The Nubian men were accomplished carvers of wood and bone. They had been told of the huge outcrop of rock in the northern Red Lands. They requested to be shown this outcrop so that they could carve the head of this woman into the stone. So it was, that they carved the head of the most impressive woman they could imagine into the stone. This is the truth of the creation of First Mother, I so swear."

The woman stopped her narrative and then asked, "So now we ask, when will her work be finished?"

Horus, still processing what he had just heard, responded, "'Her work finished?' What do you mean?"

"First Mother has protected and nurtured this ark. When will the ark be released to its destiny?"

Horus had no answer. "The Ark will stay here forever."

The woman replied, "That is not fit. First Mother releases her children into the world to stand tall and do great deeds. The Ark must be given its freedom to become meaningful. It must be allowed to climb great heights —to teach all people—to find its own destiny. Ma'at is not served until this comes to pass."

Horus stared at the woman, "You are correct, Elder Woman. Ma'at must be served. I will think about this thing. You are as wise as you are beautiful. We will place your words into our Ark with our other Truths."

They stared at one another for a long time, then the Truth-teller turned and left with her assistants.

Horus and Ishmael were left standing in silence and in thought.

After the women had departed, Hetephe found her way into the chamber. Horus handed her the parchment. She read, "The reader of these words may read but upon their honor, will not repeat the contents to any person." She somberly finished reading the parchment. She said, "The Ark is from Tallstone. First Mother depicts a woman from Urfa. Ma'at is heavy in this place."

Horus looked at Ishmael, who was eager to get back to Maribah, and asked, "This means nothing to you, does it, Prince Ishmael?"

Ishmael snapped from his daydream and truthfully answered, "Nothing. Nothing at all."

Horus walked alone from the chamber. *Here it ends. I have failed. Abram is not my heir nor is his son. The Kyrios-Olon will succeed. The world will be a world of sheep. The path of Kiya will end. My carcass will be the one rotting at the end of the path. I do not ask for forgiveness. There is none!*

Everyone returned to Memphis except Horus, who went on to Newport. *I have been too long from Azazil and our followers. With them, I can at least pretend to be saving the people.*

~~~~~~~~~~~~~

19. Vignettes

Year 186, Seasons 6-9

SONG OF THE OCEANIDS

Word of Polydore's immigration to Byblos to assist in the building of the greatest port in the world spread throughout the Oceanid community. Several Oceanids came to observe and join in the festivities. The several grew until almost all of the world's remaining Oceanids had set up residence in Byblos—or El's End as Oceanids called the city.

In gratitude for Polydore's contributions, Baalat built the Oceanids a private dock in a secluded bay north of Byblos connected to the main docks with a pretty path. The dock had a party area and a wine flask that never seemed to empty. They could wear clothes or not, depending on their mood.

In the beginning, young, muscular, male attendants would arrive toward sunset to serve wine and perform whatever tasks the Oceanids requested. The old Oceanids found this pleasant and amusing, but not too much was required of the young men.

One evening, retired Admiral Maddog Burlyman appeared at the dock bringing two barrels of wine. As a man of the sea, Burlyman had a keen respect for the keepers of the sea. The demeanor of the Oceanids changed from laughing, giddy old women staring at young men's bodies to mature self-possessed worldly women in the presence of a man of consequence.

Polydore asked, "Would you join us for a glass of wine, Captain?"

Burlyman accepted. Stories of the old days were told. There was laughter. There were memories. There was Burlyman surrounded by fascinated Oceanids, the youngest of whose left strap had accidentally slid from her shoulder exposing much of her fit body. Burlyman kept stealing glances until he noticed the right strap, too, had accidentally slipped down. Burlyman, somewhat at ease with too much wine, asked the Oceanid if she would like to dance with him.

"I most certainly would, Captain Burlyman!" She stood and her tunic accidentally slipped entirely from her body.

The Oceanids began singing a nice little dance number. They sang several different songs throughout the night.
~~~~~~~~~~~~~

~ ~ ~

In the early morning, after the Captain had left them, Polydore exclaimed, "Let's all swim home together!"

The suggestion was met with unanimous enthusiasm.

The next day, Polydore secured a seaworthy barge and equipped it with good food, water, and wine.

After sunrise the next day, the Oceanids boarded the barge. Polydore bid farewell to their friends including Baalat and Burlyman, who turned away so they could not see his face.

They set sail to the location of the now submerged Port Spearpoint, once home of the mythical Oceanus—who had perhaps released the Great Flood upon the Olympians.

Arriving, they dropped anchor, drank wine, sang, and swam naked for three days. The next morning was beautiful with a clear sky and big fluffy clouds. Polydore looked at them with boundless love and said, "Let's go find our sisters!" They dove into the water to swim across Middlesea to Tartarus; there and along the way, they met Metis and all their Sisters.

The sea, with full voice at last, sang its song.

HORUS AND AZAZIL

"The Lady of Byblos IV" docked in Byblos. Standard procedures dictated that the captain inform Baalat of all important people on board.

Horus's mind was still full of his journey to Memphis along with the meeting of Ishmael and his experience at First Mother. He desperately needed Azazil to discuss these developments and for validation that Horus was doing the best he could. He found Azazil visiting with the Byblos "Way of Horus" priests.

Azazil and the priests were ecstatic to see their teacher safe and looking well after so long a time away.

Horus visited and allowed himself to take comfort in their praise. "You renew my spirit and give me hope. I have been away too long." He told them of his recent journey to Memphis save the part of First Mother which would best be discussed alone with Azazil.

A scribe from Port Byblos headquarters found them and said, "Lady Baalat would enjoy a visit from her esteemed teacher of old. She invites you to dine with her tonight. Will you accept her invitation?"

"Yes. I look forward to it. May I bring Shaman Azazil with me?"

"Of course. I will inform my Lady. Thank you, Lord Horus."

~~~

They arrived at the dock at sunset. They were escorted to Warehouse Six and taken to Baalat's private quarters on the third floor.

She greeted Horus with excitement. "My teacher. Welcome! You fed me great knowledge in my youth. I can only feed you the fruits of the sea and the vine in return. Forgive me!"

"There is nothing to forgive, Daughter. You walk a righteous path. I could not ask for more."

She glanced away as she muttered, "You could but you didn't." She looked back at him and continued, "But come and let me introduce you to my other dinner guests. These are our two expert traders—Taone and Tatwo. I believe you know the ship's captain—Captain Burlyman. They returned on the same ship as you and have been telling me all the Memphis gossip. Your name came up."

Fine wine was served as they stood in front of a panoramic view of the harbor. Baalat changed the subject to extol the excellence of her staff. "My business ventures excel because I can recruit the right people for a job and stay out of their way as they do it." They bantered awhile until it was time to be seated for dinner.

Baalat sat at the circular table with her back to the view so that Horus, sitting across from her, would have the full view. A Trader sat on either side of Horus and then Azazil. On one side of Baalat sat Burlyman, on the other side an empty chair.

Glasses were raised and compliments were given. Then Baalat said, "My distant ears tell me that Horus went to First Mother not once but twice. Is there potential profit—or loss—in that for Byblos?"

Horus was surprised, "That was not advertised. How does Baalat know of this?"

"Don't be silly, Teacher. The quarry men live and drink in Newport—a sailors town! How could I *not* hear of it?"

"I see no profit or loss to anyone. It was nothing more than a journey to pay respect to First Mother and the Ark of Tallstone."
~~~

"Is Pharaoh Djoser doing well? We have heard he may not be in good health but healthy enough to travel with you to the quarry—along with his beloved queen and some kind of prince."

"Your ears also have eyes. Eyes that see what they are not meant to see."

Baalat laughed. "Then let's talk of Byblos. Has Azazil told you that the Urfa Church is becoming a nuisance? Their teachings are creating discontent in my city, pitting men against women, husbands against wives, wealthy against poor, *your* teachings against *their* teachings. There have been three instances of men forcefully taking a woman against her will. There was no punishment because the men told the chief that the women had asked for it by the way they dressed."

Azazil said, "I have not told him the extent of it. Tomorrow will be soon enough to address these issues."

Baalat said, "I apologize. I appear to be raising subjects no one wishes to address. I would bring dancing girls to entertain us but the Church frowns upon dancing. Dancing women lead to impure thoughts."

Azazil said, "Lord Baalat, please don't bring unpleasant times to your delightful evening."

Horus interrupted with, "It is all right Azazil, I stayed in Canaan too long. It sounds as if Phoenicia suffers the same problems as Canaan."

Baalat interjected, "And Mesopotamia and Greece and soon enough Egypt!"

Horus repeated, "Greece? Egypt?"

Baalat answered, "Greece! It is unbelievable that such an educated, culturally advanced, critical-thinking country could fall under the false teachings of the Church of Urfa! Their philosophers talk of the benevolent glory of the Olympians and the horrible actions of the Titans. They ignore the writings of Kiya in favor of the dung spread by the Church of Urfa. They turn truth on its head and the people believe it. Many Oceanids came to Byblos when Polydore arrived here. Later, she called for all her sisters to join her here in Byblos. The remaining Oceanids came from all over the world. They swam, they sang, they danced, but most of all they talked. They exchanged stories of how their lands were changing and they refused to live in such a world! The empty chair beside me is empty because my friend, mentor, and champion is dead! They're all dead! They returned to the sea—with their pride—with their dignity—

with their attitude of love and nurturing among all people. Dead! My Polydore is dead!"

Horus said gently, "She lives. They all live. There is no death. Only life in union with all other things. 'The One, The All' is true. The Land of the Dead exists."

Azazil asked, "Osiris was correct? The Land of the Dead exists. How do you know this?"

Horus quietly said, "I will not tell you. The knowledge would force you to think of yourself as a god. You would behave as the gods behave. It would destroy you."

Azazil hissed, "When did truth become our enemy?! When did knowledge destroy us?! When did Horus become the gatekeeper between knowledge and ignorance?!"

Horus said, "I will not tell you."

Baalat interrupted as she said to Azazil, "Horus took some kind of parchment to place in the Ark of Tallstone. It will contain his proof. The Pharaoh will grant me access to it. If Horus will not teach it, then Azazil can teach it. Better civilization be destroyed by truth than ignorance."

She walked to Horus and took his hands into hers. "Teacher. You taught us well. It is time for you to accept this. Be at peace."

"Peace? I abandoned Serket a long time ago."

He thought he had no tears left to cry.

Azazil watched the sick, tender moment with fury and first-time pity. Tomorrow, he would meet with his priests. The time had come to plan for an uncertain future.

ABRAM AND SARAI

Sarai happily played with her toddler son, Isaac.

Abram approvingly said, "He grows strong, Wife. He will bring you joy."

Sarai had undergone a complete transformation after Abram had impregnated her. She still despised Hagar and her bastard son, but she grudgingly admitted that she was probably impregnated because of the potions Hagar had left for her. Sarai had won the battle and Sarai had won the war; Isaac would be Abram's heir. Abram had promised her. She was at last happy, and her hatred of Sarai diminished as time passed.

Abram was ecstatic. Sarai no longer badgered him and even, at times, lay with him with a semblance of joy and pleasure. He dedicated himself to building Hebron into a righteous city worshiping only the One True God —*his* god.

Urfa missionaries would visit him upon occasion just to catch up on how he was doing. As a courtesy to Abram, they did not preach their belief in many gods. They did, however, subtly point out how much happier a man was when he had a loving, caring, obeying wife, and how much better a man could make decisions than a woman—those kinds of things. "The people of Hebron want you to tell them what to do and what to think! It is your duty to guide them in these matters, Lord Abram."

Lord Abram seemed to remember that Horus had taught him that he was to teach people how to think for themselves and make their own decisions. That each person was different and should not be judged on their beliefs. He reconciled these philosophies as best he could, but always insisted upon teaching about the One True God. Admittedly, Asherah's Birthing Pole *had* helped during Isaac's birth. The women of Hebron had noticed this and many had obtained their own "Asherah Pole." Not as an idol but just something to pray to when they wanted to get pregnant and give birth. Abram hardly noticed when Zedek set up a small church on the edge of Hebron.

An Egyptian sought out Lord Abram and was shown to Abram's house. Sarai answered the door.

The Egyptian introduced himself as a road surveyor from Memphis. "Is Lord Abram available?"

Sarai eyed the man with trepidation. "From Memphis? That's in Egypt, isn't it?"

Upon hearing, "Yes," she wanted to ask what business he had but that would be pushing the boundaries of being a good wife. She said, instead, "Yes. This way, if it pleases you."

Abram greeted the man and offered refreshments. The man sat down to talk. Sarai stood nearby listening. In case Abram needed anything.

"Lord Abram, I am surveying the land to build a road connecting Memphis to the western lands. A road to supplement the great Northern 'Way of Horus' Trade route. This road will be built through either Rusalem or Hebron. There are reasons for both routes. I am to ask your opinion on the matter."

"A trade route, you say? Hebron will be a wonderful stop along this route. We are more aggressive than Rusalem in developing our resources. Rusalem wishes to be left alone so they can live in peace. I wish to make Hebron a great city. Who will make this decision?"

"Pharaoh Djoser has not yet obligated himself to the project. He will decide when the time comes. I will have both routes mapped so he can make a wise decision."

Abram was excited about the prospect. "I am a student of the great Egyptian Shaman Horus. Horus is a personal friend of the pharaoh. Not that it matters, but still an asset for Hebron, I imagine."

"Yes, a strong asset, but this is already known. A prince of Egypt—Prince Ishmael—has stated that he prefers Hebron because of this."

Sarai's blood turned cold.

Abram said, "Ishmael is a prince of Egypt? I suppose I knew that, but I really didn't know if he and his mother had survived after they left here or not. It appears they did. How wonderful for them both. He is my first-born son, you know."

Old feelings rose in Sarai. *Isaac is your heir. Not that bastard son! I am your wife. Not that whore!*

The surveyor replied, "No, I didn't know, but that explains his desires. Prince Ishmael will build a city in the Sinai for his firstborn son. The City of Shur will be midway across the Sinai Desert. A road to Hebron would make it convenient for you to visit your son and grandchildren."

Sarai panicked. "Grandchildren? Ishmael has more than one son?!"

The surveyor, unaware of the impropriety of a woman speaking in front of men, laughed and said "I understand that the first one hasn't been born but the gossip is that the prince intends to have twelve sons and build a city in the desert for each. I hope so. That would generate endless work."

Neither man noticed Sarai trembling.

DJOSER AND HETEPHE

Princess Incense took the hidden corridors to her parents' chambers. She slipped in before the predawn light had broken. She stood staring at them sleeping in their bed, overcome with love for them. *Mother sleeps in the same bed as Father. Father never took another wife or even a concubine. They are each other's best counsel. Perhaps they really are some kind of Living Gods.*

Hetephe's eyes popped open as a mother knowing her child needed her. She glanced at Incense, then the sand clock, then the darkness, then her sleeping husband, then back at Incense. She slipped naked from under her sheet and put on her sleeping tunic thrown haphazardly to the floor. "Your father was inspired last night. At his age, I will take all the inspiration he can give me."

They walked to an adjoining room where Hetephe woke one of her attendants. "Breakfast for two. Perhaps a little fruit-wine for celebration." She looked at Incense and asked, "It will be a celebration, won't it?"

Incense happily nodded, "Yes."

They went to the dining area overlooking the Great River and sat.

The mother looked at the daughter and asked, "Do I have my first great-grandson?"

The daughter replied, "Yes. Ishmael's prophecy is fulfilled. His name is Nebaioth, and he looks just like his father only one shade darker. Ishmael wanted to introduce him to Father before the umbilical had even been cut. Maribah calmed him down. She was nursing Nebby when I left. She wants a priestess in the family and already set the date to be impregnated. Their daughter will be named Basemath in my honor. And Maribah has no intention of marrying Ishmael or being his concubine. She is a priestess committed to raising her two children with or without him—his choice. Mother and child are doing fine. Ishmael is being Ishmael."

The predawn light was beginning to show.

A third plate of food was served followed closely by Djoser walking in being steadied by two attendants. He sat and asked, "A healthy great-grandson?"

Incense answered, "Yes. Very healthy and loud. His Father's son. His name is Nebaioth."

Djoser replied, "Excellent. Unfortunately, I won't live long enough to name him Pharaoh. Do *you* want to be the next Pharaoh, Incense?

She laughed. "No. I will be busy directing various women on how to raise my grandchildren. Besides, I don't have the equipment necessary for Hathor to blow godhood into me. You should have given me a brother. Boys care more about the appearance of power than girls. What about Ishmael?"

"I have considered Ishmael a great deal, but General Sanakhte or even General Khaba would be a better choice. They are high-born and have spent their lives developing the necessary skills. Khaba may be self-centered but he *is* intelligent, dedicated, thorough, and cares for our people. Ishmael is more intelligent, less wise, and more dedicated, but only to his own projects, and doesn't care enough for his people to wave at them from his platforms. Although, they would all thoroughly enjoy, as did I, having Hathor blow godhood into them."

Hetephe slapped him on his shoulder with, "Pig! All men are pigs!"

Djoser could only oink.

Incense stared at the two with love.

NIMROD, ASTARTE, T'JARU

Nimrod was upset, as he usually was. Dyoares had commanded Nimrod to become High-Priest of the Church of Urfa. Nims were not supposed to do actual work. That was for the lower classes.

Nimrod had tried to recruit T'jaru for the job but T'jaru was black, and the church was preaching for white people to distrust black people. That, plus T'jaru had laughed in his face. "Your people preach dung, Nimrod. That's why I'm here. I'm trying to undo all the filth you have created. Are you insane? Why don't you join me and teach people to think for themselves? You might like it!"

Astarte was more accommodating. "I would love to be your High-Priestess. I'm quite accomplished with showing love!"

Nimrod gracefully pointed out that they needed a man, not a woman, to replace El as High-Priest.

"Well, if you change your mind, I would love to try out for it."

Nimrod had done well with his position. He had opened a school for young children to train them—that is brainwash them—into the teachings of the church. Missionaries had been told to bring back children from each of their assignments. They brought back castoffs and firstborns of pious families along with kidnapped children. The school grew nicely. The boys would make wonderful missionaries. The girls would be used for other things.

He was pleased with his progress in Byblos. It was slow but incremental.

Mesopotamia was going even better. The missionaries did not have to be subtle. T'jaru and Astarte would show up and undo some of the work of his missionaries, but the Church had many missionaries. The evil Horus followers had only two people of significance. Time was on his side.

He was surprised at how quickly Greek cities entered the fold. *Greeks have an affinity for the Olympian gods. Who knows why? But they do.*

The Kyrios-Olon had promoted a bright missionary to become a Nim and had sent him to Egypt to make friends with a high-level official named Khaba. Nimlad was instructed, "Don't mention religion; just trading opportunities you would have access to. You have contacts all over the world. Explain how you would be of service to Khaba and could help him to be named Pharaoh."

Nimrod was training more and more missionaries and sending them farther and farther into the world. *People are predisposed to be sheep. I's easier to love people like yourself and hate those not like you than it is to love everyone regardless of their beliefs. All those teachings of Horus sound noble but you don't get anything out of it. You're doing for others; not for yourself. That's stupid and the people know it. Horus and his people simply don't understand. That, plus it's much easier to be told what to do and think than decide for yourself. The people like it. The Nims like it. The Dyo's love it. It is the natural order of things.*

AZAZIL

Baalat had booked Azazil passage to Newport. From Newport, he went to the quarry over which First Mother watched.

The Site Chief refused Azazil entry into the chambers containing the Ark.

Azazil produced a letter from "The Lady of Byblos" requesting her emissary be granted every courtesy at the site. The Chief still refused.

Azazil produced a second letter that read in part, "If my gracious request is not graciously granted, then I shall personally call upon the Pharaoh and request that your manhood be removed and be hung upon a post for all to see and that I am the one to do it with a dull blade and happy heart."

The site chief read the second letter and said, "This way, Lord Azazil. May I get you food and drink?"

The Lady of Byblos was a persuasive woman.

~~~~~~~~~~~~

20. Mari's Children

Year 187 – Year 190, Season 12, Isismonth

YEAR 187, SEASON 12

The season of celebration had begun. Families gathered to review their year and pray that Hathor could revive Osiris when the Solstice arrived.

Incense held Nebby on her lap and gossiped with Priestess Maribah and Queen Hetephe.

Mari said to Incense, "That son of yours is insatiable. He has been insisting that I pleasure him yet again."

Incense: "You only lay with him one time, Mari. He deserves more of your time."

Mari: "He impregnated me. What more does he want? He has those Ishtar women and half the priestesses infatuated with him. He gets more pleasure than Anubis. I am busy being Priestess and raising his son."

Hete: "Mari, don't you ever, you know, get interested in laying with a man?"

Mari: "What for? I mean, I want to when I need to get pregnant."

Hete: "Did you enjoy the night you got pregnant?"

Mari: "Very much. The view was magnificent, the wine superb, and I felt much closer to Osiris; being up high and that close to his—obelisk. It was a grand time to get pregnant."

Hete: "You are dedicated to being a priestess, aren't you, Mari?"

Mari: "It is my life! Other than raising strong children, of course. But I am ready to pleasure Ishmael again. He promised me a daughter, you know. I will train her to be the best priestess since High-Priestess Hathor. When the time comes, perhaps she will be considered as her replacement. I can only dream."

Incense: "When have you scheduled your next impregnation, Mari?"

Mari: "The night after High-Priestess Hathor calls for Osiris to rise higher in the sky. She will succeed. I know she will because she is the best priestess ever. She has already told me that I can use the roof, again, and she will give me some Aphrodite wine for good fortune. I'm getting excited thinking about it. I hope it happens on the first try."

Hete: "Oh, Mari. Do it three or four times, just to make sure."

Mari: "Do you think so? I suppose it wouldn't hurt since we are already naked. I may just do that!"
~~~~~~~~~~~~

Incense: "Tell Ishmael that you want him to do it at least four times. Just the thought will inspire him to perform his mightiest!"
Mari: "I will do it! Anything to get me a daughter!

YEAR 188, SEASON 12

A year passed and another season of celebration had begun. Families gathered to review their year and to pray that Hathor could revive Osiris for yet another year.

Incense held Kedar on her lap and gossiped with Priestess Maribah and Queen Hetephe.

Nebby toddled wildly across the floor.

Mari said to Incense, "That son of yours tricked me. We had agreed that his second child would be a girl, but he overpowered my potions. I have already begun drinking my 'baby girl' potion and I'll not let him do it five times, again! I will get my baby girl!"
Hete: "Keddy looks just like Nebby except he has our skin tone, but they are both going to be strong like their father. I hope he grows to love archery like I do. You could not ask for better children, Mari. Are you sure you don't want to marry him? He wants *you* to be the mother of his children; not some random woman."
Mari: "I don't think so. But I can decide this time next year after I get my little priestess."

YEAR 189, SEASON 12

A year passed and another season of celebration had begun. Families gathered to review their year and to pray that Hathor could revive Osiris for yet another year.

Incense held Basemath on her lap and gossiped with Priestess Maribah and Queen Hetephe.

Nebby ran wild with Keddy toddling across the floor after him.

Mari said to Incense, "High-Priestess Hathor has made me an offer."
Hete: "Oh?"
Mari: "Yes. I will be allowed to move to Ishmael's city with him to raise his family *if* I will build a temple for Osiris and be its senior priestess *plus* I can be High-Priestess to any other gods I wish. She feels that this would be an opportunity for me to gain experience and become even more valuable in Memphis if and when I return *plus* I can raise little Basemath as a priestess. What do you think Mother Incense? Will you

leave the palace and come with us to that Osiris-forsaken Shur with your son and grandchildren?"

Incense: "How wonderful, Mari. Yes! The palace is so constricting and predictable. We can all blossom like desert flowers in Shur. It will be a grand experience for you and your children! When do we leave?"

Mari: "After Ishmael impregnates me during his little yearly pleasure ritual. He loves doing it up there on the roof for some reason. Anyway, the builders want two more months to finish up, so Ishmael is planning on moving in Setmonth."

Hete: "No. Ishtarmonth will be better! I will have Djoser command the builders to make the city perfect! Tell Ishmael to postpone your move for one month."

Mari: "I will suggest it, but Ishmael usually ignores suggestions."

Hete: "It is not a suggestion, Mari. The Queen commands it!"

YEAR 190, SEASON 12

A year passed and another season of celebration had begun. Families gathered to review their year and to pray that Hathor could revive Osiris for yet another year.

In the city of Shur, Incense held the babe, Adbeel, and watched with quiet pride as Ishmael chased his two older sons across the lush courtyard in wild abandon. She glanced at her "honorary" daughter-in-law holding the hand of her toddler daughter as the two watched the three males being "boys." Both Mari and Basemath wore their Priestess robes and adornments. Their community contained less than a hundred residents, but it was still important for the religious leaders to be seen by the people so that the people would be comforted and confident in the coming week until Osiris once again climbed higher into the sky and the fruits of the earth would be assured.

In the meantime, Mari and Basemath's temple was festively decorated with greenery and red berries. She performed a daily sunrise ceremony and planned for the Winter's Solstice ceremony to be memorable. High-Priestess Hathor had sent a senior priestess to help with—and observe—Mari's first big ceremony.

Bedouins routinely passed through Shur, refilling their water supplies in exchange for livestock.

Eight caravans had already passed through the city on the way from Rusalem to Memphis and back. The traders were amazed to find such an oasis as this in the middle of the Sinai. Three families immigrated from outside Rusalem to join this delightful little community in the middle of the desert. They were followers of Asherah and Anath and politely asked Mari if they could erect little idols for them in her temple.

As they watched the males, Mari said to Incense, "Ishmael is angry with me because I will not permit him to take Addy with him and the boys into the wilderness on a camping trip. Addy can barely sit up by himself. I don't know what the man is thinking!"

"They seldom think, Mari. They just do. It is their nature, I'm afraid."

"I suppose so, but Ishmael has been so demanding of my time since we moved here. He complains that I am the only woman available for him to lay with and he wants to impregnate me with another son. My duties at the temple suffer and Bassimy isn't old enough to help. I'm so afraid that High-Priestess Hathor will think I'm doing a terrible job. You are already helping me raise his four children and he wants to add another one! I need two of me, as it is."

"Perhaps you or Ishmael could take a wife. They would solve all your problems."

"A wife? But he wants me to bear his children."

"That's because you are the finest incubator he can get. Challenge his male ego to find a better incubator to have his babies. You don't want to marry. You have your little priestess. You have done your duty. Marry him off and devote your time to your work. Everyone will be happy."

"Would I have to lay with him if he gets married?"

Incense laughed. "Probably not, sweet Mari. Probably not."

~~~~~~~~~~~~

21. Ishmael's Marriage

Year 190, Season 4, Zeusmonth

The innocent young thing was the first-born child of a powerful Bedouin Chief and always astutely studied his trading technique. Although she was of age, she had never lain with a man—well, no man of consequence, anyway—and, even then, she didn't let him do anything that would get her pregnant.

She was intelligent, ambitious, and Bedouin-sophisticated. She had once traveled to a coastal city and saw the wonders of people who stayed in one place and did not travel the wilderness. She was infatuated with the city even though she was a Bedouin "princess."

On this day, Fatimah sat beside her father as he explained the finer techniques of trading. "Find out their marital status as quickly as you can —how many wives they have, how many they are allowed, what about concubines. A man's relation with women is powerful knowledge."

She saw the man and the two children approaching their camp well before her father did. *He is young, tall, and strong but he has children, Still, his wife does not appear to be with him. Perhaps there is some learning to be had.*

The man entered the camp with confidence and smiles and the attitude of "I am somebody. Don't mess with me." Her heart skipped a beat. *Dung! Where is his wife? Wives?*

She slipped into her natural unobtrusive camouflage of "all sweetness" personae as the wanderer joined her father for refreshments. The chief began his undetectable probing of, "Is there profit to be had here?"

Fatimah listened with double interest; to her father's gentle inquiry techniques, wondering, *How much trouble could I get into with him? Would the learning be worth the risk? I suppose to be with this man is worth the risk! Perhaps he can take more than one wife!*

The chief said, "Your sons are already boys to be reckoned with. Is your wife far behind?"

The world stopped. The stars fell from their courses. The future wrapped itself around Fatimah as a mother's love wraps itself around her newborn.

The man replied, "I have no wife."
~~~~~~~~~~~~

~~~

And in Shur, Incense sat outside her home watching Addy play. Nebby and Keddy were with their father exploring the great sand dunes in the south. Bassimy was in the Temple with her Priestess mother.

The small caravan stopped at Ishmael's house.

Incense saw the tall man speak to the man in the wagon pulled by the two donkeys. She recognized both. She rose and folded her hands in front of herself. *How shall I greet you, Abram? Will you even speak to me? Am I to be mad or happy or furious or imperial or cold? How shall we meet, my love?*

The tall man walked to the front door and knocked.

Incense stared at him with amusement.

There being no answer, the tall man turned and walked back to the cart for further instructions.

Incense silently watched.

The tall man nodded and walked to address Incense. "Excuse me, Lady. We come to visit the house of Ishmael. Do you know when his wife will return to receive us?"

"You are funny, Master Eliezer, but we do not play silly games here. You know full well who I am. Bring your Lord and come into our home. I will find someone to take care of your donkeys while I introduce Abram to his grandson. Come!"

"I'm afraid his wife must first grant us the hospitality of Ishmael's house before we can accept his hospitality."

She laughed. "Stay here, Eliezer. I will visit Abram." She took Keddy's hand, and walked to the wagon containing.

Arriving, she said, "Hello, Abram. This is your grandson, Kedar. Our son is in the desert teaching his two older sons the ways of the desert and won't return for at least two sunsets. Will you come in and visit with me."

She saw his face contort. "Ishmael needs a different threshold for his home. I swore to Sarai that if his wife did not properly receive me, I would return without getting out of the wagon. I expect you to understand."

"I don't understand in the least, Abram. But no matter. I will tell Ishmael that you still remember him. It would please him if you and Eliezer toured his city to see what he is creating for his son. We are proud of it and hope
~~~

you will be, too. Perhaps speak to Adbeel and then go to the temple to meet the mother of his children and his daughter."

"He is not married?"

"No. Maribah is a priestess dedicated to her profession."

"A Horpriestess with bastard children worshiping a false god?!"

"She lays with no man but Ishmael but, yes, call them that, if you wish."

"Then you admit I was correct in naming Isaac my heir and not Ishmael!"

She laughed. "I never denied it, Abram. You had every right to name Isaac instead of your bastard son."

"He is not a bastard! He is our son, and you were my …"

"Your what, Sweet? I was your what?"

"Sarai wanted you to."

"And I did. So where are we now?"

He lamented, "Nothing became what I wished it to become but I must not complain. I have fallen away from the teachings of Horus. The only thing I hold fast to is there are no gods but God. Now I find that Ishmael lays with an idolater and you have turned against me."

"Turned against you, Abram? Sarai told you to drive me and our child into a vast desert, probably to die, and you did! Turned against you, Abram? Come to my bedroom, Abram. I will turn against you. You will be pleased, but I doubt that Sarai will be. Choose what kind of life you want, Abram. Return to the way of Horus or become … whatever it is you will become."

"I must go, Hagar. I'm sorry, but I must go!"

"My name is Incense!"

Abram did not look at her. He called Eliezer, "Take us back to Hebron."

Incense watched them depart. *You could have saved civilization, sweet Abram. But you are too self-righteous.*

DECISION TIME

Year 190, Season 6, Aresmonth

Ishmael and his son returned from their adventure, not in two days, but in two quartermoons; on the second day of Aresmonth. Incense greeted them with cool drinks and dates.

She said, "I will watch the boys while you visit Mari."

"Thank you, Mother. But I found a Bedouin tribe with a friendly maiden of great worth. I can leave Mari to her peace for now."

"Is the maiden worthy to become your wife?"

"You and Mari conspire against me! I don't want a wife. I just want sons!"

"You are a witless male, Ishmael! Find a wife! Mari is beginning to show her pregnancy. I have told her to bear you no more children and that she should never lie with you again! Do as you will with that information!"

"My mother is angry with me. Is everything all right?"

"Your father came to visit while you were away. He would not get out of his wagon because you 'had the wrong threshold!'"

"What?"

"That was his obtuse way of saying that he won't come to see you until you have an obedient wife to obediently greet him at the door and obediently slobber over him as she invites him in."

"Oh, Sarai still controls him."

"Yes, she does. That he ever sired a son such as you, is unbelievable."

"Very well. The daughter of the Bedouin chief I met was young, beautiful, and so sweet that bees flew by just to smell her. I wanted to grow wings and spread them over us to protect her from the evils of the world. Her name is Fatimah, and her sweet innocence makes me feel good about myself. I will talk to Mari and get her opinion on me marrying this woman. Mari deserves a say in this, and I trust her judgment."

"You might also ask Fatimah."

Ishmael finished his drink and set off to find Maribah.

Maribah was surprised when Ishmael began happily talking about his excursion into the desert rather than trying to get her naked.

"The boys and I just kept traveling deeper and deeper into the desert. Much farther than we had ever been before. It was glorious. We found a place where Nebby says he is going to build his city. He told me that Keddy could have Shur. And nearby we came across a Bedouin tribe. There was this maiden …"

Mari's heart jumped. *Maiden?!*

She exclaimed, "Did she pleasure you?! Did you like her?!

"Well, yes. All of that. And a lot of it. Are you upset?"

She jumped up and embraced him, "You *will* make her your wife, won't you?! Then I could dedicate myself to being a priestess. Go get her right now! I will arrange your marriage. Mother Incense will want to help. How exciting! Go! Go on! Get her. I want to meet her! This is so exciting! I will get to perform my first wedding ceremony!"

THE BRIDE OF ISHMAEL

Year 190, Season 9, Anathmonth

The city of Shur grew to prominence overnight. After all, The Pharaoh and his Queen did not travel to just any city. It had to be a city of importance.

High-Priestess Hathor lost one of her few disagreements with Djoser. She wanted the wedding to be held in Memphis; he, in the city of his grandson.

The builders had planned for large transient events, but this wedding would have pushed the infrastructure of Memphis itself. Everyone would be there. Memphis Highborn, Nubian Highborn, Living Gods, representatives from Hebron, Port Jaffa, Damascus, from Byblos, Bedouin tribes from the south, and uninvited, several Nims from Urfa.

Luckily for all, the mother of the groom had been planning for this event most of her life and the mother of the groom had resources. Also, the mother of the groom fell in love with her sweet, innocent soon-to-be daughter-in-law as did the groom's incubator priestess.

With solicitous graciousness, Fatimah demurely welcomed her soon-to-be father-in-law, Abram, into the home of her soon-to-be husband, lord, and master.

She sat with wide-eyed infatuation as Living God Horus explained the Way of Kiya to her and her family.

She sat with great solemnity as High-Priestess Hathor and her assistant priestess, Maribah, extolled the virtues of greeting the sun each morning on its way to become Ra, the Living Sun.

Baalat met and treated her as an equal.

Fatimah disappeared with Astarte, Anath, and Asherah to discuss only Osiris knew what.

Finally, with great poise and confidence, she was introduced to the grandparents of her soon-to-be husband—the Pharaoh and Queen Hetephe. Hetephe thought, *Husband, if not Pharaoh Ismael, then perhaps Pharaoh Fatima.*

Fatimah was born to it. She was, after all, a Bedouin Princess.

OLD FRIENDS GATHER

The marriage ceremony was spectacular!

That night, after the sun had set, Horus, Baalat, and Abram, followed by Azazil, escaped the festivities to find a secluded place to meet in the wilderness close to the foot of the mountain.

Baalat spread a blanket for them to sit on and drink wine. She was happy, confident, outgoing, and awash with the joy of living. The men—not so much.

Baalat said, "My wonderful teacher appears to be worn down by too much life. I'm sorry, Lord Horus. I would help you if I could, but I can't. You, too, Abram. You should not have married that woman. She ruined you."

Abram replied, "Sarai is a good woman. She just couldn't have children for a long time. But she respects and obeys me."

"Respect and obey! Is that what you said, Abram? You think Sarai respects you? I don't think so. And 'obey' requires an unequal, subservient power structure. That's what those Urfa priests constantly preach. It only results in men disrespecting women. And that's why you're so unhappy, my once-friend. You need a wife that *respects* you; not *obeys* you. But do as you will."

Horus ignored the bickering. He asked, "Are the Urfa priests converting more people?"

Baalat answered, "'Influencing' is a better word. The people aren't conscious of what's happening to them at all. And, yes. Slowly. Surely. I have had to replace my dock restaurant servers with men. Low-born sailors called for my women with 'hey bitch,' 'bring me a beer, split-tail,' and 'get your butt over here, woman.' It infected the speech of even the once-respectful Greek sailors. It feeds on itself. It becomes the normal attitude. Polydore told me what was happening back when I was Horus's student. I didn't believe her, but now it is upon me. Upon all women."

Abram raised his voice. "That's not fair, Baalat! A woman is only happy when she has a loving husband and children to raise. That's her purpose in life. And her husband will take care of her. She must be pure when she marries so that she can't compare her husband with other men."

She thought, *Only a man would turn an act of affection into combat.*

She said, "Sweet Abram! You *do* realize when a thing interests a woman, they do it better than a man. Nurturing, growing, and friendship are what interests most women; not power and competing and killing and that distraction that pops up between your legs. You're funny, Abram. Most men are funny—and simple! No wonder they have to show their power over women by calling them derogatory names!"

"You're mad because I wouldn't plow you that time in the woods! You never found a man to plow you and you're blaming me! You're a whore!' Abram threw his wine on the ground and stood up to leave."

Horus quietly said, "Sit down, Abram."

Abram sat back down.

Horus asked, "Is this where my teachings led you, Abram?"

"I know there are no gods but God! I know that my first son's whore has a temple full of false idols and that my second son married a virtuous obedient woman!"

Baalat said to Horus, "Lord Horus, you need to add '*Respect* Women' to your teachings.' That would solve a lot of problems. Your 'Love Everyone' teaching can get twisted out of recognition when it comes to men's attitudes toward women."

Horus said, "Respect should be obvious, Baalat."

Abram broke in, "It is obvious. I respect women. Women just need to be obedient!"

Baalat sighed and said, "There you have it, Teacher."

A feminine voice from the darkness said, "I heard someone mention my profession."

Baalat and Horus rose immediately, faced the voice, and bowed.

Baalat said, "Great Queen Hetephe. Excuse our words. We were discussing things no gentle woman's ears should hear."

"We whores like to keep up with what's being said about us. We demand total respect, as you know."

Abram rose to acknowledge Hetephe and her companion. "Great Queen, you are known to be a loving and caring wife. You bring greatness to the house of your husband."

"Lord Abram, I believe I overheard some words about my grandson's whore and her temple. Whatever were you saying?"

"Great Queen Hetephe, the mother of Ishmael's children is not a proper woman. She did not greet me at Ishmael's house when I came to visit. She is an unmarried woman issuing bastard children. Ishmael took my advice and has married a proper woman who will be a proper wife. I can now forgive him for his improper behavior, so no harm is done."

In the light of the bright desert moon, Hetephe looked at Horus and asked, "Is this your former student, Horus? His words are not the words I would expect to hear."

Horus answered, "Lord Abram was raised in the city of Urfa, my Queen. He returned to their church after leaving me. His words are taught by the Church of Urfa and accepted by both men and women in their church."

Hetephe replied, "I see. Well, I shall introduce my good friend and sister whore, Priestess Maribah." She motioned to Maribah to speak.

Maribah stepped forward and said, "Good evening on this joyous occasion of the marriage of Ishmael and Fatimah. I greet you all with friendship."

Abram stared at her then took a step back. "You are the priestess of the temple of false gods?! You allow your children to worship false gods! You must repent and destroy your false idols! There are no gods but God!"

Maribah replied, "I will be happy to place your god in the temple for all to pay their respects to, Lord Abram. You are, after all, my children's grandfather."

"No! I do not accept your bastard children. They were conceived as you fornicated in unrighteous lust with my son. You are not pure. You are not a pious woman. You should be stoned to death. Do not come near me lest I cast the first stone."

Maribah held up her hand for silence. "I don't want to be stoned to death. I will return to the safety of my temple. Everyone is invited to seek peace in the House of Osiris. I shall personally greet each of you if you choose to come. Good evening."

Djoser, Hetephe, Incense/Hagar/Keterah
Horus, Serket, Azazil, Abram, Baalat
Ishmael, Maribah, Fatimah, Nebaioth, Basemath, Kedar | Anath, Astarte

She turned and walked away.

Hetephe said, "I'm afraid my little surprise visit didn't work out as I thought it would. Good evening, everyone."

She turned and hurried to join her friend.

Baalat said, "I have been commanded to love everyone, Abram. I must love you. But I am not commanded to respect you."

Abram stared at her in self-righteous fury, and said, "Now that both my sons have loving, obedient wives, my house is in proper order. I am a righteous man." He turned and walked into the night.

Baalat watched Abram disappear, then rose, gently kissed Horus on his cheek, said, "I'm sorry," and turned to walk back to the festivities.

Arriving, Baalat silently eased into the company surrounding Ishmael and Fatimah.

Everyone watched as Nubian maidens performed their fertility dance. Fatimah laughed and clapped in rhythm with the drummers.

After they were finished, she told her new husband, "A desert girl's parts are not connected like a Nubian girl's parts. Will you be disappointed when I cannot dance like that for you tonight?"

Ishmael laughed. "The welcome dance of a desert maiden is burned into my mind. It is a dance designed to entrap any man they dance for, and I am trapped."

"I shall perform it for you tonight, properly, and with desert-heated love, Husband." She leaned against him.

He put his arm around her.

Baalat listened and watched the couple with quiet pride. *They are bonded. Like Djoser and Hetephe. Not out of others' expectations or demands. Each respects the other. I don't foresee any "obey" from Fatimah. She will obey him when it fits their needs. He will obey her when it fits their needs. She is as much the whore as any of us. But she is not, and will never be, his slave. Poor Abram, you will never understand.*

Fatimah acknowledged her with, "Lord Baalat, you disappeared. Our Queen set off to find you."

"I was rejoicing with Lord Horus and your new Father-in-Law. Abram is so thrilled that you are joining his family. He is full of pride."

"Oh, yes. A wise woman will always find out the expectations of her husband's parents. I have learned the best I can but perhaps we can meet after this madness is over and I can learn even more. Father Abram's wife did not come to our wedding. There must be a story my husband does not share, and you have no husband, Lord Baalat. But this is my wedding night! All should be happiness! Dance with me, Husband. I will dance the desert maiden's greeting dance!" She pulled the protesting Ishmael to the center of the room and began her sensuous belly dance. A Nubian dancer ran to Ishmael and taught him the proper Nubian response.

Baalat thought, *Yes, Desert Princess, there are stories there.*

LIFE GOES ON

The morning after the wedding ceremony, life resumed its pace.

Djoser and Hetephe had been given their own room in the temple but now sat with Incense as their grandchildren played underfoot.

Priestess Maribah scurried around her temple greeting morning visitors and ensuring all went as it should.

Abram and Eliezer were on their way back to Hebron wrapped in deep self-satisfaction.

Baalat and her group were on their way to Port Jaffa to book passage back to Byblos.

Horus sat on a blanket in a secluded place in the wilderness close to the foot of the mountain absentmindedly twirling an empty wine cup.

Mostly naked, in her sleeping room, with her new husband, Fatimah feverishly practiced a Nubian fertility dance.

~~~

That evening, a contented Fatimah and exhausted Ishmael returned to Maribah's temple to eat their evening meal with their family. The Pharaoh, queen, and company would depart for Memphis immediately after the coming sunrise ceremony. But this evening, Fatimah would be welcomed into the hearts of her new family.

Fatimah, Incense, and Hetephe gratuitously inspected Maribah's growing belly, clucking at what a fine son was growing inside.

Maribah's toddlers climbed over Fatimah learning what kind of woman their new mother would be.
~~~

Ishmael and Djoser sat together drinking wine and beer proudly watching the women and children be women and children. Djoser lamented that he was aging and must soon select a successor and how Incense did not want the responsibility and how Ishmael did not fully embrace all the lands of Egypt and how Horus would not be a good pharaoh and what did Ishmael think of General Sanakhte and General Khaba.

"From what I've seen, Sanakhte is older than Egypt, and Khaba's nothing but a stiff-penny—self-absorbed, self-adoring. Knows what to do if it brings him glory. You aren't considering them for Pharaoh, are you?"

"Who would you suggest?"

"That High-Priestess woman. She would be a good one."

"Hathor would consider becoming Pharaoh as beneath her."

"Maybe that Baalat woman from that seaport up north."

"Baalat? An excellent suggestion. I'll consider her. But Nubia prefers a man over a woman and they like Khaba. They see him as a strong leader— which he is if it serves his interests."

"It's best if you don't die."

"A most excellent suggestion. I will ask Hathor about that."

Suddenly, Nebby raised his arms above his head and became a ferocious, frightening bear that rushed toward his grandfather. Keddy imitated his brother as best a toddler could and, with raised arms, toddled behind.

Bassimy, in priestess robe, watched her brothers with womanly disdain.

Djoser tried, but could not escape the onslaught of two frightening bears.

SUNRISE

Djoser watched as Maribah greeted Osiris with a ceremony of great beauty and majesty. *Are you impressed, old friend? You did not command this much respect when you were alive. Do you watch? Do you care?*

Horus and Azazil joined Djoser and Hetephe after the ceremony.

Horus asked Djoser, "Are you pleased, Father? Did you get everything you wanted?"

"Almost, Son. But not everything. Why don't you return to Egypt and live out your days in peace? Let Shaman Azazil continue your work. You have done all a person can do. Perhaps Serket would hear of it and join you."

"Azazil is going to Byblos to propose to Baalat that she build a Church to counter the Urfa missionaries. I violently disagree with him and Baalat will obey me; not Azazil. I want people to understand without a church telling them what to think. We will stop in Hebron to visit Abram and his son Isaac. I understand Isaac is even more pious than Abram. And Serket will continue to be where I am not."

Djoser listened to Horus talk of disheartening things and tried to peer into a future of cloud and haze.

As Djoser and Horus visited, Ishmael and Fatimah lay in their marriage bed doing married things—fighting off frightening bears as a small priestess sat on Ishmael's stomach watching her brothers with disdain.

Djoser, Hetephe, Incense/Hagar/Keterah
Horus, Serket, Azazil, Abram, Baalat
Ishmael, Maribah, Fatimah, Nebaioth, Basemath, Kedar | Anath, Astarte

~~~~~~~~~~~~~

22. Ishmael's Children

Year 202, Seasons 9, 10, Anathmonth, Nephthysmonth

Twelve years passed.

Ishmael had stumbled onto a ritual very much to his liking—after every Winter's Solstice, he would impregnate his woman. This worked well; it produced fine children whose birth anniversaries were easy to remember. They were all in Anathmonth.

Ishmael was the type man every woman wanted to father her children—attentive, protective, nurturing, patient—and powerful. Maribah and Fatimah were the best of friends and confidants. They had each other. Ishmael had his sons and the desert.

Maribah's children had grown into fine young adults. Nebaioth, 15, and Kedar, 14, strode the earth like their father—as if they owned the desert wastelands and endless dunes of sand. Nebaioth found desert maidens like Kedar's arrows found their marks. Basemath, 13, was consecrated as an official Assistant Priestess of Osiris. Adbeel, 12, had taken an interest in his Father's city of Shur. He continually insisted to anyone who would listen that this would become *his* city.

Fatimah's children still grew toward adulthood. Mibsam, 12, named in honor of Incense, grew toward manhood as did her other eight sons.

Shur grew into a major city servicing caravans crossing the unforgiving Sinai. Adbeel often stayed in the city rather than going with his father and brothers into the desert.

Each year, the wealth, power, and influence of Baalat grew.

Horus and Azazil grew more distant. Azazil honored Horus's wishes to withhold critical information from the people knowing full well that Horus was wrong in his belief. The breach would someday come, and it would be catastrophic to their relationship.

Baalat was more sanguine than Azazil—"Let the baby cry!"

Each year, Hebron grew and Abram became more proper. Isaac was his son in full. Sarai was the righteous matron of a righteous land. Its people had the piousness of Urfa and believed in their own self-righteousness.

Each year, Djoser grew older.
~~~~~~~~~~~~~

THE SEDUCTION OF BASEMATH

Anathmonth came.

It was time for Ishmael's major expedition with his children into the vast wasteland east of the Waters of Aqaba. This was his Birth Anniversary gift to them. The adventure lasted two full seasons. Ishmael would have added a much-needed third season but the mothers would not hear of it. With the wisdom of a husband, he compromised.

One-year-olds were exempt from the expedition. Two-year-olds were not. Nebaioth, Kedar, and Adbeel helped the younger ones keep up. Basemath provided for their other needs. Six-year-old's were expected to take care of themselves.

Basemath and her two oldest brothers were close. The three shared the self-assured arrogance of their father mixed with the self-assured responsibility of their mother. Each knew what the other thought as they thought it. To invoke the wrath of one was to invoke the wrath of three.

Basemath knew that her older brother was always excited when he found a maiden who would lay with him. She was uneasy that he had important knowledge that she did not have and which she *should*. She did not have Kedar's skill with archery, but she was close to him with his intense sense of doing the right thing and protecting the weak.

The power, strength, and self-confidence of her older brothers had long attracted her in a way she could not explain. She knew they would protect her with their lives. She wanted to return that dedication—that affection. She wanted to be somehow closer to them but didn't know how. She shared her feelings with her two mothers. They both had replied in unison: "Basemath, don't you dare lay with your brothers!"

So it was, they strode the desert as if they owned it. Bedouins and caravans were tolerated, even encouraged, but there was no doubt in their minds who owned the land. Their territory expanded year by year.

Even Basemath felt the pride and the glory. Long ago, she had obtained special dispensation from Hathor to leave her duties in the Shur temple during Anathmonth and eventually Aphroditemonth with the requirement that Basemath perform a sunrise ceremony each morning no matter where she was. This would accomplish the long-term desires of Hathor and give Basemath extensive priestess practice.

They made camp in a wadi deep within the desert. As was their ritual, Nebaioth found the most promising source of water, Basemath planted Acacia Tree seeds, and Kedar arranged the surrounding area to give the seeds the best chance for survival.

Adbeel monitored Mishma as he practiced building a fire for cooking.

All sat around the fire telling stories.

Basemath was looking in the starlit darkness as the darkness moved. She tensed. Her two older brothers tensed. Kedar found his bow.

The darkness came toward them. It said, "I am Esau. I have meat to share. May I join your camp?"

All the males stood as the large, burly, red-faced, red-haired, hairy hunter came into clearer view. Basemath did not stand. She stared.

Nebaioth replied, "Friendly greetings, Esau. All are welcome to join the tribe of Ishmael. I am Nebaioth."

Each male introduced himself. Basemath didn't. She stared. *He is more powerful than my father. Look at him! He is a real man! Not pleasant to look at but he could protect me from anything!*

The men talked. No one noticed Basemath, still sitting by the fire—staring.

Finally, the two older brothers remembered their sister. They glanced at her. Nebaioth saw the look on her face. He knew it well. Dozens of maidens had looked upon him with that look. With head and eye motions, Nebaioth and Kedar discussed the situation. Kedar uneasily agreed.

Kedar said to Esau. I am an expert archer. I can hit an enemy hidden in darkness by hearing a scream of distress.

Esau nodded without knowing what had prompted that comment.

Nebaioth said, "This is our sister, Basemath. Basemath, will you entertain our new friend while we roast his gift?"

Basemath rose without breaking her stare. "Yes, Brother. I will. Come, Esau, let me show you where we planted the Arcadia seeds. It's so dark now, you may have to hold my hand to protect me."

She took his hand and led him into the darkness.

Kedar protectively called after, "Scream if you need help!"

Away from the fire, observing his children grow, Ishmael sat; feeling the mixed emotions of a father watching his children grow into a world much larger than they.

~~~

Basemath rose at first light to prepare for her sunrise service. She woke Mishma, the oldest boy who had not yet reached manhood, to restart the morning fire and warm their freshly roasted meat. Mishma kicked Dumah awake with, "Get up, fat-butt, help me!"

Ishmael already sat unobtrusively by the remains of the fire watching over his children and the dawning light.

Nebaioth rose next and inquired of Basemath, "Did things go well last night?"

"Yes. You no longer know things I don't."

"And …?"

"And … it was pleasant enough. Mother Mari was correct. I will not at all mind laying with a man when I need to become pregnant."

"I see. Get ready. Here comes the sun." Nebaioth coughed a loud cough; loud enough that all the boys awoke and ran toward Basemath. Esau groggily sat up to see what was going on.

Basemath raised her arms toward the east.

Esau thought, *Oh, No! She's a Priestess!*

Osiris burst forth between two mountain peaks.

<div style="text-align:center">MECCAH</div>

They broke camp. Nebaioth led them to the southeast toward the mountains.

He said to his brother and sister, who walked on either side of him, "Our new friend Esau came from this direction. Sister, did he ever mention where he is from?"

"Yes, Hebron. His mother doesn't like him so he stays away as much as he can. He hunts a lot. His mother favors his twin brother because he isn't red and ugly."

"Hebron. That's where Grandfather Abram lives. I sympathize with Esau. Grandfather Abram doesn't like *us*, either. 'Bastards,' I believe he calls us."
~~~

Kedar said, "Mother Mari tells me that I bit him on the ankle at Mother Fati's wedding. I suppose that didn't help."

Nebaioth said, "He is a long way from Hebron. Change places with him, Sister. Esau knows things that I need to know."

Basemath stopped and let her brothers pass by.

She stepped in beside Esau and said, "Great Hunter and manly Esau, my brother Nebaioth requests you join him at the head of our exploration, if it pleases you."

Esau was flustered. *She's smiling at me. Shouldn't we be formal so that nobody knows what we did last night? What if her father finds out? Is she a whore? What if my father finds out? What if Grandfather Abram finds out that I lay with a Priestess?!*

He said, "A-All right. I will go." He nervously hurried to the front.

Ishmael looked at his daughter and said, "It appears you may have had a good time last night."

Looking straight ahead, she noncommittally answered, "It was all right."

Esau joined Nebaioth and Kedar.

Nebaioth asked, "Hunter Esau. This is the direction you came from. It appears to be mountainous. Hard walking, I would guess. Do you think our young ones can keep up?"

Esau exhaled. *They don't know what we did. Basemath won't dare tell. Everything will be fine.*

He said, "I know these mountains really good. It's my favorite place in the world. There is a valley there. It's pretty and peaceful and full of trees and animals and things. It sounds just like the Land of Eden that my grandfather talks about. I know the passages through the mountains to get us there. I hope you like it."

Nebaioth was more interested in terrain and markers and distances than he was in Esau's grandfather's tales.

Kedar thought, *I wonder if his grandfather has teeth marks on his ankle.*

The progress was difficult. They stopped often to let the young ones rest. They made camp overlooking a vast beautiful wasteland with the Waters of Aqaba on the distant horizon. It was beautiful.

After all was quiet, and everyone sleeping soundly, she went to him.

Phoenicia, Jaffa, Rocky, Burlyman, Polydore | Astarte, T'jaru
Terah, Amathlai, Haran, Terahson, Nahor, Sarai, Isaac, Jacob
Kyrios-Olon, Teumessian, Nimrod, Nimbal, Nimlad, Nimisis, Asherah, Set.

SUNRISE

Basemath could not perform a proper sunrise ceremony because mountains blocked her view. Her Priestess mind whirled in thought. *What is proper here? At what moment do I greet Osiris?*

The proper answer would require deep, philosophical conversations with Mother Mari and perhaps even High-Priestess Hathor. But, as always, she would do what she thought was right at the time when she had to do it.

They hiked. They reached the top.

They looked into a valley of makkah—a serene sanctuary encouraging quiet contemplation of one's life—of one's ancestors—of one's god.

Basemath stared at the makkah with religious intensity. *Perhaps this is where Osiris lives when he is not shining above us.*

She could sense her oldest brother trembling, her next brother staring in awe, and her father in disbelief.

Esau was babbling, "… favorite valley … so pretty … I'm not ugly here … at peace … grandfather's god … hope … love … Father Isaac will not come … and on and on …"

Even the children stared in appreciation. Everywhere they looked was a shrine to nature's glory.

Finally, Nebaioth muttered, "Take us into this place, Esau."

Esau led them down from the mountain into the makkah.

No one spoke as Esau led them along a brook under towering trees, past fruit trees, past flowering shrubs. They came to a clearing where Esau had arranged rocks upon which he could sit while watching the small river flow past. Mountains towered on either side of the valley, protecting it from the evils of the world. Here was sanctuary. Here was life. Here was makkah.

Nebaioth walked to Ishmael, fell to both knees, bowed his head, and whispered, "Father, I am home."

~~~

Basemath slept with the youngest boys away from the men.

After all were sleeping soundly, she rose, gathered her clothes, and walked neck-deep into the gently flowing river. She washed her clothes, her body, and her hair. She returned and sat on the bank drying her long flowing
~~~

hair, staring into the moonlit river, contemplating the nature of life. This was a good place to question everything she knew. Or thought she knew. To smile with joy for her older brother and the enchantment this place brought him. To rejoice that her mothers were *her* mothers, and her father was *her* father. To consider the boy-man Esau with whom she had lain. The why of it. The so-what of it. The what-now of it.

She rose and gathered her clothes. Any sound would wake the hunters, but she was a priestess. She would not make a sound. *Father will be awake. I don't know what wakes Father but he will know where I am with his eyes still closed. Maybe even my mothers know.*

She walked naked and stood for a while staring down at the sleeping Esau. *Should I wake you? Would it please you? Would you please me? Probably. But this is not the time or place.*

She returned to her sleeping blanket and lay down wrapping it around her. Basemath slept soundly until the predawn light.

~~~

She performed a beautiful sunrise ceremony. Mishma prepared an excellent morning fire. The meat was delicious. The talk was subdued.

Nebaioth stood. "Father. I am failing as a leader. Basemath must be in Shur in two quartermoons. We are three quartermoons away. I have not addressed our relationship with Hunter Esau. It is apparent that we are related." He glanced at Basemath's sudden look of concern, and added, "But not *that* closely related."

He continued, "Esau's father is Isaac. Your brother's name is Isaac. Esau's grandfather must be our Grandfather Abram. I am remiss in not already celebrating the meeting between our families. My inadequacies must be addressed." He looked at Ishmael, who sat in silence.

Finally, Basemath asked, "What will we do?"

Nebaioth breathed deeply and said, "When we break camp, Cousin Esau will lead Mother Fati's sons to Hebron; they will introduce themselves to Grandfather Abram and Uncle Isaac. I will lead the rest of us back to Shur within two quartermoons. I know the way. I will not let us tarry."

He glanced at Ishmael for approval.

Ishmael shook his head with approval as he studied the fire.

They broke camp.
~~~

Baalat decided it would not be appropriate to kiss Esau goodbye. Besides, it would embarrass him.

Ishmael hugged his children, starting with the youngest. When he came to Nebaioth, he held him at arm's length, smiled, and nodded his head with approval. He embraced his son, then turned and said, "Hunter Esau, take me and my boys to meet their grandfather!"

The two parties departed, in opposite directions, into the future.

Djoser, Hetephe, Incense/Hagar/Keterah
Horus, Serket, Azazil, Abram, Baalat
Ishmael, Maribah, Fatimah, Nebaioth, Basemath, Kedar | Anath, Astarte

~~~~~~~~~~~~~

23. Ishmael's Reunion

Year 202, Season 10, Aphroditemonth

Ishmael took careful note of their journey through the mountains. *There will someday be a road here. I must know the best way.*

Away from Basemath and her intimidating brothers, Esau became more talkative. Ishmael pushed the conversation toward Esau's family. After a while, Esau became comfortable and didn't realize he might be becoming a little *too* familiar with his new uncle.

Esau talked. "Mother doesn't like me because she says I'm not pious like I'm supposed to be. Brother Jacob is very pious just like Father and Grandfather want him to be, but I'm not. I hear Mother talking to Father in the night about how the other women whisper about her behind her back because I'm not at all pious. I mean, I would be pious if I knew how to be. I don't talk ugly to anyone or anything, but I think maybe I'm rough and coarse and don't look pious. I tried hard but I'd rather be out hunting and exploring and things. My new cousins look pious, but I don't really know. You're pious aren't you, Uncle Ishmael? Father and Mother will like you if you are really pious."

"It's easy to pretend the part. Does Isaac ever talk of his brother?"

"He and Grandfather talk about you, sometimes. You had bastard children by a whore idolater, but you finally married a virtuous woman that obeys you, so Grandfather forgives you. Where do you keep your unrighteous bastard children, Uncle?"

Ishmael thought, *They just left us, Nephew.*

He answered, "The customs of Egypt and Canaan are much different. As long as I'm in Egypt, all my children are respected and loved, equally. I don't apply labels to people. My four oldest children are by Priestess Maribah, the younger ones are by my wife, Fatimah." *So that's why Nebby sent only Fati's sons with me. Well done, Son.*

"Basemath's a Priestess, isn't she?

"Yes. Like her mother. And a good one, at that."

"Father and Grandfather won't like that. Priestesses are idolaters who should be stoned to death. Is Basemath a whore?"
~~~~~~~~~~~~~

"A whore?"

"Yes. Grandfather says that priestesses are whores. That doesn't sound nice, but I think Basemath is nice even if she *is* a priestess."

"You are correct, Esau. Basemath is an extremely nice, caring person. But you need not defend her honor in Canaan."

Ishmael looked at Mibsam and said, "Mibby, you're the oldest. You are responsible for the words and actions of your brothers. You will be in the land of Canaan and the house of Abram. You must respect their customs, their beliefs, and their religion. Do you understand what will be expected from all of you?"

Mibsam asked, "If somebody calls Basemath a whore, can I hit him?"

"No. 'Whore' is only a word. Neither agree nor disagree. Ignore it. In Egypt, you can hit them. In Canaan, we will respect their customs. Do not embarrass the family of Ishmael by being a poor guest. If a conversation grows too uncomfortable for you to bear, ask Esau to take all of you out and show you around. Esau is more clever than he realizes and will be able to extricate you and your brothers from difficult situations."

This was the first compliment Esau had ever received in his life. He was embarrassed but pleased. Late in the day, as they descended the mountains onto the plains, Esau received his second compliment. "You are an expert guide, Hunter Esau. Your path is true and sure."

He decided that a pious response might be, "Thank you, Uncle Ishmael."

~~~

Esau and his guests traveled fast. In less than two quartermoons they arrived in the lands of Hebron. Ishmael insisted they camp beside a stream so they could wash themselves and their clothes. The boys, including Esau, had great fun splashing and playing in the river.

As the others played, Ishmael and Mibsam dried on the bank discussing tomorrow's plans for introducing themselves. Ishmael guided Mibsam to come up with the plan. Finally, Ishmael said, "Yes, I believe that to be a good plan, Mibby. It should work well."

~~~

After morning meal, Mibsam, with guidance from Esau, led his troupe to the home of Abram.

Ishmael whispered to his son, "You are prepared. You will do well."

With that, Mibsam marched to the door as his companions stood a respectful distance behind.

Mibsam knocked.

Sarai answered.

Mibsam said, "I-I am Mibsam, son of Ishmael and the g-good woman Fatimah. My Father wishes to extend his warm regards and introduce my younger brothers to their grandfather, Abram. Will this be permitted?"

Sarai stared at the boy. *Ishmael dares return to my house?! The insolence! The ... the ...*

She said, "Wait here!" and hurried to find Abram to repeat the request.

Abram rejoiced. "Ishmael is here with his sons by the woman Fatimah. Fatimah is pious and righteous. Of course, I will receive them. Bring them to me. All of them."

Sarai returned to the door, opened it, and stiffly said, "Lord Abram will receive you. All of you."

With that, Mibsam motioned for his father, brothers, and cousin to follow Sarai into the visiting room where Abram sat.

Abram rose and let Ishmael bow before him and kiss his hand.

Ishmael said, "Father Abram. You continue to prosper in the land of Hebron. I strive to bring honor to your name in the lands of Egypt. These are four of your grandsons by my loving and obedient wife, Fatimah."

Mibsam walked to Abram, said a few words of praise, and introduced himself. He was followed by his younger brothers.

Mibsam announced Esau, "We were joined in the wilderness by our cousin, your grandson Esau, who brings pride to his father's house."

Abram said, "Yes. Yes. Esau. My big, ugly grandson by Isaac and his good wife, Rebekah. He is much like you as a child, except he is not a bastard. Isaac will probably bless Esau as his heir. Rebekah favors Jacob, her pious son, but Isaac will do what's best." Abram looked at Sarai and commanded, "Where are the refreshments for my guests, woman? Bring them immediately! And have Eliezer summon Isaac and his family to meet his brother."

Abram settled back in his chair to hear stories from his firstborn son, his bastard Ishmael.

~~~

As Ishmael told the story of their adventures in the southern mountains and meeting the great hunter Esau, there was a knock on the door.

Sarai answered.

Her voice could be heard saying, "Oh, Isaac. I'm so glad you and Jacob are here. I will show you to Abram and bring you refreshments right away." She did not acknowledge Rebekah who followed her into the food preparation room.

Ishmael stopped his storytelling, stood to face Isaac, and held both arms wide in greeting.

Isaac walked to face his brother, ignored the implied embrace, and thumped his chest in a halfhearted greeting. He said, "I am Isaac, your younger brother by our father's wife, Sarai. I have heard much about you, Brother. You brought my mother untold grief."

"Yes, I did. But she was rewarded for her piety and patience with your birth. I suspect you make her life a blessing. Am I correct?"

Isaac was taken aback. "Why, yes. I try to. *I* will receive our Father's blessing, you know."

Mibsam listened to the conversation with frowning confusion. *This man rejects and belittles you, Father. But you do nothing. How can this be?*

Ishmael glanced at Mibsam and winked. He continued talking to Isaac, "Of course. But let me praise you for this fine son of yours. He is an expert and powerful hunter. You must be proud of him."

Ishmael did not acknowledge his nephew, Jacob, sitting primly beside Isaac.

Isaac answered, "Yes. I am proud of both of my sons. Esau brings endless meat to my home and Jacob, here, brings his mother and me endless pride. Say hello to your uncle, Jacob."

Jacob stiffly said, "Hello, Uncle."

Sarai and Rebekah stood in the background with folded hands, listening and beaming with pride.

Ishmael replied, "Hello, Jacob. Do you often sit with your grandfather listening to stories of his student days with great Shaman Horus?"
~~~

Jacob replied, "He rarely speaks of those trying days. He prefers to teach how one should live in order to live a righteous life."

Ishmael looked at his father, "Trying days?"

Abram said, "We grow older. The season of youth is behind me. The season of responsibility is upon me. You will understand one day. SARAI! Are you preparing highsun meal for our guests? Include Isaac and Jacob. Visiting distant relatives can be trying."

Mibsam glanced at his father and smirked.

The morning, meal, and afternoon visits went well.

Isaac warmed to Ishmael once Isaac understood that Ishmael had not come to claim Abram's blessing—that is, inheritance— and that Ishmael did not appear to be angry with Abram or Sarai even though they had once condemned Ishmael and his mother to die in the desert, and that Ishmael had no intention of exposing him or the House of Abram to any idolaters or priestesses.

But Ishmael did courteously explain that if any of his family came to visit *him*, the visitors would be expected to respect the customs of Egypt—that is, respect idolaters, priestesses, whores, and treat women equally to men. There would be none of that "loving" subservience.

By evening meal, there was some actual laughter. Not by Sarai, but by everyone else.

After evening meal, the men retired to the garden to talk of manly things. This included Esau, Jacob, and, to his surprise, Mibsam.

Mibsam had never been invited to join "the men" before. He could now drink wine. *Father considers me a man now. I can drink wine and everything. Oh no, I will have to lay with a woman. I don't know about that part.*

Sarai and Rebekah served the men wine. Rebekah was all charm, smiles, and graciousness.

The men sat back and admired the garden, the view, and the night sky.

Ishmael said, "Father, will you teach the Way of Horus to Mibsam?"

Abram was delighted, "Yes, but I no longer call it the Way of Horus. I call it the 'Path of Righteousness.' The words are the same. I would not change the words." He settled into the teachings so ingrained in him. He was at peace as the words flowed forth.

Mibsam and Esau were both riveted. Neither had ever heard the complete teachings.

After Abram finished, Esau asked, "But Grandfather, you did not mention your god. Shouldn't you do these things because your god commands you to do these things?"

Abram had never been asked that particular question. He had no ready answer. But he said, "Horus teaches there is no god. Only the light from the Land of The Dead that comes to all people when they die."

Esau asked, "Is the light god?"

"Well, the light is everything that has ever come before. I suppose you could call it god."

"Can this god make it rain?"

"No. I don't think so."

Esau pressed on, "What about wind and lightning, and crops to grow and a woman to have a baby? Can your god do those things? And is this god a man or a woman?"

Abram suddenly wished that Horus was here to answer these complex questions. He said, "My god gives you eternal life. You simply have to believe in him and obey his commands, and you will live forever in him."

Esau asked, "What happens if you don't obey his commands, Grandfather?"

Abram was growing agitated. "All will go to the light when they die but I suppose the righteous will be rewarded with more than the unrighteous. I don't really know. But that's enough teaching for tonight. I don't want to overburden your untrained minds. Just trust me. There are no gods but my god. Don't worship idols and don't lay with whores. Your life will be righteous and well lived."

Isaac said, "That's enough. Your grandfather is tired from a long day entertaining his bastard son and grandsons. Let him rest."

Ishmael said, "All of this is recorded in writings contained in a chest in Egypt. I have seen them, myself."

Mibsam exclaimed, "Take us there, Father. Have someone read the words to us!"

Ishmael said, "If you improve your reading skills, you can read the words for yourself." For the first time, Mibsam and Esau understood the advantages of book study.

Ishmael rose and said, "Father, it's late and we have stayed too long. I'll take my sons and retire for the evening. We will leave after sunrise. Will you see us off or should we say farewell to you now?"

"Yes. I will see you off. Perhaps, I may even replenish your supplies."

"You are very righteous, Father. Thank you." *But don't let Sarai draw our water!*

Ishmael turned to Isaac and said, "Consider allowing Esau to travel with us back to Shur. He could teach me a great deal about the lands in the far south and exposure to Egyptian customs in Shur would be educational for him. My sons like Esau a great deal. Consider it. Tell me your decision in the morning."

Esau was thrilled but said nothing. Isaac was irritated for a reason he did not understand. Jacob and Rebekah were excited about the prospect of the rough-hewn Esau not being around to embarrass them. Rebekah would talk with Jacob that very night!

So it was that the next morning, Ishmael set off with his sons and Esau to return to Shur.

Ishmael filled his own water bags.

Calling after his departing son, Jacob offered Esau some fatherly advice: "Stay away from Priestesses and other whores!"

Phoenicia, Jaffa, Rocky, Burlyman, Polydore | Astarte, T'jaru
Terah, Amathlai, Haran, Terahson, Nahor, Sarai, Isaac, Jacob
Kyrios-Olon, Teumessian, Nimrod, Nimbal, Nimlad, Nimisis, Asherah, Set.

~~~~~~~~~~~~~

24. The God of Basemath

Year 202, Season 12, Isismonth

Djoser had called for a meeting of his Full Council on the day after the Winter's Solstice. Everyone of importance was commanded to come to Memphis. The purpose was to discuss Djoser's successor.

Egyptian cities were already being dressed in greenery and red berries. Families were gathering for celebration and reflection.

REUNIONS

Ishmael and his family arrived in Memphis a full quartermoon before the official season began. He set up camp outside the white walls of Memphis even though they could have been housed in the palace. "Palaces make you soft."

Fatimah dressed in her finest. Basemath dressed in her priestess robes. The men and boys dressed as they would in the wilderness. Their welcoming by the pharaoh, queen, and princess was a spectacle—common men and high-born women greeting the Pharaoh. The crowd was elated. Ishmael and his family followed the Pharaoh into the palace; the women waved gaily to the crowd.

Horus and Azazil were already there. Esau and Mibsam stared in silent awe at Horus. Azazil noticed their interest and walked to the two young men to introduce himself. Azazil was delighted to be suddenly hosting a deep and quasi-learned discussion on gods and the nature of death.

Horus asked Ishmael, "Who's the red-headed man?"

"That's Esau; a grandson of Abram. He took up with my priestess daughter and suddenly developed an interest in religion. We are all traveling to First Mother tomorrow to do a little question-answering. He and Mibsam heard the gospel from Abram but had more questions than Grandfather had answers. Can you go with us?"

Horus suddenly took an interest. "They have questions? Are they the questions of sheep?"

"I couldn't answer them, and I have read the Tallstone writings."

"Then, of course, I will go."
~~~~~~~~~~~~~

Djoser and Hetephe walked into the room and accepted salutations and embraces. Their two oldest grandsons followed.

Ishmael stood before his grandfather.

Djoser said, "You have raised these boys to be men to be feared. They insist on taking every coin I have in the treasury to build Nebaioth a new city somewhere in the wastelands beyond the Sinai."

Ishmael laughed. "Not that far, Grandfather; just across the Red Sea. Build a few river ports and you will open an entire new world of trade and wealth. Have Mother and Grandmother find Nebby three or four worthy concubines; you will have a new growing city almost overnight; a beautiful city at that."

"High-born women and wilderness do not fit well together. Incense had a duty."

Nebaioth joined the conversation and, again, sang the praises of the Valley of Makkah.

Adbeel asked Incense, "Mother, when do I get a concubine? If I am going to become the Chief of Shur, I need a concubine; a good one; and soon!"

"You are correct, Son. I will ask Mother to find you a high-born wife. You need a wife, not a concubine."

Horus joined Azazil and his new followers to discuss the coming excursion.

The evening was delightful.

~~~

Hete, with her mustache and companions, set off for First Mother after morning meal. She listened to the discussions of learned men and their students. She was sure that all of this was extremely important, but she was content to know that Osiris rose each morning to become the living god Ra, that her husband had been imbued with godhood, and that she would someday die and go to the Land of the Dead and be united with everything that had ever been and then live forever. If all of that could not be true, then surely some of it was true. She would leave it to Horus to work out the details.

The site manager knew the mustached one and immediately allowed them entry into the chambers containing the chest.
~~~

The young ones entered in awe. Hetephe knew it would be a long day and had brought food and drink. She settled in to listen to men and a priestess.

Azazil first removed the writings of Kiya and placed the scroll on the table. He pointed to the words for Mibsam and Esau as he read aloud. Basemath read along with him as best she could.

Azazil said, "These were the first instructions on how to live a good life. Death, gods, and religions are not mentioned. Just instructions that are necessary to be a person of goodwill. This is the basis for the Way of Horus which he still teaches today. But the world grew more complex. Black and white things became more and more shades of gray. People invented gods to explain why things were the way they were."

Azazil then removed pages containing the transcribed words of Dionysus. "Horus's father was the great lord Dionysus who fought in the war against the Olympians. His half-brother and enemy was the strongest man in the world, Heracles. Heracles picked Dionysus up above his head and slammed his body into Pumi's stone table at Tallstone. Dionysus lay there between life and death when a light came to him. Dionysus thought it might be his ancestors welcoming him to the Land of the Dead. Dionysus spent the remainder of his life searching for the Land of the Dead. A search that Horus continues to this day. These are some of the writings of Dionysus." Azazil read from the writings.

The audience sat mesmerized as was Hetephe.

Azazil retrieved the Testimony of Set. "Here is where our knowledge now stands. You will hear words Horus will not teach. Abram has heard the words but does not teach them. Do with this information as you will." He read the Testimony of Set and said, "Such is our current understanding of death. Gods are not mentioned. Do with this as you may."

There was subdued murmuring from the listeners.

Basemath finally asked, "Gods are not mentioned. Doesn't High-Priestess Hathor call forth Osiris to become the God Ra?"

Hetephe quietly answered, "No. That was Hathor's invention for Djoser to control and unite Egypt. It was a necessary lie. The people believed it because the people need to believe in gods."

Basemath said, "Oh."

Esau asked, "What about Asherah and El and Anath and the old gods?"

Azazil answered, "Those are only people claiming to be gods to in order to control people."

Horus added, "The powerful know what they do. They call people sheep because the people accept their words without question. They are evil."

Basemath said, "Oh."

Esau said, "Then there is no god. Even the god of Abram."

Azazil said. "Abram may call The Tree of Life god if he wishes to, but the Tree of Life is the experience of everything that has ever been. It does not grant wishes nor cause storms nor control anything. It's simply everything that has ever been."

Basemath said, "Oh."

Hetephe was more interested in Basemath's reaction than she was with any words being said. She walked to embrace Basemath.

Basemath sobbed, "My life is a lie. What I was no longer is. My life is without meaning. I am nothing."

Esau would not have it. He walked to the two women and forcefully pulled Basemath from Hetephe. He looked at her and spat out more words than he had ever before stung together, "You are life! You are meaning! You are Truth. You learn and grow and become more than you were with each breath you take. Teach those who seek to understand! To the others, bring them comfort and hope. A priestess must take care of her gods and her flock! Don't confuse people who simply want to live a good life."

Basemath grabbed him and clung tightly to him. Her body shivered as tears flowed. "I tried so hard to be a good priestess. I tried so hard! I need my mother!"

Hetephe watched the two play out their drama, then turned and refilled her wine glass.

~~~

They walked slowly back to Memphis in the late night.

Mibsam and Azazil walked far in front talking. Azazil was excited to finally have someone who knew what Azazil knew and was, like Azazil, unsure of how to proceed with this information. "Horus will not teach these things and doesn't want me to, either. Lady Baalat knows these things but will not take any action. I am alone in wanting to teach the people."
~~~

Horus and Hetephe walked behind; she was filled with the warmth of too much wine; he, with the discontent of too little.

And far behind, Basemath walked, tightly holding Esau's hand. "Should I discuss this with Mother or maybe you and I could run away from everything to that Makkah place? I *could* question High-Priestess Hathor but I would face her wrath. That's what I *should* do. I'm not afraid of her but what if she cries? I couldn't stand her crying. She is everything I wanted to be. Mother won't believe it; any of it. And maybe it's not true. Do you believe it's true, Esau?"

"I am a simple man, Basemath. I do not understand the complexities of life. The truth is simple. These teachings are simple. I believe them."

"So do I, Esau. My life is a lie."

CRISIS OF FAITH

The next morning, immediately after the sunrise ceremony was completed, and as Lady Baalat and her staff were arriving in Newport, Priestess Basemath demanded an audience with High-Priestess Hathor. The Assistant-Priestess replied. "This is an extremely busy time for the High-Priestess. She cannot see you."

Basemath replied, "I shall wait until she sees me, or I die." She sat down.

The Assistant-Priestess stared at her, turned, and left. In a few minutes, the attendant returned and asked. "What is the reason for this audience?"

"I have heard the Testimony of Set."

"Is there more?"

"No."

The Assistant-Priestess hurried away.

A long time later, the attendant returned, and said, "Follow me." Basemath followed her into a room deep inside the Mastaba.

Hathor stood in front of an alcove staring at many fine articles of clothing. She asked Basemath, "Did you cry?"

"Yes."

"Good." Hathor lovingly caressed the clothing. "Touch these things."

Basemath tentatively touched a piece of clothing.

Djoser, Hetephe, Incense/Hagar/Keterah
Horus, Serket, Azazil, Abram, Baalat
Ishmael, Maribah, Fatimah, Nebaioth, Basemath, Kedar | Anath, Astarte

"These are clothes Isis wore. She left them here and died before she returned." Hathor's voice became distant. "To be alone. To touch her robes. To have to do things no mortal can do. To speak words that have never been spoken. To tell lies because someone must tell them. To have the weight of Egypt on your shoulders. To know the words a god would speak. To sink to the floor under the weight of it all. To sit there helplessly clutching these clothes to your face. Sobbing. To silently scream, 'Great Isis ... You must not leave your people ... You must speak to them ... Only your words will bring my master Osiris back to me and bring hope and dreams to the poor ... Let me be your voice, my queen ... make me Priestess to the Living Word of Isis.'"

Hathor continued, "To rise and do that which cannot be done. To tell a broken man that you speak the words of his dead wife. To say to the people words only a god would say to her people. To have the people believe and celebrate her words. To do these things and not yet even be a woman. You *dare* come here to tell me my life is a lie. That Isis did not give me the strength to do what she wanted me to do. That Isis did not give me the wisdom to know what to say. That Isis—dead—and I—living—were not one."

Hathor stared defiantly at Basemath, and said, "Do not look upon me and see anything other than the High-Priestess of Osiris. And do not look upon yourself as anything other than a great life lived greatly. You have knowledge that I did not have, Priestess. Take it, add it to what you already know, and teach those who will listen. Do what you must do as I do what I must do. You may go!"

Basemath curtsied deeply and kissed the ring of power.

Basemath left Hathor.

~~~

Lady Baalat and her people happily arrived at the finest, most expensive inn in Memphis. Baalat had retained the entire third floor—with access to the roof.

She could have stayed in the palace. Djoser almost commanded it, then thought better of it. Baalat had business interests in Memphis she would be entertaining throughout the season. That, plus this trip was a reward for her hardworking staff with whom she wished to spend the holidays.

Baalat expected Horus to come sniffing around, soon. Probably with Azazil. And was disappointed, but not surprised, to learn that Abram
~~~

would not be in Memphis. She sent a courier to the High-Priestess that Baalat of Byblos would enjoy a short visit anytime during the holidays if the Priestess could schedule the time. She expected an invitation after the Winter's Solstice and was surprised to be invited immediately after sunset. *I must be special or maybe Djoser is getting on her nerves.*

She inspected the facilities, making sure everything was in order and her people were properly being taken care of, and then climbed to the roof to enjoy the view and a glass of wine. Captain Burlyman joined her. She pulled his favorite beer and a pouch of nuts from her bag. "I have an invitation to Hathor's after sunset. I suppose she will feed me, and we will visit for a while. Tomorrow late, I have to gather at the head of the Grand Concourse for the parade to meet the Pharaoh and attend the reception. The next morning and the entire day and night, there is a general meeting of council members. After that, I don't have anything. Schedule our clients and entertain them. Give them their gifts. Keep notes on what I need to follow up on and any issues that I need to address. Give Horus access to the roof and wine. If Abram shows up, him, too. Make sure the staff has fun. By the way, Season's greetings."

Burlyman silently nodded and gave a lifted beer salute.

~~~

Baalat arrived back at the inn late in the evening; maybe one glass of wine too many. Burlyman greeted her with, "Horus and Azazil are on the roof." She nodded her understanding and went to her room to change out of formal clothes into an Oceanid approved tunic. *Serket, I promised I would take care of Horus if he ever needed you.*

She went to the roof, sat down, accepted the proffered glass of wine, and said, "Well, now, Horus. Tell me about this Priestess-in-crisis friend of yours with the testicles to call the High-Priestess of Osiris to task."

They talked into the night.

RESOLUTION

The next mid-morning, Baalat sat on the roof holding her fruit-wine drink —thinking. *I have no meetings until my highsun meal with the Damascus trader and then the Grand Reception tonight. A slow day.*

Taone appeared. "There is a priestess and a rough-looking red-headed man inquiring if you will see them."
~~~

She considered. "I can't handle a rough-looking red-headed man this early. Show the woman to me. Ask the Captain to entertain the man. Find out his story."

Taone left but soon returned with Basemath and introduced her. "Lady Baalat, this is Priestess Basemath of Shur. She understands that you were once a student of Horus, and she seeks your advice on religious matters."

The two women exchanged greetings. Basemath accepted a glass of fruit-wine and the women sat down to talk.

Baalat said, "You are the woman of the moment, Priestess Basemath. Both Hathor and Horus brought up your story. They are far more interested in religions and gods than me but how can I help you?"

"Shaman Azazil recommended you. He believes you can solve any problem in the world. I can think of no bigger problem than if there are no gods. Will you advise me on this matter?"

"Well, my position is this. There are no gods, but it doesn't matter what you believe as long as you don't use your beliefs to harm or belittle other people. Religious leaders can bring their people hope and peace, which is good. They can also use their influence to gain wealth and power, which is bad. The question appears to be not what god you worship but rather does your religious leader respect the teachings of Horus, which is good, although even his teachings can be twisted for evil purposes. That's all I know. Did it help?"

"If there are no gods, then why am I a priestess?"

"Silly woman, to bring hope and peace to those that need to believe in a god. Simply pick your god well."

"I will not live a lie. Great Lord."

"Hmm. Well, then be a priestess to all gods. Teach that all gods and all people are united together when you die. That's what the Testimony of Set proclaims, isn't it? Go with that concept."

"Be a priestess for the Land of the Dead?"

"The 'Tree of Life' sounds better than the 'Land of the Dead,' don't you think? All that light and everything."

"Being priestess to all gods would not be living a lie?"

"That depends on your message, Priestess Basemath."

The women talked on for a while.

Eventually, Taone appeared and said, "Your appointment is waiting in the dining room. Chief."

Baalat said, "Dung! I've got to go change and get his gift. Introduce Priestess Basemath to him as my spiritual advisor. Basemath, join us for our meal. Go entertain him until I get there. He is a major trader from Damascus. Maybe his caravans go through Shur. Take care of me, ladies. Scurry. Scurry."

Baalat hurried to change waving at the two women to 'scurry.'

Taone hurriedly led Basemath to the dining room, told the table captain to add one to their party, left Basemath there as hostess, and scurried off to retrieve their guest.

The captain added another place setting, setting them equidistantly apart.

Basemath said, "No. no. The guest must directly face his host. I will sit between them."

The captain quickly obeyed and was finished as Taone walked up with the trader and made introductions.

They sat and the Trader inquired, "Spiritual advisor! How interesting. What god do you advise her on?"

Well before her crisis of faith, Basemath had graduated from being a priestess-in-training. She was, in her own way, a force within the priesthood. A minor force, but an up-and-coming force. She was not a reclusive tentative priestess. She was the daughter of Maribah, a potential heir to Hathor. As her father often told her, "Never let them see you unsure."

She engaged. "All of them. A single god without all other gods is weak and useless. All gods must be respected, even the ones you don't like because it is the people relying on the supposed good-will of the god that you are respecting; not the god itself. In death, all people are joined together as one, even with those who would be gods."

"Fascinating. I have never considered these things. What is the name of your church? Do you have more than one?"

"I am High-Priestess to the 'Church of Light.' My church will one day cover the world."

Baalat arrived and sat down. "Sorry, I'm late. What have I missed?"

Djoser, Hetephe, Incense/Hagar/Keterah
Horus, Serket, Azazil, Abram, Baalat
Ishmael, Maribah, Fatimah, Nebaioth, Basemath, Kedar | Anath, Astarte

The trader exclaimed. "Your advisor has gained a disciple! Where can I attend a service."

Basemath glanced at the trader and then at Baalat. She said, "My first church will open next year in the magnificent city of Makkah."

The remainder of the meal was, as was the beginning, delightful.

Phoenicia, Jaffa, Rocky, Burlyman, Polydore | Astarte, T'jaru
Terah, Amathlai, Haran, Terahson, Nahor, Sarai, Isaac, Jacob
Kyrios-Olon, Teumessian, Nimrod, Nimbal, Nimlad, Nimisis, Asherah, Set.

~~~~~~~~~~~~

25. The Succession Committee

Egypt came to watch.

They sat on rooftops; on barges in the river; in the trees. Even if they could not see, they wanted to be near. There were drummers and singers and dancers and flags waving.

Hathor had loaned her drummers and announcers to the Pharaoh for this momentous gathering. The name of each person introduced walking the Great Concourse to meet the Pharaoh would be announced from the Mastaba of Osiris, to be repeated by the announcers again and again until every person knew who was being introduced.

Sunset approached. It began. It was glorious.

At long last, all had been introduced and led into the place. Queen Hetephe and Princess Incense waved to the crowd. People fainted. Djoser, Pharaoh of Egypt, turned and walked to his palace.

The large meeting room was filled with the high-born, the powerful, the want-to-be's, and the influential. They drank their beer and wine and chatted away amicably.

Djoser entered the room.

All talking stopped. Everyone turned to face him. Djoser walked to his elevated throne and sat—stone-faced. Queen Hetephe walked to stand beside the throne. She placed her hand on his shoulder.

He did not speak. He gazed out over the room. Making eye contact with them all.

He spoke. "The two-hundred-sixth Winter's Solstice will be the fiftieth anniversary of my ascension; a good time to die."

The crowd murmured.

"Silence!' He paused. "On that eve, I and my queen will drink the wine of life. At sunrise, High-Priestess Hathor will call for Osiris to rise higher than he did the morning before—ensuring the continuation of life. At highsun, the new Pharaoh will be crowned, and Hathor shall blow the godhood of Osiris into him as Isis blew life into Osiris. The only decision remaining is this—who shall be Pharaoh? This is my decision and my decision alone. But I am not a foolish Pharaoh. I have gathered the wisest,
~~~~~~~~~~~~

smartest, most far-seeing, brilliant, caring minds in Egypt. By sunrise tomorrow, you will all agree on the three best candidates from which to choose. These three will study directly with me for the remaining three years of my life in order to prepare them. One of the three will be chosen on Winter's Solstice eve of the fiftieth year of reign. Choose wisely."

He rose. Hetephe followed him out the door.

The crowd was stunned. A lone voice was heard to exclaim, "Dung!"

The somber crowd talked among themselves.

Later, common man Djoser entered the room with Hetephe and twelve scribes. Those who saw them knew not to approach but to wait until they were approached. Incense was their visitation advisor. She led her parents to greet Hathor. The scribes separated Hathor from her group and surrounded Hathor and Djoser as they talked.

Djoser and Hathor quietly talked. He said, "Let's make it official, Little Trader Girl. Who?"

Hathor no longer bristled at the phrase. It was, she knew, his term of endearment and he only used it when no one else could overhear.

She replied, "T'jaru, Rafah, Baalat."

The scribes wrote.

"I agree. But Baalat will laugh at me and T'jaru is dedicated to his current mission."

"You will not know their measure until the prize is before them."

"And what of Hathor? She would be a wonderful Pharaoh."

She looked at him and laughed. They continued talking for a short while. Then, Djoser took her hands and leaned over to kiss her ring. "We did well, didn't we, High-Priestess?"

"This is the high point of civilization, my Pharaoh. Do not despair when it is over. Thank you for the glory of it all."

He again took her hands, squeezed them, and sadly smiled.

Esau had been invited due to his relationship with Ishmael and Abram. He stood quietly beside Priestess Basemath as she watched Djoser and Hathor in deep discussion. Basemath was fearful and envious. *She has the ears of gods and Pharaohs and I shall dare approach her and tell her what I am going to do. Be with me then, Mother—Father—Nebaioth—Esau. Be with me.*

Phoenicia, Jaffa, Rocky, Burlyman, Polydore | Astarte, T'jaru

Terah, Amathlai, Haran, Terahson, Nahor, Sarai, Isaac, Jacob

Kyrios-Olon, Teumessian, Nimrod, Nimbal, Nimlad, Nimisis, Asherah, Set.

Incense guided Djoser from Hathor and led him to an influential Nomarch where the drama was repeated.

After a while, Hetephe led those whom Djoser had talked with into a smaller meeting room where they could sit and visit more intimately. As the crowd thinned, Hetephe recruited twelve scribes and began talking with the lesser Nomarchs and less powerful. Then Princess Incense joined in. Finally, Djoser had spoken to each of their guests, and everyone had been quizzed by either Djoser, Hetephe, or Incense.

Toward the end of the night, an Announcer loudly announced that an office of Succession and Future Development was being opened in a storefront on Dividing Street. Every citizen with comments was encouraged to visit and share their thoughts on the future of Egypt.

Everyone knew this was the official end of the meeting, but they were all still having such a lovely time. "Just one more wine, please."

~~~

By mid-morning the next day, all of Memphis and much of Egypt knew of the coming death of the Pharaoh and queen. This plan was not met with disbelief or incredulity. Human sacrifice was sometimes necessary.

The words in everyone's mouth were:
"It is the way of the gods."
"Don't you remember it was Djoser who pushed the king from the ledge to his death?"
"He sacrifices himself so that the next Pharaoh will prosper."
"One Pharaoh dies. A new Pharaoh is born. Ma'at is preserved."
"Our Pharaoh sacrifices himself for the glory of Egypt."
"Our Pharaoh loves us more than he loves life."
"Better to die a man of power and strength than to become a doddering old man who urinates in his tunic."

On the contrary. Now there was something to look forward to. Continuous entertainment for the masses.

VIGNETTES

Djoser, Hetephe, and the chief scribe sequestered in their most private room considering the results of the previous night.

Hathor worked in the frenzy of her most demanding season of the year compounded by almost an entire evening taken by the Pharaoh plus that little priestess issue. She could no longer allow herself to be distracted.

Djoser, Hetephe, Incense/Hagar/Keterah
Horus, Serket, Azazil, Abram, Baalat
Ishmael, Maribah, Fatimah, Nebaioth, Basemath, Kedar | Anath, Astarte
~~~

Ishmael and his sons had a grand time. Mishma was introduced at the House of Ishtar. They got back to their camp in time to watch the sunrise ceremony.

Basemath would make no announcement of her intentions to her family until she officially resigned from her priestesshood. She could give her resignation to her mother, Priestess Maribah, but Maribah was in Shur with her temple, so Basemath went to the Mastaba to seek an audience with Hathor. But Hathor was not currently accepting any appointments. Basemath had said to no avail, "But I need to resign my priestesshood!"

~~~

Fatimah watched her family with pride. *Ishmael and my sons are so important. Imagine being an advisor to the Pharaoh.*

She was overjoyed when someone who appeared to be a powerful man came calling. She said to the man, "Yes, Lord Horus. Ishmael will be thrilled to offer you hospitality. I will wake him right now and bring you refreshments."

Later, everyone in her tent went on nervous alert when an official-looking priest came calling and said, "By command of the High-Priestess, Priestess Basemath will come with me!"

Horus and Ishmael looked at one another with concern as Basemath obediently followed the priest out of the tent. Nebaioth and Kedar exchanged glances. Esau was terrified.

~~~

Basemath was led through the frenzied activity of the Mastaba to stand beside the center of control—Hathor. Hathor did not look at her as she continued to direct and handle problems. She simply asked, "Why?"

Basemath knew to be direct and concise. "I will create my own church which honors all gods and no gods. I can no longer be faithful to my vows as a priestess to Osiris."

"You will be Priestess to all gods *but* Osiris?"

"No. To all gods. But I can no longer say that Osiris is a god."

"If you call yourself Priestess to *any* god, then you will remain a Priestess to Osiris. Your vows call only for your respect for Isis and Osiris as the embodiment of the hope and joy their story brings to the people. If your new understanding of the gods honors that vow, then I will not accept your resignation. You will remain a Priestess to Osiris plus whatever other living and dead so-called god you embrace. Am I understood?"

"Yes, High-Priestess. I shall be honored to represent the glory of Isis and Osiris."

"May your 'Church of Light' thrive and bring hope and joy to your people. Do well, Priestess Basemath. You may go."

"Thank you, High-Priestess." Basemath was escorted out of the Mastaba.

She was strangely invigorated as she absentmindedly walked back to her camp with purpose. She did not notice crowds automatically make way for her. *My vision is worthy. My path is straight. My courage will not falter. The most powerful people in the world believe in me. I believe in myself. I know what I must do. Isis and Osiris would want me to succeed. I cannot fail.*

Basemath entered her father's tent. Ishmael and Horus were deep in discussions.

Basemath interrupted with, "Father, command the Pharaoh build Nebaioth a city in Meccah. It must contain a temple to all gods and must be completed before this time next year. Come with me, Nebaioth. We must discuss the details of what we are going to do."

She marched from the tent with Nebaioth obediently following. Kedar nodded to Esau, and they followed behind.

Horus laughed. "Your daughter is thunder and lightning, Lord Ishmael."

Ishmael replied, "Esau has been telling me stories, Shaman Horus. You appear to have had a hand in whatever is happening here."

"Indeed I did, my friend. I stayed out of her way!"

At the Mastaba of Osiris, Hathor looked out over her people and smiled.

WINTER'S SOLSTICE EVE

All families gathered together on Winter's Solstice Eve to rejoice in familial love.

Djoser and Hetephe, too. On this night, they had no servants, attendants, or handmaidens. They, too, were with their own families.

Incense had provided her parents with Ishmael who fathered children by Priestess Maribah and then by Fatimah. All but Maribah were gathered in the House of Djoser and Hetephe to reflect and celebrate without rank or privilege but as family.

Djoser, Hetephe, Incense/Hagar/Keterah
Horus, Serket, Azazil, Abram, Baalat
Ishmael, Maribah, Fatimah, Nebaioth, Basemath, Kedar | Anath, Astarte

The family room was decorated with festive greenery and red berries. Egypt reflected on itself and the faithful prayed to whatever gods they prayed to that Hathor would call forth Osiris to rise higher in the noonday sky than he had on this day. Regardless, this night belonged to the family.

So it was that Hetephe, Incense, Fatimah, and Basemath sat together gossiping and laughing; that frightening bears ran wild through the room; that the men stood together, drank, and solved problems of the world.

Fatimah: "It would be so wonderful if Maribah were here. She takes her duties so seriously."
Hetephe: "Her duties are critical to the well-being of the people. To forsake them is to forsake Ma'at."
Incense: "The people of Shur love your mother, Basemath. She brings them their hope and dreams."
Fatimah: "She is overworked. She has no Assistant to help her."

There was an awkward silence.

Basemath answered the questioning silence. "I will return to Mother in two days but not as her Assistant. The High-Priestess has designated another Assistant Priestess to go with me to replace me in Shur. If all works out as I shall make it work out, I will leave my mother, forever." She choked on "forever," but just a little.

Fatimah rushed to embrace her stepdaughter. "All will be as it will be, Daughter. All will be well."

Djoser kept half his attention on the men and the other half on the women. He noticed the embrace. He asked, "Ishmael, if you convince me that this ridiculous plan can be made to work, how will your daughter and sons react?"

Ishmael laughed. "'Made to work,' Grandfather?" How can it *not* work? Nebaioth and Kedar want it and Basemath demands it! Adbeel will be thrilled because, with his big brothers out of the way, he will become Chief of Shur. What could be finer?"

"You're sure Basemath wishes for this to happen?"

"Basemath *demands* it, Grandfather. She is the one that drove me to bring this up to you. I would have waited for a more opportune time but with your proclamation and Basemath's insistence that Meccah be completed before your retirement, I hope you will trust my judgment and grant me this project to be completed as quickly as possible."

Nebaioth added, "Grandfather, this will be the greatest city in the world!"

Djoser said, "I'll discuss it more with Hetephe. If the sun rises higher tomorrow, I'll give my decision." He glanced at the women. He noticed Basemath talking to Hetephe. He could not hear her words.

What she said was, "Let us rejoice. I am High-Priestess to the Church of Light and before my grandfather dies, he shall experience the all-welcoming Church of Light in his city of Meccah!"

On the night before Winter Solstice, families grew closer.

Djoser, Hetephe, Incense/Hagar/Keterah
Horus, Serket, Azazil, Abram, Baalat
Ishmael, Maribah, Fatimah, Nebaioth, Basemath, Kedar | Anath, Astarte

~~~~~~~~~~~~~~

26. Meccah

Year 203, Season 2, Setmonth

Fatimah stood beside Ishmael, thrilled that she been had invited to be part of her stepchildren's great adventure.

But Ishmael was not happy. Nor Nebaioth. Nor Kedar. Nor Basemath. Esau was Esau.

The builder was apologetic but "what-am-I-supposed-to-do?" He said, "The dock is finished, my lords. In record time I might add. The road is almost complete. Through extremely rough terrain, I might add. Building material is being delivered. As we speak, I might add. But three years may not be possible. All building materials must be imported and carried over mountainous terrain. The Temple you demand is expansive. I am an Egyptian. It will be well-built before it will be quickly built. I know this is what you want me to do, my lords."

The three looked at one another with frustration.

The builder asked, "Perhaps the Priestess could pray to Osiris for some kind of godly assistance."

She replied, "No god will help or hinder us. We will continue to work with our greatest strength and plan with great wisdom. Are you doing these things, Builder?"

"Yes, Great Priestess. I am"

"Then you can do no more. I express my gratitude for the significant progress you have made."

He replied, with some relief, "Thank you, Great Priestess. I will continue to do all possible to complete your city within three years."

"Including the Temple."

"Yes, Priestess. Including the Temple."

Kedar headed back to the dock to again imagine what improvements could be made. Nebaioth and Basemath headed toward the valley to continue to lay out the streets and buildings. The temple would be on the north side, a coliseum on the south. The builder returned to oversee the road-building workers and to spur them on to smarter efforts.
~~~~~~~~~~~~~~

THE COMING

It came silently, without fanfare, without warning. Those that saw it, took no notice because they could not see that which they could not imagine.

Still, it came.

~~~

High-Priestess Hathor and her priests and priestesses had completed the ceremony and retired from the stage, pleased with another successful calling of Osiris to become Ra. They had, yet again, delivered the thrill, the pageantry, the love, the hope. As always, the crowds were thrilled with the sunrise ceremony. They mingled and visited and rejoiced.

But Hathor was uneasy. "Something's not right."

It was more of a feeling. Perhaps a change in wind or air pressure or sound of the wind or color of the sky. She summoned her Senior Priestess to walk with her through the passages to the eighth level of the Mastaba.

Arriving, Hathor looked up.

She saw its coming.

~~~

The guard and vizier rushed into the room as the Pharaoh and queen were completing their sunrise ritual—an inexcusable and intolerable invasion of privacy.

Djoser rushed to put on his tunic as Hetephe casually retrieved hers. She asked the Vizier, "Is there a good reason for this Vizier Menkasonson."

Both Menkasonson and the guard fell prostrate to the floor. The vizier whispered, "My lords. They have returned."

~~~

Pharaoh Djoser and Queen Hetephe hurriedly walked onto the Great Concourse. The crowd saw them and were elated. A great cheer went up. The crowd saw them staring into the sky. The crowd followed their gaze.

They fell to their knees.

~~~

"Target east-northeast. Slow descent rate."
"Confirm. Target east-northeast. Slowing descent rate. Do we have a landing site?"

Djoser, Hetephe, Incense/Hagar/Keterah
Horus, Serket, Azazil, Abram, Baalat
Ishmael, Maribah, Fatimah, Nebaioth, Basemath, Kedar | Anath, Astarte

"Confirm. Landing site clear. Hold descent rate."

"Confirm. Holding decent rate."

"Directly over target on my on my Mark."

"Confirm. Waiting on Mark."

"Wait. Wait. Wait. Mark."

"Confirm. Over target. Stopping lateral displacement. Initiating slow descent. Prepare for tethering."

~~~

What normally took days of advanced planning was improvised. The ambassadors, advisors, scribes, performers, singers, drummers, and color guards began appearing.

To welcome their returning.

~~~

Without ceremony or plan, Djoser walked to the landing site. Hetephe walked with him. He stood at the appropriate location and gave appropriate landing signals. Hetephe took up a supporting position.

The tethering ropes were thrown. Djoser expertly tethered two of the four as Hetephe copied his motions. They pulled Airboat 113 into its docking station. The gate opened, a rope ladder was thrown down, and the pilots descended. The two couples faced each other

The people watched this unbelievable sight in silent awe.

The Pilot said, "Hello, Prince Djoser. It's good to see you."

"Hello, Pilot Rhodos, I mean—*Eagle* Pilot Rhodos. You remain as accomplished and beautiful as ever."

"More accomplished. Beautiful on the outside. Very old on the inside. You remember my husband, Eagle Pilot Iapyx."

"Yes, of course, your very attentive husband. This is my wife, Queen Hetephe of Egypt."

"So the prince became the king."

"Oh, no. Much more than a king. A god, actually. I will request you to demonstrate proper respect when I acknowledge you to my people."

"Of course, we will be delighted to bow and curtsy. I know gods adore adoration. But Iapyx and I are old and exhausted beyond our endurance. May we be allowed to adore you and then collapse from exhaustion?"

Phoenicia, Jaffa, Rocky, Burlyman, Polydore | Astarte, T'jaru

Terah, Amathlai, Haran, Terahson, Nahor, Sarai, Isaac, Jacob

Kyrios-Olon, Teumessian, Nimrod, Nimbal, Nimlad, Nimisis, Asherah, Set.

"Of course. I will present you to our people when we reach the foot of the concourse. Sixty steps later, you may both collapse and be carried to your Quarters. Follow me."

Djoser and Hetephe led Iapyx and Rhodos down the concourse followed by the improvising pageantry of Egypt. They reached the foot and separated so the pilots could face the crowd.

One pilot bowed. The other pilot curtsied.

Djoser then led the three the sixty steps into the palace. Both pilots, true to her word, collapsed. They were carried to the guest suite, there to sleep.

~~~

Two days later, Rhodos wandered out of her guest room and was greeted by a handmaiden.

The handmaiden said, "Come with me Great Pilot. I will wash your hair, bathe, massage you, and then dress you in fresh clothes. Your morning meal will be served when you are ready. Shall I retrieve your husband?"

"No. Have someone check on him but let him rest. He's tired. But *my* morning sounds like just what I need. Let's go."

Rhodos followed the handmaiden to where she was bathed and pampered.

The strong fingers of the masseuse were reinvigorating. There was a stir at the door, the masseuse excused herself to greet the new visitors. She returned and said, "My Lady. I will dress you now so that you may confer with your visitors."

Rhodos complied, not sure if she was ready to confer with visitors.

Dressed, she was escorted to the door where three priestesses of powerful presence stood waiting with folded hands.

Arriving, the most powerful priestess intoned, "Eagle Pilot Rhodos, we come to inform you that Eagle Pilot Iapyx has discarded his constraining body so that he can enter the Land of the Dead and continue his life eternal. You will rejoin your husband when you discard the body you currently wear. His emptied shell will be prepared and cared for as you so direct. We are at your service."

Eagle Pilot Rhodos fell to her knees, closed her eyes, and continued to exist.

<div align="center">
Djoser, Hetephe, Incense/Hagar/Keterah
Horus, Serket, Azazil, Abram, Baalat
Ishmael, Maribah, Fatimah, Nebaioth, Basemath, Kedar | Anath, Astarte
</div>
~~~

MECCAH

The family ate highsun meal on the ground in the center of the someday-to-be Church of Light. Esau had painstakingly selected nice rocks with which to define the circular outline of the church. The seven surrounding mountains provided peace in the valley by protecting it from virtually everything, including the works of men. Once there, it was so very nice. Getting there—building there—not so nice.

Ishmael stared in the direction of Memphis listening to his wife talk and his children play. He saw the bird in the distance. It attracted his absent-minded attention because it did not swoop or soar as one would expect. The bird grew larger. Ishmael nudged Esau and nodded toward the oncoming bird. They began following the bird with close attention.

It was not a bird, or a reflection, or a cloud, or anything possible. It was a giant egg. Flying toward them. The men stood. Kedar prepared his bow and arrows. The children gawked.

It came.

Ishmael stood to his fullest and motioned his family to gather behind him except for Kedar, Nebaioth, and Esau who stood beside him. Each man looked as formidable as he could.

A sling carrying a massive amount of wood dangled beneath the giant egg. The egg arrived, hovered, veered toward the clearing being made for the road, lowered itself, released the sling containing the wood, hovered again, and flew over to a clearing where a rope was thrown from a carriage beneath the egg. A figure slid down the rope, placed four boxes on the ground, and hit one box with a hammer. The four boxes exploded exposing a large metal stake driven into the ground. The figure looped the rope under each stake and looped it back to a metal bracket on the rope.

The figure shouted, "Clear to initiate pull-down!"

Nothing happened.

"Repeat. Clear to initiate pull down!"

From the carriage, a voice replied, "How do I do that?"

"Pull the green lever."

"Oh, yeah. Initiating pull-down!"

The metal bracket began to slowly be pulled upward pulling the carriage toward the ground. Finally, the pulling and creaking stopped. The voice in the carriage asked, "Can I get out, now?"

"Pull-down secure. Co-pilot is clear to egress."

"Egress means that I can get out, doesn't it?"

"Confirm. Egress means you can exit the craft."

A rope ladder was thrown over the side. A second figure emerged and scrambled from the basket.

Ishmael and his family had watched and listened to all of this with terrified fascination. The two human figures walked towards them; one pulling off her helmet to let her long hair flow over her shoulders. She decided that Ishmael was the ranking person in the group, walked to him, hit her chest with her fist, and said, "I am Eagle Pilot Rhodos of the Egyptian Flying Corp under the command of Pharaoh Djoser. I have been assigned to transport material from lower Egypt to support the building of the city of Meccah. I am at your service."

Everyone stared at her in silent terrified wonder except Basemath, who walked to face Rhodos and said, "Greetings. I am Basemath, Priestess to the Church of Light. Welcome into the service of all gods and all people. Come with me. I will provide you with refreshments."

Rhodos followed Basemath to the improvised eating area in the outlined temple. Fatimah suddenly remembered that she was the hostess and was the person who should be entertaining the newcomer, no matter how exotic she might be. She hurried to join the two women and introduce herself. The men watched the women depart in dumb astonishment, trying to make sense of what was happening. The pilot-in-training scribe joined the men to talk of men things like "flying that thing is more fun than—you know."

The women sat with fruit-wines, talking.

Rhodos told her story. "My husband and I—he died recently—retired from the 'Titan Flying Group.' In the early days, we dealt with Egypt on a great many projects, but we moved our base of operations to Farland and our priorities shifted. Airboat 113 is old and outdated and was to be scrapped. My husband and I requested it as our retirement gift and asked permission to make the long journey back to our youth. If we died on the way, nothing would be lost. If we lived, perhaps the airboat could still perform useful things in Egypt. Prince Djoser assigned me to train pilots and transport building materials to your new city. Finding a source for pilot candidates will be slower than I had hoped, I'm afraid. So I request your patience until I can find and train pilots."

Basemath looked at the pilot-in-training laughing with the men and asked, "Where did you get the happy one?"

Rhodos answered, "He is a scribe. A good scribe as I understand. Not so good a pilot."

Basemath said, "Priestesses would be too enchanted and distracted with rising closer to the gods. Perhaps military men. They appear to be disciplined and like taking orders. How long to train a trainable man?"

"Four to eight flights for a co-pilot. Many seasons in the air for a Pilot."

The two women continued discussing logistics and timetables.

Fatimah listened with admiration.

~~~

Even with Rhodos limiting her working flights to one every other day, building progress increased tenfold with the efficiency of Airboat 113. She gave daily courtesy sightseeing flights for the highborn and children. Vizier Nimisis overcame his fear and flew with her many times. She was an expert at answering his questions without giving any real information, such as "Where are there more of these things?" "What else can you make?" "Who controls this land?" "What gods do you worship?"

But even with the courtesy flights, a dozen military archers were soon trained as co-pilots. Half were pilot material. The training was focused and arduous. After three seasons, the first pilot trainee was allowed to take off and land without Rhodos. After another season, he was allowed to perform a working flight assisted by three co-pilots of pilot caliber.

Eagle Pilot Rhodos retired from the Egyptian Flying Force.

~~~

Basemath's temple took shape. She acquired an idol of each Canaanite and Egyptian god. Azazil came to Meccah to assist her in the development of proper rituals, protocols, and theological concepts. They held endless discussions on her vision.

Today, Ishmael, Nebaioth, Kedar, and Esau stood on the crest of the road watching the construction of their city.

Phoenicia, Jaffa, Rocky, Burlyman, Polydore | Astarte, T'jaru

Terah, Amathlai, Haran, Terahson, Nahor, Sarai, Isaac, Jacob

Kyrios-Olon, Teumessian, Nimrod, Nimbal, Nimlad, Nimisis, Asherah, Set.

The road was as good as it could be for the terrain it traversed. Incense's port was operational and transported workers to and from the work site. Many of the young women workers were enthralled with Meccah and redoubled their efforts to find a husband who wanted to settle in Meccah. Many married workers agreed that this land was good. With daily airboat deliveries, the city would be completed within the next four seasons.

The men were elated. High-Priestess Basemath was satisfied. Incense was fulfilled. Djoser was pleased. Both with his current investment and the ones made long ago.

~~~~~~~~~~~~~

27. Vignettes

Year 204, Season 1, Osirismonth

Osiris rose higher on the day after Winter's Solstice. The mood of the people shifted from somber reflection to abandoned rejoicing.

IN MEMPHIS

Djoser sat with Hathor and Rhodos at Osiris's table.

Hetephe surreptitiously watched them as she chatted with Incense.

Rhodos said, "I am at last free of all responsibilities, Prince. Oceanids were not designed to have responsibilities. Dionysus seduced me into another world. But now, I am free to return to the sea."

"It was a rewarding world, I hope."

"Very. But Lord Nimisis is constantly trying to obtain information I shall not give him. Once his friend Khaba becomes Pharaoh, his questioning techniques will become more aggressive. That, plus I am told that I am the last of my kind. I long to greet my sisters."

"I understand. But in the meantime, you have helped complete my grandson's city two years ahead of schedule and I shall be able to visit his city before I greet my ancestors. Life is good, Pilot Rhodos. More wine?"

She replied, "Still. I am a long time from my sea and my sisters." She held out her wine cup. "Yes, Please."

IN THE SINAI

Ishmael and his younger sons explored the desert and wastelands of the Sinai. Each son practiced selecting a possible location for his someday-city. Ishmael's younger children grew ever more confident, self-sufficient, and ready to take on the world.

IN SHUR

Adbeel walked the city of Shur with his wife, the daughter of a high-ranking handmaiden to Queen Hetephe.

He said, "My people love me being their chief. I have a natural talent for leading people. They follow me even if I am younger than they are."

His wife enthusiastically agreed with Adbeel's assessment.

Phoenicia, Jaffa, Rocky, Burlyman, Polydore | Astarte, T'jaru
Terah, Amathlai, Haran, Terahson, Nahor, Sarai, Isaac, Jacob
Kyrios-Olon, Teumessian, Nimrod, Nimbal, Nimlad, Nimisis, Asherah, Set.
~~~~~~~~~~~~~

Neither considered that even though Adbeel's mother, High-Priestess Maribah, had no political power, she probably *could* command fire to rain from the sky, wells to run dry, pestilence to come, and crops to die in the field. Those sorts of things.

That, plus Adbeel's father was Ishmael.

IN MECCAH

In Meccah, Nebaioth was in serious discussions with Basemath and Kedar as Esau and Azazil listened.

Nebaioth: "We all agree, then. I will proclaim Meccah to be *my* city and then Basemath will perform her first ceremony in our city's temple at Summer's Solstice. I like it. Ma'at will be well served."
Kedar: "And the other part, Brother?"
Nebaioth: "Oh, yes. I must find a wife before then."
Basemath: "And you must recruit settlers and plan a massive opening ceremony and invite every one of significance. I will ask Grandmother to find you a wife. Men are poorly equipped to do these things!"
Nebaioth: "Am I allowed to marry my sister?"
Basemath: "Yes. But I would never lay with you, Brother. You might find that to be bothersome!"
Kedar: "A wife and ten concubines would solve that problem."
Basemath: "Send word for Grandmother to select your wife. She will know exactly who you should marry plus she can make political gold with the marriage ceremony of Ishmael's first-born son. You can meet your bride at the wedding. Meccah will get a great deal of attention. That will help build attendance at Meccah's Summer Solstice ceremony."

IN HEBRON

The House of Abram was righteous and proper. Isaac, Rebekah, and their children often visited Abram and his extremely righteous wife, Sarai. Everyone said all the proper words.

During this festive season of love and brotherhood, men were more accepting of the company of women. Sarai and Rebekah were thrilled to be allowed to sit with the men and discuss meaningful things.

Isaac reminded everyone Esau was exploring the world with his cousins.

Rebekah offered, "I am so happy that Jacob chose to stay here learning proper thought. Jacob is so proper, especially compared to his twin brother. I suppose some whore has seduced your poor Esau, by now."

Isaac defensively answered, "Esau is a strong accomplished hunter. There aren't many loose women in the wilderness."

Rebekah asked, "Father Abram, who do you think would better honor Isaac's blessing? You are so wise in these matters."

Sarai smiled.

IN BYBLOS

Baalat and her close advisors sat on her roof drinking wine and laughing.

Taone asked Horus, "Lord Horus, how should I have responded? This strange man slaps me on my bottom as I pass him on the street. I turned and stared at him in disbelief. He thrust his pelvis at me – leering! I walked away but his actions left me feeling violated. It still bothers me."

Horus answered, "This is a season of love and affection. He did no harm, and you are commanded to love everyone, even this somewhat coarse man. You did correctly, Lord Taone."

Tatwo offered, "What if she cut off his testicles? Would that be allowed? If she were loving him while she did it, of course."

Baalat was somber. "I disbanded my street patrol who were supposed to protect women from assaults by men. The men in the patrol were admonishing the women for creating the situation. There were three cases of the patrol men attacking the women they were sworn to protect. The day of castration may be closer than you think, Shaman."

Burlyman said, "The attitudes in Byblos have reached the level of Port Jaffa. Poseidon only knows what the women of Port Jaffa suffer."

Tatwo said, "A castration patrol! That's what every city needs. A man forcefully takes a woman and then she can castrate him! Everybody wins!"

Baalat said to Horus, "The Church of Urfa preaches the subservience of women to men, louder and louder. This message changes the nature of people and not for the good. The nature of our kind continues to degenerate, not improve. The Oceanids were correct."

Burlyman looked at Horus and said, "It's not your fault, Lord Horus. You have tried to teach people the correct way to live. It's not your fault."

Horus stared at his wine as he said, "If not mine, Captain, then whose?"

~~~~~~~~~~~~~~~~~~~~~~~~

28. Summer Solstice Festival

Year 204, Season 6, Aresmonth

Meccah contained two large inns built specially to handle surging visitors for special events, including the upcoming Summer Solstice Festival. One inn for the influential and high-born, the other for the common people.

Basemath had conceived the concept of a large Summer Solstice Festival to complement the Winter Solstice Festival celebrated in Memphis and throughout the world. It would give people another significant festival and bring in much-needed traffic to remote Meccah. The city was an isolated paradise in a vast wasteland traveled only by Bedouins. Ishmael planned on developing a trade route from Hebron through Mecca to Upper Egypt, but that would be a long time coming. In the meantime, there was a festival to hold, a city to found, a temple to consecrate, and a new, higher religious concept to introduce.

The affluent commoners were the first to arrive. They loved a good festival and here were games and competitions and exhibitions and music and street food and everything.

Young women who were attracted to Basemath's teachings and wanted to be considered for priestesshood answered people's questions about Basemath and Azazil's new religious concept—one without traditional gods. Can you believe it? Basemath taught these young women how to maximize their natural beauty with paints, creams, and oils; all essential tools in a priestess's arsenal.

Azazil was solicitous of all these young women; but especially for ones that might understand and embrace the "Revelation of Set." Ones that might become a true believer.

Basemath and Azazil practiced the upcoming Summer Solstice Ceremony over and over; attracting more interested young maybe-priestesses with each repetition.

More commoners came, followed soon by the affluent who were interested in the potential profits this new city and religion might offer.

Ishmael and Amenirdis, his new extremely high-born elegant, intelligent, ambitious Egyptian Priestess wife, greeted each guest as they arrived at the inns. She was a weapon unleashed.

Djoser, Hetephe, Incense/Hagar/Keterah
Horus, Serket, Azazil, Abram, Baalat
Ishmael, Maribah, Fatimah, Nebaioth, Basemath, Kedar | Anath, Astarte
~~~~~~~~~~~~~~~~~~~~~~~~

Amenirdis chatted:

"What must we offer to attract your most wealthy caravans?"

"We are on excellent terms with the extremely wealthy Nubians toward the south and have ports to support even the largest caravans."

"There are no bandits in this area. Just the occasional Bedouin tribe."

"Our excellent pastures are designed to refresh even the most weary beasts of burden. And men."

"Be sure to try our spas and baths."

Then, wonder of wonders, the almost Living-God Horus himself arrived. With none other than the highly respected Chief of Hebron—Abram.

Forewarned by Ishmael, Amenirdis charmed Abram and his son, Isaac, graciously assuring them that the Church of Light recognized that all gods were false gods even if they did display the many gods of Canaan. This was simply to demonstrate that they were all replaced by the "Light," which was actually the god of Abram. But be sure to stay away from the potential priestesses since they were not yet well trained and might lead a man to think impure thoughts.

Amenirdis was unable to charm Horus.

Ishmael strode the city as if he owned the world which, of course, he did.

The Pharaoh's caravan arrived the day before Summer Solstice and established their camp to the north of the city. Everyone enjoyed the festivities except the Pharaoh, who remained in his tent greeting those he should greet.

Hetephe donned her mustache and loose-fitting clothes and wandered the new city looking for an archery competition. Her disguise did not fool most people, but they honored her desire to be left to herself.

General Sanakhte, his son, General Khaba, and *his* son, Huni regally walked the city. General Khaba strode the city as if he owned the world which, in his mind, he did.

INCENSE AND ABRAM

Abram walked the river pathway with Isaac, Jacob, and Esau. He saw Incense and Ishmael sitting on the riverbank. He said, "Continue your walk. I deem to speak to my oldest son. I will join you later."

Isaac replied, "Father, Ishmael is with his mother. Are you sure that is acceptable? Mother isn't here and I'm sure she would not be pleased."

"Do not correct your father, Isaac. I will speak to them and join you later."

"Yes, Father."

The group continued as Abram left the path to join Ishmael and Incense.

Abram piously approached the two. "I extend my greetings to you, Son Ishmael. This is an eventful time in your life."

"Father Abram! You pay me and your grandchildren a great honor. Welcome to Meccah."

The two men chatted away about manly things. Incense stood obediently listening to the weighty conversation of men.

Finally, Abram spoke to Incense. "You appear to have taken on the attributes of a pious woman, Hathor."

She replied, "I am Princess Incense, Lord Abram. But yes. I am well trained in what pleases men such as yourself and I truly want you to enjoy my grandchildren's new city. Your goodwill toward them is important to them. I will play the part that best serves my family."

They continued their civil conversation. Abram did not notice, but Ishmael did, when Incense glanced at Ishmael, then toward the distance, and raised an eyebrow. Ishmael interrupted with, "Excuse me while you two remember old times. I will go speak to my brother."

Abram almost panicked, realizing he was to be left alone with this "woman." He started to protest but Incense offered, "I am now a pious woman and will not seduce you." She softly muttered, "Perhaps."

Incense said to Abram, "We are alone now, Abram. How are you? Really?"

He stared at her. Conflicted. He felt safe with Incense, but Sarai would be furious with him. He could already hear her tirades.

Incense offered, "We cannot make her any more furious than she already will be, Abram. Let us enjoy the company of one another while we can. Come. Sit with me and we can talk."

He stared at her. Conflicted, but safe, he sat with her.

"Are you at peace, Abram?"

"Certainly. Well, I am righteous. Being righteous is hard, sometimes."

"You betrayed the wishes of Horus. You teach one thing and live another. Your wife does not respect you. Your youngest son is an empty shell whose wife and son plot against him. Lord T'jaru tells me that the Church of Urfa uses you as their best example of a man with a happy marriage. A man with an obedient wife and obedient children. Did not Horus teach you to destroy the wicked teachings of the Church of Urfa? How do you reconcile all these things, Sweet Abram? You cannot change your nature, but you can, at least, try to understand it."

Abram stared at the flowing water. "Did you ever feel affection toward me, Hath … Princess Incense?"

"I loved you, Abram."

Abram stammered, "S-Sarai did not come because she is older than her years. She would not be physically able to make the trip. I fear she will die too soon. If she does die, are you …" His voice trailed off.

"I will be in Meccah and will seduce you if you come here again. A wanton woman will climb on your body and do everything you have ever imagined a whore doing to a man. I shall go ahead and select names for the sons I will give you. Will you have pleasant dreams tonight, Sweet Abram? Will you dream of me?"

He rose and without looking at her, replied, "I am a righteous man!" and walked briskly to rejoin his family.

ISHMAEL AND KHABA

As Ishmael walked away from his mother and father, he saw the two Generals of Egypt, one striding the city as if he owned it. Ishmael changed course to walk over and welcome the two men and their group to Meccah.

"General Sanakhte and General Khaba, welcome to Meccah. I hope you are finding my son's city to your satisfaction."

General Khaba sniffed the air as General Sanakhte exchanged pleasantries with Ishmael. Ishmael said, "Lord T'jaru tells me you Lords are two of the leading candidates to succeed Grandfather Djoser as Pharaoh."

Khaba snapped out of his superiority stance. *He knows we are competitors! What are his plans to eliminate us? I must show him that I do not fear him! Or should I camouflage my ambitions as my good friend Nimisis continually tells me to do? Oh, the weight of greatness! How shall I proceed?*

Khaba said, "Lord T'jaru would make a far better Pharaoh than my humble self. It is a pity he is said to prefer the potential in the far eastern lands than the established authority of Egypt. But what of you, Prince Ishmael? Rumors have it that you are the Pharaoh's favorite."

"Yes. I spread that rumor constantly. It keeps my mother happy and the enemies of Egypt nervous. I can see it in their eyes." Ishmael watched Khaba's eyes dilate.

Khaba quickly added, "Well, yes. But being Pharaoh appears to be all duty and ritual; not exciting at all, like opening up new worlds as you and your sons are doing in Sinai and these lands south of Midian."

"Yes, it is all exciting. But I shall retire from my exciting adventures as soon as my last son has a tribe or city of his own. My youngest is seven years of age so I could not possibly retire in time to become Pharaoh. But when the next Pharaoh retires, perhaps you will think kindly of me and *my* contributions to Egypt." He looked at Khaba and grinned.

Khaba thought, *You mock me, you bastard son of the princess. You think my contributions are not as great as yours. You anger me, Prince Ishmael. My day will come, and you will not like it!*

Khaba grimaced back.

NEBAIOTH, KEDAR, ISAAC, JACOB, AND ESAU

Nebaioth and Kedar walked their city welcoming everyone they met. This day was glorious. Their vision was complete.

Nebby and Amenirdis planned to have many children and live here forever; guiding their city, nurturing their people, and helping Basemath grow her church. Meccah would become a place of greatness; not as great as Memphis or even Byblos, perhaps; but, still, a place of greatness.

Kedar planned to maintain a permanent residence here as he explored the southern lands where lay powerful tribes and the kingdom of Saba. He and Cousin Esau would begin a new adventure after this one was finished.

A future of brotherhood, inclusion, and peace lay before them.

Esau hailed them. Esau was showing his father and twin brother the glories of Meccah. His brother, Jacob, was impressed.

Isaac had his nose in the air. "There are so many smells in this city. How are you able to stand it?"

Nebaioth and Kedar joined the three men.

Djoser, Hetephe, Incense/Hagar/Keterah
Horus, Serket, Azazil, Abram, Baalat
Ishmael, Maribah, Fatimah, Nebaioth, Basemath, Kedar | Anath, Astarte

Nebaioth said, "I hope you are enjoying yourself, Uncle Isaac. Father instructed us to keep women of questionable morals away from you. He doesn't want you to think badly of our people and what we have built."

Isaac glanced back in the direction he had left Abram. "Well, I *am* afraid your mother may be tempting our father, even as we speak. But Father is extremely righteous. I doubt if he would notice a wanton suggestion."

Kedar's eyes flared at this reference to his virtuous grandmother. Nebaioth subtly reached over to touch Kedar's hand as he said, "Grandmother Incense is a pious woman, Uncle."

Kedar added, "And she could have any man in Egypt she wished. I doubt Grandfather Abram is making her wanton blood rise."

Wide-eyed, Jacob stepped back and asked, "May we go now, Father? We have acknowledged our relatives as pious men are obligated to do. Perhaps the smells will not be as bad nearer the river."

Kedar asked, "Do you have something on your upper lip, Cousin Jacob?"

Isaac quickly said, "Your city is most interesting; especially this temple to a new god that doesn't exist. Father and Lord Abram have discussed it constantly and are anxious to hear the details of it. But come, sons, we must go now. Good day, Nephews."

Kedar and Nebaioth watched the three men depart. Kedar asked, "Is Cousin Esau really related to them?"

HORUS, AZAZIL, AND BASEMATH

Azazil and Basemath sat in the temple discussing possible positions and attitudes she might take while sitting on the platform of the Hubal; standing, sitting, or prostrate. All-giving or unapproachable or welcoming? Her maybe-priestesses sat around them listening.

Horus entered and unceremoniously interrupted their meeting. Horus, with simmering deep theological differences rising, said to Azazil, "So my once-devoted follower has finally rejected my command and will become a destroyer of mankind!"

Basemath stood and commanded, "Welcome to the Church of Light, Shaman Horus! Here you shall experience the endless love of all people for all other people. Here the truth of 'Love One Another' is made real. Sit. Join us in peace."

Horus's long-pent-up anger rose, "You create an abomination, priestess. You intend to teach things that men are not meant to know. Hearing and understanding your teachings will give men reason to believe that they are gods. They will become the abominations I seek to destroy. Evil! Corrupt! Self-centered! Greedy! Without love! You will teach a truth that mankind is incapable of understanding. It will destroy them! Destroy us all!"

Azazil, now standing, replied, "Horus, you are angry with me. This temple is not a place for anger. Walk with me. Castigate me outside." Azazil began walking out of the temple.

This enraged the already angry Horus. He spat out all manner of contempt for all manner of things.

Azazil walked outside of the temple knowing that Horus would follow.

Basemath sat serenely watching the two men from her Hubal. Her maybe-priestesses observed everything with wide-eyed wonder. One, then two, and then three of the maybe-priestesses stood and positioned themselves to protect entrance into the temple from further anger.

Horus grew angrier as he followed Azazil into the street.

People were attracted to the commotion including Isaac, Jacob, Esau, Sanakhte, and Khaba.

Horus followed behind Azazil to the river shouting, "You betray me Azazil. I told you of the Testament of Horus with the understanding that you would not repeat his words. You agreed that the words should be hidden from the knowledge of men!"

Azazil replied, "Your memories have grown dim, Teacher. None of those things are true. Lady Baalat gained me access to the Chest of Tallstone because you would not tell your most devout followers the Testament of Set. Old age has flawed your judgment by every measure. Your two most ardent, trusted followers tell you this, yet you will not even consider our arguments. Have you grown afraid that your life's work will come to fruition and men other than yourself shall understand the nature of life and death? How does their knowledge diminish your life?"

Horus shouted, "You are evil, Azazil. I cast you out of my company. You can no longer claim to be a disciple of Horus. You are condemned to lead mankind into eternal evil!"

Horus turned and stormed away.

~~~~~~~~~~~~~

29. The Founding of Meccah

Year 204, Season 7, Ishtarmonth

Horus stood outside the temple in the predawn light facing eastward.

He thought, *Father, I am old. I wait. My patience is gone, as is my peace, my love, my hope. I celebrate Abram as my greatest student. But a student who continues to destroy the ancient bond between male and female. I revile my student Baalat. The person who does the most to hold back the subjugation of the feminine to the masculine. I publicly cast off Azazil, my student who still trusts men to hear truth and be elevated by it. He does not know the nature of men as I do. He still believes. Is it to be the Priestess, who I have never taught, that brings the message of "The Light" to the people? Will they believe? Will that care? Will they embrace "The Way of Kiya?" If she succeeds, then I was wrong and I was hiding the very knowledge that might liberate the minds of all men. The way is long, Father. And I am old. Help those that can best serve you.*

The sun breached the horizon. Horus raised his arms. "Greetings Osiris. Shine your love on your people so that they may rejoice …"

Many people gathered to witness Horus greet his father. Horus finished his ceremony, acknowledged the people, and invited them to ask any questions they might have. He never noticed the woman standing behind him. Watching. Wondering. Questioning.

After a long time listening, Priestess Basemath turned and reentered her temple.

THE NAMING OF MECCAH

The Temple was located at the northernmost part of the city, the Coliseum at the most southern. The procession of the Pharaoh from his northern camp, past the temple, through the city to the Coliseum was a spectacle complete with everything necessary for a spectacle. Nebaioth, Basemath, and Kedar led the procession. They were followed by Princess Incense, Ishmael, and Amenirdis—followed by drummers, by dancers, by singers, by the Egyptian influential and high-born, followed by Egypt, itself—Pharaoh Djoser and Queen Hetephe.

The procession with its countless guests and revelers entered the Coliseum. Amid the mass confusion of finding seats, Nebaioth, Basemath, Kedar, Incense, and Ishmael mounted the center stage facing the area where Djoser and Hetephe would sit.
~~~~~~~~~~~~~

Horus was the last to enter and found a place to stand near the entrance.

As the crowd settled down, Ishmael strode to the front of the stage, and began the ceremony to establish the city of Meccah by holding a flask high, and loudly announcing, "Grandfather Djoser, tell your friend, Dionysus, that it is I, Ishmael, who brought the wine this time."

Most Egyptians understood the reference and howled with merriment.

Near the entrance, the last measure of self-worth drained from Horus, the only begotten son of the gods of Egypt—Isis and Osiris.

THE CHURCH OF LIGHT

As one major event was ending, another was to begin immediately.

Basemath, her three priestesses, and many maybe-priestesses gathered at their positions at the temple. Although practiced many times, they knew that complete chaos waited patiently to find any weakness in their ritual.

The honorees were escorted from the coliseum to line up for admission to the temple before the crowd was released.

Only three hundred sixty people could participate in a ceremony. Three hundred-sixty prayer carpets circled the outside of the temple. Of the three-hundred sixty, the first one hundred eighty to enter would be the current permanent residents of Meccah, ranked oldest to youngest. The next ninety were selected from the interested workers who had built the city and its roads, including Pilot Rhodos. The remainder would be family and friends led by Ishmael and Priestess Maribah of Shur and their families. The group included Abram and political allies such as General Sanakhte and General Khaba. Horus had declined his invitation. The last two to enter would be the Queen and the Pharaoh.

As preparations to enter the temple were being finalized, the crowd was stunned to see attendants strip the robes of power from the Pharaoh and the Queen leaving them clothed only in the simple linen tunics of beggars. Horus watched with an empty heart and emptier soul.

The waiting participants circled the temple. A maybe-priestess explained that even if a god they would soon bow to did not exist, they had parents or sisters or brothers or aunts or uncles or ancestors who worshiped this god. It was not the god they bowed to; they were respecting those who did worship the god.

A single bell rang.

Maybe-priestesses instructed each person to pick up the prayer carpet beside them, follow the person in front of them into the temple, and repeat their actions each step of the way.

A second bell rang.

Azazil led the people into the temple

Each idol along the wall was illuminated by a single candle. The room was blackness but for three-hundred sixty flickering candles illuminating three-hundred sixty gods.

Azazil stopped before the Canaanite idol of Yahweh and bowed. He then turned and went to the next idol, Asherah, and again bowed. Each person, in turn, repeated these actions until Azazil reached the three-hundred sixtieth idol where he fell in behind the Pharaoh who was just then bowing to Yahweh.

As the last person moved to the second idol, Azazil picked up the candle illuminating Yahweh and turned to walk toward the center of the room, the candle lighting his way. The candle light hinted at a circular platform in the center of the room. Azazil placed his candle on the platform, turned, and then slowly began to move on. The second candle arrived and was placed on the platform and the man followed the almost unseeable Azazil. As more and more candles were added to the platform, the High-Priestess, sitting cross-legged in the center of the platform, began to be illuminated.

Azazil continued his slow walk around the platform followed, in step, by the three-sixty. The once giddy, excited, curious, thrill-seeking participants were now humbled and quiet, filled with the wonder of gods, filled with the bond between themselves and all of humanity.

Azazil completed his circuit around the Hubal and stopped. Three hundred-sixty candles illuminated the Hubal. Three hundred sixty people surrounded the Hubal. Azazil motioned for them to place their prayer rug on the floor and sit.

They sat.

A bell sounded three times. The Hubal began to slowly rotate and rise as it rotated.

The High-Priestess began. "I am Basemath, High-Priestess of the Church of Light.' My Church contains and celebrates the Tree of Life. The Tree of Life was born from a seed at the beginning of all things. The tree grows and creates all things. The Tree of Life is all things—The One, The All, The Light."

The Hubal continued to turn and to rise higher.

She spoke louder, "Close your eyes and bow your heads to the majesty of The Tree of Life!"

The participants obeyed

In the stillness, there was no sound but the surprisingly loud voice of a High-Priestess from on high.

She thundered:
"Those that follow the Path of Kiya are enlightened and worthy.
Honor your ancestors. They are your past. You are their future.
Kill nothing you do not consume unless it will harm you. Each life is precious unto itself.
Honor your vows. Do that which you say you will do.
Take nothing that is not yours.
Say nothing that is false.
Pick up those who have fallen.
Give to those who ask.
Love everyone, even those who despise you.
Be worthy."

The thundering voice stopped and gave way to stillness.

A disembodied voice from on high then said, "You shall soon shed the body that constrains you and you shall be welcomed into eternity. Open your eyes, stand on your feet, and behold!"

The people stood. All was in total darkness but for the ceiling, high above. The ceiling had been designed to reflect the light of three hundred sixty candles: an encompassing light from an unknowable source. Warm, inviting, peaceful, without condition, without guilt, welcoming. The Tree of Life. The One. The All.

The candles were instantaneously extinguished leaving the room in total darkness. For a moment. Or an eternity. Or maybe it never even happened, the people were without reference to life or death, existence or oblivion. knowing or unknowing.

Then, a disembodied voice thundered from on high, "BEHOLD THE TREE OF LIFE."

Djoser, Hetephe, Incense/Hagar/Keterah
Horus, Serket, Azazil, Abram, Baalat
Ishmael, Maribah, Fatimah, Nebaioth, Basemath, Kedar | Anath, Astarte

To the clash of cymbals, hidden directional lights illuminated only the space between the floor and the Hubal, now raised to the ceiling. Three hundred sixty strands of gold and silver fell from the circumference of the Hubal in a vortex, wrapping themselves around each other to become a single strand originating at the center of the temple floor.

Three Priestesses faced the crowd with their backs to the strands of silver and gold. They began to sing Kiya's "Song of Enlightenment." As they sang, Azazil led the people around the periphery of the temple for the Third time and back outside the temple into the gathered crowd.

The excited, curious crowd parted to make way for the exiting solemn, reflecting congregation.

~~~

Each of the three hundred sixty participants were moved in their own way.

Azazil hoped that his once-teacher Horus would come to him.

Abram walked in studious silence, needing his teacher to explain what he had just witnessed.

Maribah said to Ishmael, "I must go to my daughter!"

Esau became excited and said to his cousins, "Basemath did that! Did you see her? Did you hear her? Our Basemath did that!"

Nebaioth and Kedar looked at one another with validation.

An unknown person sidled up to General Khaba and judiciously inquired, "Did she say anything of significance?"

Inside, attendants quickly dressed Djoser and Hetephe in their robes as the priestesses and the want-to-be priestesses reconfigured their temple.

VIGNETTES

What a day this had been! A new city. A new religion. A new everything. The stars were in their courses.

Horus and Azazil walked together beside the river, talking.

Khaba was lost in thought, unsure of what he had just witnessed.

Nimrod found Abram and said, "How did she address the role of the female to the male?"

Basemath saw her mother and ran to embrace her.
~~~

Esau stopped and stared at nothing. He muttered to Nebaioth and Kedar, "W-would she would look on me with pity if I asked her to consider ... taking me as her husband?"

Nebaioth and Kedar stopped with their cousin, Esau. Kedar said, "Priestesses don't leave their temples unattended, Cousin. She won't go exploring the world with you!"

Alone, Ishmael walked to the crest of the road.

From there he could see his son's city surrounded by seven mountains. Down the road, in the distance would lie the sea of Aqaba. Beyond, Egypt. He was surrounded by infinite possibilities.

He stood, he was sure, at the center of the world!

Djoser, Hetephe, Incense/Hagar/Keterah
Horus, Serket, Azazil, Abram, Baalat
Ishmael, Maribah, Fatimah, Nebaioth, Basemath, Kedar | Anath, Astarte

~~~~~~~~~~~~~~

30. Djoser's Last Year

Year 205, Season 1, Osirismonth

Six seasons passed.

In Memphis, High-Priestess Hathor performed a magnificent Winter Solstice Festival sunrise ceremony. Osiris rose higher in the sky than the day before. The world rejoiced. The joyful revelry began.

THE HOUSE OF DJOSER

Ishmael, Fatimah, and their sons celebrated with Princess Incense and her parents in their private quarters.

Djoser was lamenting. "I have witnessed my last Winter's Solstice sunrise ceremony. This time next year, Hetephe and I will be celebrating with our ancestors and perhaps with Isis and Osiris! It will be glorious reliving old times, won't it Archer Hete!"

Hetephe: "Reliving old times? I may have some old times I don't wish to share with my husband."

Djoser: "You were young and foolish, Wife. Exactly which old times are you referring to?"

Hetephe: "Let it be a surprise, Husband."

He laughed. She didn't

Ishmael lamented, "I have failed you, Grandfather. Only two of your twelve grandsons have a city of their own and you have only one more year as Pharaoh. Building almost a city a month will be difficult, but I suppose I could try."

Djoser said, "You built two cities that Egypt did not have before. Wonderful cities, at that. Give your sons whatever time they need. They will make their own future, with or without the help of a Pharaoh."

Ishmael said, 'Kedar doesn't want his own city. He's interested in exploring the lands south of Meccah with some young woman. But both Mishma and Dumah are continually looking for places for their city. Mibsam is like his older sister, more interested in the Land of the Dead and gods than in leading a tribe. Nebaioth insists that the Chest of Tallstone should be moved to Meccah because Basemath's church is
~~~~~~~~~~~~~~

based on its writings plus Basemath is hungry to read the writings for herself. What do you think? First Mother or Meccah?"

Hetephe would not have it. "Move the chest from First Mother who has protected it for so many years? No! The chest is the child of First Mother!"

Ishmael laughed. "May I remind my grandmother of the words of the old woman Truth-teller; 'First Mother wishes to release her children into the world to stand tall and do great deeds. The Ark must be given its freedom and allowed to climb great heights—to teach all people—to find its destiny. Ma'at is not served until this comes to pass.' I thought the woman to be somewhat addled, but still …"

Hetephe snorted, "She *did* say that. But if you move it, let it be after my passing."

Mibsam listened with excitement. *My name is being discussed beside affairs of state. Maybe I can be in charge of moving it! Brother and Sister will be proud!*

Nine-year-old Napish admonished his younger brother, Kedemah, "Stop pretending to be a scary bear, Keddy. You aren't fooling anybody."

Ishmael looked at Fatimah and suggested, "We should have more children!"

Fatimah laughed.

Ishmael rounded up his family, took a beer for himself, and fruit-wines for his wife and mother. They departed the palace to walk the streets of Memphis and join in the singing of holiday songs. The people of Memphis adored Prince Ishmael and his family.

Times were good.

Times would change.

THE MASTABA OF OSIRIS

Hathor retired with Horus to her place of safety, Osiris's Mastaba.

Horus sat a glass of wine on his father's chest and sat down beside his body. Hathor leaned back against Horus's chest as his arms wrapped around her, protecting her from the world. They sipped fine wine.

She talked of melancholy things. "I did the best I could with the words Osiris told me, but Lord Set's testament has added more words to my knowledge of death, of life after death, of the nature of gods. It's all so complicated yet all so simple. I think Priestess Maribah's young daughter in Meccah understands it better than I. She conducts a ceremony more relevant than mine. I—High-Priestess of Osiris—replaced by a novice priestess in a city past the ends of the earth. Of course, her religion is unproven, and I don't fully understand it, but more wine, please."

Horus said, "Priestess Basemath and Azazil teach that a person's concept of god is limited by their experience, but it doesn't matter what they believe because all gods are twigs on the same Tree of Life. In the Land of the Dead, all people who honor a particular god are connected by their belief in that god. All that matters is we respect other people's god, and not believe that our god is the only god. Eventually, all who are enlightened will realize there are no gods, just all things united for eternity."

"Yet it was you that drove Set to deliver the Testament to the living. It's you who brought forth her religion. Azazil told me that it completes the Way of Kiya perfectly. It is the answer to the 'why.' It is you who should be teaching this to the people, but you were too frightened. You did not trust their worth."

"Do you believe I should embrace the teachings of Basemath?"

"You have always taught the 'how.' You need only add the 'why.' Besides, it would please Serket."

He thought, *You do not understand, Mother. Azazil does not understand. Sheep are sheep easily misled into false thoughts, self-destroying thoughts. They would not understand, and if they did, the Kyrios-Olon would not be far behind.*

He said, "I will *not* teach it! It would not bring the sheep peace."

"Teach it. It will bring Serket peace."

THE HOUSE OF GENERAL SANAKHTE

General Sanakhte and his three favorite concubines hosted a gathering for General Khaba, his wife Meresankh, his son Huni, and the support staff of both houses.

The general sipped his wine as he reflected on days past. "Perhaps it was best that Djoser became Pharaoh instead of me. The Pharaoh's responsibilities are relentless and unending. It wears one down. He is older than his years. His mind is no longer always quick. He could live on and become a doddering old man wandering around his land, but he insists that he is no longer best for Egypt. But I understand that my son is under consideration. An honor on us both, Khaba."

Phoenicia, Jaffa, Rocky, Burlyman, Polydore | Astarte, T'jaru
Terah, Amathlai, Haran, Terahson, Nahor, Sarai, Isaac, Jacob
Kyrios-Olon, Teumessian, Nimrod, Nimbal, Nimlad, Nimisis, Asherah, Set.

Khaba replied, "I do not deserve such consideration, Father. I am content to help Egypt in whatever small ways I can."

"That is why you are being considered, Son. Djoser places a high value on those who would serve Egypt and not their self-interests. You matured almost overnight. From a boy reveling in self-glory to serving the land of Egypt. Even the queen admitted it. Djoser was most impressed that you solved Pilot Rhodos's problem by offering her soldiers from your guard."

Khaba fought back his self-righteousness. *You were correct Servant Nimisis. You advised me correctly in these matters. Always praise Egypt, never myself. My day of supreme glory will come! You will be my Vizier.*

Khaba said, "Everyone knows that Djoser will select you as his successor, Father. You are the wisest, most respected man in Egypt—other than Pharaoh Djoser, of course."

"Who would be your second choice, Son?"

Khaba choked on the forthcoming word "me" and spit out instead, "Rafah would make an excellent Pharaoh. He will live several more years, I believe."

Huni asked his grandfather, "What must I do to become Pharaoh, Grandfather?"

Sanakhte laughed. "Live long, be wise and just, follow the path of Kiya, but mostly, be fortunate."

Khaba thought, *And have a Pharaoh as your father.*

His faithful, ever-present servant, Nimisis, refilled Khaba's wine glass.

THE NAMING

Year 205, Season 6, Aresmonth

They sat at their table looking over the great river. He told her his decision.

She asked, "Are you sure he is the one, Husband?"

"Doubt is for the weak, Hetephe. I am not weak. Let us drink!" He held up her glass of wine to salute her.

She responded in kind. "I will take comfort in knowing that no one is worthy to replace you. He has his weaknesses, but also many strengths."

"Incense would have been perfect if she were mean enough. Ishmael simply isn't aware enough of the needs of Egypt."

Djoser, Hetephe, Incense/Hagar/Keterah
Horus, Serket, Azazil, Abram, Baalat
Ishmael, Maribah, Fatimah, Nebaioth, Basemath, Kedar | Anath, Astarte

"Mean? When were you ever mean?"

Djoser laughed, "I left a trail of blood and tears. I destroyed people. I manipulated lives. Didn't you notice? Maybe I was too nice to you."

"Oh, yes. You were prepared to let me entertain the entire Nubian Army on a table at Hostess House. I had forgotten about that."

"You *do* understand. I believe Khaba will build the glory of Egypt, if only for his own glory. Had I named Sanakhte, he would be dead soon enough and Khaba would become Pharaoh, anyway. This is why we have wine, woman!"

HEIR TO THE KINGDOM

This sunrise ceremony would be momentous. Everyone knew it. Everyone gathered. Waiting. The next Pharaoh of Egypt would be named.

The sun reflected off the peak of the obelisk and began its slow slide down. Women touched their husbands. Everyone held their breath. Waiting.

Hathor stood where she always stood. Hands clasped. Head bowed. Waiting.

On the next level, a figure knelt prostrate, head on the floor, dressed as a beggar. Waiting.

On the level above the beggar, the Pharaoh stood, stone-faced, arms crossed, holding crook and flail. Looking out over his people. Waiting.

Osiris continued to slide down his obelisk.

Hathor stepped forward and raised her arms.

Osiris breached the horizon. Waiting ended.

With Ra on his way into the morning sky, the normal ceremony would now end. But on this morning, when the High-Priestess lowered her arms, there were cymbals and drums. She turned to face the beggar and the Pharaoh and to the raising of her arms, the beggar rose to his full height.

Attendants rushed to remove the beggar's tunic and replace it with a robe of power. The heir to the throne of Egypt. The heir in which the godhood of Osiris would be blown in the coming Winter Solstice. The future Pharaoh of Egypt raised his arms to his people.

The crowd erupted with tumultuous excitement and praise for their soon-to-be Pharaoh. General Khaba of Egypt.

Phoenicia, Jaffa, Rocky, Burlyman, Polydore | Astarte, T'jaru
Terah, Amathlai, Haran, Terahson, Nahor, Sarai, Isaac, Jacob
Kyrios-Olon, Teumessian, Nimrod, Nimbal, Nimlad, Nimisis, Asherah, Set.

PILOT RHODOS

Pilot Rhodos was granted an audience with Pharaoh Djoser. She strode in all smiles and happiness. "Take me on an airboat ride, Pilot Djoser!"

"I may be out of practice, Pilot Rhodos."

"Look, Djoser. I brought you bags of the weed of paradise, a lifetime supply of room lights to light those Mastabas of yours, and that big supply of ambrosia pills. You owe me!"

Hetephe asked, "Will he have a chaperon?"

"No. Just him and me. Up there in the big fluffy clouds. Just like when we were young and innocent and adventuresome."

Hetephe looked at Djoser and snarled, "What man could refuse *that* invitation?"

Djoser looked at Rhodos and said, "I will be delighted to fly in big fluffy clouds with you, Rhodos. Even without all those expensive gifts you gave me. I am at your disposal. Give me a time."

"Tomorrow before first sun. We can get to altitude and watch Hathor's ceremony from up in the sky. Bring wine!" She turned to Hetephe and said, "He turned out nice. Didn't he? I knew he would. And don't worry. I will take good care of him." Rhodos smirked, turned, and confidently strode out.

Hetephe glared after her.

Djoser innocently said, "I've always had a weakness for strong women."

FINALE

Airboat 113 hovered below the big fluffy clouds. They sipped wine as they watched the sunrise ceremony play out far below. She leaned back against his chest; his arms encircled her body. The ceremony finished, she broke his embrace and said, "You still can't have me, Djoser. Set course to Port Spearpoint location."

He studied the map and onboard compass, moved the rudders, and said, "Course set to Port Spearpoint location."

"Pour me more wine."

"More wine poured."

"Hold me again."

"He slid in behind her and embraced her. "Holding until further notice."

She pressed her back against his chest and cried. "I loved him! I loved him so much. He was a Pilot! He took me to the sky and taught me everything!"

Then they were quiet for a while.

She said, "But he died. I can go back to the sea now. I am an Oceanid, you know. At least, I was. I miss my sisters and the Sea. Djoser returns me to the sea. To my sisters. He was once a little boy trying to seduce me. Now, he's a Pharaoh and he *still* can't seduce me. So sad. We have traveled far but I want to go home." She fell asleep in his arms

They sailed on.

~~~

They stood side by side as they hovered above Port Spearpoint, now submerged far below the water's surface. She opened the boarding gate, looked out over the sea, and said, "I would enjoy another glass of wine with you, Djoser, but I have a long swim ahead, and I am out of practice. I will settle for a brotherly kiss."

"Must it be brotherly?"

She laughed. "Still trying! I like that in a Pharaoh." She dropped her tunic, placed his hands on her breasts, pecked him on his cheek, stepped back for a moment letting him inspect her body, turned, and dove into the waiting sea.

He watched her graceful dive. Watched her enter the sea and, in his mind at least, saw her surface, blow him a kiss, then begin her long swim toward Tartarus. *Soon, Oceanid, I will see you soon.*

He set course back to Memphis.

SUMMER SOLSTICE—MECCAH

Year 205, Season 6, Aresmonth

In the early days of Aresmonth, every member of Ishmael's family gathered in Meccah, even Abram.

For the special Summer Solstice service, the three hundred citizens of Mecca let Ishmael's family enter their temple first.

High-Priestess Basemath sat cross-legged in the darkness on the Hubal as her six priestesses lit the three-hundred-sixty candles. Love flowed from
~~~

her heart across the idols, over her family, over her people, and over the world. She sat in the reflected shadow of the boundary of the power and glory of the dead – of "The Tree of Life." *I'm glad I didn't let Azazil convince me to engage in ritual fornication on the way to the ceiling. That's for fertility rituals. Not this. Besides, Esau had a better suggestion.*

Outside, High-Priest Azazil and his six priests coordinated the line of people waiting to enter the temple. The citizens needed no more training. Their entry and circumnavigation were second nature to them. They never tired of the ritual. It renewed them. Refreshed them. Removed their doubts and anger toward others. It brought them peace. And with peace, universal love of all humanity. The Church of Light was the primary reason people migrated to Meccah. Its reputation grew slowly but surely.

And on this special day, the city overflowed with visitors, all potential immigrants. There would be three services on this day alone and that many again on the next day, and the next until all desiring entry were accommodated.

High-Priest Azazil prepared himself to lead Kedemah, and those behind him, into the temple. *I still think the fornication suggestion would have worked. Nothing brings a man and woman closer together than that. But Esau did offer the better suggestion. Have the male High-Priest lead the people to the female High-Priestess and have a priest for each priestess. Male and Female. Life and Death. The One, The All. Ma'at, I suppose.*

The bell rang. The High-Priest led the people on their long journey to the High-Priestess to experience the reflected shadow of "The One."

The ceremony was magnificent!

~~~

Outside, Pharaoh-to-be General Khaba bristled with the indignation of being scheduled for the second ceremony rather than the first. "I should have led the way! How dare those people put me in the second group!"

His faithful servant Nimisis calmed him. "Your patience and understanding have brought you to the pinnacle, Great Pharaoh-to-be Khaba! This time next year, you can do whatever you wish to do to this city and especially this temple where the High-Priestess has so greatly insulted you! But until that day. A smile and misdirecting praise will serve you well, as it did to bring you to the pinnacle."

"But I am the designated Pharaoh, now. People should bow before me!"

Djoser, Hetephe, Incense/Hagar/Keterah
Horus, Serket, Azazil, Abram, Baalat
Ishmael, Maribah, Fatimah, Nebaioth, Basemath, Kedar | Anath, Astarte
~~~

"You are too intelligent for that kind of thought, my Lord. Especially expressing it out loud. One potentially insulting word will reach the ear of Ishmael, then Princess Incense, then the Pharaoh himself. You have worked so hard to get here. Don't allow lack of patience sabotage everything you have worked for."

"As always, Servant Nimisis, you are correct." *I didn't add, "I was wise to select you." I must not say things like that out loud. I'm getting good at this!*

WINTER SOLSTICE EVE

Year 205, Season 12, Isismonth

The day came as it must. The final day in the lives of Djoser and Hete.

High-Priestess Hathor celebrated their lives on this, their final, Sun Rise Ceremony. They stood tall on the level above her saluting the people, loving the people. Finally, as the concluding act, Horus came to the Pharaoh, took his Crook and Flail, and laid them upon an altar.

The Pharaoh and queen waved their final goodbye and retired into the Mastaba that would, soon enough, be *their* Mastaba.

Hathor concluded the ceremony and led the Priestesses and Priests into the soon-to-be Mastaba above Osiris. They drank ceremonial wine and said ceremonial things.

Hathor came to face Djoser. She held her arms out to her sides. Attendants came and disrobed her down to her undergarment—a dirty tunic of a beggar woman. She fell to her knees and kissed the feet of Djoser. She rose. "This is how the Great Trader from Memphis found me. Without Egypt, this is who I am."

She turned and walked to the Mastaba below to join Horus and Osiris.

The remaining dignitaries spoke to Djoser. Last was his heir, Pharaoh-to-be Khaba. Well-rehearsed Khaba asked, "Tell me what I must do to become as great as you, Pharaoh Djoser!'

"Love your people, Khaba. Always do what is best for your people."

Khaba bowed and kissed the ring. *This is disgusting. But soon enough ...*

Ishmael's Family

Djoser and Hetephe retired to their palace to eat their last highsun meal.

Princess Incense, Ishmael, and his family waited for them in the family room. Both Priestesses Maribah and Basemath had left the care of their

Temples to their assistants. This day was too momentous not to make personal sacrifices to be with two of the greatest people to have ever lived. This might well be the last time Ishmael would have his entire family in one place. How fitting that it be with Djoser and Hetephe.

The adults let the boys run to embrace their great-grandparents as they entered the family room. Everyone settled in, Kedemah and Napish stood beside their great-grandmother; Jetur and Tema beside their Great-grandfather. All the children sang a well-rehearsed song of praise. There was joy and laughter.

Basemath rose, took Esau's hand, marched to Djoser, and announced, "Esau seeks to marry me, Great-grandfather. Will you permit it?"

Djoser rose and intoned, "I, still-Pharaoh-of-Egypt Djoser, command you, Esau, to marry this woman, Basemath; to protect her and her children, to have enough sense to do whatever she wishes you do; and to always follow the path of Horus—and Basemath— until the moment you join us in The Light."

Esau asked, "Are we married, now?"

Maribah said, "That sounded like a marriage ceremony to me, Daughter."

Basemath exclaimed, "It was! You may kiss me, Husband!"

Esau, embarrassed and confused, to the sound of applause, did as he was commanded.

The family retired into the eating room for their highsun meal.

Joy, laughter, and merriment filled the room; along with …

Incense: "We will visit you in your Mastaba tomorrow, but will leave you before the midday coronation. The less Khaba sees of us the better."
Djoser: "Khaba will not dare violate the sanctity of anyone's Mastaba. It would set a precedent."
Incense: "The Sinai and the lands south of Midian will be safe. Khaba is not interested in those lands. They are too wild for his tastes."
Ishmael: "We will disappear from the land of Egypt and create the land of Ishmael."

After the meal, Djoser took Incense aside and instructed her, "Horus will be in my Mastaba, tomorrow. Follow him when you leave. He will take you to a wagon that contains your inheritance. The wagon contains the usual riches plus a special bag Rhodos gave me that contains pellets of ambrosia. A pellet every quarter moon extends life tenfold. Do with this gift as you will. No one knows of the wagon but Horus. Khaba would be infuriated if he found out. Take care of your family as best you can but know that Egypt is no longer safe for you. Even Shur may be too close to Khaba. You will be safe in Byblos or Meccah or even Hebron. Perhaps go to T'jaru in the Far East. I love you, Daughter. You have had a far greater influence on humanity than you can imagine. Soon, my daughter, I will see you soon."

He turned and rejoined the others.

The party rejoiced on. Everyone left before evening meal.

Djoser and Hetephe

They sat at their table looking out over the great river as they prepared to drink the wine of life.

He asked, "Are you sure this is what you wish, Hetephe?"

"Doubt is for the weak, Djoser. I am not weak. Let us drink!" She held up her glass of wine to salute him.

He responded in kind.

They drank.

He took her hand and pulled her to stand before the bench that had always faced the river.

He stood behind her and wrapped his arms around her. "Do you remember the many times we greeted the rising sun here? They were the best times of my life."

"I remember them. Every one. So good."

"You would have lived many more years, my love."

"Yes. Yes, I would have. But without you, and with a tyrant ruling over the land you created, and with that Oceanid-pilot-hussy constantly running her hands all over you in that Land of the Dead place. A woman must protect her interests. Besides, if Priestess Basemath is correct, I am only now about to live. It will be exciting to find out."

"We have done so much, lived such wonderful lives, known so many wonderful people."

"Yes. But the wine makes me think of Ibis heads. There's one around here someplace. I know there is."

Phoenicia, Jaffa, Rocky, Burlyman, Polydore | Astarte, T'jaru
Terah, Amathlai, Haran, Terahson, Nahor, Sarai, Isaac, Jacob
Kyrios-Olon, Teumessian, Nimrod, Nimbal, Nimlad, Nimisis, Asherah, Set.

She reached behind her and started exploring his body.

He laughed. "Is that to be our final act, Great Archer Hetephe?"

She turned and stared into his eyes as she slowly slid her hand down his body. She whispered, "Oh, yes, my immature little prince. Oh, yes, it is."

The walls began to glow with soft light. But death is considerate. It waited until they were ready to come into the light together.

Djoser, Hetephe, Incense/Hagar/Keterah
Horus, Serket, Azazil, Abram, Baalat
Ishmael, Maribah, Fatimah, Nebaioth, Basemath, Kedar | Anath, Astarte

~~~~~~~~~~~~~

31. Pharaoh Khaba

Hathor knew more of power and politics than even Djoser.

Nimisis's appearance was transparent from the moment she first learned of it, which was immediately. *Nimlad, Nimbal, Nimrod, Nimisis? How obvious. Of course, Nimisis had been sent by those Church of Urfa Kyrios-Olon people to seduce the weakest link in Egyptian power to their desires. So it is Khaba, is it? What shall I do?*

What she did was to bend Khaba and Nimisis to *her* desires. As the time drew near, her staff began lamenting how inappropriate that an old used High-Priestess was to breathe the life of Osiris into the new Pharaoh; it should a younger, prettier priestess who would then be designated to replace Hathor as High Priestess.

After Khaba was chosen to become the new Pharaoh, she allowed Khaba to come to her and explain why another priestess might be better to perform the sacred ritual; someone younger, perhaps. Hathor was delighted to parade her younger priestesses before him; Hathor's favorite was made up even more so than the others. Hathor's favorite being the priestess Hathor had already decided would become her successor. The Priestess was as accomplished in all things as Hathor, including knowing beauty was a weapon to be used to insulate all Mastabas from any manner of disrespect or desecration.

So it was that the young priestess, behind Khaba's back, became infatuated with the very air that Nimisis breathed. Hathor imagined Nimisis's eyes becoming slits as he imagined having complete control over High-Priestess Tentysis. *How silly men are.*

~~~

So it was that High-Priestess Hathor called forth Osiris to become Ra, the living sun

Horus smiled. *Remember Father, at highsun a priestess will blow your godhood into a new Pharaoh. The last one died last night. But you already know that.*

As Hathor concluded her morning ritual, Horus led the family from Djoser's Mastaba through the back passages onto the Grand Concourse. From there he led them the back way to the river.

A priest whispered something into Hathor's ear as she orchestrated the mayhem between completing the Winters Solstice ritual of the calling forth of Osiris and initiating the planned highsun ritual of the Anointing of Pharaoh Khaba. Hathor whispered something back.

As Horus and the family of Djoser approached the road to Shur, they were overtaken by Members of Khaba's guard. "Great Princess Incense, where are you going?"

Incense replied, "I will answer your impertinent question with one of my own, why do you hail me?"

The guard, coached by Nimisis in the way of "if you aren't allowed to kill them, then show them respect," answered, "I apologize for my unintended impertinence, Princess Incense, but General Khaba just learned of your departure, and he was so looking forward to speaking to you after his Anointing. Will you be able to accept this invitation?"

"Is this an invitation or a command, Guard?"

"*General* Khaba would not dare command a Princess, Princess Incense."

Incense considered the emphasis on "General" and her options. "The Pharaoh desires only *my* presence? My son and grandchildren are free to return Shur?"

"Yes, Princess Incense."

Ishmael growled, "I will escort you, Mother!"

Multiple scenarios played out in her mind. She decided, and said, "Very well, Ishmael." She turned to Horus and commanded, "Shaman, please escort my grandchildren to Shur carrying with them only that which is theirs. Am I understood?"

Horus answered, "Yes, Princess Incense, and I have many followers in Memphis. They will be there to assist you in any way you might need." He stared at the guards.

She said, "We will do whatever is necessary to maintain peace and goodwill with our new Great Pharaoh Khaba. All of us are in complete agreement, I'm sure."

Horus nodded and said, "Pharaoh Khaba is just and wise." He led all but Incense and Ishmael away toward Shur.

Incense and Ishmael were marched toward the Palace. They worked their way through the mass of people awaiting the spectacle of the anointing of

Djoser, Hetephe, Incense/Hagar/Keterah
Horus, Serket, Azazil, Abram, Baalat
Ishmael, Maribah, Fatimah, Nebaioth, Basemath, Kedar | Anath, Astarte

the Pharaoh. No one noticed them enter the palace where they were left in an empty receiving room. The Guards took up position outside the doors.

Soon, a hooded shadow appeared in a shadowed doorway. The figure put its finger to its lips and motioned violently for Ishmael to leave. Ishmael stared at the figure with mounting anger. The figure repeated the unequivocal gestures with even more vehemence. Ishmael glanced at his mother who nodded for him to obey. He stormed from the room and demanded of their guards, "Show me where they keep the beer!"

The figure motioned for Incense to come to her. Incense accepted the urgency of the drama and went to her. The robed figure's head was covered with a veil. Through the veil, Incense saw the face of an achingly beautiful woman. The woman leaned and whispered, "I am Tentyris, heir to Hathor. This meeting does not happen, nor can it ever be imagined to have happened. Any word I say which you even suggest you heard, either to your son or Horus or a dead crow in an earless forest, will find its way back to Nimisis and my resulting painful death will be meaningless compared to the damage incurred by all humanity. Your exit from Memphis was not anticipated by Hathor. She commanded you be brought here so that I may steal precious seconds from my day to tell you things before the wheels of Nimisis's plans begin to turn. Queen Meresankh is to die by a scorpion sting before Osirismonth is ended and you will become Kahbah's wife. Khaba will celebrate his first anniversary as Pharaoh by re-carving the head of First Mother into Khaba's image. The Chest of Tallstone will be destroyed or relocated to Urfa. The Church in Meccah will be destroyed. With these things done, Nimisis can control all religious thought in Egypt. Khaba knows none of this but will blindly follow the advice of his Vizier. A fool could make *some* use of what I have told you. You are the rightful Pharaoh of Egypt. Osiris is with you." The figure disappeared into the shadowed doorway.

Incense walked to the double doors and opened them to find Ishmael drinking beer with the Pharaoh's guards. She said, "My woman's problem is over, Son. Thank you for my privacy during this period."

Ishmael laughed as he walked to follow his mother back into the room.

As she closed the door, Incense assumed her position as a Princess of Egypt exclaiming, "I have no idea why Pharaoh Khaba commanded us to return. Perhaps he wishes to ravish me on the great concourse in front of all of Memphis. If so, it is his right. But no matter what may come, you are a Prince of Egypt, and you will be gracious and subservient to power."

Phoenicia, Jaffa, Rocky, Burlyman, Polydore | Astarte, T'jaru
Terah, Amathlai, Haran, Terahson, Nahor, Sarai, Isaac, Jacob
Kyrios-Olon, Teumessian, Nimrod, Nimbal, Nimlad, Nimisis, Asherah, Set.

After the door was fully closed, she quietly said, "You will always remember I asked you to leave me and my problem in the privacy of an empty room. Do you understand?"

"I understand, Mother. Wine?"

Both changed from their traveling clothes into formal clothes and waited to be summoned.

They waited a long time but finally, their guards escorted them to the fifth level of the multi-level Mastaba. The level which Khaba could now claim.

The reception in progress was impressive. Everyone sought to tell Pharaoh Khaba how wonderful he was and that they were there to serve him. On one side stood Queen Meresankh, on the other, a priestess of immense poise and presence, and directly behind, Vizier Nimisis stood, listening to every word uttered.

A priestess took Ishmael and Incense from the guards and marched them directly to the Pharaoh. Ishmael obediently walked three steps behind, his trademark imbecilic grin plastered on his face. Incense arrived, curtsied, said all the appropriate things, and ended with, "I am so pleased that you are now Pharaoh. Egypt and the world are fortunate to have you."

Khaba was not, nor would ever be, by any measure, the Pharaoh that Djoser was. Khaba was childlike in his excitement of his crowning and anointment. He giddily responded, "Princess Incense, Hathor told me of your abrupt departure and then I was horrified to hear that you fear that I might command you to fornicate with me on the Grand Concourse for the enjoyment of my people!"

Incense blushed and responded, "Well, it is your right, of course. Even if I *have* promised a great Lord and significant ally of Egypt that I would marry him when Ma'at allows him to take me as his wife. I did not know your mind in this matter."

"Sweet Princess Incense. I have a wife—a Queen, no less. You need not fear me. A significant ally of Egypt, you say? Who might that be?"

She blushed again. "Great Pharaoh, you might be better served in affairs of state if your Vizier hears and comments on my proposal of marriage. Such a union might be useful to him."

"Yes, yes. You are correct. But my people must see the House of Djoser rejoice in my ascension. The absence of you and your son might confuse the people."

She curtsied deeply to him and motioned Ishmael to bow. She rose, almost in tears, as she said, "Oh, my Pharaoh! I had not thought of that. You are so wise! We departed because we did not wish to be a distraction from this glorious day. I did not realize that our presence might add to your glory. Forgive us for our ignorance!"

Incense, being a princess, could navigate the system.

Ishmael glanced at Nimisis. Wheels seemed to be turning in his mind.

The party roared on.

High-Priestess Hathor took time to greet Ishmael and then introduce the princess to Senior Priestess Tentyris, the priestess who had commanded the spirit of Osiris into Khaba, making him a living god. Senior Priestess Tentyris then escorted Incense to meet the wonderful Vizier Nimisis, whom she touched on the shoulder as she introduced him.

All the beautiful, wonderful people had a beautiful, wonderful time that day. Save, perhaps Vizier Nimisis, who attempted to absorb everything, and Prince Ishmael wearing his imbecilic grin as he *did* absorb everything.

Hathor was pleased.

As the designated ending time for the reception approached, priests and priestesses unobtrusively began directing their guests toward the palace. As Incense was leaving, Hathor found her and quickly said, "Your father gave me life. I will see him soon," and departed.

The last guest gone, Hathor took time to look lovingly across her city.

ON THE ROAD TO SHUR

Meanwhile, Horus and the family of Ishmael had reached the juncture where one road led to Newport and the other led to Shur.

Horus said to Nebaioth, "I must leave your good company here. I am going to Newport and find a ship bound for Byblos. Take care of your family Nebaioth. They are the best hope for truth and the Way of Kiya."

There were the usual protestations and goodbyes and sentiments. Those things being said, Horus waved goodbye and set off up the road to Newport. Nebaioth led his family down the road to Shur.

A while later, three "travelers" came to the fork and immediately followed Nebaioth down the road to Shur.

Even later, a wagon pulled by two cows emerged from overgrowth near the river. It came to the road to Shur and took it.

Night came. The wagon continued until the old, disheveled farmer saw a fire on the distant horizon and movement off the side of the road. He stopped the wagon, got down, and relieved himself by the side of the road.

A voice out of the darkness demanded, "Hey, old man. What have you got in that wagon?!"

The farmer answered, "The finest dung in Egypt, Good Master. I buy it from Newport and the quarries to take to my farm in Shur. Perhaps I could trade you some dung for a meal and drink."

A drunken figure appeared from the night, looked at the old man, smelled the nearby wagon, and said, "I think not, old man. Your smell is disgusting. Get that wagon out of here!"

"Perhaps a drink before I go, Good Master?"

"Go on! Get out of here!"

"The old farmer sniffed, "Perhaps those at yon campfire will be more gracious!"

"Perhaps they like the smell of dung, Old Man. Get out of here!"

The old, bedraggled farmer mounted his wagon and set off to see if the campfire people might be more gracious.

HATHOR AND THE GUTTER GIRL

Hathor, dressed in the robes and jewels of her office, sat in a high-back chair facing Osiris's body. The room was lit by candlelight. All of her Priestesses filed in and lined the wall of the chamber. A nude woman came in last and walked to face Hathor across from Osiris. Hathor studied the woman, candlelight reflected off them both; the room was in total silence.

Hathor asked, "Are you prepared?"

"Yes, High-Priestess. I am."

"Do you know all that you must know?"

"Yes, High-Priestess. I do."

Hathor stood and raised her arms to her sides. Priestesses rushed to her, each one removing a piece of clothing or jewel. Hathor stood naked facing the woman across from her.

Djoser, Hetephe, Incense/Hagar/Keterah
Horus, Serket, Azazil, Abram, Baalat
Ishmael, Maribah, Fatimah, Nebaioth, Basemath, Kedar | Anath, Astarte

Hathor took a step forward, and said, "Into you, I deliver the glory of Osiris." With parted lips, the two women kissed as Hathor exhaled her breath into the other woman.

The other woman picked up a glass of wine and said, "Into you, I deliver the glory of Osiris."

She held the wine for Hathor to drink and then Hathor sat down.

Hathor looked at the woman as the woman was dressed in Hathor's robes of power.

Hathor's limbs grew heavy. Her eyes closed. *I was the best Priestess I could be. He never cast me down.*

Her thoughts drifted back to her mother and her sisters—to the little gutter girl who decided to be a hostess. Someone flooded her chambers with light. She opened her eyes to see the little gutter girl standing looking down at her.

The gutter girl said, *"We did well, didn't we? I am pleased with us. But I have come to take us higher."*

Hathor opened her eyes to look across the body of Osiris as the Red-orbed crown of the High-Priestess was placed upon Tentyris's head.

Hathor then rose. The gutter girl took her hand.

~~~~~~~~~~~~~

32. Memphis to Meccah

Before daybreak the next morning, Incense and Ishmael sleepily followed the still-excited Pharaoh Khaba and his party from his palace to the Grand Concourse to watch the High-Priestess call forth Osiris.

Incense and Nimisis were two of the few people to notice that the High Priestess appeared to be somehow different this morning. She was taller, her voice deeper, the cadence of her words slower.

A subtle fear shuddered through Incense's body. *That isn't Hathor! That's Tentyris! Where is Hathor?* Incense remembered, *"Your father gave me life. I will see …"* Incense repressed a gasp.

As High-Priestess Tentyris performed the beautiful sunrise ceremony calling forth Osiris, so did Priestess Maribah perform a lovely sunrise welcoming ceremony on the road to Shur. Ishmael's family basked in the radiance of love and brotherhood. The smelly, bedraggled farmer stood by his wagon and cows admiring the actions of high-class people.

He offered to let the two women ride in his wagon if they liked.

Basemath said to Maribah, "It is the fragrance of the earth, Mother." They graciously accepted.

The group departed on the last segment of their journey to Shur. After they were underway, the old, bedraggled said in a raspy voice, "I have found women to be usually freer with knowledge than men but priestesses extremely careful with what they say. What type of mouths sit beside me?"

The two women looked at each other. Maribah asked, "What type of mouth is needed?"

The raspy voice answered, "Closed. Very, very closed."

Maribah answered, "Then closed they shall be."

The old man said, "This, then, is my story. You are being followed by three spies of the Pharaoh. My wagon carries Djoser's gifts to Incense. Incense is detained in Memphis by the Pharaoh. I must find a safe place for her gifts and rely on the wisdom of the gods to direct me."

Maribah said to Basemath, "Shur is heavily traveled by traders, soldiers, and all manner of people. Meccah is remote and peaceful. Can this wagon make it to Meccah? Roads are almost nonexistent and difficult at best."
~~~~~~~~~~~~~

Basemath answered, "Grandmother will be more at peace in Meccah now that her parents are dead. Send Esau, Kedar, and the boys with the wagon to Meccah. I will sail to Grandmother's port from Aqaba. The land south of Aqaba is wilderness, the wagon will be safe enough. If the cows die, my husband can pull the wagon. The boys can have a grand wilderness adventure."

Maribah said to the old man, "The gods direct your wagon to Meccah."

The old man said, "I will get your wagon safely past Aqaba, then pass the reins to Ishmael. The fragrance of earth will stay with me to Hebron."

~~~

In Memphis, Incense turned to Ishmael and said, "It's morning. We have no place to sleep, we have not been commanded to do anything, and I am exhausted. I will go congratulate Khaba and his wife again. You give our regards to Vizier Nimisis and let's find a place to sleep for a while and then make some plans."

"I have a plan. To leave this place as soon as we can. Saying goodbye to Nimisis will be a pleasure."

They parted, said their respective goodbyes, and met again at the foot of the Concourse.

She said, "Khaba has given my old room for my use. He seems to think that my presence lends authority to his position. I don't know how to respond to that."

He said, "Nimisis invites you—it was a command, I think—to eat evening meal with him at the palace. He wants more information on this marriage proposal. I told him that was your business; not mine. I thought your influence in Egypt was finished, Mother, but you appear to be still in demand. So, do you want to leave this place, or not?"

"Let's get some sleep. I will decide what to do after I talk with the charming Vizier."

~~~

Incense arrived at the palace for evening meal. She was concerned to find Khaba and his wife at the table with Nimisis. No one stood to greet her when she was seated. Everyone but Nimisis exchanged the customary "How nice …" pleasantries and settled in.

Nimisis bluntly asked, "Who wishes to marry you?"

Phoenicia, Jaffa, Rocky, Burlyman, Polydore | Astarte, T'jaru
Terah, Amathlai, Haran, Terahson, Nahor, Sarai, Isaac, Jacob
Kyrios-Olon, Teumessian, Nimrod, Nimbal, Nimlad, Nimisis, Asherah, Set.

She laughed, "Well, Pharaoh Khaba is happily married to a queen that will bring him greater respect and power than I ever could. So what of you, handsome Vizier? Do you wish to marry a princess of Egypt?"

Taken aback, Nimisis stammered, "No, that would ... I mean ... You mentioned a powerful ally of Egypt. I was wondering who that might be—for diplomatic purposes, of course."

"Abram of Hebron. He is a righteous man whose wife is still living but is badly ill. I was her handmaiden in my youth and bore Abram's first son because she was barren at the time. He has an affinity toward me, I suppose."

"You were a handmaiden? You bore the son of Abram of Hebron? That means Prince Ishmael is Abram's son!"

"You sound surprised. It is a vizier's duty to know everything of possible interest to the Pharaoh. Oh, dear. I didn't mean to put your position in question! I apologize."

"You ... you ... Great Pharaoh Khaba, this changes ... I mean, this marriage would greatly benefit Egypt. I recommend it. Perhaps it could take place in the temple in Shur for the enjoyment of the masses. When will she die? Will it be soon?"

Incense said, "I planned to travel to Hebron after leaving Memphis so that I could pay my respects to Abram. Abram delights in visits from Ishmael and trying to convince Ishmael of the worthiness of following Abram's pious guidance. But I wish to serve Egypt, as best I can. What would you have me do, Great Pharaoh?"

Khaba looked at Nimisis for guidance.

Nimisis asked Incense, "What does Lord Abram think of this new church of Ishmael's in Meccah?"

"It is his *daughter's* church. My son cares little for gods and their teachings. My sweet Abram does not approve of *any* teachings whereby the wife is not subservient to the husband. So, it is not Abram's favorite church."

"Ahh. Interesting. Where will you live after your marriage?"

"*If* Sarai, dies and *if* Abram and I marry, then I would wish to live in Meccah with my oldest grandchildren, but I imagine Abram would prefer to continue living in Hebron."

"So you would live in Hebron?"

"Perhaps, but probably in Meccah."

Nimisis almost showed emotion. He said, "Great Pharaoh Khaba, the plans of the princess will add to the value of Egypt as will the plans of Prince Ishmael and his sons. It would be of great benefit to Egypt if their marriage were to take place in Meccah in that new church there. The last Pharaoh was remiss in not establishing administrative presences in Shur and Meccah. They grow in size and influence and need closer ties with Memphis." *This marriage will be wonderful! The Church has no stronger tool than Abram in subjugating women to authority. We can strengthen our influence when he has an Egyptian wife. This marriage MUST happen!*

Khaba said, "Yes, Princess Incense. Continue with your plans. I will send emissaries to Shur and Meccah to establish lines of communication."

And on and on.

Incense replied with all the proper words.

The evening meal and meeting finally ended.

Nimisis, at the command of his Pharaoh, commanded emissaries to travel to Shur and Meccah and establish communication channels with Memphis—and provide intelligence reports back to Nimisis. Unknown to his Pharaoh, Nimisis also sent a Messenger to Nimrod in Urfa saying, "Abram's wife is no longer useful. She is now a major hindrance."

Incense immediately returned to her room to plan.

Ishmael returned to his room much later, after having added to the wealth of the House of Ishtar.

~~~

The next morning, Incense and Ishmael attended the Sunrise ceremony performed by High-Priestess Tentyris and then bid a formal farewell to the Pharaoh. Nimisis silently monitored.

Those things being done, Incense and Ishmael returned to her room, requested a late morning meal, and laid out their plans as they ate.

"You need to return to Fatimah, Son. Your eyes will begin to wander if you are away too long."

He hesitated, "Well, yes, Mother. My eyes have already wandered but I need to get back to Meccah, regardless. Nebaioth and Basemath are probably already back. The village cannot function well without at least
~~~

one of them there. They are returning through Shur with the rest of the family. They won't be back in Meccah yet."

Incense replied, "Then let's take a barge from Gulfport to my port. We can be in Meccah in three days or so. We may arrive before Nebaioth."

"I'm ready, Mother. This city life is no place for a real man. I want to get back to the wilderness with my sons. Maybe Esau will return with Basemath. Things will be right again."

"If Esau comes, I'll ask him to take me to visit his grandfather. I need to check on Abram for old times' sake. He *is* your father, after all."

"There's not much of a road between Meccah and Hebron and I don't have the resources to build one, anymore. That's unfortunate."

She laughed. "You and I once crossed burning sands with nothing but salted water. I'm sure you aren't suggesting that I'm not woman enough to take a pleasant stroll through the wilderness protected by the fiercest hunter in the southern lands."

Their plans made, they journeyed to the northernmost port on the great gulf and made passage on a barge that would take them to Incense's port serving Mecca. They boarded the barge to take them down the coast of the great body of water separating the Sinai from Midian and the southern lands. They looked forward to the passage. It would be good to get home.

In Shur, Adbeel had competently managed the city, but the Temple had been without a Priestess. Maribah was thrilled to be back at her temple. She missed performing her duties. Basemath and Fatimah would delay their departure by a day so that Basemath could share in her mother's glorious sunrise ceremony.

Fatimah's sons were conflicted. The thought of returning to Meccah through the wilderness with that smelly old man and big brother Kedar and Cousin Esau was exciting, but the thought of an inspiring barge ride down the water with their mother and big sister also interested them.

Excitement would win the day.

ON TO MECCAH

The next morning after the sunrise ceremony, the group set off for Aqaba.

Kedar rode with the smelly old man with whom he had developed a tight bond. The boys walked with Esau who was teaching them wilderness things. Fatimah and Basemath walked with Nebaioth.

Djoser, Hetephe, Incense/Hagar/Keterah
Horus, Serket, Azazil, Abram, Baalat
Ishmael, Maribah, Fatimah, Nebaioth, Basemath, Kedar | Anath, Astarte

As they neared Aqaba, Kedar asked that they camp overnight well outside the other side of Aqaba.

The next morning, after another wonderful sunrise ceremony, everyone gathered around the smelly old man and his wagon. The old man would part ways with the company and travel on to Hebron, perhaps to bathe and change clothes. The wagon would become the responsibility of Esau who was now charged with taking the wagon through the wilderness and on to Meccah.

The old man, with a conspiratorial voice, pulled Esau and the boys closer to him and whispered, "Hidden beneath the dung, is Egyptian treasure. The wagon contains the inheritance of Princess Incense. You must tell no one lest they bring an army that Esau cannot fight off and kill you and take the treasure. Do you so swear?"

The big-eyed boys "so swore."

Esau felt the weight of responsibility. *My life is getting too complicated.*

Nebaioth suddenly realized who the smelly old man was. *Stupid! How could I be so blind?*

Kedar asked his big brother, "Shall I go with you or with the wagon?"

Nebaioth said, "You knew, didn't you?"

"I figured it out. We had nice discussions."

"Which path do you think is best?"

Kedar said, "I prefer going with you and Sister because there is a great deal that we need to discuss. But I am probably better equipped to handle unforeseen issues, and if the cattle die, it will take two men to pull the wagon. So, I feel my duty is with the wagon."

Decisions made, goodbyes said, Nebaioth, Basemath, and Fatimah watched as Esau and Kedar commanded the wagon toward Meccah through the land of Midian and on through the southern wastelands.

Basemath whispered to herself, "May The One be with them."

Nebaioth responded, "Let it be."

Then, they and Fatimah set off to Port Aqaba to secure passage to Incense's Port and then on to Meccah.

The One was with them.

~~~~~~~~~~~~~

33. The Secret

Osirismonth

The citizens of Meccah rejoiced with the return of Ishmael and Incense.

They rejoiced a great deal more with the subsequent return of Priestess Basemath. Azazil had cared for the Tree-of-Life temple in her absence but there had been no Ceremony since she had departed for Memphis almost a month earlier. People were hungry for renewal and validation.

Priestess Basemath basked in the warm knowledge that what she did was meaningful. She was innocent of political intrigue.

Ishmael basked in the glory of his oldest son's city. *Let those who would bring unrest or evil to Meccah journey on to Tartarus.*

Fatimah was reunited with her husband who wished only for his contentment and satisfaction.

Incense and Nebaioth talked. They knew political intrigue would soon come to Meccah and it seldom brought contentment or satisfaction. Would it help Nebaioth and his brother's fortunes if Incense married Abram as she had suggested to the Pharaoh? Abram had only hinted at such a thing, but Incense leveraged the hint to alleviate the possibility of Khaba's wife accidentally dying. The Vizier appeared visibly delighted that Incense might marry Abram. Both wondered, *Why is that?*

They needed Kedar.

In the meantime, there was reunion and rejoicing and ceremonies and living life. And waiting for a mysterious wagon of treasure.

Esau, Kedar, and the boys killed a mountain goat, a bear, and a lion. Life was exciting in the wilderness. Unfortunately, all good things must come to an end, and the wagon, pulled by two contented cows, arrived in the wilderness oasis of Meccah.

And as always, there was reunion and rejoicing.

~~~

The cows were rewarded with their own pasture. As it turned out, they were both pregnant. The wagon of fertilizer found a welcome home in the crop fields. The tarp separating the fertilizer from the treasures was removed revealing many boxes and urns. These were moved, unopened to Incense's house. These were the gifts from her beloved parents.

She opened them in the solitude of quiet reflection and memories. There was the usual gold, fine jewels, and riches. These things she showered upon Ishmael and his family.

There were other treasures requiring explanation and instruction. These things she held close to her heart and did not share.

There was also a chest.

~~~

Incense hosted a special evening meal for her three oldest grandchildren.

Kedar was the suspicious grandchild. "What a nice meal we are having, Grandmother. One wonders why Father and Second-Mother are not here, too."

Incense laughed. "Can a grandmother not entertain her special loved ones away from the others?"

Everyone bantered on.

Finally, Incense somberly announced, "In my inheritance was something greater than my power. You are the wisest in my family, Basemath. Between you and Kedar, we will know what to do."

Nebaioth ignored the slight and remained silent.

Incense said, "Nebaioth, take your sister and brother into my sleeping room. Discover the nature of power."

The three looked at each other, rose, and followed Nebaioth into their grandmother's sleeping room.

Kedar's voice could be heard, exclaiming, "My god!"

Then there was silence. Then muttering. Then waiting.

They returned to the table. Incense refilled their wine glasses. They sat in silence for a while.

Nebaioth asked, "Who knows of this?"

Kedar replied, "Horus does not know. He would have told me in the wagon."

Nebaioth asked, "Does the Pharaoh know?"
~~~

Incense handed a papyrus to Nebaioth and said, "It's in Father's writing."

Nebaioth read the scroll aloud. "This chest is a grave threat to the Church of Urfa as long as it exists. I fear that Khaba will be heavily influenced by his Vizier-elect who is undoubtedly an agent of the church. It is no longer safe in Egypt. Horus will not entertain discussion on its disposition, and I will neither ask him nor trust him to meet the coming future. There is no right course in this matter. I entrust the next generation to do whatever is right to the best of their abilities. This is a great treasure of civilization and must not be lost. Into the hands of Princess Incense, I place the Golden Chest of Tallstone."

Once more, Kedar muttered, "My god."

~~~

Basemath recruited builders to build her an underground vault. "This will be my private room where I may retire to consider the immensity of all things and grow in knowledge and worthiness. To be alone with The One. Build it well."

They built it well. The trap door leading beneath the floor of the Hubal was unobtrusive and well-disguised. The room was large enough to display the chest in its full glory with a table and chairs for scholars and Shamans to inspect and read the contents. There was an oil trough to provide ample lighting with ventilation shafts to circulate the air. It was well hidden but accessible to those invited to know of its presence.

After it was completed, Basemath invited her older brothers and grandmother to sit with her in the presence of the chest. They somberly commented on its majesty and the responsibility they bore. Nebaioth joked that Basemath should welcome it with ritual fornication.

Basemath indignantly retorted, "Both my mothers forbade me to lay with my brothers and our secret would not be safe with Esau!"

The chest, taken care of at least for now, was relegated to secrets kept by keepers of secrets.
~~~

~~~~~~~~~~~~

34. Incense visits Abram

Year 206, Season 6, Aresmonth

Basemath spent as much time with her husband as she could. They were often separated for long periods, so their time together was precious. A time of separation grew near.

Esau would lead Incense, Ishmael, Kedar, and the boys to Hebron to visit Abram, Isaac, and Jacob.

Kedar paid a courtesy visit to the new Memphis Building located near the western gate. The representative greeted Kedar with open arms. "You are going to see Abram? How delightful! The Vizier, I mean the Pharaoh would be delighted with stronger relations with Hebron. With Abram, especially. Give him the Pharaoh's salutations! And your mother, how is *she*? I simply must give her a reception when she returns from her visit with Abram. I hope she has a delightful time!"

Kedar met with his grandmother. "The Vizier wants this marriage. I don't know why but he thinks it would benefit him. I suppose that would be beneficial to our family, but I'm uneasy as long as I don't know why."

"I miss the warmth of a man. Not that Abram is that warm, but still, he *is* a man. He needs a great deal of training and forgiveness, but still …"

Plans were made and the day arrived.

Basemath, Azazil, Fatimah, and Nebaioth waved goodbye as the expedition set off.

THE DEATH OF SARAI

Year 206, Season 7, Ishtarmonth

The long journey to Hebron was wonderful. The boys were all experts in reading trails, dunes, clouds, temperatures, sun, and moon. They were already laying claim to areas their tribe would control and where their water and sustenance would come from. They entertained their mother and grandmother with their infinite knowledge of the wilderness. Even Esau was impressed with them, but, still, he taught them hunting techniques and how to always be successful in a hunt.

Kedar had little interest in these things and spent his days and nights considering the implications of his sister's church as it related to the
~~~~~~~~~~~~

teachings of Horus and the teachings of his Grandfather Abram. All three teachings were rooted in the same basic words but resulted in wildly different practical applications. And, unknown to anyone other than three people, his sister was now caretaker of "the words."

In less than a month, they made camp outside the city of Hebron.

In the early morning, Ishmael and Incense formally called upon the House of Abram. Eliezer formally answered Ishmael's knock. Ishmael formally stated, "I am Abram's son, Ishmael. I came with my mother, Incense. We wish to visit Abram. Will he receive us?"

"My master is in mourning, but I will inquire."

Eliezer closed the door. Inquired. Reopened the door and said, "Yes, he will see you. Come with me."

As they entered Abram's visiting room, Abram stood. On either side of him were Isaac and Jacob. Children quietly played in the corner of the room where Rebekah and two younger women stood with their hands folded in front of them looking with disapproval at these two interlopers come to interfere with their pious mourning.

Isaac and Jacob looked at Ishmael with defiance.

Both Ishmael and Incense immediately noted that Sarai was not there and that Abram was in mourning. This could only mean ...

Ishmael intoned, "Father Abram. I fear this is a bad time to call upon you. Master Eliezer suggested that you are in mourning. If this is so. I apologize for the invasion of your grief."

Incense stepped between them, curtsied to Abram, took his hands into hers, and said, "Oh, Abram. I am so sorry for your loss. She was a righteous, pious woman; always respectful of her place in your household. I grieve with you and your family."

The three women in the background wrung their hands and fidgeted, glancing at each other for this gross breakdown in proper protocol. *This woman approached Father Abram before being acknowledged and invited. She is a woman of the worst kind!*

Abram responded, "She died suddenly. A scorpion sting in the night. I was fortunate that it did not sting me instead of her. It was a horrible experience. She died within two days. It was distasteful to watch!"

"Oh, you poor man. How you must have suffered!" *Marry you, Abram? Am I that desperate?*

Abram, Incense, and Ishmael said all the proper words to one another as the remainder of the room listened in quiet outrage.

The proper words being said, Ishmael turned to Isaac and said, "Brother, the weight of responsibility is heavy upon you and your house. Are your responsibilities met or do they continue?"

Somewhat mollified with the recognition, Isaac replied, "Mother is buried in the cave Father purchased for his House. Our seven days were almost beyond bearing but our thirty days of mourning ends in two more nights. Perhaps then, we can begin living our lives again and greet you with greater courtesy."

"You are wise, Brother. I and Mother will leave your House to its mourning and return in three days." He turned, took Incense's hand, and led her out the door. Their departure was followed by righteous eyes.

Outside, he said, "Well, that was brutal. Are you all right, Mother?"

She absentmindedly replied, "Yes, but take me to a quiet place." *Dead? You died, Sarai? Nimisis asked me how much longer you would live. A scorpion sting? Khaba's wife was scheduled for an unexpected scorpion sting. Nimisis, how badly do you wish me to marry Abram? What are you capable of to make this happen? Father, what is a Princess of Egypt to do?*

Ishmael, Kedar, and Esau left Incense by the town well where she could sit in quiet contemplation and visit the women who came to draw their water. Incense had several nice conversations and learned all the local gossip as the men took Ishmael's younger sons on adventures throughout Hebron; a place that was pious, righteous, and women knew their place.

After evening meal at their camp, Incense asked Kedar to walk with her. Their stroll through the city attracted many eyes; Incense did not follow the appropriate three steps behind the man; although it appeared she *might* be his grandmother, so it wasn't *that* inappropriate.

Incense said, "Someone had Sarai killed by the sting of a scorpion."

Kedar replied, "I told you, the Vizier wants you to marry Abram."

"Why? Khaba could marry him to any high-born Egyptian woman with rank and achieve the same ends."

"Obviously not. Through you, the Vizier has direct control over Abram."

"What does he need from Abram that doesn't already have?"

"Maybe direct control over your grandchildren."

"My children's churches! Their churches are a threat to the Church of Urfa. Control the churches and control the thoughts of the people. Nimisis will use Abram's natural inclinations to weaken Basemath's and Fatimah's churches and I won't interfere because my sons are at the mercy of the Pharaoh. How devious! How obvious!"

They walked in silence.

Incense said, "Abram is more rigid than he was when he threw me and Ishmael out. He no longer even recognizes a woman's existence as independent of a male. Everything revolves around what the man wants. He has no respect for a woman."

"So marrying Abram would be like marrying a pig."

"Marrying any man is like marrying a pig, Son. Sleeping with Abram would be worse. I would be sleeping with the enemy."

"The enemy of women?"

"Of all enlightened people."

"So, what is it you want and how will you get it?"

They walked for a while in silence.

Incense finally said, "I want Fatimah's Church to flourish. I want Basemath's church to spread throughout the world. I want my son's children to each become leaders of a great nation. I want Meccah to rival Memphis in greatness. I will prevent Nimisis from interfering with these things and I will fulfill my destiny. I will marry Abram."

~~~

On the third day, Ishmael accompanied Incense to Abram's house. Protocols were observed.

Only Abram and Eliezer remained in the house. Abram's family had retired to their respective homes. Abram and Ishmael exchanged salutations.

Ishmael said, as he had been instructed, "It would not be appropriate for my mother to visit my father without a proper chaperon. I will observe while the two of you talk. Is that satisfactory, Father?"
~~~

"Yes. As long as the talk does not turn to our marriage. I must not consider marriage until my year of mourning is complete."

Incense respectfully asked, "After your mourning is righteously complete, will you enter into marriage with me?"

"A man such as myself needs a loving obedient woman as a wife."

"Would you consider a loving woman who is not as obedient as you would like? Perhaps you could train her in your ways."

"Yes. That would be possible."

"Good. Would Summer Solstice be an appropriate marriage date for the two of us?"

"Yes. My year of mourning will be complete then."

"Should the marriage ceremony reflect the glory of Hebron?"

"Yes, I think so."

"Then our Wedding Ceremony must be performed in Hebron before your pious and righteous people. I shall spend the year preparing my mind and body to enthusiastically mentally and physically greet my new husband with all of my womanly righteousness mixed with a somewhat disobedient woman's naughtiness. Is this satisfactory?"

"Y-yes. I suppose that would be acceptable."

"May Eliezer announce me to Isaac's wife as you visit your first-born son?"

"Yes."

Eliezer escorted Incense to Isaac's home.

Incense engaged full Egyptian Princess diplomatic training tactics as she manipulated Rebekah into suggesting that the marriage of her Father-in-law to the powerful Egyptian Pharaoh would be extremely beneficial to Rebekah's status in the world. And her Father-in-law's, of course.

Elsewhere, Esau innocently visited with his twin brother, Jacob, and their father, Isaac.

~~~~~~~~~~~~

35. Conversations in Meccah

Year 206, Season 8, Astartemonth

So it was, the travelers returned to Meccah.

They were welcomed by Fatimah, Basemath, Azazil, and Nebaioth.

Fatimah and Ishmael walked off together to physically discuss some urgent things.

Basemath and Esau walked off together to physically discuss some urgent things.

Azazil walked with Kedar toward the temple to discuss religious things.

Nebaioth, Incense, and his younger brothers walked off together to discuss the results of their grand visit.

FATIMAH AND ISHMAEL

The exhausting discussion of urgent things was completed to the satisfaction of both parties. Fatimah lay in the crook of Ishmael's arm contentedly telling him Meccah gossip.

"Maribah visited Basemath and told her that a priestess from Memphis had visited *her* and told her that Vizier Nimisis had told High-Priestess Tentyris that she should also tell the people each morning to be thankful for the blessings of Pharaoh Khaba along with the love of Osiris. Can you believe that? A Vizier telling a High-Priestess what to do! Not *telling*, really. Just suggesting. But still …"

"Uh-ha …"

BASEMATH AND ESAU

The exhausting discussion of urgent things was completed to the satisfaction of both parties. Basemath lay in the crook of Esau's arm anxiously telling him Temple gossip.

"The quartermoon ceremonies are going so well. Azazil is such a help. We keep making improvements to the ceremony. Everyone in Meccah comes to every service. They bring anyone passing by. Bedouins, travelers, occasional traders. Everyone is so impressed with the message. It's so inclusive, they say. It brings everyone closer together. Even closer to people they may not have respected before. You aren't jealous of Azazil,
~~~~~~~~~~~~

are you? I mean he *is* the High-Priest in my church, and we must work together—closely sometimes. You aren't jealous, are you? You don't have any reason to be jealous."

"Ha-uh."

AZAZIL AND KEDAR

Azazil and Kedar entered the temple.

Azazil volunteered, "I'm High-Priest in your sister's temple. The Priestess showed me secret things of great interest."

"She believes you can keep high-secrets and you are not her brother. Secret things are interesting."

"Basemath is the High-Priestess of the temple and a keeper of secrets. A priestess must fulfill her responsibilities."

"My sister always fulfills her duty. Vigorously, I imagine."

Azazil gave no reply but looked around to make sure the Temple was empty, then slid open a hidden door. The two men entered the vault of the Chest of Tallstone.

NEBAIOTH AND INCENSE

Amenirdis served wine to her husband and Mother-in-law.

Amenirdis: "My husband has been uneasy since you left for Hebron. I try to calm him, but he remains concerned for you and the safety of Meccah and his people."
Incense: "Abram's wife accidentally died the month before we arrived. I have decided to marry Abram next summer to help prevent the mischief my son is concerned about. We must make plans to protect ourselves."
Nebaioth: "Intrigue arrives in Meccah in the form of Abram and Khaba and that vizier of his. Egypt is a relentless enemy."
Incense: "We must maintain peace until all your brothers are grown with their own tribes. This will give you time to grow Meccah and add impenetrable defenses to the safety of the city's already significant natural defense."
Nebaioth: "The Memphis diplomat has made several inquiries into your progress. How he expects me to know these things, I cannot imagine."
Incense: "He is under pressure from Memphis. I will visit him tomorrow and make sure he understands that Abram's daughter-in-law is thrilled with the prospect the marriage might make her an Egyptian princess and

that Abram is adamant that if this wedding takes place, it must be in Hebron, but Abram won't discuss these things until his year of mourning is over. The Vizier will assuredly make use of this information to ensure Abram marries me. But we must keep Abram away from Basemath's temple at all costs. Even if her service *does* celebrate only one god, the mixture of men and women in the same service and the presence of idols would be more than Abram could stand."
Amenirdis: "I suggest Kedar begin training all boys and girls in the sport of archery. He can have competitions and make it fun for everyone involved. Archery has so many useful purposes, don't you think?"

Djoser, Hetephe, Incense/Hagar/Keterah
Horus, Serket, Azazil, Abram, Baalat
Ishmael, Maribah, Fatimah, Nebaioth, Basemath, Kedar | Anath, Astarte

~~~~~~~~~~~~

36. VIGNETTES

Year 207 to Year 211

THE DEATH OF TENTYRIS

Year 207, Season 1, Osirismonth

The death of High-Priestess Tentyris was as horrible as it was unfortunate. She had performed such a magnificent Sunrise Ceremony. Osiris was forced to rise higher than he had the day before. Everything was going so beautifully until she tragically fell from the top of the Mastaba and broke her neck. She must have slipped, most people said. And there was no truth to the rumor that she was still alive after the fall. How could she be? Her neck was broken.

Pharaoh Khaba immediately called a council of all Priests and Priestesses, headed by Vizier Nimisis, to select a new High-Priestess before the coming sunrise.

The meeting was not at all calm like the Priestesses expected it to be. Three Priests loudly selected their favorite, a Priest no-less, to become High-Priest to Osiris. "It's time for a man to have this position! It isn't fair that it is always a priestess! We must select a priest!"

No one was in favor of their nominee, but the three priests were so loud, and Chairman Nimisis kept deferring to them. As morning approached, Chairman Nimisis declared that Priest Nebwa had been unanimously selected to be the High-Priest of Osiris; a declaration disputed by many of those involved. Nebwa was well-liked by all the priestesses and priests but was thought to be a little on the simple and compliant side.

His first sunrise ceremony was a complete disaster, but the priestesses improvised to bring it to an almost acceptable closure. The priestesses immediately began rigorously training Nebwa on how to properly conduct this extremely important ceremony. The three loud Priests later took Nebwa aside and instructed him to add copious praise for Pharaoh Khaba. They said, "It's only fair!"

THE MARRIAGE OF ABRAM AND KETERAH

Year 207, month 6, Aresmonth

In Hebron, at Summer Solstice, in the sixth month of the second year of the reign of Khaba, the pious man Abram married the sometimes-naughty

Phoenicia, Jaffa, Rocky, Burlyman, Polydore | Astarte, T'jaru
Terah, Amathlai, Haran, Terahson, Nahor, Sarai, Isaac, Jacob
Kyrios-Olon, Teumessian, Nimrod, Nimbal, Nimlad, Nimisis, Asherah, Set.
~~~~~~~~~~~~

woman Incense who accepted the name Keterah which in the language of Abram's people held the same meaning.

In the years to come, Keterah would bear Abram six sons whom she would allow to be raised with their cousins, the twelve sons of Jacob. Jacob's wife, Princess Rebekah of Hebron and Egypt, would piously monitor the raising of these righteous children.

THE REPLACEMENT OF MARIBAH

Year 207, Month 7, Ishtarmonth

After the suspicious death of Tentyris, Maribah began adding a reference to the glory of Pharaoh Khaba to her ceremonies but to no avail. After the marriage of Abram to Incense, Maribah was notified that High-Priest Nebwa was sending her replacement to Shur and that she should properly train the priest so that he could take over her duties without interruption. A candidate once considered by Hathor as her heir, had been unceremoniously fired. She was, however, not that unhappy about it. Her neck had not broken and there were no scorpions in her bed. She could peacefully retire to her daughter's church in Meccah.

The consensus of Nebaioth and his advisors was that Nimisis still feared the potential wrath of Ishmael and his sons.

Once-Priestess Maribah was welcomed to her new home with coordinated, precision exercises by the Meccah Archery Team.

She noticed that a nice new wooden walkway had been built running the length of the ridge on both sides of the gate into the city. There was a protected nice place to rest every twelve paces. The archers stored their extra training arrows there.

WINTER SOLSTICE CEREMONY

Year 208, Month 1, Osirismonth

Another Winter's Solstice came.

High-Priest Nebwa was pleased with himself. He had performed the entire Winter Solstice ceremony without one significant error. Much to his own delight and the priestess's relief, Osiris had risen higher in the sky. The high-sun reception on the Osiris Mastaba was festive and raucous.

While Nimisis was busy controlling everything else, Nebwa was able to approach Khaba without permission. Nebwa asked the Pharaoh if his praise was adequate. Khaba happily engaged Nebwa in conversation. He was the High-Priest, after all. Nebwa naively informed Khaba that now that this important event was over, he could begin replacing all of the Mastaba priestesses with priests like Vizier Nimisis wanted him to do.

Nimisis became furious when he saw Nebwa talking to Khaba without any supervision. *Ares, strike them all dead. The incompetent fools, Zeus only knows what that imbecile is telling Khaba. Do I have to do everything!*

In the background, three priests stood laughing with three young priestesses. Drinking wine.

THE DEATH OF FIRST MOTHER

Year 209, Month 1, Osirismonth

Another Winter's Solstice came.

Nimisis was happy with Nebwa's performance of the Solstice celebration. There were almost no mistakes of any note. And, it was performed without the support of any priestesses. They had all been replaced. Well, three priestesses did remain, but they were very young women whose primary duties were as servants to the priests.

Nimisis suggested that Khaba make his important proclamation at high-sun on the last day of celebration. He said, "This would be a wonderful time to give your wonderful gift to your people."

On the last day of celebration, the people of Memphis gathered to hear an important proclamation from the Pharaoh. Khaba announced, "I have commissioned a magnificent gift to be created for the people of Egypt. This will be the greatest monument in the entire world. A great figure will be sculpted in a massive outcrop of rock near Newport where our quarries are located. This outcrop will be fashioned into the likeness of your beloved Pharaoh before year's end. It will become an important place in Egypt. This will demonstrate my endless love for my people."

Vizier Nimisis listened to the speech with his chief builder. He said, "That went well enough, I think. Can you really do it in a year?"

"I doubt it. We don't have enough skilled sculptors. All my people can work with stone but it's all rough cuts, not intricate, detailed cuts."

"Just make it recognizable. That's all that matters."

"That's a shame. The craftsmanship in that woman's head we are cutting away is exquisite. The finest I have ever seen. I hate to destroy something without replacing it with something better."

Phoenicia, Jaffa, Rocky, Burlyman, Polydore | Astarte, T'jaru
Terah, Amathlai, Haran, Terahson, Nahor, Sarai, Isaac, Jacob
Kyrios-Olon, Teumessian, Nimrod, Nimbal, Nimlad, Nimisis, Asherah, Set.

"Are you questioning my orders, Builder!?"

"No! Are you questioning my pride of craft, Vizier!?"

"Complete it within a year!" *Insubordinate bastard! Your replacement is walking around somewhere! You are safe until I find him!*

Nimisis continued, "And bring that Chest of Tallstone thing of theirs to me. I want to inspect its contents."

"That was moved from First Mother years ago. I thought you knew."

Nimisis froze.

ISHMAEL'S CHILDREN

Year 210, Month 7, Ishtarmonth

Another Winter Solstice came as did a Summer Solstice.

Nebaioth was the Chief of the City of Meccah and Adbeel the Chief of the City of Shur.

Kedar did not wish such responsibility. He was interested in studying his sister Basemath's Church of Light teachings and refining his archery skills.

Ishmael, himself, was the titular head of the great tribe exploring the lands south of Midian, but Ishmael often left the tribe to visit Shur and Meccah and charged Misha with leading the tribe in his absence. Misha eventually became its unofficial chief.

The tribe had grown to over two hundred people. It had been agreed that those who wished could follow Misha's younger brother Dumah and form a new tribe. Now, both tribes had again grown to the point that they were becoming too large. Massa and Hadad offered themselves as worthy to be chiefs of the two new tribes. There was much discussion and challenges of worthiness. They eventually prevailed.

Brothers Tema and Jetur wanted none of that nonsense. They announced that they would both journey to the extreme south and marry well. They and their high-born, beautiful wives would leave the tribe of their wives and set up their own cities down there somewhere.

Ishmael swelled with the pride of a father having such naive, but self-assured, sons. And, who knew, maybe they would succeed.

The two youngest sons remained with their mother in Meccah to explore the great surrounding wilderness.

VISIT TO HEBRON

Year 210, Season 8, Astartemonth

Ishmael and Esau visited Abram in Hebron. Keterah, obviously pregnant, sat in a chair in the corner as her sons by Abram, Zimran and Jokshan, fought for the attention of their big brother Ishmael. Esau sat on the floor play-fighting the toddlers.

Abram remained concerned over Basemath's church in Meccah. "I would like to watch her perform a service, but Keterah insists that I would not enjoy it and it might upset me. I understand their priestess celebrates the one true god, so I don't understand why those idols have to be there. Keterah explains it over and over, but still …"

"Actually, Father, The Church of Light is Maribah's church now. Basemath gave the priestesshood to her mother so Basemath and Esau could travel the wilderness teaching the people of your one true god. Surely this pleases you. Your grandson carries on your teachings. Everyone who hears the word is enchanted with the knowledge. They say they knew *how* to live but now they understand why. Their Church grows across the wilderness and even into Egypt and Canaan. Some say into Byblos, itself. Are you pleased?"

"Esau teaches these things?"

"Yes. Basemath came with us. She is at the town well talking to the women who come there."

Abram became agitated. "At the well talking to the women?! Is she pious? Does she teach the woman's proper role in the home of her husband?"

"I have instructed Basemath not to address this subject in Hebron, Father. Such things are best left to the custom of the lands in which she teaches."

"Still, she is a woman teaching about the nature of God. It is not fitting that a woman instructs in these matters."

From the corner of the room came the word, "Abram!"

Abram looked at Keterah and replied, "Well, I don't think it's proper! It makes women think they are as good as men!"

"ABRAM!"

Abram looked at Ishmael and said, "I sometimes choose inappropriate words, but I still put up with a lot from your mother. She is wise but sometimes disrespectful to her husband. But she bears me fine sons."

Ishmael laughed. "I have seen Pharaohs back down from Mother Incense ... I mean Keterah. Something about her usually being right."

There was a knock at the door. Eliezer answered it. "Of course you may visit, Lord Isaac. Your grandson Esau is also here."

Everyone but Abram rose. Everyone said all the proper pious words.

Those words being said, Esau inquired, "Grandfather Isaac, would brother Jacob receive me if I call upon him?"

Isaac replied, "Wait until your next visit. Your brother and mother are both still upset with you because you tricked me into giving Jacob my blessing instead of giving it to you."

"But it is Jacob that tricked you; not me!"

Isaac was adamant, "No matter. They blame you for forcing them to do it. They say that it's God's will that Jacob receives my blessing, and you stood in God's way. So it was your fault."

Esau laughed a hunter's laugh. "I shall make my own blessing, Father. Uncle Ishmael is helping me."

Ishmael listened to his brother and nephew talk and then stole a few moments to visit privately with his mother. He then said his goodbyes well before an evening meal would have to be offered.

He and Esau found Basemath at the well. The three began their journey back to Meccah.

They camped in the village outside of Hebron and enjoyed the hospitality of the villagers. The local women were quick to note that Basemath talked with the men as if she were their equal. They soon decided that she *was* their equal. Several of the younger, more brazen, women joined in the fireside conversation. They were emboldened when they were not commanded to "keep their place." The innocent presence of Basemath seemed to validate their brazenness.

The next morning, Basemath greeted the sunrise and then they continued their long journey home.

RETURN TO MECCAH

Year 210, Season 9, Anathmonth

Their return to Meccah was met with jubilation.

Djoser, Hetephe, Incense/Hagar/Keterah
Horus, Serket, Azazil, Abram, Baalat
Ishmael, Maribah, Fatimah, Nebaioth, Basemath, Kedar | Anath, Astarte

Fatimah and Maribah ran to embrace Ishmael. Maribah graciously said her welcome and let Fatimah lead Ishmael off to discuss an important matter that had just arisen.

Maribah joined Azazil and Kedar in greeting Basemath and Esau. The work of their church was expanding and never-ending.

Ishmael's sons, Massa and Hadad, were jealous of their big brother, Nebaioth, who had his own city here, in the wilderness. That's what they wanted and they studied their oldest brother's every move. Ishmael's two youngest sons, Kedemah and Napish, also lived in Meccah. Kedemah waited with excitement to inform his father that he had now entered into manhood and wanted to discuss his next steps in building a city in the East. Napish was close to Kedemah and would travel with him probably to join either their brother's Misha or Dumah's tribes or else settle with Brother Adbeel in his city of Shur.

Ishmael's sons were all now men and well on their way to glorious success.

His life was as wonderful as it could be.

Or would ever be again.

REPORT TO MEMPHIS HEADQUARTERS

Year 210, Season 10, Aphroditemonth

The Egyptian Ambassador observed the happy return of Ishmael and his group to Meccah. Basemath seemed ecstatic, probably not a good sign.

The ambassador traveled to present his report directly to headquarters. Vizier Nimisis, himself, attended the meeting.

The ambassador nervously reported that interest in the Meccah church was *not* shrinking; if anything, it grew daily. "The church grows in influence throughout the region. The excommunicated Priestess from Shur moved to Meccah and took over the church services and now her daughter and daughter's husband travel the land teaching her religion. This influence reaches throughout the Sinai, Median, and lands to the south. Women who hear this message are quick to lose their willingness to be subservient to men."

Nimisis considered the situation. *I have delayed direct confrontation with the old order long enough. It's time to act. The old order must give way to the new.*

"Your report is informative. I will inform the Pharaoh. You may go."

Relieved, the ambassador left the vizier and staff.

Phoenicia, Jaffa, Rocky, Burlyman, Polydore | Astarte, T'jaru
Terah, Amathlai, Haran, Terahson, Nahor, Sarai, Isaac, Jacob
Kyrios-Olon, Teumessian, Nimrod, Nimbal, Nimlad, Nimisis, Asherah, Set.

Nimisis sat in silence making his plan. He withdrew pen and parchment and wrote.

He sealed the message with wax, handed it to a messenger, and said, "Deliver this to Nimrod before the end of next month."

He dismissed his remaining staff and sat back in his chair; fingers clasped together, thinking. *Lord Horus, I thought getting rid of that bitch priestess in Shur would weaken you. It only made you stronger. I thought marrying the bitch princess to Abram would make you weaker. It made you stronger. This will end, our persistent adversary. This will end!*

THE INVITATION

Year 210, Season 12, Isismonth

During the yearly celebration of Winter's Solstice, the joyous word went out to all people.

The Pharaoh would celebrate and pay high honor to his beloved predecessor, Pharaoh Djoser. He would personally attend the next Summer Solstice Ceremony performed in the Temple of Meccah

The city, temple, and ceremony were all created by the son and grandchildren of Princess Incense. These were new and glorious additions to the kingdom of Egypt which Pharaoh Khaba wished to personally extol to all people. This was the highest honor the Pharaoh could bestow upon Princess Incense and Prince Ishmael and his children.

The news took Nebaioth by surprise. He had not been informed of this event. He and Kedar went immediately to the Egyptian Ambassador's office. Words were said.

Kedar and Azazil traveled to Hebron to discuss the situation with Incense. Her quick, political mind instantly considered intrigue and hidden motives. *Why? For the self-centered Khaba to honor someone else? I think not. It must be for his self-glory ... or ... Abram ... or ... Oh, my god!*

They made plans and contingency plans. In all their family, they were the only three who understood this was not the joyous event as it had been presented. Keterah could see into the possible why of it and envision the outcome that Vizier Nimisis hoped for.

She said to Kedar as he departed, "I can usually control the thoughts and actions of my husband. But if Nimrod accompanies us, then he will whisper behind my back. If Nimrod comes, prepare for chaos."

Djoser, Hetephe, Incense/Hagar/Keterah
Horus, Serket, Azazil, Abram, Baalat
Ishmael, Maribah, Fatimah, Nebaioth, Basemath, Kedar | Anath, Astarte

~~~~~~~~~~~~

37. Abram and The Tree of Life

Year 211, Season 6, Aresmonth

Summer Solstice approached.

All preparations that could be made, had been. Meccah was prepared for a massive turnout.

The first ceremony would be performed by Maribah and Azazil during the Summer Solstice. This would be for the Pharaoh and three hundred fifty-nine of his guests. The first being completed, then Basemath and Esau would perform the standard Tree-of-Life ceremony. This ceremony would be repeated until high-moon and then begin again the next day at sunrise. Ceremonies would be ongoing until everyone had attended one.

Basemath's eyes glistened with the joy of teaching so many new people the wonderful news of the Tree-of-Life.

The time of celebration approached.

Ishmael stood with Nebaioth greeting the countless people as they arrived from the west. Fatimah and Kedar greeted those arriving from the north.

The head of the Pharaoh's security guard entered the western gate with smiles and salutations as he greeted Ishmael and commented on the wonderful reception, the beautiful city, and the outstanding friendliness of the people.

He did not, however, comment on the heavy gate surrounded by fortified wooden runways placed on top of inaccessible ridges overlooking the open wilderness where an intruding bear could be saturated with arrows over two hundred paces distant nor on the slingshot rocks or pots which might contain oil for burning. That wouldn't be prudent to comment on.

Aja presided over her Welcome Maidens at the city park by the river. Any person wishing a tour of the city or environs had only to ask Maiden Aja and an appropriate guide would be assigned to happily show them around. The Egyptian builder had a surprising request, "The river through Meccah is so beautiful. Can you show me the headwaters?"

The request was so unusual that Aja, herself, volunteered to be his guide. "Oh, five other builders wish to go with us? Well, I will need some help."

Phoenicia, Jaffa, Rocky, Burlyman, Polydore | Astarte, T'jaru
Terah, Amathlai, Haran, Terahson, Nahor, Sarai, Isaac, Jacob
Kyrios-Olon, Teumessian, Nimrod, Nimbal, Nimlad, Nimisis, Asherah, Set.
~~~~~~~~~~~~

The builders were given their tour of the headwaters of the stream. They were a most unusual group of tourists.

~~~

The camping areas, the playing fields, and the inns filled with visitors. Summer Solstice approached. Then more crowds came to Meccah, as did the Pharaoh and his court. The people responded with proper love and awe. The Pharaoh was thrilled. His vizier took note of all things.

~~~

A young boy sought Kedar. Finding him, he said, "Lord Kedar—Father Abram, and Mother Keterah follow close behind. Mother Keterah requests your greeting before they enter the city gates."

Kedar sent for Ishmael and Nebaioth to join him at the northern gate. As he briskly walked to the gate, he called for Aja and other Welcome Maidens to join him.

The group arrived at the gate and quickly discussed responsibilities. They were prepared as Abram's palanquin came into view.

The palanquin was motioned to the pleasant welcome garden outside the gate. There were facilities where the visitors could rest, relieve, and refresh themselves before entering the bustling city. The four bearers set the palanquin on the ground and Keterah walked up to pull back the curtains. She smiled at Kedar as she did so. The palanquin contained Father Abram and his old acquaintance, Nimrod.

Enthusiastic, righteous, pious greetings and salutations were exchanged by all parties. Kedar glanced at Aja and nodded.

As Abram and Nimrod were being helped to the ground, Welcome Maiden Aja impiously moved forward, wantonly grabbed the hand of Nimrod, and said, "You are the most handsome man I have ever seen, I demand that I be allowed to show you the glorious sights of Meccah. No man dare refuse the Supreme Welcome Maiden lest I have one of the gods rain fire upon your head. Come with me! We will have a delightful time." She pulled him away before he had time to access the situation or refuse.

Keterah was thrilled. *She is a natural. A true Weapon of War!*

Ishmael had distracted Abram by embracing him and gushing pious things. They all sat on the park benches to talk and rejoice in their reunion and of the coming Solstice.

Djoser, Hetephe, Incense/Hagar/Keterah
Horus, Serket, Azazil, Abram, Baalat
Ishmael, Maribah, Fatimah, Nebaioth, Basemath, Kedar | Anath, Astarte

Kedar innocently said, "Grandfather, you allowed Lord Nimrod to ride with you instead of Grandmother. He must be interesting."

"Yes, he is, young man. We talked about many things. He reminded me of the time in Harran when he became so angry with me when I destroyed all of my father's idols. And he *was* angry. He was extremely angry." Abram gurgled a laugh. "But he admits that I did the righteous thing. The One God is very proud of me. Destroying all those ungodly idols."

Keterah asked Ishmael, "How is your daughter doing with her Horus-loving, One God, Tree-of-Life religious teachings, Ishmael? Do all righteous people support her as the One God would wish them to do?"

Kedar answered before his father could open his mouth. "Evil people oppose her teachings, Grandmother. They twist her ceremonies away from the universal love and respect all people should have for one another. Her adversaries prey upon the fear and insecurities of those insecure in their belief in their own god. Happily, you and Grandfather Abram are here to support her and bring the truth of the One God to all righteous people."

As the conversation continued along these lines, down by the river, Nimrod kept looking back trying to extricate himself from this woman. This woman who stood too close and smelled of jasmine and who was intensely interested in his profound thoughts on using religious thought to affect and control the actions and responses of multi-cultural populations.

CELEBRATION

The time neared.

Three hundred sixty chairs befitting the rank of the participants surrounded the outside of the church. Azazil and Esau assisted Nimisis in seating the participants in the order the Pharaoh had commanded according to the recommendations of his vizier.

The Pharaoh's Honor Guardsman, for security reasons, would be first, followed by Princess Incense who was now named Keterah, wife of staunch Egyptian ally, Abram of Hebron. Third would be her son, Prince Ishmael followed by Chief Nebaioth. Then Queen Meresankh and then Pharaoh Khaba, himself.

Jacob sat one-hundredth in line followed by Abram, Nimisis, and Isaac.

A priest came to Keterah, said, "three hundred heartbeats, my Lady," and walked off.

Keterah rose and commanded the Security Guard ahead of her, "Escort me to pay my respects to the Pharaoh!"

The guard had no choice but to rise and obey.

Keterah bowed before the Pharaoh. "Your magnificence is without limit, Great Pharaoh Khaba. You are the greatest Pharaoh to ever live. Thank you for allowing me to share this moment of glory with you."

Khaba beamed peacock pride as Keterah rose and asked, "Oh, and may I speak to my beloved husband before this begins?"

Khaba vigorously nodded, "Yes."

The guard had been out-maneuvered. His command from Nimisis had been overridden by the Pharaoh. He had no choice but to take the woman to speak to Abram. Nimisis could only observe from the background as Keterah approached Abram.

She knelt and whispered in his ear. "The One God watches and approves of your reverent participation in this ceremony, my husband. Your understanding and approval for the ritual use of idols to strengthen the concept of your One-God is righteous and just."

Keterah had done all she could do. She straightened herself, smiled sweetly to Nimrod, and returned to her seat.

Nimrod leaned over and asked too loudly, "Has your wife always been this insolent, Lord Abram?"

"She isn't too insolent. Usually."

Nimrod glanced at Isaac, and said, "Abram was wise to give his blessing to you rather than that unrighteous Ishmael."

To Jacob, he loudly whispered, "I hear Ishmael worships every idol in this temple."

Abram said, "Ishmael is a good boy."

Nimrod replied, "They say Ishmael goes to Byblos and plows that Baalat woman often. They say her screams of pleasure cover the entire city of Byblos. She claims to be a living god. Blasphemy!"

Abram began fidgeting, but he didn't know why.

The bell rang. The people rose. Azazil led the Honor Guardsman into the Church. The procession began.

Djoser, Hetephe, Incense/Hagar/Keterah
Horus, Serket, Azazil, Abram, Baalat
Ishmael, Maribah, Fatimah, Nebaioth, Basemath, Kedar | Anath, Astarte

Azazil expertly kept the procession moving then: Stop. Respectfully nod. Move. Repeat.

Keterah came to the one hundred-second idol. *Abram will now be facing the first idol, Yahweh. And Asherah is next. Good, good. Abram knew them both and knows they aren't really gods. Just revered people. Good, good.*

Abram respectfully nodded to Yahweh. *I am just showing respect to people who believe you were a god. I am to love everyone. I'm just showing my love to those misguided people.*

Move. Stop. Respectfully nod.

Abram respectfully nodded to the idol of Asherah. He heard a voice beside him mutter, "I am forced to bow to a female god. This is not right!"

Move. Stop. Respectfully nod.

Abram faced Aphrodite and respectfully nodded.

Move. Stop. Respectfully nod.

The voice behind him muttered, "I am forced to bow before the mother of whores."

Abram faced Anath and nodded. In a moment, the voice muttered, "The whore of Canaan. How much more can a righteous man endure?"

A priestess quietly approached Nimrod, leaned over, and whispered, "Please respect the silence, Great Lord."

As she left, Nimrod muttered loud enough for Abram to hear, "Disrespectful unrighteous whore priestess!"

Abram grew more agitated.

Keterah nodded to the three hundredth statue. Dionysus.

The scream and the subsequent sound of a heavy object hitting the floor on the other side of the church was the sound of the wrath of the righteous destroying the works of the unrighteous. More screams and more thuds. The sword of the righteous was thundering and unrelenting.

Move. Stop. Respectfully nod.

She nodded to Nephthys. *I didn't know you could scream that loudly, Husband. You are certainly indignant over all these idols. You destroyed them once. How foolish to think I could prevent you from destroying them again.*

Move. Stop. Respectfully nod.

She nodded to the statue of Set.

Nebaioth broke out of the procession to hurry to the commotion on the other side of the church.

Maribah sat serenely on the Hubal emanating the peace of the Tree-of-Life as the fury of the Tree-of-Life played out around her.

Azazil pushed the protecting Nimrod aside and calmly said to Abram, "Lord Abram, I have prepared a place by the river for all righteous people to gather. They are impatiently waiting for you to address them and teach them. Come. Go with me and teach your people!" He aggressively pulled Abram by the arm toward the exit.

Abram stared wide-eyed at the next statue, wanting to topple it. There were so many. So much work to do.

Azazil said, "You can lead the people gathered to hear your guidance!"

Abram decided. He would go with this nice young man and teach the righteous by the river.

Nebaioth stood glaring in pure hatred at the destruction. He grabbed Nimrod by his neck and hissed, "You caused this!"

Nimrod gurgled, "Not me. The Pharaoh commanded it!"

Nebaioth stared at Nimrod for a moment, released him, and strode to confront the Pharaoh who was continuing to follow behind Keterah.

The Honor Guardsman, of course, was on high alert.

The guardsman took Nebaioth but not before Nebaioth grabbed the pharaoh's shoulder and spun him around.

Nebaioth hissed, "You caused this thing! You are evil, itself."

Khaba had no idea how to respond to this madness. He was Pharaoh. These words could not be said. Where was his Vizier?"

Nimisis came rushing up to the Pharaoh. More words were said.

Nebaioth was constrained from physically attacking the pharaoh, but not before he spit in Khaba's face. Nebaioth's world went black.

Keterah came to the last idol. She graciously nodded to Osiris.

<p style="text-align:center">~~~</p>

Djoser, Hetephe, Incense/Hagar/Keterah
Horus, Serket, Azazil, Abram, Baalat
Ishmael, Maribah, Fatimah, Nebaioth, Basemath, Kedar | Anath, Astarte

The Pharaoh and his court immediately departed Meccah. Nebaioth was not killed for his insolence. Keterah negotiated with Nimrod that Nimrod escort Abram and Abram's family back to Hebron leaving her behind. Basemath and Maribah lovingly put the pieces of their broken statues back together. The townspeople helped them.

Meccah was empty of visitors and eerily quiet.

Kedar conducted the meeting. Nebaioth stood at the door, looking out consumed with guilt. Ishmael sat beside Keterah. Esau and Aja sat against the wall in case they were needed.

Kedar finally asked, "Grandmother, what will they do?"

"Destroy Meccah and the Church. That's what Nimisis had been trying to achieve, destroy Basemath's church and her teachings. They will kill the priests and priestesses and anyone else who might continue their teachings. After that, kill Ishmael and his sons? Kill me? If Nimisis sees us as a threat, then we will be killed. If an asset, we won't be killed."

"Can we negotiate a truce of some kind?"

"Perhaps deliver the tortured headless bodies of Nebaioth, Basemath, Maribah, and Azazil to Nimisis. Throw in the body of Lord Horus. That, along with Ishmael's undying allegiance to the glory of Pharaoh Djoser, might be enough."

Kedar laughed a bitter laugh. "A Forever War until Meccah falls or Egypt falls. No more trade with Egypt. Isolation. We can live with that."

Aja offered, "They know they can't take the Western Gate. The builders were amazed at its defenses. But I showed them the path from the mountains into the city. They could attack from the south. They were extremely interested in the river and how it flowed. They were interested in seeing the northern approach and commented on how the wooden path encircled the city overlooking every approach. One of them said, 'They could move pretty fast to any point in the city.'"

Keterah said, "Very good, Maiden Aja! Excellent insights!" *A weapon of war, indeed!*

Aja swelled with pride.

Kedar called to Nebaioth and Esau, "Explore the path to the mountain. Plan what we need to do to protect ourselves from attack in that direction. We will also need a plan for attack from the north. Father, all your tribes need to be alerted to this development. Have them swear allegiance to the Pharaoh but develop a plan to send us information about all encounters. We need to know Egypt's attitudes toward my brothers. Better yet, you are now the enemy of Nebaioth. Let it be widely known that you can't forgive him for disrespecting the Pharaoh. Swear allegiance to Nimisis. Meccah must now consider you to be an enemy."

Ishmael was incensed. "I will not turn my back on my oldest children! I will fight with them to the death!"

Kedar barked, "And Egypt will hunt down your other children and kill them and everyone in their tribes! Grandmother, command your son to do as I say."

The room was silent for a long time. Keterah then said, "Khaba considers me an ally. I am safe in Hebron. You may visit me at any time with any information you might have that would be of interest to Meccah. You can live on in peace while protecting your younger children or you can die beside your older children defending Meccah and leave your younger children exposed to the wrath of Egypt. But my son is wise. He always obeys his mother. I command you to grant immortality to your oldest sons and daughter. Tell them farewell and leave them to their destiny."

Kedar said, "Meccah is unassailable, Father. Plus, we know the wilderness and they don't. We are safe, enough. Go in peace. Turn your back on Meccah. Protect those who need your protection."

Ishmael, Prince of Egypt, grandson of Djoser and Hetephe, survivor of expulsion into the wilderness with salted water, proud father of many children, father of nations, lover of life, obedient son, slowly fell to his knees and cried.

~~~

So it was, that Keterah and Ishmael traveled to Memphis and sought out Nimisis, who they knew had the ear of Khaba. They expressed their horror over the occurrences in Meccah. Ishmael confessed he still loved his children, but could not tolerate insolence to the Pharaoh; that he wished to prostrate himself before Khaba and beg forgiveness. Nimisis immediately saw that he could use Ishmael and Incense to his advantage.

So it was, Ishmael laid on the floor in front of Khaba's throne and, in front of Khaba's court, said all the words he needed to say which would protect his younger children while damning his three older children.

Djoser, Hetephe, Incense/Hagar/Keterah
Horus, Serket, Azazil, Abram, Baalat
Ishmael, Maribah, Fatimah, Nebaioth, Basemath, Kedar | Anath, Astarte
~~~

So it was, Ishmael returned to Hebron with his mother, a broken man.

So it was, Kedar, Nebaioth, and Aja prepared for the eternal defense of Mecca.

So it was, Maribah and Azazil continued performing beautiful Tree-of-Life services for the adoring townspeople and visitors.

So it was, Basemath and Esau wandered the wilderness teaching the gospel of The Church of Light.

~~~~~~~~~~~~~

38. The Destruction of Meccah

Year 211, Season 9, Anathmonth

On the day of the first anniversary of the fateful incident with the Pharaoh, there was a massive Egyptian troop buildup near their port. But Meccah was as prepared as it could be. Visitors were welcomed into the city for the Summer Solstice celebration, but it was nowhere the size of last year's. The Welcome Maidens had been trained to recognize concealed weapons and suspicious visitors. Aja was in her element of intrigue, intelligence gathering, drama, play-acting, and being pretty.

The Meccah Defense Committee had done a superb job of planning, but they were not generals nor tacticians nor did they know the depth and breadth of the mind of a Nim. Nimisis had planned for this day long ago.

The Summer's Solstice approached. Word came that many barges carrying troops had set out from Memphis headed toward Grandmother's Port.

Kedar said, "They plan on attacking during the celebration. They hope to catch us off guard and unprepared." Kedar sent word throughout the city, "We will be attacked by the Egyptian army. Leave now, through the Western Gate or Northern Gate. Leave now for your own safety."

Many people left. A surprising number of the faithful stayed, saying, "To die in the Church of Light would be an honor."

Kedar was correct that the attack would begin at Summer's Solstice.

He was incorrect that they would be prepared.

SUMMER'S SOLSTICE IN HEBRON

In Hebron, Keterah sat in sadness with her four children as she listened to Abram, Isaac, and Jacob discuss the sins of the world. Jacob was not at all sure that he should allow his many sons to associate with any of those Ishmaelite tribes. His sons were much more pious than those Ishmaelites. Rebekah and Judith sat cluckingly agreeing with Jacob's wise concerns knowing the grandmother of the Ishmaelites was sitting with them.

Isaac, the gratuitous son he was, brought up the fact that his father had once more destroyed evil idols. This time, exactly one year ago today, in that unrighteous city of Meccah. "All pious people are so proud of you, Father. You are indeed the righteous Patriarch of the House of Abram."
~~~~~~~~~~~~~

Abram basked in the praise. "I only do what Lord Horus taught me to do, fight the many false gods and bring love and peace into the world. It's the Way of Horus, you know."

Cluck, cluck, cluck.

Abram continued, "I expect Lord Horus to visit me soon. He pays his respects every year or so. He is getting old, but he still travels a great deal. It is about time for him to call."

Cluck, cluck, cluck.

SUMMER'S SOLSTICE IN MECCAH

The people began their procession into the Church.

Fireballs saturated the Western Gate, setting the walkway ablaze.

Kedar looked up. *We are doomed.*

Too late, he commanded the archers to fall back and to bring down that thing in the sky delivering the fireballs. It hovered just out of range of the arrows. He grabbed extra arrows and climbed to the church roof top.

Airboat 113 methodically dropped fireballs onto the archers, buildings, and infrastructure. Kedar patiently waited until Airboat 113 drifted into range. He composed himself, relaxed, and let his arrows fly. The arrows found their mark. A hissing sound emanated from the airboat. Then it erupted into a giant fireball. Debris began to fall all around him.

Kedar's world went black.

HEBRON PASTORAL

Ishmael and Fatimah lived in a room in Hebron to be near his mother and her children by Abram. He had seen Abram only once since his return. The meeting had been full of self-righteous justifications and explanations and fault-finding of adversaries. Ishmael had listened politely, said, "Yes, Father. I understand," and left him. He longed to return to the purity of the wilderness, to see his children, but he honored his agreement not to return to Egypt. He was pleased that, as far as knew, Meccah still stood.

Keterah and her sons were visiting Ishmael and Fatimah in the park. Her sons observed the easy, loving relationship between Ishmael and Fatimah; their banter and exchanged glances and camaraderie; the laughter and mutual respect of a man and a woman. The boys were enchanted.

Keterah was pleased. Her battle for the minds of her children with Rebekah and Eliezer was never-ending. Abram's support consisted of "Whatever will be, will be." Her sons responded more easily to Ishmael and Fatimah's worldview than that of Rebekah and Eliezer. Her sons had learned quickly that they were expected to politely agree to that side of the family even—especially—when they spoke of the intellectual inferiority of women. Keterah taught and influenced the minds of her children with the skill of an Egyptian Princess in full. The influence of Ishmael and Fatimah was invaluable.

Ishmael spent the day watching the children and the women with him. His heart was filled with love.

Night came.

MECCAH DEVASTATION

Kedar recognized that he was alive. Not alive enough to turn his head or move his body. But alive.

He lay still, harvesting strength to open his eyes.

He turned his head and opened his eyes. He saw the fires in the south. He lay still for a while longer, then sat up, then shakily stood up. The flames illuminated the night sky. The Western Gate, walkways, and archers were burnt charcoal.

The Egyptian soldiers were resting. They had had a busy day and were tired. They were in the south of the city methodically removing the Coliseum and the existence of Meccah, removing any sign that the city had ever been. The waterfall feeding the stream through the city no longer existed; dammed or diverted or, for history, never was.

Kedar climbed from the rooftop to the ground. He noticed that the walk leading to the Church was red. He had to be careful not to slip down in the redness. He entered the church. It was dark in the night. He found the flint and lit the oil in the trough built into the sides of the church. The soft fire provided just the correct amount of light to light the interior in a peaceful glow. The source of the red slipperiness was now apparent. It had flowed from the bodies of the peaceful congregation gathered to rejoice in the oneness of all humanity. Most of them had gathered in the back of the church making their harvesting easy. Easy, at least, for well-trained swordsmen.

One random body had been tied to a pillar beside the Hubal stage.

A drop of blood plopped on the Hubal. Kedar looked up to see what appeared to be the bodies of two people hanging from the ceiling. *That's probably Basemath and Maribah.*

He looked at the bound body, again. *That's Esau. He would have had a good view of everything.*

He walked the floor to see if anyone was still alive. Finding no life, he walked to and opened the door to the vault beneath the Hubal, entered, and retrieved the Chest of Tallstone. *Tomorrow they will come and turn the church to dust. I should save something. This is a good thing to save.*

He dragged the chest to the entrance, decided he could drag it out the North Gate without being seen, and, with the last of his strength, pulled the chest to a secluded area outside the city. He knelt, found more strength, and returned to the church.

He created a pyre on the Hubal including the robes and garments of two priestesses that had been haphazardly thrown aside. He lowered the bodies of two women and lovingly lay them on the pyre. He lay their clothes and robes beneath their heads.

He dragged a body from the front of the heap and placed it on the pyre. The clothes suggested it might be his brother. Since the head was missing, he could not be sure, but no matter.

Then he remembered Esau tied to the pillar. He stumbled over and untied the ropes holding him up. The body fell to the floor and seemed to emit a cry. *Hmm. He may still be alive. I might as well take him out to the chest.*

With strength coming from no one knows where, Kedar pulled the body to possible safety and returned to the Church. The oil had burned down, the light softening. Kedar went and kissed the lips on the remains of the faces of the two women.

He went to the storage room, overturned all the urns of oil, found and lit a torch, and threw it onto the pyre.

He stood peacefully watching the pyre ignite and the flames gently embrace the three bodies. *Soon, my family, I will see you soon.*

He stumbled out the door and found his way out the North Gate to the secluded area. There he lay down beside what might, or might not be, the still living body of Esau.

He rested.

AFTERMATH

The morning sun came to light the Chest of Tallstone and the sleeping bodies of Kedar and Esau.

Inside the Northern Gate, the soldiers of Egypt were preparing for another busy day. Every stone that had been Meccah had to be removed along with all vegetation. The land had to be salted to prevent the land from recovering. There were bodies to chop into small pieces so that no bones could be found. Fortunately, the soldiers would be allowed ample time to eat, rest, and play with the young women they had captured alive.

The Major surveyed the site with mixed emotions. *That big, red hairy hunter inflicted my biggest losses. He took out half my Special Forces. The corporal said they chained him alive inside that church so he could watch the wrath of Egypt. Presenting the head of Chief Nebaioth to the Pharaoh will ensure my mission is a complete success. And my report on the priestesses and their church will make the Vizier ecstatic for months to come. It's a pity that the inside of the church caught fire last night. I could have selected some nice souvenirs for the vizier. Oh, well, sometimes bad things happen.*

Night came.

The soldiers were tired from a day of exhausting work. They rested, ate, sang soldier's songs, and played "pass the woman."

Beyond the Northern gate, two men still slept.

BEGIN!

Morning light came. Esau sat staring at the sleeping Kedar. He listened to the distant sounds of a city being removed. He did not think. He could not think. He could not remember. *I will not remember until the wrath of every god that has ever existed rains down upon Egypt!*

There was no food in this place and little water. They were weak and injured. Their options were limited. Esau fashioned two poles with which to drag the Chest, shook Kedar, and said, "We must begin."

Kedar awoke, stood, and nodded to Esau in brotherhood.

They began.

HEBRON PASTORAL

On a beautiful Hebron afternoon, Ishmael sat in the park with his mother.

Passing women would certainly report this impropriety to their husbands. *Poor Lord Abram is married to this woman. She is not pious at all!*

Djoser, Hetephe, Incense/Hagar/Keterah
Horus, Serket, Azazil, Abram, Baalat
Ishmael, Maribah, Fatimah, Nebaioth, Basemath, Kedar | Anath, Astarte

News traveled slowly to Hebron, but still it traveled. The gossip, such as it was, was that the Airboat thing had been used and that Meccah had fallen, the temple destroyed, and its people dispersed.

The official account arrived soon after the gossip and was officially presented to Lord Abram of Hebron. The account was read aloud to Lord Abram and his officials.

Abram nodded sagely and righteously in the correct places. Refreshments were served and everyone discussed the events that had transpired.

Women were not allowed in the same room as men doing official business. Keterah could only sit in anguished silence as the fate of her children was officially presented in a distant room.

After all the meetings were over, Keterah was allowed to join her husband who told her of the official report.

She did not cry. She merely said, "I see," rose, and left.

So it was, that on a beautiful summer afternoon in Hebron, Ishmael sat in the park with his mother forlornly drinking wine.

A nervous, young man approached them and asked, "Lord Ishmael?"

"Yes. I am Ishmael."

The man fell to Ishmael's feet, grabbed his legs, and said, "My lord. I am a messenger from the village in the west. I bring you joy. I bring you pain!"

REUNION

Ishmael arrived in the village late in the evening. Kedar and Esau sat by the cooking fire, drinking beer.

Ishmael sat down and joined them. "My sons, I give all thanks that you are here. Keterah sends love to each of you."

Kedar acknowledged his father and said, "It is good to see you, Father. We are in need of wise counsel. We will speak nothing of the past; only the future. We salvaged the Chest. Other than us and the chest, Meccah no longer exists, and the past is over. What shall we do?"

Ishmael reached deeply into his memories and pulled out, "We will drink beer. We will do what is right."

~~~~~~~~~~~~~

39. Horus

BAALAT

Year 212, Season 9, Anathmonth

Baalat said, "Teacher, I will use your visit to announce my withdrawal from all my offices. Your presence will make this an announcement of interest throughout the land!"

Horus saluted her with his glass of wine. "Byblos without Baalat? Horus without his best student? The world without your power? Is this even possible, Living-God Baalat?"

"I told you I would do it, Teacher. Do you remember way back then? I said, 'I will become a Living God that follows the path of Kiya.' Well, here I am. Are you proud of me?"

"I would stand and embrace you with joy and pride, Baalat, but that would involve my standing. I will simply say you are the one thing in my life that made my life worthy. I will greet my parents with pride because of you."

She stood and walked over to pull his head into her breasts for a moment. She stood back, walked to her third-story window, looked out over her port, and answered, "You always were a crying baby, Teacher. Your teachings will live on forever. Probably twisted and used entirely out of context. But still, no one has ever done more. Except Kiya, who knew the way from the beginning. You were the catalyst for the Testament of Set, the answer to everything. No, Teacher. You have done well. You simply cannot accept the truth of it. Now, should I announce my retirement at our little Tree-of-Life Church or at that monstrosity Lord Ahiram is building in my honor?"

"At the monstrosity. That will give more power and influence to Ahiram which is the entire point of building the Temple. No Phoenician believes you are really a god, but the Temple gives his claim credence. And don't draw unnecessary attention to that church. Urfa won't like it and I don't like it."

"Too bad, Teacher. I am a regular attendee along with most of my staff. You were wrong and Shaman Azazil was right. That Meccah incident was an abomination. I considered sending an official Phoenician condemnation to Egypt, but I have nothing to gain and influence to lose."

Djoser, Hetephe, Incense/Hagar/Keterah
Horus, Serket, Azazil, Abram, Baalat
Ishmael, Maribah, Fatimah, Nebaioth, Basemath, Kedar | Anath, Astarte
~~~~~~~~~~~~~

"I will pass along your thoughts to Princess Incense. She can only mourn her loss in silence. That's the way of princesses, you know."

"You will see Abram?"

"Yes. It may be the last stop on 'The Way-of-Horus.' My body and my will have grown too old. I will visit Abram and then retire to Rusalem. Who knows, perhaps Serket will return to me."

She looked upon the old man, and, filled with love, answered, "Yes, Teacher. I believe she will join you there."

~~~

The announcement that Lord Ahiram would replace Lady Baalat shot through the city and environs with lightning speed. Everyone who ever was anyone, gathered at the Temple of The Lady of Byblos to witness this life-changing event.

Horus was given a premiere seat. He would be recognized during the program as the man who had set her on her path and that everyone should follow the Way of Horus. Baalat had assigned a priestess from their small Church of Light to be his aide. Her name was Maysarah. They chatted while waiting for the program to begin. Maysarah knew everything about the Church and its Tree of Life. She was interested that High Priest Azazil had once been a follower of Horus. She grilled him for information.

Then to deafening recognition, the Lady of Byblos strode confidently onto the Temple floor.

The program began.

Baalat orated, "My senior staff was aghast—'You will replace yourself with a *man*?' they screamed. I asked each of them if *she* wanted the job, which of course she didn't. I told them, 'But think of the power you would have!' They were adamant in their refusal. They are all too refined, caring, empathetic, and intelligent to want nothing but raw power."

The crowd laughed.

She continued, "So, what was I to do? What I did was find the best person to replace me who would accept the position, It happened to be a man!"

More laughter.

Baalat talked on, "He can do all of the jobs as well as any woman. He is dedicated, competent, caring and has a vision for the future where all Phoenicians will share the fruits of the labor and contributions of all

<div align="center">Phoenicia, Jaffa, Rocky, Burlyman, Polydore | Astarte, T'jaru
Terah, Amathlai, Haran, Terahson, Nahor, Sarai, Isaac, Jacob
Kyrios-Olon, Teumessian, Nimrod, Nimbal, Nimlad, Nimisis, Asherah, Set.</div>
~~~

Phoenicians, And as a bonus, he can be loud and opinionated. And we all know how lessor minds—like the Egyptians and Canaanites—are quick to obey the loudest voice in the room."

Tremendous laughter.

She held out her arm to the side and announced, "People of Byblos and Phoenicia—This is Lord Ahiram. The future of the glory of Phoenicia!"

The applause was deafening as Ahiram walked to join Baalat.

He acknowledged the audience and then said something no one could hear. He repeated it. People strained closer. He bellowed, "I said, Canaan, can you hear me?!!!"

The laughter was deafening.

He orated, "Civilization is the process which we change from tribal attitudes of 'us against them' to the civilized attitude of 'we are all one people.' An attitude of 'if one suffers, we all suffer.' These attitudes will not change easily. Many people simply wish to be left alone, told what to do, and will gladly obey 'the loudest voice.' Those tyrants who wish power and glory for themselves know this and their attitude will always be, 'I want it all! I am not going to share!' The 'Lady of Byblos' is civilized and enlightened. As did the great Queen Kiya before her, Baalat brought civilization to her people. Now, it is up to her people to keep it. I will not use my loud voice with civilized people, only against tyrants. Only against the Kyrios-Olon who stay hidden in the rotting fabric of our world but use their lackeys to command in loud shrill voices, 'Do as we say!'"

The program went on, including a standing ovation for Shaman Horus whom Priestess Maysarah helped to stand.

The program ended. Maysarah and Horus remained in their seats until the crowd had cleared out.

As darkness approached, Baalat brought Ahiram to introduce him to Horus. His adulation was sincere.

Maysarah said to Baalat, "I wish to go with him, my Lady."

Baalat looked at Horus and said, "I know you are somewhat disappointed in Abram's teachings, so I give you a new student. You will find her to meet all of your qualifications. Perhaps she will want to marry one of those Ishmaelite people I hear so much about."

She nodded to Maysarah, embraced Horus goodbye, and turned to hurry off before something got caught in her eye.

Horus, with passion, called after her, "Baalat, you were never a whore!"

Her words drifted back, "You will never understand! You're only a man!"

ABRAM

Year 212, Season 10, Aphroditemonth

Abram was in his element as Patriarch of the city; planning festivities, meetings, and learned discussions with the pious city elders.

The arrival of Lord Horus in Hebron was always an event of much importance.

Maysarah, however, was not allowed into these discussions but instead, visited with Keterah.

Their visit was so delightful that Keterah rose and told Eliezer that they would be visiting Ishmael, Kedar, and Esau in the city and he must take over her hostess duties.

Eliezer would have a great deal to cluck about with the women.

The two women found and joined Ishmael and his sons sitting in the park. Keterah listened with interest as Maysarah told Ishmael, Kedar, and Esau about her life and hopes and dreams.

After three days of visiting and learned discussions, Horus made an unusual request, "I would like to visit the ruins of Meccah."

Abram thought this to be a grand suggestion. He could show Horus where Abram had once more destroyed the unrighteous idols. The expedition was planned. Esau and Kedar, in quiet agony, would lead the palanquin containing Abram and Horus so that they could hear their words and provide any requested services.

After they agreed, Esau retired to a private place and vomited.

The expedition set off after Horus's sunrise ceremony.

They were halfway to the closest western village when Abram began telling Horus of his visit to that Meccah church with all its false idols.

Esau tried not to hear.

Abram furnished great detail. "Nimrod was once angry with me because I destroyed all those idols in Harran. He threw me in the furnace and everything. But now he understands. I was prepared to nod to all those idols like Keterah wanted me to do, but with each idol, Nimrod grew more righteous and agitated. So finally, I realized that I was being unrighteous and that I must destroy all of those false idols. Without, Nimrod's guidance, I would never have …"

Esau suddenly stopped and set down his corner of the palanquin with a thud. Everyone looked at him, standing ramrod straight, face frozen without expression. Kedar signaled one of the accompanying Meccah survivors to take Esau's place, went to Esau, and said, "The God of Vengeance is with you. Go!"

Esau turned, and without a word, started back to Hebron.

Abram was confused. Everyone was confused. But Kedar commanded the expedition on to their next stop at the western village.

THE CHEST OF TALLSTONE

The villagers were thrilled to greet Patriarch Abram and the legendary Shaman Horus. A sheep was sacrificed and prepared.

Later, Ishmael went to Kedar and asked, "What's the matter with Esau?"

Kedar answered, "Grandfather Abram told Lord Horus that it was by Nimrod's words that he destroyed Sister's idols. Esau is on his way to deliver a long and painful death to Nimrod."

"Oh."

Kedar said, "Now, we must make a decision. Grandmother says that we should tell Lord Horus. I agree. Do you?"

"About the chest."

"Yes."

"That's more your and Esau's decision."

"Then it is decided. Come. I will present it to the Shaman."

Kedar motioned for Keterah and Ishmael to sit on either side of Horus by the cooking fire as it burned low. Maysarah stood behind her teacher.

Kedar talked to the village elders.

Two villagers retreated to a hut and removed a covered heavy sack. The two men carried the sack and set it down before Horus, who questioningly looked around at the group.

Kedar addressed Horus, "Once an old man drove a wagon full of dung to Aqaba. He carried more than he knew. By order of the Pharaoh, he not only carried the inheritance of his daughter but of all mankind."

Realization came to Horus. *Father, forgive them. Forgive us all.*

Kedar told Horus, "We placed it with honor in the Tree-of-Life Church. Our plan did not work. Now we don't know what to do with it."

Horus muttered, "Khaba disfigured First Mother. I was told the Chest was not found; that the Pharaoh believed I had stolen it. Now it is obvious. Of course, Djoser would not leave the Chest to the care of those who did not honor it. So here it is. Where does it belong?"

Maysarah messaged her teacher's shoulder to relieve his increasing stress.

All were silent as Horus considered the question.

He said, "Maysarah?"

She replied, "You were foolish to have no heir to watch over it, Teacher, and Lord Abram neither honors its heritage nor is Canaan a proper land for its home. The Temple of the Lady of Byblos would be nice. It would be honored there, and close to from where it came. The children of Lord Ishmael provided a perfect home except for the wars of men. A remote mountain top, safe from men's vanities, a secret resting place protected by a mighty few. I don't know where that might be, but I believe the Chest would be at peace in such a place."

Ishmael muttered, "The mountains of Midian …"

Horus stared into the dying fire. *There will never be peace. The Kyrios-Olon do not profit from peace.*

The next morning, after the sunrise ceremony, the expedition left the Chest in the care of the villagers. Upon their return, the destination of the chest would be decided, and it would be taken to another resting place.

MECCAH

Year 212, Season 11, Dionysusmonth

Kedar stopped at the Northern Gate, or where it would have been if it still were. He fell to the ground and sobbed.

Everyone in the expedition was somber except Abram, who looked on with a mixture of pride and righteousness. *Behold the wrath of the One True God. The vengeance of the righteous over idolaters!*

Phoenicia, Jaffa, Rocky, Burlyman, Polydore | Astarte, T'jaru
Terah, Amathlai, Haran, Terahson, Nahor, Sarai, Isaac, Jacob
Kyrios-Olon, Teumessian, Nimrod, Nimbal, Nimlad, Nimisis, Asherah, Set.

Keterah would remain beside her husband and contain his comments as best she could. *Many suffered horribly in this place; some beyond horror.*

Ishmael and Fatimah walked to Kedar and picked him up. The three entered a city now level. Nothing grew. The river was gone. All that remained was a level field of gravel and salt.

Fatimah lamented, "This place is barren now. Nothing will ever grow. There is no water!"

Keterah overheard and replied, "There is always water! Ishmael, find water for your people!"

The obedient son, with his staff, began searching the desolation. He finally stopped, studied, and drove his staff into a shallow depression. Water began bubbling up into the depression.

Keterah commanded, "Fill! Fill!"

Fatimah giggled. "My husband is clever. My Mother-in-Law is mighty!"

The depression filled as Ishmael dug deeper into the source of water. Birds soon saw and began circling this new source of water.

The refugees, once residents of Meccah, went into the mountains to gather stones. Others began reclaiming the charred wood of the city.

Those with stones laid them to lay an outline where they remembered the buildings once were. The best stones were used to outline the church that had once stood there. They worked throughout the day. The outline of the once-city slowly took shape.

Those with charred wood brought it to where a church once had stood. Kedar directed the Hubal to be reformed. It could not rise toward the sky, but it would be a charred, black stage upon which one could sit in quiet contemplation of The Tree-of-Life. Maysarah observed, with interest, the intense reverence that a mighty archer could achieve.

The more Abram spoke of evil idols the greater their love grew for their once-city, their once-church, their understanding of the nature of god they carried with them. Keterah ceased attempting to keep Abram from speaking. It was as if the more he spoke, the more the people understood that Meccah had been the hope of humanity; not Hebron; not Canaan; not Egypt. Meccah. Perhaps nothing could grow in this place for a thousand years, but they would remember, they would tell their children.

Djoser, Hetephe, Incense/Hagar/Keterah
Horus, Serket, Azazil, Abram, Baalat
Ishmael, Maribah, Fatimah, Nebaioth, Basemath, Kedar | Anath, Astarte

"This is where we would circle the temple, paying honor to the people who worshiped different gods."

"We walked around it three times!"

"I remember it was seven times!"

"It contained the words of the prophets and all truth."

Kedar completed the laying of the new Hubal and sat quietly in its center. Maysarah took Horus to sit beside Kedar on the Hubal. She quietly told Kedar, "I am a Priestess of The Church of Light."

Keterah led Abram around the Hubal three times insisting he praise the god of Basemath who he conflated with the One God. Everyone gathered to watch this spectacle, including a stranger.

Ishmael saw the stranger join them and walked to introduce himself. "I am Ishmael, once of Meccah. Welcome to the remains of my son's city."

The stranger answered without taking his eyes off the unfolding spectacle, "I am Jurhum. I saw the birds circling. There is water here."

"A great deal more, Chief Jurhum. You shall take all the water you wish. There will be no quarrels in this place. It is a place of peace for all tribes."

A well was built over the water. The tribe of Jurhum drew their fill.

Kedar and Maysarah chose to remain here, in the ruins. So did several families who once lived in Meccah. The others returned with Abram and Horus to Hebron.

~~~

Tribes learned of the well and that they were welcome to draw all the water they wished but there would be no quarrels in this place.

Maysarah performed a lovely ceremony under each full moon. Tribes in the area would attend. The tribes began coming under a full moon to trade and resolve any disagreement their tribe might have with another.

Within the Church of Light, the Tree-of-Life grew.

HORUS'S DECISION

Year 212, Season 12, Isismonth

The expedition finally returned to the village west of Hebron and made camp. The women made their own little fire away from the men so they could talk of women's things.
~~~

Villager: "How long will it take for them to decide?"
Fatimah: "They have already decided, they need only say it."
Keterah: "What will you do Fatimah. You can come live with me."
Fatima: "Thank you, Keterah. But I have sons throughout the land. One will want their mother to live with their tribe. I will be quite comfortable."
Villager: "How will you find them?"
Fatima laughed: "How will I *not* find them? They are everywhere and they all know where each other are."

At the men's fire, Horus sat in torment. He had just lost an eager, learned student when he needed her most. He realized, too late, that Azazil was correct and that he had made a grievous decision. An impossible choice lay before him. The end of all journeys lay before him. His once hoped-for-heir-to-his lifelong work neither understood what was at stake nor did he comprehend his misguided thoughts. And, unfortunately, Serket was not with him. *Father, were you pleased I selected a pillow the color of wine?*

Abram: "What will you do with your chest, Lord Horus? It is a valuable treasure. I will be happy to keep it in Hebron. It will bring much trade through my city."
Villager: "Does it really contain the writings of the ancients? Can we open it?"
Abram: "It contains the Testament of Yahweh, himself. It is a wonderful treasure that should not be looked on by anyone but the most pious priest! And then, not often."
Refugee: "It should be kept under the Hubal in Meccah! That's where it belongs."

They talked on, drinking what passed for wine.

Finally,

Ishmael: "Will you join me, Lord Horus? It will be a difficult journey."
Horus: "No. It has been delivered into *your* hands. Do the best you can. Its destiny is beyond my saying."
Ishmael: "I don't honor the chest like Kedar does, or even Esau, Certainly, it is not as meaningful to me as it is to you. I understand it's priceless. But not to me."
Horus: "Will you protect it with all the ardor of a prince of Egypt?"
Ishmael: "Yes."
Horus: "That is all I can ask, Prince Ishmael. And that is more than enough."

Djoser, Hetephe, Incense/Hagar/Keterah
Horus, Serket, Azazil, Abram, Baalat
Ishmael, Maribah, Fatimah, Nebaioth, Basemath, Kedar | Anath, Astarte

Ishmael rose, walked to his mother, and held out both hands to her.

Keterah took his hands, pulled herself up, looked into his eyes, and said, "I will miss you. I will send your inheritance to Adbeel with the next caravan. It contains jewels, contentment, long-lasting life. Magic things like that. Remember to ask it for it."

Ishmael said, "I may not see you again, Mother."

Keterah replied, "I *will* see you again, Son. In this life or the next."

"Do you really believe in those teachings, Mother?"

"I choose to believe them. How else could I let you leave me?"

He embraced her and returned to the men.

Later, when he retired to his bed, Fatimah, overcome with love, welcomed him long into the night.

THE LONELINESS OF MEN

At sunrise, Ishmael met with Fatimah and said many lovely things and made many lovely promises. She chose to believe every word.

Keterah was not to be seen.

The expedition, save Ishmael, departed for Hebron after Horus's uplifting sunrise ceremony.

Ishmael remained behind until the villagers could fashion him a cart he could pull by himself through the wilderness. He would, soon enough, find the tribe of one of his sons and, if not, he knew well the way to Shur.

His world had changed. No one waited for, looked for, or expected the arrival of Ishmael. His only company would be a useless chest full of meaningful-to-somebody-else treasures.

The cart was finished and loaded before high-sun.

Ishmael tested it, smiled broadly, thanked the villagers, and set off on another adventure. Pulling a cart containing a golden chest.

~~~

To the East, Horus rode in the palanquin with Abram silently listening to Abram's pious summary of their expedition.

But his mind was to the southwest. *The most meaningful writings and thoughts to ever exist are in the protection of a man who doesn't believe a word the chest contains.*

Phoenicia, Jaffa, Rocky, Burlyman, Polydore | Astarte, T'jaru
Terah, Amathlai, Haran, Terahson, Nahor, Sarai, Isaac, Jacob
Kyrios-Olon, Teumessian, Nimrod, Nimbal, Nimlad, Nimisis, Asherah, Set.
~~~

How did this happen? Does it matter? Does anything matter? Father, help me to understand!

They would arrive in Hebron later in the day,

Horus would travel on to Rusalem after greeting the next sunrise.

ISHMAEL

Year 213, Season 3, Tehutimonth

Ishmael found and joined the nomadic tribe of his son, Mishma, as he traveled west toward Shur. Mishma and Ishmael greeted as powerful men greet. With bravado and strength; not love nor affection.

Mishma's tribe arrived near Shur and set up camp. Ishmael and Mishma continued into the city where they met Adbeel. Adbeel greeted them as powerful men greet.

The father and his two sons would visit for a day, and then Mishma would turn his tribe southward. Ishmael would travel southeast toward Aqaba.

Ishmael remembered, "By the way, Son. Your grandmother sent me a wagon full of supplies. She said I might be able to use it during my travels. Did she send such a thing?"

"Oh, yes. She did. It came with two donkeys to pull it. I have it stored somewhere. I'll find it before you leave. You can ride instead of walk."

The three men attended the sunrise ceremony at the Church of Shur. The Priest greeted the sun extolling the virtues of Pharaoh Khaba and the virtue of wives who obey their husbands. The Priest taught, "A disobedient wife should not always be stoned to death but could instead sometimes be shunned by the righteous." The church had no priestesses.

Ishmael remembered to get the wagon and loaded his equipment and the disguised chest into the back.

He rose at sunrise the next day and traveled past Aqaba southward toward the mountain range of Midian. After traveling for a while, the top of the great mountain range appeared on the horizon rising out of the plains. *What have I agreed to do?*

He knew the mountains well after a lifetime of exploring the wildernesses with his sons. He selected the best mountain peak upon which to place his "treasure." He traveled until he arrived at the small stream dividing his chosen peak from the plains. He stopped and unharnessed the donkeys to allow them to rest and graze while he sat and studied the ascent.

Djoser, Hetephe, Incense/Hagar/Keterah
Horus, Serket, Azazil, Abram, Baalat
Ishmael, Maribah, Fatimah, Nebaioth, Basemath, Kedar | Anath, Astarte

Aloud, he said, "All right, Paiou, all right, Kyiry, you two pull our wagon up the mountain until you can't. Then we will hide it and carry our cargo by foot. We have ten feet. That should be enough. Maybe everything in one trip. Or two trips if I get tired."

After resting, he harnessed the donkeys, slapped Kyiry on the rump, and commanded, "Let's go climb a mountain."

HORUS AND SERKET

Year 213, Season 3, Tehutimonth

The people of Rusalem honored Horus by always keeping Serket's old room available for the occasions Horus would visit them.

That evening at dusk, Horus sat in the park listening to the local priest call forth the children of Shalem and Shahar to come and play across the night sky. One by one, the children of Shalem and Shahar began appearing. It was a beautiful evening. *I have become nothing. But I did not lose my soul to the Kyrios-Olon. That is triumph enough, I suppose.*

Late in the night, he lay in Serket's bed. He was old. He was tired. He slept. He dreamed dreams. *"You slept enough, Master Horus. Now we gotta watch Grandfather call the children of Shalem and Shahar. It'll bring you some peace. Let's get outside, right now!"*

Dreams of things past. *You tryin' to flatter me, Mister Horus. I like that."*

Thunder rolled from the lightning from the night storm. He woke. He was alone. He wept.

Lightning reflected from the wall. The light attracted his attention. He rolled his head toward the wall. *Serket's nose was close to his. She was staring at him with love in her eyes.*

He asked aloud, "Where have you been? I have missed you."

"I have been bringing peace to people who did not have peace. Healing them from sickness and scorpion stings. I have come to get you."

"How did you die?"

I was saving scorpions from the abuse of people. Three of them stung my hand.

"They were never the brightest of creatures."

She smiled and said, "I love them still. And you."

"Are you really here or are you the imagination of a dying mind?

We are all here, Silly. I'm just the easiest for you to see. To understand.

Feminine voice: "I am here, my son. Waiting to wrap you in my love."

Masculine voice: "I wait to experience everything you have experienced, Son. And the wine-red pillow was an excellent choice."

Serket: "We tarry, Husband. Come. We are waiting."

Djoser, Hetephe, Incense/Hagar/Keterah
Horus, Serket, Azazil, Abram, Baalat
Ishmael, Maribah, Fatimah, Nebaioth, Basemath, Kedar | Anath, Astarte

~~~~~~~~~~~~~

40. The Lord

The long years passed.

Ishmael still took the life-extending ambrosia his mother had given him so long ago.

Now, ancient in days, he looked westward with love and hatred.

In the Sinai, his descendants lived. *My sons' descendants are there with their cities and tribes They survive famines well enough. They are accustomed to thriving in the wilderness. But they are infected with the teachings of the Canaanites.*

Beyond that, Egypt. *My enemies crawl across Egypt like maggots on a long-dead carcass. Oh, that I could turn it into a lake of fire and make them regret they ever heard my name. They killed those I loved. They humiliated me and drove out the very best who ever lived. Oh, that I could bring down evil!*

He returned to his tent and removed some of his mother's long-ago gift, the Grass of Paradise. This alone could relieve his mind, unharden his heart, and calm his soul. The sun began setting to his left, the night rising from his right. He slowly walked to a massive throne he had chiseled from the mountain stone, sat in it, returned his gaze westward, and loaded his pipe with the grass. He lit his pipe and let the sweet smoke fill his lungs.

Peace came to him. *They only do what men do. Lie. Fight. Betray. The mighty subjugate the weak. It has always been so. What difference?*

He remembered those he had loved. *They were caring, nurturing people. Helping those around them. Teaching them. Sharing. What happened? Why did it happen?*

He sank deeper into his stupor. *Horus knew what was happening and why. Mother knew. I should have paid more attention to them. I thought it didn't matter. That humans could not grow worse than they already were. But no matter how evil they become, they can always grow worse.*

He slept.

~~~

He woke. The day had begun. His anger returned. *I have lived too long, seen too much. Pharaohs come and go. To what end? Everything is bitter in my mouth.*

He stood and walked to stare toward the east where his mother and her six sons had disappeared long ago. Some said Abram had cast them out. Ishmael believed what the others said, that she had set off in disgust for

Mesopotamia with her sons to build their own blessings. *Grandfather should have anointed Mother as Pharaoh.*

After Abram had died and was placed in his tomb, the Church of Urfa had permeated religious thought in Canaan to their liking. The basis of Abram's teachings remained but that was basically, "Be righteous." The subjugation of women, the fear of "Others," and the superiority of men were now inseparable from their political and religious thought. The Church had varying degrees of success in other parts of the world, but in Canaan, all resistance was gone and success was total.

Only around the once-city of Meccah did the teaching of the Tree-of-Life dominate. Or at least it did the last time he had visited his once-son's once-city. There, Ishmael had encountered Esau who was growing a large following. Esau had led Ishmael to the once-eastern gate where there was a post in the ground. Upon the post was a skull. Esau had said, "Nimrod freely embraced the Way of Horus in the end. I kept him alive until he understood. I was filled with love when I mercifully removed his head."

Ishmael had made the mountain his home; created caves for his treasures, carved massive chairs out of stone to overlook the land; one facing west toward Egypt with the Sinai; one facing south toward the lands of most of his sons; one facing east toward Midian and Canaan; one facing north toward Midian and Middlesea. He sometimes read the writings from the Chest of Tallstone he kept in the ornate cave he had carved out for it. He was not proficient in reading the old languages, but simply holding the writings brought back the feeling of hope for humanity. *Where are Basemath and Azazil when I need them? Oh, yes. Long dead. Is that Tree-of-Life belief true? Perhaps. It would be wonderful to see them again. All of them. I loved them so!*

With melancholy, he began his morning stroll. *I don't travel anymore. Once, I traveled at least every Solstice. To Hebron and Shur. To Meccah. Even to Memphis. But no more My peace is here, on my mountaintop; not on the plains; not in civilization.*

He wandered down the mountain admiring his wilderness home.

At the sound of a human voice, he froze.

"Lord, I search for a lost lamb. Pray, have you heard one crying for its shepherd?"

Ishmael looked up and into the eyes of a young, strapping shepherd. "Don't look at me, Shepherd! It is not for your eyes to behold me."

"I'm sorry," said the shepherd, moving his gaze to the ground. "I did not mean to offend you, but I must find my lamb. Without me, it will die in this place."

"Who are you that I should acknowledge your existence?"

"Lord, I am a shepherd exiled from the land of Egypt which enslaves my people. My wife is Zipporah, oldest of the seven daughters of Jethro, a man of wealth and standing in Midian, at the foot of this great mountain. I mean you no trouble. I will take my leave. Shalom, Master."

"You are a Jacobite, Shepherd?"

"Yes, my Lord, an Israelite of the House of Israel, once named Jacob.

"You people change your names with the coming of a new month. You are a Jacobite!"

"Yes, my Lord."

I knew Jacob and his father, Isaac, and his grandfather, Abram. Fine men. Well, honest men, anyway. Much unlike today's poor excuses for men. Abram's wife, Keterah, was the finest person to ever live. Not so much his first wife, Sarai, but certainly Keterah."

"You knew my ancestors, Lord. But they lived in the distant past and all died long ago!"

"Well, yes. I have have been alive for a long time and lost whatever little patience with people that I may have once had. If I am short with you, well … then I am short with you."

"You honor me by speaking with me, Lord. I shall tell my family of your graciousness toward me and the House of Isra -- Jacob."

"Well, yes. That is permissible. Just don't disturb my walks. I am of great importance. Self-importance, anyway."

"What name shall I tell my family, Lord?"

"I am who I am. You need know nothing more. Leave me."

As the Sun set, Ishmael again retrieved his pipe and sat outside his tent. On this night, he stared northward toward an angry sky. As he began to drift into peace, he was surprised by his lack of anger. *The visit with the shepherd was nice. He appears to be a good man. Perhaps we can visit again.*

Phoenicia, Jaffa, Rocky, Burlyman, Polydore | Astarte, T'jaru
Terah, Amathlai, Haran, Terahson, Nahor, Sarai, Isaac, Jacob
Kyrios-Olon, Teumessian, Nimrod, Nimbal, Nimlad, Nimisis, Asherah, Set.

He slipped into a restless sleep. *The Ambrosia pills. I must stop taking Mother's Ambrosia pills and allow death to come for me. But the chest, who would protect the chest? I must live until my duty is complete.*

THE LOST LAMB

The next morning, pitiful bleating woke Ishmael. Thoughts of damnation flashed through his mind as he woke to stare into the forlorn eyes of a lamb. He could not think of a curse worthy of this scene. He simply rose, threw some leftover greens to the lamb, and then began shepherding the lamb the long walk down the mountain.

~~~

The late day found the man and the lamb in the foothills.

In the distance, sheep grazed. He pointed the lamb toward the flock, kicked it, yelled, and returned to the long climb back up the mountain.

The lamb was discovered at dusk by its shepherd. "Praise be to the gods. That which was lost has been found."

At evening meal, the shepherd discussed this improbable event with his wife. "I know the lamb was on the mountain because I found its footprints there. It had to have been returned by the great Lord living on the mountain. It had to be."

Zipporah agreed. They discussed how such an act could be repaid. It was decided that at the proper time, the lamb would be sacrificed, and a portion of its cooked meat would be given as an offering of thanks to the great Lord named, "I Am Who I Am."

THE OFFERING

Seasons passed.

One evening after dusk, Ishmael sat in his tent reading an ancient scroll by his artificial light, part of his priceless inheritance from his mother along with the weed and the Ambrosia. He had only to insert rods into urns and the artificial light glowed with the light of a small sun.

In the distance, Ishmael detected the smell of cooked meat. He walked outside his tent. Behind him, the glowing light inside the tent turned the entire tent into a glowing source of warm light. He walked to the trail head, crossed his arms, applied his frown, and waited for the source of the wondrous smell.
~~~

The shepherd crested the trail's end, saw Ishmael, and turned his gaze downward.

He said, "Lord, please accept this unworthy offering for the honor you have bestowed upon my house."

Ishmael eagerly looked at the shepherd's backpack overflowing with all manner of fragrant cuts of meat. "Your offering is worthy, shepherd. I will continue to look over your flocks and your family."

Turning, he said, "Come, sit with me and we will sample your offering."

The shepherd looked up to follow, then froze with fear and awe. No word could come to his mouth. Behind the ancient man stood a burning bush. A fire that did not flicker or change, that did not consume the bush, that was as bright as a coming morning sun, that was beyond his concept to understand. "My Lord!" said the shepherd as he fell to his knees with head bowed, "My Lord."

Ishmael looked at the prostrate shepherd and then turned toward the "burning tent." *Ah, yes. Of course you would be confused. Perhaps visiting during the day would be better.*

"Come back in a quartermoon during the day. We will visit then."

The shepherd hurriedly departed as Ishmael returned to his tent and eagerly considered the burnt offering.

THE THOUGHT

On one of his thrones, in the night, Ishmael awoke and stared into the darkness. His mind was sharp, clear, and aware. Inspiration flooded his body, turning it rigid. Afraid to think, afraid to breathe, lest the thought be lost to him forever. *A Jacobite fled from Egypt. Egypt, who slaughtered my oldest son and his people. Egypt, whose great people have long vanished. Egypt, whose wealth now relies on indentured Jacobites. Canaan, once occupied by the children of Jacob. Canaan, now overrun with evil vermin. Jacobite, I shall free your people from their bondage and give you and your people a land of milk and honey. Jacobite, I shall give you the land of Canaan.*

TEACHER

Ishmael built a meeting place on a southerly outcropping below the high points that contained his thrones. The outcropping gave a panoramic view toward the directions of the lands of Egypt and Canaan. His vigor had returned full force. He now had a goal worthy of his power; worthy of the first-born son of Princess Incense and Patriarch Abram; worthy of the grandson of Pharaoh Djoser and Queen Hetephe.

Worthy of a Prince of Egypt.

The shepherd arrived and was directed to stare at the great vistas toward the west.

Once Ishmael began, he could not stop talking. He told the stories that his mother had told him. He shared the stories of ancient knowledge, of the creation, of mankind's forgotten history. He told the shepherd how to be a righteous man, and how to treat the poor, the afflicted, the widowed, those without power of their own. He may have embellished his own role a little, but only a little.

As best he could, Ishmael taught the shepherd of the Tree of Life; of the All, of the One, of what Horus had once taught him. "Civilization is the process by which we change from tribal attitudes of 'us against them' to the civilized attitude of 'we are one people.' An attitude of 'if one suffers, we all suffer.' These attitudes do not change easily. Most people simply wish to be left alone inside their own tribe, told what to do, and will gladly obey 'the loudest voice.' Tyrants who wish power and glory for themselves alone, whose attitude is, 'I want it all' know this. A true leader will not use a loud voice with civilized people, only against tyrants such as the Kyrios-Olon who stay hidden in the rotting fabric of our world but use their purchased lackeys to command the sheep in a loud shrill voice, 'Do as we say!'"

The shepherd's keen intellect absorbed it all, making the stories his own.

Finally, Ishmael shifted the subject to the shepherd. *What use can I make you, shepherd? How can I use you to set the Jacobites free?*

Ishmael said, "Now, tell me your story."

The shepherd told of how the great famine of long ago forced his people to leave their lands in Canaan and indenture themselves to the Pharaoh for seven years. But when the seven years ended, the Pharaoh would not grant them their freedom. They were held against their will.

The shepherd talked of his sister, Miriam, and of his older brother, Aaron, a man of many eloquent and forceful words.

As the shepherd spoke, Ishmael studied him and listened to the passion of a quiet man as the shepherd repeated Ishmael's teachings back to him exactly as he had heard the words adding his insights and thoughts to Ishmael's teachings.

He then described the reason for his exile from Egypt. "An overseer had mercilessly whipped an Israelite into unconsciousness. I commanded him to cease but he continued the beating. I broke the overseer's neck with one blow. My adopted father, the Pharaoh, was greatly displeased with me. He sent me into the desert with only my staff."

Ishmael stiffened, "Your father was a Pharaoh?"

"Yes, my Lord. His future wife, Thermuthis, found me in the reeds near her bath. My sister had placed me there to escape the killing of the firstborn. Thermuthis raised me as her own."

"You are the adopted brother of the new Pharaoh of Egypt?!"

With humility, the shepherd responded, "Yes, my Lord. I have been blessed that I need no longer wear a mantle of great power. I have been set free to live a life of simplicity and truth."

"The Pharaoh would know you if you came into his court?"

"Oh, yes, my Lord. Many were the days we played and fought and rode together. It was as if we were of the same father and mother, brothers by blood. It was only later in life when I became more beloved than he by our father, that we became rivals."

Thunderstruck, Ishmael commanded, "Leave me now! Come back in a quartermoon. I must think about this! I must think!"

The shepherd rose and turned to leave but Ishmael commanded, "Wait, shepherd, what is your name?"

"My name, blessed Lord, is Moses."

THE COMMANDMENT

Moses returned at the appointed time. His Lord waited. Staff in hand. Rigid back, Stern look. Great white mane and beard flowing in the wind. Moses averted his Lord's eyes.

"Look at me, Prince of Egypt. Hear my words and understand. You will go into Egypt. You will take Aaron and make Aaron your voice. You shall speak to no man but Aaron. Aaron will say to the Pharaoh with a loud voice: 'Let my people go!' When the Pharaoh refuses, have said to him, 'My Lord is fearsome, great and mighty. He is mightier than all your puny gods. Release the Jacobites or my Lord will bring a plague upon your land.

Phoenicia, Jaffa, Rocky, Burlyman, Polydore | Astarte, T'jaru
Terah, Amathlai, Haran, Terahson, Nahor, Sarai, Isaac, Jacob
Kyrios-Olon, Teumessian, Nimrod, Nimbal, Nimlad, Nimisis, Asherah, Set.

Pestilence, death, and great suffering. My Lord commands you: 'Let my people go!' Look closely at the land and the people. At every sign of trouble, hunger, sickness, or sadness command Aaron to proclaim loudly that this is because of my wrath. Exaggerate every misfortune as my doing as punishment to the Pharaoh. And in every audience with the Pharaoh, have Aaron demand loudly: 'Let my people go!' Say these things often and loudly and then again! The louder his voice, the more they believe! If, after a season, your demand is not met, leave with Aaron loudly exclaiming, 'When we return, it shall be with the vengeance of my great and mighty Lord. Run away, Egyptians. Hide from his terrible wrath!' Return here with Aaron. I am not without resources to fulfill this promise. The Pharaoh may release your people. If so, bring them here, to the foot of the mountain. I shall give them their promised land."

Moses stared into the eyes of this fearsome, great, and mighty Lord.

In those eyes, Ishmael saw the future of the House of Abram. And, too, he who would become the custodian of the golden Chest of Tallstone.

THE CHOSEN PEOPLE

Moses departed for Egypt to command the Pharaoh to let his people go.

Ishmael sat on his a throne and reflected. He finalized his decision. *The House of Moses shall protect the Chest of Tallstone and the teachings of the ancients.*

Ishmael would send Moses into the lands of his sons and raise a mighty army of expert archers in the name of Ishmael.

If Moses returned *without* the Jacobites, then Moses could use the army to attack Egypt.

If Moses returned *with* the Jacobites, then the archers could be used to conquer Canaan.

Ishmael suddenly knew how a Pharaoh felt with great people doing his bidding to accomplish great things. *Pharaoh Ishmael. That's funny.* He considered Moses. *Pharaoh Moses. That sounds right.*

As he reflected, he saw a cloud of smoke form in the far distance. It reflected red from the annihilation of a distant exploding mountain. The sky began turning to smoke-filled darkness.

From his mountaintop, Ishmael could see desolation falling on the land. He knew not from where the darkened sky came, but all unknown things would work in the favor of Moses. Surely, this was a sign of times to come.

Djoser, Hetephe, Incense/Hagar/Keterah
Horus, Serket, Azazil, Abram, Baalat
Ishmael, Maribah, Fatimah, Nebaioth, Basemath, Kedar | Anath, Astarte

He became lost in thought. *When I give the chest to Moses, will he understand the words? Can he? Can any of them? Can they do what Horus and Abram could not? How will this work out? Not as I plan, but as it will be. Will enlightened people understand? Will they act? Will they hear the words as they are written? The Kyrios-Olon still seek the chest. It is a threat to them as long as the writings exist. I fear for you, Moses. For you and your people. But you are the best of us. If you fail, it is the failure of all men who would not listen and understand. Men who listened to the loudest voice rather than reason. Nobility will be lost in the dust of time. Truth is always distorted into something that it wasn't.*

He became more and more agitated. *Make them understand, Moses. Make them understand The Tree-of-Life. Don't let it remain hidden. Give them the knowledge, and with it, reason will come and civilization will continue until all people are finally enlightened and free.*

He slept a fitful sleep.

FUTURE IMPERFECT

The sky eventually cleared.

And on this day, in the far distance, on the plains below, Ishmael could see a great cloud of dust rising from the march of many peoples.

With a hammer and chisel, he created two stone tablets from the mountainside. Upon these tablets, he engraved the teachings of Kiya. He inspected his work, was pleased with it, and spontaneously added across the top, "You will worship only One God."

Into a chest once protected by First Mother, and then by the Church of Light, and then by a mountain, into this chest of wondrous things and wondrous knowledge, he placed, too, his commandments.

Without anger, without hubris, without emotion, Ishmael entered his tent, collected his wondrous gifts, dressed in his mantle of power, prepared the ark, and threw the pills of Ambrosia from the mountaintop. He then watched the coming of his chosen people to whom he would entrust a promised land and the golden Chest of Tallstone.

The Lord waited in anticipation for "what will be."

As did the Tree of Life.

And Civilization.

###

Phoenicia, Jaffa, Rocky, Burlyman, Polydore | Astarte, T'jaru
Terah, Amathlai, Haran, Terahson, Nahor, Sarai, Isaac, Jacob
Kyrios-Olon, Teumessian, Nimrod, Nimbal, Nimlad, Nimisis, Asherah, Set.

~~~~~~~~~~~~

Here ends the story of *The Beginning of Civilization: Mythologies Told True.*

Civilization remains under constant attack by those the original gods devolved into. Without enlightened good work, it will not survive.

Be worthy.

Peace. dw.

Djoser, Hetephe, Incense/Hagar/Keterah
Horus, Serket, Azazil, Abram, Baalat
Ishmael, Maribah, Fatimah, Nebaioth, Basemath, Kedar | Anath, Astarte
~~~~~~~~~~~~

~~~~~~~~~~~~~

APPENDIX

Mythologies and traditions are italicized.

Abram was a follower of Horus. His parents were Terah and Amathlai. His siblings were Terahson, Haran, Nahor, and Sarai.

Aqaba is the city located at the top of the Gulf of Aqaba.

Alashiya was the unflooded, surviving highlands of Tartarus. A source of Egyptian copper.

Amathlai was Terah's wife and Abram's mother.

Ambrosia was a potion created by the Olympians to reduce the effects of aging tenfold. Furure chemists converted it from a potion to pills.

Amenirdis was Nebaioth's wife.

Anath was the second daughter of Ishtar and became 'Dispatcher Anath,' a feared warrior of the Egyptian army and subsequently the Sinai virgin goddess of war and strife. She was sometimes consort to Set.

Anubis was the son of Set and Nephthys.

Asherah was the Horpriestess of the Church of Urfa and the last consort and wife to Set.

Asherah *was the consort of Yahweh but was deconstructed and eliminated by later Hebrews who became jealous of the feminine. She was widely worshiped by Canaanite women as the goddess of childbirth. Asherah poles were a common altar item in households.*

Astarte was the oldest daughter of Ishtar

Azazil replaced Rocky as Horus's primary follower and became Horus's enemy due to a difference of opinion.

Azazil *was the adversary of God.*

Baalat was a girl concubine to Teumessian in the Temple of Urfa and a subsequent follower of Horus. She was the force that developed Byblos into a major trading center and ally of Egypt. She became "Lady of Byblos" and a living god.

Baalat Gebal*, "Lady of Byblos," was the Goddess of the City of Byblos who was also recognized in Egypt.*

Phoenicia, Jaffa, Rocky, Burlyman, Polydore | Astarte, T'jaru
Terah, Amathlai, Haran, Terahson, Nahor, Sarai, Isaac, Jacob
Kyrios-Olon, Teumessian, Nimrod, Nimbal, Nimlad, Nimisis, Asherah, Set.
~~~~~~~~~~~~~

Blackwater was a strong non-alcoholic beverage containing caffeine and sugar.

Brown-wine was brandy.

Byblos, aka Els End, was originally a small fishing village created by the Oceanids for refugees after the Great Flood. Baalat grew the village into a major port, sea power, and trading partner to Egypt. It became a key city in Phoenicia. See Baalat.

Calendar, as referenced in this work, is contrived to fit the narrative and is not based on historical evolution. The "political calendar" was an invention of Djoser to standardize and formalize time references across Egypt and beyond. The Year begins at the Winter Solstice and is divided into twelve months of 30 days with five days added on immediately before the Winter Solstice and are universal Egyptian holidays. The years are referenced from their best estimate of the First Winter Solstice Festival. The **Months** were named for Osiris, Set, Tehuti, Zeus, Poseidon, Ares, Ishtar, Astarte, Anath, Aphrodite, Dionysus, and Isis. In this work, a Season is the period from one new moon to the next making twelve seasons in a year with a few days left over. Historically, the Egyptians had three seasons starting with the flooding of the Nile. Mathematically, a New Moon does not correlate to the beginning of a calendar month and will occur on any particular calendar date once every 29.5 years.

The **Church of Urfa** was founded in ancient times by Teumessian who sought to resolve the lessons learned from the Olympian gods. After the death of the Olympians, the children of Teumessian assumed the mantle of the Kyrios-Olon and used the power of the church to control the masses for their own purposes of maintaining power and control. They sent missionaries throughout the world to establish their church and to control religious and political thought.

A **Cubit** is 1.5 feet, 45.72 centimeters

Crook and Flail were symbols of the pharaohs power. The Crook represents the staff used by shepherds to protect their flocks and the flail represents the tool used to thresh grain.

Damascus, "City of Jasmine."

Disciples of Horus were the ardent followers of Horus who formed in each camp along the trade route from Kemet to the Sinai. The chief was Rocky and then Azazil.

Djoser, Hetephe, Incense/Hagar/Keterah
Horus, Serket, Azazil, Abram, Baalat
Ishmael, Maribah, Fatimah, Nebaioth, Basemath, Kedar | Anath, Astarte

Drink referred to in this narrative: **Ambrosia** was an Olympian potion extending life by a factor of ten; **Aphrodite-wine** was a wine containing an aphrodisiac; **Bitter** was a nonalcoholic drink made by mixing various herbs with water; **Blackwater** was a coffee-like drink; **Sweet** was a nonalcoholic drink containing honey; **beer; wine; fruit-wine** was wine mixed with fruit juices containing only a little alcohol; **brown-wine** was brandy; **Red Elixir** was Kiya's potion extending life by a factor of two.

Dyo was the Name-prefix the people gave to themselves upon their initiation into the Kyrios-Olon. See Kyrios-Olon. The original major Dyo's were Dyoares, Dyohestia, and Dyoathena.

El's End is the name for the Oceanid's tent city which became Byblos. "El" is a reference of unknown etymology to Elder Titan Cronus. "End" refers to the end of all his Olympian children. See Byblos.

El was used as a generic title for 'god,' but El Set evolved into the name of a specific god.

El is the supreme Canaanite God. The god above all others. His consort was Asherah. He founded and was the shrine god of Byblos and was associated with the Greek Cronus.

Eliezer, "Court of El," was given to Abram by Nimrod and became Abram's majordomo.

Esau was Isaac's oldest son and twin brother to Jacob. He was a great hunter who fell in with Ishmael's family and married Basemath.

Esau was Isaac's oldest son and twin brother to Jacob aka Israel. His first wife was Judith, his second was Basemath. He was said to be "hairy and red" and needy. He was righteously tricked from his inheritance by Jacob and his mother. Immediately after Abram died, he killed Nimrod, denied the resurrection of the dead, denied God, raped a betrothed woman, and spurned his birthright. While Jacon studied the Torah, Esau worshiped with idolaters.

Hagar. See Incense.

Hathor was the youngest daughter of Ishtar. She eventually became High-Priestess to Osiris.

Hathor, in Egyptian traditions, was a major Egyptian God.

Hetephe aka Hete was the finest archer in Nubia, the home to the finest archers in the world. She became a Major in the First Egyptian Army and finally the only wife to Djoser.

Haran was Terah's oldest son. Terah worked for Nimrod in a high position and dealt with selling idols.

Harran, in this manuscript, is a city a half-day journey south of Urfa and the gateway into Mesopotamia. Terah resettled his family there because the village became the center of Terah's idol manufacturing industry. Traditionally, the city where Terah died on his way to Canaan.

Hebron was the land given to Abram by Horus if Abram ever defied the Church of Urfa, which he did. After Haran was burned in the furnace, Terah led his family toward Hebron where he died. The famine diverted the remainder of the immigrants temporarily to Egypt. It is the location of the tomb of the Patriarchs.

Hor is a prefix-title designating a female who could counsel with the Kyrios-Olon.

Horus was the son of Isis and Osiris. His stepmothers were Hathor and Nephthys. He dedicated his life to teaching the way of Kiya and searching for the nature of death.

Horus's Parents were Isis, his birth mother; Dexithea/Nephthys, his nursing mother; Hathor, his nanny; Osiris, his natural father, and Djoser, his godfather.

Horus's Consorts were Anath and Serket.

Horses were named Shalom, Arrow, Djoser the Horse, two unnamed, plus a later one for Shalom named Scorpion.

Incense was the daughter of Djoser and Hetephe and was subsequently renamed Hagar and also Keterah. See Initkaes.

***Initkaes,** in Egyptian history, was the only child of Djoser and Hetephe. No suggested etymology was found.*

Ishmael's Family aka Ishmaelites:
Ishmael's wives are poorly and contradictorily documented. My names are arbitrary and their backgrounds fictitious: Maribah and Fatimah.
    Children by Maribah
Nebaioth, b. y186, "Prophecy."
Kedar, b. y187, "Black."
Basemath b. y188, "Sweet Smelling." Ishmael's only daughter.
Adbeel, b. y189, "Servant of God."
    Children by Fatimah
Mibsam, b. y190, "Smelling Sweet."

Mishma, b. y191, "A Thing Heard."
Dumah, b. y192, "Silence."
Massa, b. y193, "Oracle."
Hadad, b. y194.
Tema, b. y195, "South."
Jetur, b. y196, "Mountainous."
Napish, b. y197, "He who rests."
Kedemah, b. y198, "Eastward."

Jacob*, later renamed 'Israel,' is the son of Isaac and the younger twin brother of Esau. He fathered the twelve tribes of Israel by his two wives, who were sisters, Leah and Rachael.*

Jaffa was a seaport in Canaan and its southernmost major town.

Jaffa the Eighteenth was the Chief of the town of Jaffa

Khaba was the Pharaoh nemesis of Ishmael.

Keterah aka Incense aka Hagar was the wife of Abram, the mother of Ishmael, and the only child of Djoser and Hetephe.

Kyrios-Olon means 'Master of All" and is the name Teumessian's children called themselves as the self-proclaimed heirs to the extinct Olympian gods. See Dyo. Dyoares, Dyoathena, and Dyohestia.

Living Gods were men and women who captured the imagination of the populace and were elevated to high position of power.

The **Living Word of the Gods** was one of the titles assumed by Teumessian, the High-Priest of Urfa. See Teumessian.

Maddog Burlyman was Polydore's bodyguard and then Baalat's Admiral of the fleet.

Makkah, the city, was the city of Ishmael's oldest children, Nebaioth, Basemath, and Kedar, and home of the Temple of The Tree-of-Life.

Makkah, the place, is an invented word meaning "a serene sanctuary encouraging quiet contemplation of one's life, ancestors, and god."

Megiddo was a major trading city in Canaan.

Moloch *was the Canaanite god of fire and is associated with child sacrifice, perhaps by "passing through fire." Current thought is that this may be the name of the sacrifice rather than the name of the god.*

Murex was the owner of the dye manufacturing facility in Jaffa.

Phoenicia, Jaffa, Rocky, Burlyman, Polydore | Astarte, T'jaru
Terah, Amathlai, Haran, Terahson, Nahor, Sarai, Isaac, Jacob
Kyrios-Olon, Teumessian, Nimrod, Nimbal, Nimlad, Nimisis, Asherah, Set.

Nebwa is an invented priest who became the first High-Priest to Osiris and then began the removal of women from church hierarchies.

Nim is a prefix title given to a male who could counsel with the Kyrios-Olon. They were candidates for Kyrios-Olon membership if they performed well.

Nimrod was the Nim assigned to control Abram. He begins as Abram's best friend, then mentor, and ultimately his adversary throwing Abram into the furnace.

Nimbal was the Nim assigned to control the powerful women of Port Jaffa.

Nimlad was the Nim assigned to control God Set.

Nimisis was the Nim assigned to control General Khaba

Ninurta. See T'jaru.

Nubians were the people of the Upper Kingdom. Notable Nubians in this story are King Kerma, Queen Nima, Rafah, T'jaru, and Hetephe. Djoser and Hotep were half Nubian through their mother, Nima.

Oceanids were a sisterhood of independent, worldly, exceptionally competent women who formed a worldwide network of like-minded women. Polydore and Rhodos were notable Oceanids in this narrative.

Pharaoh was a king of Egypt into who had been blown the breath of Osiris making him a Living God.

Phoenicia was the older sister of Serket. She became a powerful woman in Port Jaffa.

Phoenician city-states: *By the mid-14th century BC, the Phoenician city-states were considered "favored cities" by the Egyptians. Tyre, Sidon, Beirut, and Byblos were regarded as the most important. The Phoenicians had considerable autonomy, and their cities were reasonably well-developed and prosperous. Byblos was the leading city; it was a center for bronze-making and the primary terminus of precious goods such as tin and lapis lazuli from as far east as Afghanistan. Sidon and Tyre also commanded interest among Egyptian officials, beginning a pattern of rivalry that would span the next millennium. (Wikipedia entry)*

Polydore was an Oceanid who came early to Kemet (Egypt), returned later as Portmaster of Jaffa in Canaan, and eventually became the advisor to Baalat. She was the last Oceanid other than Pilot Rhodos.

Djoser, Hetephe, Incense/Hagar/Keterah
Horus, Serket, Azazil, Abram, Baalat
Ishmael, Maribah, Fatimah, Nebaioth, Basemath, Kedar | Anath, Astarte

Quartermoon is the equivalent of one week as opposed to a 'quarter moon' which is a phase of the moon.

Rocky was the original disciple of Horus who became the consort to Phoenicia in Port Jaffa.

Rusalem was a small town in the Sinai out-lands whose gods were Shalem and Shahar.

Shalem was the god of sunset. His twin sister and consort was Shahar, the god of sunrise. Shalem is the root word of Shalom, "Peace."

Set, biy 70, is considered a Living God in South Memphis, married to Nephthys, and presumed father of Anubis, uncle of Horus. He eventually goes to Urfa to become consort to Asherah and High-Priest of the church of Urfa. He dies, resurrects, and tells Horus the nature of death. Aka Charon aka Ell Set aka El aka Yahweh.

Serket was the wife and love interest of Horus.

Serket was a Canaanite god. She was consort to Horus the elder and younger. She could cure scorpion stings. She had no temples but many priests, she became associated with Nephthys and Isis.

Shekel was a measurement of weight. When referring to coinage, one shekel equals three Denarius. A typical laborer's wage was one denarii which is roughly eight shekels a month.

Shur was the first city built by Ishmael for his oldest son. It was located in the Sinai wilderness midway between Egypt and Hebron.

Stiff-penny is a euphemism for 'Penis-Head.'

Sur aka Tyre was South of Byblos. Malqart was the local 'El.'

Tentyris was heir to Hathor as High-Priestess to Osiris.

Terah was Abrams's father, a merchant for idols, and the titular chief of Urfa. In this narrative, Terah lived in Hebron but traveled to Hebron where he died of malnutrition.

Teumessian became the High-Priest of Urfa after the Great Flood and sent his missionaries into the world to preach his version of the will of the gods. See The-Living-Word-of-the-Gods.

The One-God was God as understood by Abram and was based on the teachings of Horus; conflating "The One, The All" concept with the traditional concept of a god who embraced righteous pious men. He was heavily influenced by the Church of Urfa which taught the necessity of a wife's complete subservience to her husband.

The One, The All was God as understood by Azazil, Basemath, and Horus. It was based on the Testament of Set, Shamanistic thought, the writings of Dionysus and Pumi, and the teachings of Queen Kiya.

The Tree-of-Life is treated as the continuum of the body of "The One, The All" God from its birth to the current instance of time.

Titles:
> **Dyo** is the name prefix signifying a member of the Kyrios-Olon.
> **Nim** designates a male who may deal with the Kyrios-Olon.
> **Hor** designates a female who may deal with the Kyrios-Olon.

T'jaru was Nubian Chief Kerma's youngest son and a Major in the First Egyptian Army. He became a general and then an Egyptian emissary to Mesopotamia where he became known as Ninurta, "Mighty Hunter."

Tophet *was a village in the Valley of Gehenna outside of Jerusalem where child sacrifice by "passing through fire" was practiced, perhaps to God Moloch.*

Waters of Aqaba, in this narrative, is the Gulf of Aqaba separating the Sinai region from current-day Saudi Arabia' The ancient city of Aqaba lies on the northernmost point of the gulf.

Way of Horus aka War Road is a road across the upper Sinai desert linking Egypt with (then) Canaan. It became a reference to the teachings of Horus which was a retelling of the teachings of Kiya.

Way of Horus teachings: Horus taught the philosophy of Kiya throughout his life to the extent it became known as the Way of Horus. See Way of Kiya.

Way of Kiya:
"Honor your ancestors. They are your past. You are their future.
Kill nothing you do not consume unless it will harm you. Each life is precious unto itself.
Honor your vows. Do that which you say you will do.
Take nothing that is not yours.
Say nothing that is false.
Pick up those who have fallen.
Give to those who ask.
Love everyone, even those who despise you.
Be worthy."

Djoser, Hetephe, Incense/Hagar/Keterah
Horus, Serket, Azazil, Abram, Baalat
Ishmael, Maribah, Fatimah, Nebaioth, Basemath, Kedar | Anath, Astarte

Winter Solstice Season is the period of reflective family gatherings the quartermoon before the Winter Solstice followed by a quartermoon of celebrating and reveling.

Zedek was Nimrod's primary assistant within the Church of Urfa.

* 9 7 8 1 9 6 5 6 1 9 1 0 0 *